Dedication:

I would like to thank so many people. The first one is Lyndsie Stambaugh for helping me with this book and dealing with my ramblings.

I would also like to thank Mrs. Hayes for a simple little project in the 6th grade of making a short story that started this love of writing.

I would also like to thank Penny Mays, if it wasn't for her pushing me and showing me that dreams do come true then I would not be here.

Lastly, I would like to thank the love of my life, Bo Mower. Without your constant love and support, I would not have been able to publish or follow my dreams. Thank you for being that constant support that I needed.

Prologue:

In my time on this planet, my father never told me what he did. I always thought I knew or at least, could make a very good, educated guess. I never really wanted to truly know; I never wanted my suspicions to be confirmed. I didn't enjoy the attention or the money that came with his job. It only provided him with the excuse to neglect his wife and children. All I ever wanted from him was to see me; what a stupid naïve child I was. I wanted him to spend time with me and get to know his daughter. That small simple thing that I craved seemed impossible.

As I grew, my hope of my father wanting to get to know me, or my brother, began to dwindle. The more time went on, I stopped asking my mother when he would be home, or when we would do stuff as a family. I began to live my life as if he didn't matter. I let myself grow numb with all the things that concerned my father. I followed my other passions and focused on school. In one simple gesture, my father messed up my entire life, with one stupid mistake. He messed with the wrong family, and that threw me and my family into my father's business and the day I dreaded came true. My suspicions were confirmed.

I now understand the dangers that came with his job much more than I had. It made me hate him more than I thought possible. He had willingly involved himself, and, by association, his family into the mafia that existed within the United States. Even though I told myself that I hated him, I couldn't lie that I did still have some love in my heart for him. That little girl, who just wanted her father, was still inside me, just buried deep down. My heart shattered when he died, talking on the phone with me. Telling me how much he loved me. That's when the realization set in that this was no joke. This was a matter of life and death. The one goal was to keep my family safe.

This turned into a strategy game. One I had currently been losing, but now, I was in it for real. I was done being mad, scared, and pathetic. I was about to start playing and that idea terrified me; I didn't want to be my father, and yet, I had no other choice. It took me too long to figure out how to play the game properly, but once I started, I was finally leveling out the playing field. I was dedicated to the game, and I was determined to win.

Content of Table

Dedication: 3

Prologue: 4

Chapter One 8

The Talk 8

Chapter Two 28

Mourning 28

Chapter Three 55

The Kill 55

Chapter Four 77

The Accident 77

Chapter Five 99

The First Meeting 99

Chapter Six 125

Reunited Again 125

Chapter Seven 141

The News 141

Chapter Eight 159

Taken Again 159

Chapter Nine 180

The Family Reunion 180

Chapter Ten 199

The Truth Comes Out 199

Chapter Eleven	221
The Damage	221
Chapter Twelve	246
The Surprise	246
Chapter Thirteen	262
The confrontation	262
Chapter Fourteen	282
Back on the Road Again	282
Chapter Fifteen	298
Trapped	298
Chapter Sixteen	317
Fighting the Monster	317
Chapter Seventeen	333
Back on the Road	333
Chapter Eighteen	349
Almost there	349

Chapter One

The Talk

I was up in my room looking at the photos I had taken from my trip to Central Park. I smiled at how much I had improved since the day my mother gave me my first camera when I was eight years old. My peace was shattered as I heard my father and mother arguing downstairs. "Anastasia and Dominic get down here please," I heard my father call us down from what sounded like his office. That was strange, and my body immediately went on high alert as the anxiety coursed through my brain. We were not allowed in his office; he got mad if we even got too close to the door sometimes. It was completely out of the ordinary to be called down to it. My anxiety got carried away and I was just trying to keep my breathing under control as I got off my bed and headed downstairs. I thought I was moving too fast, not giving myself enough time to compose my emotions, but I was moving too slow for his liking. When I finally walked through the office doors, I found my entire family in the office and my heart rate spiked even more if that was possible.

"What is going on?"

"I must send you to Texas for a little while. We are going to visit the beach house in Rockport. You guys will be down there, and I will join after I finish some business. I made some mistakes in the business trade and now we have some problems forming. I want to stop it before they get bigger. I would rather not have you around while I do it," Dad said his voice tense.

"You are sending us away? I don't want to go to Texas. I want to stay here and spend time with my friends before we all go off to college. I got into my dream school, the School of Visual Arts. I just graduated high school and the first thing you do is piss someone off and try and send me away. Why can't I stay here? It was your mistake, how is that my problem," I asked, the anger growing in my voice. I could hear the volume of my voice growing increasingly louder.

"Ana, you will listen to me now. I told you what you will be doing, and you will do it. Especially if you want me to pay for that dream college of yours," he said, his voice growing louder with mine. He stood looking between the three of us, but I could see his nostrils flaring with anger. He pinched the bridge of his nose to try and calm down. I heard him take a deep breath, "I am sorry for this, but it is something that must happen. Each of you will be taking a group of my men. I tried to pair you up with people closer to your age but will still be able to protect you. You will be leaving separately and meeting in Rockport. I want to make sure you are all protected. No more arguing, go pack your things. Do it now."

I stormed out of his office and back up the stairs. I went to my room, grabbed my luggage set and began tossing things in it. I was so angry and frustrated. I didn't understand why this was happening. He helped run a simple marketing company. How much of a problem could he create? Why was he being so ridiculous? I guess part of me always knew that the work that kept us living very well was not always legal. That was not something I wanted to talk to myself about today though. I was so angry I could feel the invisible steam coming from my ears. Then there was a knock on the door that brought me out of my thoughts, "Go away."

The door opened despite me yelling at the person. Whoever it was, was not afraid that I was mad. I turned to yell at the person again and explain that I was pissed off.

That they were invading my space. I went to yell, but I froze when I saw Luca. I hadn't seen him in years, but he had been my best friend when I was a kid. Then my father took him under his wing and hired him, and we stopped talking and hanging out. Luca had grown into a handsome man, and I couldn't help but remember the small crush I had, had on him, "Hey Anastasia. I am going to be the leader of your team. I just wanted to see how you were doing?"

"Hi, Luca. So, you get to go to Texas. Yay you," I said with enthusiasm leaving my voice. I was trying not to snap at him at the same time, not stare at him.

"Well, I love warm weather. I know it sucks but this small town is what you need right now," he said, watching me closely.

This annoyed me, "You don't know what is good for me. You disappeared eight years ago when my dad took you in and trained you. I want to stay here and live my life in New York while I can, but no. I must spend my last summer before college in Rockport away from all my friends," I said as calmly as I could. I could feel my anger beginning to boil and I didn't want to explode.

I turned my back on him before he could see me collapse, "Come on Anastasia. It's a chance to have some fun in a new place. Why can't you try and look at the positive side of this."

"Luca, I am desperately trying to look at the positive side. No matter what I do I will be in a small town because of something my father did. I am trying to pack. I have a headache. Can you please go away and let me have some peace before I am stuck in a small space with a bunch of people who are supposed to watch me like a hawk," I said, trying to turn my attention back to packing my suitcases, "I will see you in the morning."

I heard his footsteps then my bedroom door closed and that is when I let my body relax. I quickly returned to putting more clothes in my large suitcase. I finally filled them with everything I could think of and kept me entertained in this small town. I went and sat on my bed and grabbed the Nikon I had left sitting there. I slipped it into its camera bag and wrapped the bag around my suitcase handle. I tried not to dwell on the fact that I was leaving for Texas without saying goodbye to everyone. I lay down feeling utterly defeated and felt that burning need to grab the razor blade I kept tucked into my purse. I covered my face with the pillow and screamed as loud as I could. I closed my eyes and tried to slip into unconsciousness, but I couldn't get myself to calm down enough to fall asleep. I was just about to give up when I heard gunshots ring throughout the house. I jumped out of bed as my heart began to race, Luca and Xavier ran into the room with two other guys behind him. Apollo was one and the other looked like my friend Jace, "Jace, Xavier grab her bags and get them to the car now!" Luca moved to me, "Anastasia we must leave now. I do not have time or energy to argue with you."

"Who is here Luca? Why did I hear gunshots?"

"No time. We can talk later. We need to leave. Now please be quiet and follow me," he pulled me to the side of my room, so we were hugging the wall. It was set so that Luca was in front of me, and Apollo was behind me. He pressed his earpiece to help him hear what was being said. Then he responded, "I have the package. Let's get safely out of here."

He pulled me slowly through the house, always hugging the walls. He was holding a gun and always had one hand behind him keeping me back. He took a step, and I went to follow him when someone shot the wall between our heads. I screamed and ducked down as he pushed me back behind the wall, "Luca?!"

"Shh, please I need to focus," he said looking at me for just a moment.

I was breathing heavily as the panic began to fill my chest and made it harder to breathe, "Luca what the hell is happening?! Why are we being shot at?"

"Ana, I need you to be quiet now!" As he turned to yell at me a man jumped out and shot between us again. It grazed my arm and hit the wall. I screamed and hit the floor as the pain seared through my arm. I watched Apollo jump in front of me and shot the man three times and he collapsed to the ground. A puddle of blood quickly formed under him. Apollo stood guard as Luca kneeled next to me, "Ana?! Are you okay?"

My arm felt like it was burning and my whole body was shaking as I did a mental check, "I think so… Luca what the hell did my father do?"

"We can talk about this when you are safely away from this house and these people," he said, tearing part of his shirt off and tying it around my bicep where the bullet grazed my arm. Apollo was still standing at the ready with his gun, "You good Apollo?"

"I'm good, let's get moving."

Luca pulled me to my feet, but the fear crept through my body, and I was frozen in one spot, "Come on Anastasia. We need to get out of here."

"I-I can't. Luca-"

"I will keep you safe. I promise, but the only way for me to do that is to get you out of here. Please come with me," he said, pulling me to him.

This time Apollo was taking the lead and Luca stayed behind me. We moved slowly through the house again. It was a slow walk, but we finally made it to the garage, and I was surrounded by a large group of men. I didn't quite know how many men my father had but I was surprised by the sight of it. I could see them packing cars and it looked like the garage was huge. Luca didn't hesitate and pulled me to the car and opened the back door. I quickly got in the backseat and Luca got in next to me. Xavier and Apollo were in the front; Apollo was driving, and Xavier was in the passenger seat. Then we sped quickly away from my home. Apollo had a phone to his ear and when he hung up, he said, "Everyone made it out okay. The boss says he will call when we are all safely away."

"Thank you," Luca said as he turned to look at me. "Let me see your arm," he said gently, grabbing my arm and untying the piece of shirt. "Xavier please hand me the first aid kit," I watched as Xavier listened and handed him the first aid kit. He cleaned my arm and wrapped it back up. "It doesn't look bad. It just needed to be cleaned. Take these," he said, handing me some little white pills.

I slowly took the pills and swallowed them, "Luca, what did my father do?"

"He started a war with the wrong family. The death of your mother and brother is the prize."

I swallowed the lump that was forming in my throat, "What about me?"

He looked out the window as his whole body tensed up, "He has other plans for you."

I shuddered at the thought. I turned my attention out the window by my head. I watched as we were heading to the highway that led out of the city, "Aren't we taking the jet?"

"Not this time. It is too dangerous," Luca said, his voice cold and irritated.

"We are driving from New York to Texas?!" I was astounded that we were not going to be there in just a few hours.

"Yes, now please be quiet. I need some quiet while I think of the next step of what we need to do," Luca snapped at me.

I sat quietly with my hands folded on my lap. I looked out the window and watched the world fly by me. The sun was setting before I realized that I had been in the car for hours already. I finally let myself fully register what had happened to me that day. The night overtook the bright day, and I was glad no one could see me as the tears flowed freely "When should we stop for a break Luca."

Luca sighed, "Not until a little later. Are you hungry, Anastasia?"

I swallowed trying desperately to get the lump out of my throat and I wiped at my eyes to get rid of the tears, "No, I am fine." But as I was finishing my sentence my voice was growing thick again.

"Apollo, I want you to pull the car over at the next rest stop," Luca said, keeping his in-charge role.

"Yes sir," Apollo said, his voice sounding almost robotic.

Then we sank back into silence as we drove further and further from my home and everything that I loved. I couldn't stop my tears and honestly wasn't sure I wanted to. I thought about my life and family, wondering if I was ever going to get either back. Even if I did manage to get it back, I would never be the same as it was before. Before I knew it

Apollo was pulling off the highway. I began to wipe the tears away and get rid of the evidence of me crying, "Everyone get out and stretch. We will come up with a game plan of what to do next."

Apollo and Xavier got out of the front of the car and went to the group of people that was forming in the little clearing. My door opened and I hadn't even realized that Luca had gotten out of the car and yet he was now kneeling in front of me, "Hey you."

I slowly look at his eyes. He was tall, about six feet three inches. He was muscular like he spent all day at the gym. He was of medium build, with olive skin, and spiky brown hair. He had tattoos that were barely poking out at the bottom of his shirt. His eyes were hazel but looked nice and goldish brown. "Hi," I barely whispered.

"How about you get out and stretch your legs? Get something to drink, maybe some fresh air," he had done a 360 and now his voice was gentle as he spoke to me.

"Is it safe?"

His eyes grew sad, "Yes, it is safe. Come on, let's get you out of the car for a minute. You need to get out of this car."

He stood up and held out his hand to me without waiting for me to answer him. I looked at it for a minute before I convinced myself to take it. I was pulled out into the cold air as summer was not in full force yet. The weather was chilly compared to the warmth of the car and my house. I was dressed in a tight pencil skirt, heels, and a low-cut t-shirt. He handed me some money and I muttered, "Thank you." I looked away from him and began to walk towards the building.

"We will be right out here if you need anything," he said trying to reassure me, he stopped me before I could go any further.

"Okay, go to your meeting. I will be out in a few minutes," I said proceeding back towards the building.

I quickly went into the building to get out of the cold air. I went into the bathroom to relieve my poor bladder and to look at myself. I saw that I had turned into quite a mess. I had long black hair that went just below my shoulders. My olive skin looked harsh in this light and my green eyes were very red. I had mascara running down my face, I sighed and began to clean the makeup that had smeared down my face. I finished and there was nothing I could do about the redness, so I gave up. I went out to the vending machines and the thought of food made me feel sick, so I went to grab a soda. I decided a 7up was the best option. After I hit the button, my phone went off in my purse that was strung over my shoulder. I pulled it out without looking at the name of the caller and answered the phone, "Anastasia?"

I froze at the unfamiliar voice, "Who is this?"

"Your future husband," the man said. "Do not worry sweet Anastasia. I will find you. You will not get away from me. No matter where you go. I will always find you."

I tried not to let the panic take over, but the tears filled my already red eyes. The soda began to slip from my fingers, and I felt dizzy. I looked out the door which also doubled as a window. I saw Xavier watching me and he walked over to Luca. I watched as Luca said something to the group before he turned and moved quickly towards me. He opened the door, and he slowed down the closer he got to me, "Leave my family alone. Please don't hurt them. We don't know what he did to you."

"No can-do sweetheart. Your dad must pay for what he did to me and my family. This will not just go away. You are mine now. Remember that," then the phone went dead, and I could feel myself shaking.

I stood there frozen as one tear slipped down my face with my phone up to my ear. I was staring at Luca as he approached me slowly as if I were a deer he did not want to scare away. He pulled my hand away from my face slowly and took the phone, "Anastasia?"

I somehow managed to keep my eyes and mind focused on him, "Yeah?"

"Go get back in the car," he said, his voice tight.

"Okay," I said as I left the building as fast as I could. I was shielding my face with my long hair, and I got back into the backseat of the car. I made myself as small as possible against the door. I grew furious with myself and that I needed to feel in control with that tiny little razor blade so close to me. My father would be horrified if he had seen me in my moment of weakness and I knew there would be a lecture if he ever found out. Everyone got back into the SUV and the Limo we had taken. Luca got back in the backseat beside me and with his bossy voice said, "Let's move out."

Time seemed to have sped up in the silence. My eyes began to grow heavy, but I knew that I could not sleep. My anxiety spiked and I felt myself collapsing in on myself. I could not stop thinking about my family and the insane people with guns. The worry began to destroy my stomach and I knew I would make myself sick. I fought with every fiber of my being not to give in to sleep then I heard, "What do you want us to do?"

"Get her stuff up to the suite. I will wake her up and get her up in the suite," Luca said quietly somewhere next to me.

I realized that my eyes were closed and then I was very disappointed in myself for falling asleep. I let my eyes flutter open and tried to focus on him, "Where are we?"

"We are at a hotel. I would like to put you into bed. So, can I please take you upstairs," Luca asked as he got out of the car. I watched him walk around the car and he stopped at my car door. He opened the door and once again held out his hand to me. I took it slowly not wanting to move and he pulled me gently out of the car to my feet. I quickly let go of his hand once I was steady on my feet, "Come on Ana. You look dead."

"I am fine. Let's go," I said. He put his hand on my back and guided me through the front doors. We went through the lobby of this pretty hotel and didn't waste any time getting into the elevator.

"We will be here for a couple of days. Give you some time out of the car. I think we are far enough away from him that you can have a break. You are not going anywhere alone though. Someone will always be outside your bedroom door and always with you. Do you understand," he asked as he was very intense. Granted I hadn't seen him since I was ten years old.

I nodded as the doors to the elevator opened and once again, he gently pulled me out of the giant metal box. We went down a long hallway to the last door at the end of the hallway. He opened the door for me, "Luca?"

He pushed me through another hallway to a room with a bed. I realized we were in a penthouse and couldn't imagine how much this was costing my father. He turned to look at me after he closed my bedroom door. His eyes had softened ever so slightly, "What Ana?"

"I-I don't understand."

"We will talk tomorrow. You have had a long day. I need you to get some rest," he said, putting an effort to make his voice gentle even with his frustration.

"I am not tired! This is my life! I demand you tell me what is going on right now?!"

He moved to me swiftly, "Ana you need sleep and food. Please."

"Luca, I need to know what is going on in my life. Who did he piss off?! Why are you being so difficult?"

He just stared at me for a long moment searching my eyes for something. "We will talk tomorrow," he said softly, staring down at me.

I looked away not wanting him to see me looking defeated, I was tired of being left in the dark, "I'd like to be alone. Please don't bother me."

I saw him reach for me but stopped himself. I quickly turned away from him and went into the bathroom that was attached to my room. I waited until I heard the door close, and I knew I was alone. I moved to and grabbed my purse and grabbed the razor blade that made me feel happy from the control it gave me. I pulled my skirt up and pushed the blade into my skin. I bit my lip as the pain calmed down the anxiety I felt. I kicked off the shoes and laid down on the king-size bed. All the events of the day came rushing back in a flash. It came back and completely took me by surprise by the amount of pain I was in. I pressed my skirt into my thigh to help stop the bleeding. I curled up in a small ball and a sob escaped. I let myself cry until I finally was so exhausted, I had to let my body fall asleep.

****

I woke up with a scream as I tried to protect myself from the bullets flying through my house in my dream. Luca busted through my door with a gun in his hand as he scanned the room for the threat. He was on alert mode and when he saw that I was alone and safe, he set the gun down on the night side table next to the bed, "Are you okay, Anastasia?"

I took a deep breath to try and slow my heartbeat. I threw the blankets over my head as the tears filled my eyes. I did not want him to see me crying. I needed to be the girl my dad raised me to be. I was thinking about the dream of my family dying in front of me and being shot at. I swallowed the lump in my throat, "I'm fine Luca. Go back to sleep."

"If you are fine, how about you show me your face," he said softly.

"No-" My voice betrayed me by breaking as the tears spilled over and down my face.

He sighed and pulled the blanket down, "Anastasia, don't lie to me."

"What the hell is happening?!"

"Shh, okay," he said as he sat down on the bed. "Look, your dad is in some risky business. He does work for a legal company, but we also work for a not-so-legal company. This led to the death of the Balzarini family. The son was away on business and survived the attack. It was an accident, but now he is all about revenge. Your dad gave me a small team of men to keep you safe and to get you to Texas," he said softly.

"I am scared, Luca. I am not supposed to cry or show fear. I have broken his rules. He would be so angry with me," I said slowly, hearing his voice in my head. "I am supposed to be better."

"Ana, you silly girl. You are allowed to be yourself. You are allowed to feel free to cry. That doesn't mean we don't take you seriously. You are still our boss, and we still do what you want within reason," he gently tipped my chin up, so I had to look at him, "Don't doubt yourself now."

"Are my bags up here? I would like to take a shower," I said looking at his hazel eyes which had lightened a little.

"Of course. I will be right back, Ana," he said standing up and walking out of the room.

I slowly got out of bed and pulled my skirt down to cover myself and my scars. The door opened and Xavier came in with my bags and sat them down on my bed. He grabbed my arm as I went to my suitcases. The fear he instilled made me freeze, "Want to have some fun?"

"Let me go, Xavier. We aren't dating anymore. There's a reason for that," I said, pushing him away and sighing. He pushed me aggressively against the wall and fear shot through my body. He held my hands above my head and kissed my neck. I could feel my legs shaking as the fear began to take over. I used the last bit of strength I had and broke my arms free. I shoved him as hard as I could and shouted, "I said no! Get away from me! Now get out!"

"What's with all the yelling," Luca came in looking around the room.

His eyes landed on us, and I was shaking uncontrollably, "Nothing." Xavier said, quickly leaving the room with his head down.

"Are you okay, Anastasia," he said, watching me closely.

I collapsed on the floor, and he quickly moved to me, shocked that I hit the floor, "I-I'm okay."

"Hey, you. Can you tell me what happened?"

"I-I... Nothing," I said, trying to gather myself enough to be able to look at him.

"I don't believe you. Anastasia, tell me what happened please," Luca said, trying to keep his face soft, but I could hear the tension in his voice.

"I just want to shower, please. Can we just drop it for now," I said close to begging him to just drop the subject.

"Okay, Anastasia. I am going to wait for you out here though," he said, helping me to my feet.

I felt some relief knowing that he would be out here waiting for me. I went to my suitcase and grabbed my lace blue thong with the matching bra, a pair of low-riding jeans, and a burgundy crop top that hugged me tightly. I went into the bathroom and closed the door. I took a deep breath and turned the shower on. I set my clothes down on the counter. I undressed and moved my tense body under the nice hot water. My muscles finally relaxed and loosened. I washed my hair, and body, and shaved. Once the water started to turn cold, I got out and wrapped a towel tightly around myself. I dried off and quickly got dressed. I was drying my hair and doing a low ponytail, so it was off my face. There was a light knock on the bathroom door, "Yeah?"

"Can I come in," Luca asked, his voice soft.

"Sure," I said, putting on a little bit of makeup. He opened the door and stopped to look at me.

"I have a phone call for you," he said.

My heart stopped as he handed me back my phone which I hadn't seen since he took it last night, "Thank you, Luca." I slowly put the phone to my ear trying to not shake from fear, "Hello."

"Ana," I heard my dad's voice, and the stress instantly left my body.

"Hi, Dad! Are you okay?!"

"I am okay, princess. I have been worried about you all. Your mom and brother are safe. You were my last call. I am so happy to hear your voice," he said, the relief flowing into his voice.

"I have been worried about all of you. I am so glad you called," Before I had the chance to stop myself, my eyes filled with tears as the words came out of my mouth, "I love you, Dad."

"I love you too, Ana. I am so sorry I caused you this pain. I promise that I will keep you all safe," he said, his voice the softest I have heard since I was a little girl.

I went to respond when I heard the gunshots ring off on the other side of the phone. At first, I wasn't even sure that was what I had heard, "Dad? Dad, please say something." Then more gunshots and I could hear people screaming on the other side of the phone. I felt frozen in place as I realized what was happening, "DAD?!?!"

"Daddy is a little busy sweetheart. Can I take a message for him," I heard that sick sound of his voice. Anger and fear flooded my body all at once.

"No," I yelled into the phone with all the strength I had left in me. Luca came running back into the bathroom, "Leave him alone. Just leave my father and my family alone."

23

"I'm afraid that is not possible. See I wanted my family to be left alone too. Instead, I came home to find my father, mother, and baby sister dead along with half a dozen of my father's men. This is an eye for an eye," he said, his voice sick with rage. "Say goodbye to your daughter Vinny. It's the best and last thing you will hear."

"I love you, Anastasia. Stay hidden. Do not come out of hiding. I am so sorry I caused this. I did not want to do this to any of you. If you are safe, I will die happy," he barely got the words out when two loud gunshots ran causing me to flinch away from the phone. My hand went to cover my mouth to stop myself from screaming in anguish. That's when I realized I had tears streaming down my face.

"Don't worry about it, love. We will see each other soon. I will have you. I don't care how long it takes, I will have my vengeance," the man said. Then the phone went dead.

I was shaking and I tried to steady myself, but I wasn't close to anything to stabilize against. A sob escaped as the phone slipped out of my hand and I collapsed once again. Luca caught me before I hit the floor, "Anastasia what happened?"

I couldn't blink or focus on any more words that were coming out of his mouth. I was caught up in the last five minutes. I went from hate, and relief to fear in a short five minutes. My father was mine. He brought my childhood dream and told me how much he loved me, and it was about me. I went from having a father that drove me mad to the man that I wanted to be my father. Then in a few freaking minutes, he was gone, "I think my dad just died... He-He made him say goodbye."

Luca was still holding me gently to him and I felt his arms tighten ever so slightly, "I am so sorry. I have you, Ana. It's going to be okay."

"I just listened to him die. The bastard let him say goodbye and then shot him," I said, hiding my face in his chest as I kept repeating the words that he was dead. I was unable to stop as my mind went a million miles a minute.

"Shh, it's okay," he cradled me up in his arms and took me back to the bed. He sat me down gently and pulled my face up so I was looking at him, "I will be right back. Do not move."

I pulled my knees to my chest and wrapped my arms tightly around them. I felt my heart and head breaking at the same time. I watched him quickly leave the room and I just kept staring at the door he disappeared behind. Before I could focus on getting the tears to stop, the door opened again. I looked up to see Luca and Angelo coming into the room, "What is going on? What do you want him to give me?"

They both approached me with caution from opposite sides of the bed in case I tried to run, I'm sure. Luca stood next to me while Angelo sat down in front of me, "I want you to take some pills."

"What will they do to me," I said sniffling, trying to recognize the sound of my voice.

"They are going to help you relax. You haven't gotten much sleep or had any time to process anything since we got on the road," Angelo said, his voice gentle like he was worried he would scare me.

"I don't want to sleep," I looked at Luca with more tears in my eyes and I was completely baffled that I wasn't dehydrated from crying.

"I understand Ana, but you need to relax. We are all here for you and to keep you safe. That means mentally too. Please take the pills," Luca said, his voice tense.

"It won't bring my dad back," I said, as the words left my mouth. I wish I could take them back and I looked between the two men and saw both of their bodies tense up.

Angelo carefully reached out and took my hand, "No it will not, little boss. It will not bring him back, but he lives on through you and your brother. This will just make it easier to process without overexerting yourself."

I looked at him for what felt like forever. I took a deep breath and wiped the tears away that spilled over. I slowly took the blue pills from him and put them in my mouth. I was handed a glass of water and washed it down before I could change my mind, "Can I be alone?"

Angelo stood up and nodded, not saying anything else. He watched me for a moment too long and then quickly turned to leave the room. I heard the door close, and I stared after him for a moment wondering how I could get Luca to leave me alone. I turned to him but before I could say anything he intervened with, "I am going to stay for a little while. I promise not to bother you."

I sighed, seeing no point in arguing with him. I had no energy for it and hoped he would just leave me alone. I lay down in a small ball in the middle of the bed. I refused to let the sobs escape causing pain in my throat as a lump was not able to escape. A few more tears managed to somehow slip out of my tear ducts. I let my eyes close in the hope that that would finally stop the tears and I hugged myself tightly. I could feel exhaustion begin to take over or that little pill I was unsure of. I felt a hand, safe to assume that belonged to Luca on my forehead. I barely managed to open my eyes, "Luca?"

"I didn't mean to wake you. Please close your eyes and get some sleep. Ana, I will be here when you wake up," he said quietly.

"I do not want to sleep. Luca, I don't want my imagination to take over when I finally fall asleep." I said as my eyes unwillingly slipped shut, "I'm scared."

I felt his hesitation before he started to talk, "I know. I understand Anastasia. You don't have to sleep. Just lay here on the bed. No need to be scared. You have a group of people who are all here to make sure you are safe," he said, his voice low and soothing.

I suddenly didn't want him to leave me alone in this room, "Promise you won't leave?"

"I promise I won't go anywhere. Now relax," he said as he turned on the TV that was in the room. I felt the bed shift as he made himself comfortable somewhere next to me. "Good night, Ana," he said as I slowly and unwillingly slipped into unconsciousness.

Chapter Two

Mourning

I woke up with a scream and Luca moved to me and put both of his hands on either side of my face, "It's okay Anastasia. You are safe. Nothing is here but me and you."

"I don't want to do this anymore. I just want this all to be over," I said my voice barely above a whisper as I felt my heart exploding in my chest.

"Hey, don't say that. It's just been a rough couple of days. It will get better I promise. How about we try eating some food," he said, holding his hand out to me. I slowly took it, and he pulled me out of bed.

I sighed, "Okay... I guess I can try to eat." I looked over at the clock on the nightstand next to the bed and I saw that it read two in the morning, "How long have I been asleep?"

"You have been asleep on and off for twelve hours. So not too long. Just half a day without food. When was the last time you ate?" Before I could respond he was pulling me through the suite and straight to the tiny little kitchen. He pulled out a chair at the bar. I sat down and he helped push me closer to the counter. He walked around the counter into the small kitchen, "What do you want to eat?"

"I am not that hungry. I think I will be fine. I ate breakfast the day the house was shot up. I think you should get some rest. You look exhausted," I said while he was actively looking in the cupboards.

"Okay, I can make you some soup. That will be easy on your stomach," he said ignoring my statement about him sleeping, "You need food in your body."

"Sure, I can try some soup," I said as a headache began to set in at the temples. I laid my head on the counter to feel the coolness of the tile on my head.

"Is she all right," Anthony asked somewhere behind me. He was one of my dad's favorite men. He and Luca were the top two that I knew. It's amazing how you can track a person's voice and know who it is.

"As okay as she can be. It's going to be difficult to get her to start acting normally. I am trying to get her to eat some food," Luca said softly. After a little bit, "Anastasia dinner is ready. Come on, eat some soup."

I slowly lifted my head and rubbed my eyes, "Thank you. Now please get some rest, Luca."

He was watching me like I was a bomb about to go off, "I am fine. I don't need sleep. I got some rest while you were sleeping."

I took a deep breath and tried to muster my father's energy, "Luca I order you to sleep. I need you at your best and right now you look like you might collapse."

He smirked at me as I tried to take some authority, "Alright little boss. Anthony you up for a shift?"

"Of course. Go get some sleep, Luca. I got her," Anthony said, coming up closer behind me.

I watched as Luca walked away and down the hall. A cross between relief and anxiety hit me all at once. My stomach began to churn, and I hoped the soup would help. I took another bite and slowly chewed the noodles and chicken. I finally managed to swallow as Anthony sat down next to me, "I am sorry Anastasia. We are all here for you."

I could feel his eyes on my face, "You should eat a little more."

"I am not hungry. When did you arrive here, Tony?"

"Yesterday... I was at the house when it got hit. It was awful. Gunfire everywhere, people dying and screaming," I looked up to find him staring at his hands. "Luca will be mad if I don't at least try and get you to eat more."

"I am not hungry. I do not need to eat more food. We need to be on the move again. I don't want to sit in one spot. Not with Balzarini on the hunt," I pushed my chair back and got to my feet. I felt exposed and vulnerable so I walked away from him before he could say any more to me. I went back to the room I claimed as mine in the short time we had been here.

I was restless and could not stay still, so I began to pack up my suitcase one more time. Before I knew it the sun was coming up and brought natural light into my room from the windows across from me. There was a light knock on my door, "Can I come in?"

"Sure," I said knowing that I might be a mess.

Luca entered the room with Angelo. I could not stop the sigh that escaped my body, "You ready to hit the road?"

"Yes, I think we have spent too much time here. Angelo, can you please grab my bags," I said, not looking at the man next to Luca.

"Of course, miss," he said, going over to the suitcases I had at the end of my bed and grabbing them in one fluid movement. Before I could even register, he was out the door.

I looked down at my hands when I saw Luca break his façade and run his fingers through his hair, "Ana, I know you barely ate last night. It doesn't take much to see you haven't slept either."

I took a deep breath and all the courage I had in myself. I looked up at him and gave him my best, don't mess with me, face. I paused for half a second when I saw him dressed in a tight black shirt that showed off the tattoos I could see on his forearms and some on his biceps, "Luca I am capable of making my own decisions and know what is best for me."

"Ana, stop. This is not you," he said as he moved closer to me. It was instinct to take a step back, "You are only eighteen. You don't need to be making any of these decisions besides you needing to be careful and stay alive."

I could feel myself losing my nerve and I looked back down at my hands folded in front of me, "I have to now. Dad is gone. Someone must make these decisions and God knows Dominic is not capable of handling anything to this degree. He left as soon as he turned eighteen. He was only visiting for the summer," I took a deep breath and looked back at him, "It's my job to make things right."

"No, you don't. Your mother and brother can and will step up and do what they need to, to keep you safe. This is not on you. Please stop trying to close yourself off," he said, grabbing my arm and pulling me into a hug. My body tensed up and after a few minutes, I hugged him back, "Relax. We will figure this out. No point running yourself ragged."

I felt the emotions all at once of how grateful I was to have my best friend back. Even if it was temporary. I swallowed the lump in my throat, "Let's go. We need to hit the road. I don't like staying in one place. Makes me feel like a sitting duck."

"Alright let's go," We left the room and navigated our way through the suite. Once we found our way out and got into the elevator all this anxious energy hit me. I felt myself become fidgety as I was stuck in one place waiting for those metal doors to open. Once the doors opened, I felt his hand on my back as he guided me out of the elevator and into the hotel lobby. Apollo appeared out of nowhere and was to my right. Luca was to my left and slowly my father's men appeared as they watched us. Angelo had my car door open for me as I walked from the front of the hotel to the car. I got in and the door closed behind me. My automatic response was to look out the window to watch the world go by. Apollo got behind the wheel while Angelo got in next to him. Luca had just closed the door beside me when the window by my head shattered causing me to scream. Everyone ducked and Luca pushed me down on the floor and covered me with his body, "Get us out of here now!"

Another shot ran through the air and Luca yelled out in pain. I felt some pressure particularly on my lower back as he put more pressure on me, and the middle lump was digging in. The panic took over, "Angelo Luca's been hit!!!" I yelled as the blood began to cover me a little.

"I am okay. Do not stop this car! Get us out of here now!" Luca yelled and I heard the tires squeal on the pavement as the gas pedal was pushed to the floor.

Luca stayed my human shield until Apollo slowed down and was outside the city limits. He leaned against the door and was looking a little pale. I got off the floor and sat down next to him on the seat. He was breathing heavily, and the panic began to bubble more as I saw blood coming out of his shoulder, "Luca... I am so sorry. Why would you do that? You better not die."

I couldn't stop watching the blood ooze out, "Hey calm down. I am not going to die. I will be okay with just a little bit of pain and a little bit of blood," he said, his voice soothing. Even in pain, he was trying to calm me down.

My body was tense, and I couldn't stop my mind from wondering how they found us. Then it struck me like a brick wall. It took all the air in my lungs, and I felt the hatred and fear gripping my heart, "Luca…"

He was analyzing his wound and must have heard something in my voice. He looked up at my face and I saw a flash of concern cross his face quickly, "What is it, Anastasia?"

I felt the blood drain from my face as the realization made more sense and I came to terms with the words I was about to say, "Anthony told me. He was with my dad when they took him out. Then suddenly there happened to be an attack on the hotel we were staying in. How could he find my dad and me so quickly? It doesn't make sense unless someone told him. The common factor is Anthony," I said each word as if my life depended on it and at this point it did.

I watched the surprise flash on his face as he realized he missed the most obvious clue there is, "Apollo I need you to get us lost in the woods for a little bit of time please." When he spoke, I did not recognize the harshness of his voice as that of Luca. The man I have known my whole life has been nothing but kind. Yet, at that moment he terrified me.

"I also need to get you fixed up," Angelo said, his voice leaking concern.

It was incredibly quiet as we drove. The silence was beginning to drive me to the verge of madness. We came to a stop in the middle of the forest. I was trying to hold myself together, "Alright Anastasia. I need you to play dead. I need to hear it to see if this is the truth. He may confess if he sees you like this."

"What if he doesn't? Luca, it must be him."

"It's going to be okay."

"Okay, Luca. I can do this," I said more to myself than him.

I was already covered in the blood that spilled from the wound on his shoulder, "Everything will be fine. Just close your eyes and try not to move your body as you breathe in and out."

"Let's do this," I said, lying down and closing my eyes.

The door opened and someone picked me up. I tried to keep myself from moving and to just remain limp in the arms of my old friend, "What the hell happened back there?! How the hell did they know where we were?" Xavier said somewhere in the distance.

"Is she okay?"

"She was shot. I couldn't stop the bleeding. She didn't make it. We need to bury her and find the other family members to keep them safe while we fight this invisible war," Luca said, his voice dark and angry. "But first to manage the problem. Someone snitched. Who was it? Who can live with this on their soul?"

It was dead silent for what felt like an eternity. The silence was finally broken by a sob, "I am so sorry. They threatened my family. She was never supposed to get hurt. Let alone die," Anthony said, his voice growing quiet with each word.

I felt such rage course through my body that my eyes snapped open before I could stop myself. I had thirty seconds before they could stop me. I rolled out of Luca's arms and grabbed the gun he kept holstered at his ankle. The tension rose as I stood and aimed the gun at Anthony, "You bastard!"

"Whoa. Take a deep breath. Give me back the gun," Luca said softly.

I heard him move towards me and I turned around to point it at him, "Stop! This isn't fair!" Everyone's hands went up like they could see the crazy in my eyes. I didn't care. My focus was completely on the man that caused the death of my father. I turned back to Anthony pointing the gun back at him, "How could you do this to my family?! How could you let that man kill my father? Then let him attack me and my men!"

I felt myself begin to shake with rage as I shouted at him. I had the gun aimed right at his head. I could only see the man who betrayed my father, who betrayed me. He went to say something, but I decided I was done and nothing he could say would be enough for me. I pulled the trigger and watched the blood begin to pour from right between his eyes. It was the first time I had shot a gun, and I was stunned when I hit him. A wave of shock came over me and I was frozen in place while everyone registered what I had just done, "Anastasia? Ana, give me my gun back."

I could not move. I couldn't seem to do anything. I just stood there and stared at Anthony who was gathering blood under him. The tears began to fill my eyes as Luca approached me slowly. Luca took the gun from me, and my hands went to my mouth as I stared again at the man who destroyed what I had of a family, "What-" I stopped myself at the start of the sentence not sure how to phrase my question.

I collapsed to the ground and watched as the group dispersed now that I didn't have a gun. I was left sitting on the ground to fully register what I had done. I had ended a man's life. A life I had no right to take from him. The bile rose in my throat, and I crawled towards the nearest ditch and completely emptied my stomach. I threw up until I was just dry heaving and I hurt with every heave. Someone pulled my hair back and patted my back, "Angelo you are needed over here when you are done with Luca," Apollo said.

I curled up on the ground on my side and just lay on the Earth that was growing cold underneath my body, "What the hell did I just do?"

"Shh, it's okay Anastasia," Apollo said, his voice gentle as he sat next to me rubbing my back to try and ease the guilt that was squeezing my chest.

Someone touched my head and I let my eyes stop at the source. I tried to focus on the person in front of me, "Are you done throwing up Anastasia? You are going into shock," Angelo said. I couldn't bring myself to say anything back. I just looked at him and forced my head to do a nodding motion as a few more tears slipped from my eyes, "Let's get her in the back of the car with Luca. We can't stay here or wait for her to come out of it."

I stared at the place Anthony had stood as I took away the life I thought deserved to be ended. Someone picked me up and cradled me to their chest. I felt the motion as someone moved across the path. I was sitting in the back of the car, and I hadn't registered that someone was talking to me. Luca grabbed my face and forced me to look at him, "Ana?? Are you okay??"

A few more tears spilled over as I refused to blink, "I-I killed someone. I didn't even think twice. I just pulled the trigger and now he will never draw another breath. He won't have kids."

His face melted as I wiped the tears away to no avail, "Hey it's okay. It's all going to be okay. Just try and breathe," he said softly. "How about you lay down?"

I didn't know how to respond. I didn't want to lay down, but I didn't have it in me to argue. I didn't want to sit here and think about the awful crime I had just committed. During my confusion, I laid my head on his lap and just cried some more. I let the sobs out to be free and to expel the poison I had in my body, "I don't know what happened…"

I could feel the motion of the car as we moved back toward civilization, "Shh just rest. I promise it will be okay."

I let my eyes close, and I tried to force my body to relax. I thought if I willed it hard enough I could get it to relax. I was exhausted from the emotional trauma of the day. I tried to push my thoughts away, but they kept creeping up that I had ended a man's life. A man who was trying to protect his family the same way I wanted to protect mine. Would I have done the same thing? My heart sank and my stomach churned as I realized I would. I had just done it. I am worthless. I am a killer, "I am not meant for this life…" I whispered to myself unsure if anyone was listening and not caring if they were.

I felt Luca's body tense up, "Ana…"

I took a deep breath and sat up. I moved against the door and stared at the world flying past me. I pulled my knees up to my chest and wrapped my arms tightly around them to keep them close. I wanted to be as small as possible. I reached up to my ponytail and pulled the hair tie out letting my hair hang loose around my face to cover the turmoil that was clear on my face. I knew what he was thinking but I felt disgusted with myself. I killed someone who was protecting those they loved, "It's true. I am a failure... I have lost myself in just a few simple days."

The silence was louder than the words have ever been. I felt myself collapsing in on myself and I wasn't sure how to make it stop or even if I wanted to make it stop. Luca moved my hair out of my face and tucked it gently behind my ear, "You are not a failure. You are not lost. Sometimes we do things of which we are not proud. It doesn't change who you are. You are still in shock and having a tough time processing."

I stared at the seat in front of me and processed what he was saying, and it didn't make me feel better. I had taken life away from someone whose life was only a quarter of the way through it. His family would never know his sacrifice. I turned my gaze out the window without another word to Luca. I watched the world run by and thought of the murder, "Is she okay?" It was Apollo who was speaking from the front seat of the car.

"I don't know. Angelo, what do we do?"

"We need to let her process this the best way she can and hope she comes out not too scared by the experience. We just need to be open and available when she is ready to talk and just hope for the best," Angelo said quietly.

I heard someone sigh and was not exactly sure where the sound came from, but I felt numb. It felt the best way to protect my heart and my head from any further damage. I continued to watch the world fly by until the sky began to change from blue to orange, to red, until it slowly got darker and darker. My feeling of being numb faded and I was crushed by the utter depression. Silent tears slid down my face and didn't even care to wipe them away, "Ana," Luca said softly, and I could feel as though someone was watching me.

I closed my eyes and counted to ten. Once I was at ten, I opened them and turned to look at him. I said the only thing I could think to tell him, "I'm okay Luca." My voice sounded dead, lifeless, and completely hopeless.

Before I had any time to react, he pulled me away from the door to him. It was a weird side embrace, and I could feel my body tense up under the sudden human contact, "Don't lie to me, Anastasia. We used to be best friends. I know you better than that."

I felt his arm around me, and I couldn't make myself relax any more now than I could before. I thought of everything, and I laid my head down on his shoulder, "What do you want me to say, Luca? That I am a mess? That is quite clear. I want my father back, my family back, and most importantly I want my life back."

He was quiet as I lashed out at him for doing nothing, but the job to keep me safe and whatever else my father had convinced him to do, "I know Ana. I just wish I could do something to help you. I want you to process this healthily. You are not alone though. We are all here for you."

Once again, my body was completely exhausted. I had experienced something I never thought I would have to. I somehow made more tears like my body was nothing but water. My body slowly loosens and relaxes. My face grew red as I realized his arm was still around me with my head on his shoulder. My shame was quickly replaced by embarrassment. I went to move, but his arm tightened around my waist and the blood rushed to my face, "Luca?"

He moved us around so that we were both lying down in the back of the car. He laid on his back and I was laying on my stomach on top of him. My face was red as a lobster, I was sure. I didn't think I could sleep or slow my heart rate at this point, "Do not move. Do not attempt to move. You need to relax. Just clear your head and lay here with me."

"Luca I-"

"No. Do not argue with me. Anastasia just lay right here with me," he wrapped his left arm around my body to hold me tightly in place. I swallowed trying to swallow my embarrassment of lying with him. I gave up and just listened to his heartbeat. I let my eyes slip shut as the rhythm relaxed me, "That's more like it, Ana. You are safe. Please try and get some sleep," he said, his voice soothing and quiet.

It wasn't that I hadn't been intimate with a man before. This just felt different. Luca was the first person I had ever loved that wasn't my family and nothing ever came of it. I had forced myself to move on and give up on something that was never going to happen. I felt the fear that came with having this emotion and the situation I was in, "Luca I'm scared."

"I know. You have had a lot all at once. You are safe. I promise that you are safe. You need some sleep," he responded to me as he rubbed my back.

The heat rushed to my face once again, "Okay Luca."

I focused on my breathing rather than the fact that I was lying on Luca who was rubbing my back. With my eyes shut I could feel myself begin to sink into a world of unconsciousness. I jumped with the feeling like I was falling just before I fell asleep, "Shh it's okay. Just go to sleep," he started to hum softly in my ear and that was all I needed to let myself begin to fall asleep and say a quick prayer that it was dreamless.

****

The brakes squealing pulled me out of a surprising dreamless sleep. Luca threw his right arm and leg out to brace against the seats in front of us, to keep us in place. His left arm tightened around my waist keeping me in place and so I hid my face in his chest, "What the hell was that?"

His body slowly relaxed as he managed to keep us on the seats and returned to a more comfortable position. "Sorry, Luca. I got cut off and had to slam on the breaks. Are you two okay," Apollo asked from the front.

I was breathing heavily as my heart jumped from the adrenaline coursing through my blood at the sudden wake-up call. "Are you okay Ana," Luca whispered in my ear, completely ignoring Apollo.

The blood rushed to my face again and I just nodded for a moment. How can this happen? I worked so hard to get over him. I can't just fall back into old patterns, "Are you okay? How's your shoulder?"

"I am fine. Are you ready to get up," he said, his voice was sweet and gentle as if I was ready to break again at any minute.

"Yes, I think I need to get up," I said looking up at him, my hair sliding into my eyes and covering my face.

He pushed it back and tucked it behind my ear again, "Alright Anastasia. Let me help you up."

We slowly began to rearrange ourselves without causing pain to Luca and his gunshot wound. Once I was sitting back up and on the seat by the door, I was trying to see our surroundings. I didn't recognize anything around us, "Where are we?"

"We are in Virginia," Angelo said. "How are you feeling? Ready for some food?"

The day before came flooding back and the shame and depression came flooding back with it. "I could use a shower," I said, avoiding the question altogether. I looked over at Luca, "Can we stop and get off the road please?"

He looked at me for a moment searching my eyes for something, "Apollo let's stop at the next hotel. The lady needs a shower and I need to make some calls."

"You got it, boss," Apollo said.

I was uncertain of what was going on or what would be happening as the previous day came flooding back like a rogue wave. My emotions began to swim again, I remember how sweet he was and now he couldn't be bothered with me. Then the emotions following the fact that I had killed a man. Great. I just can't take this right now. So, to start the practice of being numb, I shut down. I couldn't have feelings for Luca, it would just hurt. I needed to stop and focus. I had killed a man, was on the run from another one, and my father was dead. That was something I had prayed for at one point in my life and now all I felt was grief and despair at the thought. The words slipped out before I could do anything to stop them, "What am I doing?"

He looked up and caught me looking at him, "Nothing. We will be at a hotel soon. It will give you some time outside of the car. That's what you need."

I looked away quickly and focused on my hands which were on my lap. I let my hair fall in my face, as a way to build a wall between him and me. I decided to just stare out the window and try not to get lost or drowned in thought. Hours flew by and before I could think to ask them how much longer, we came to a stop in front of a giant hotel with a name listed as the Dolphin Inn. The car was put into the park and fear set in as the memories of being shot came back. My heart began to pound as the adrenaline took over my body and I just wanted to keep going more than anything now.

My heart stuttered and I couldn't keep myself from ducking below the window as the panic attack overtook me and all rational thinking. I looked around the car to see if there was somewhere I could hide, instead, I met the sad eyes of the three men set out to protect me, "You are safe Anastasia. We will keep you safe, remember? Let's get you inside," Apollo said softly.

Luca got out of the car and walked around to my side. I watched Angelo and Apollo get out of the car next. Before I could even register what I was doing, I locked the doors and sat on the floor of the car, and tried to get my breathing under control. I could hear someone curse, "Anastasia open the door," Angelo said.

"I can't. I'm sorry... I can't do this. I just can't do any of this right now," I said repeatedly on the floor squeezing my legs tightly to my chest.

I was facing the door with my knees to my chest. I heard another knock at the window which gathered my attention. I looked up to see Luca watching me, "Ana... Just open the door. One step at a time. Let's start with that one." I took a deep breath but couldn't seem to make myself move. I shook my head and he sighed, "I know. Okay? This isn't easy and you have been through a lot already. Please let me get you inside." After a moment of watching him, I slowly moved and unlocked the doors, "Good." He kneeled so he was down to my level and held out his hand, "Now take my hand so I can get you inside where it's safe."

I stared at his hand for a few minutes and finally took it. He helped me carefully out of the car. I was immediately surrounded by a group of men. Apollo was in front of me, Angelo was to my right, and Luca was to my left. Luca had his hand on my back guiding me towards this hotel. My anxiety was beginning to rise again, "Luca..."

"Just keep walking Anastasia. Do not stop. I want you inside and as quickly as possible," Luca said as he pushed harder on my back without looking at me.

We were inside faster than I thought possible. Angelo checked us in, and we had rented the entire top floor, and we all went to the elevator to go up there. We entered the top floor, and I broke away from the group and found the first empty room I could claim as my own. I didn't stop to take a breath. I went straight into the bathroom off to the right side of the room, not caring that I didn't have my clothes. I turned on the hot water, and I quickly took my clothes off and was under the hot water. I didn't leave the shower for at least an hour. I kept scrubbing trying to make myself feel clean. I finally gave up and got out of the shower, my hands and feet were all pruney. I got out and dried myself off with a towel and grabbed the fluffy robe from the back of the bathroom door. I went out to my room, and I stopped dead in my tracks when I saw Xavier in the middle of it. "What are you doing in here," I asked, tightening my arms around me.

"I brought your suitcases in here. I figured you'd need them," he watched as I took a step back away from him. He looked at me like a confused dog. Then he smiled, "I know you still love me. What is stopping us from being together?" He took a step towards me, and my heart began to race.

"No, I thought it was love but I was wrong. We were toxic and abusive to one another. It was unhealthy and it was just a substitute for the love I thought I needed, and you thought you needed. We are nothing to each other. We will remain nothing to each other Xavier. I am so sorry that I hurt

44

you, but this is for the best. I am sorry," I said, taking another step away from him.

His face screwed up in anger and he lunged at me. I had to move quickly, and I didn't have time to think. I ran back into the bathroom as fast as I could. I slammed the door shut and twisted the lock. I heard his body slam into the door, "Open this door, Ana. Now!!"

"No! Go away!" I desperately searched for my cell phone and hoped someone was close by to hear the noise. I heard him slamming repeatedly against the door and I could hear the wood beginning to splinter under his constant weight. My heart sank as I remembered Luca took my phone and I never got it back. The door flew open as he broke it down with one final smash, "NO!!"

He grabbed me and pushed me to the wall with my hands above my head. I kicked him as hard as I could and tried to headbutt him. He slapped me hard, and I lost my balance and hit the floor since he had let my hands go. I tried to crawl away, but he grabbed me by my ankle, and he flipped me on my back. I spit in his face, and he hit me again so hard my head bounced off the tile. I kept fighting even though my vision was a little spotty from the impact. He wrapped his hands around my throat and squeezed. My air supply was being cut off and the panic set in, "You are mine, Ana. I will be making you mine again. Don't worry, they are in a meeting and no one will hear you." I thrashed and tried everything to get him off me. I scratched his face. I managed to knee him in the groin and was gasping for air when he released my throat to grab himself in pain. He recovered faster than I did and punched me in the face. Then he moved my hands above my head when I was disoriented. I felt his hands untying the robe and pushing it up. I tried to scream again when his other hand went back around my throat, cutting off my air supply once again. I clawed at his hand desperate to get air.

I was about to give up, painfully aware he was stronger than me and I stood no chance against him. I had lost and was going to pass out when I heard the click of someone who had loaded a gun. I felt Xavier freeze, "Get away from her now Xavier. I will not ask again."

The sound of Luca's voice brought both fear and relief through my body. Xavier released my hands and neck when he got off me. I crawled away gasping for air and making sure I was covered by the robe. My wet hair was sticking to my face. "What should we do with him," asked one of the men, not one that I recognized and was too afraid to look up.

"Get him out of here. I will be with you all shortly," Luca said, his voice dark and harsh. All I could hear was footsteps and Xavier talking about how we belonged together. I had my hands around my neck as if that would help heal the pain. I could feel the tears and knew this was karma for killing a man. The silence began to drown me, "Ana?"

I hadn't realized a lump had formed in my throat until I went to speak, "Y-yeah?" I said my voice was raspy, and it was painful to talk and swallow.

"Can I help you up?" He asked, his voice was gentle as if he were talking to a child who was lost at an amusement park. I could only nod in response. He scooped me up in one fluid movement and moved me back to the room. He sat me down on the mattress and when he reached for my face I cringed away. He gently pulled my face up, he didn't move my hair and made me look at him, "Honey are you okay?"

I sat and thought about his words, and I realized that I had nothing to answer him with. I thought about what had just happened and what had happened yesterday. If Luca hadn't come to see me, I would be worse off than I am now, "I-I am sorry..."

"Shh, let me see you," his voice was soft as he pulled my face back up. He gently pushed my hair out of my face. I watched his expression change as the anger set in at what he was looking at, "How about you lay down?"

I hesitated after I saw a flash of anger, "Luca..."

He took a deep breath before he looked back at me, trying to calm down for me, "Yes?"

"I am sorry. I should have said something. I understand that now, but Xavier and I were over, over a year ago. I thought he was over it. I thought I could handle this one thing on my own after I got a glimpse of his psycho behavior," I said trying not to sound like I was strangled and hit in the head as I rambled on.

Before I could get my next sentence out, he put his hand over my mouth, "Stop. This is not your fault. I will have it taken care of. Please don't keep something like this away from me again. Angelo or Apollo will always remain outside your door. I will be back in a little bit. If you need something, you only need to open the door."

He turned away from me once again and I grabbed his hand this time to stop him, "Luca...?"

I watched him swallow and slowly turn to look back at me once again with no expression, "Everything is okay Anastasia. I will be back soon, and I don't want you to worry."

That did not ease my anxiety at all. Sure, what Xavier did was awful, but I didn't like the look in his eyes, "Okay. If you say so."

He must have seen the look in my eyes, and I saw his eyes harden with what I assume was frustration, "Please stop. I need you to try and relax. Everything is okay now."

I looked away from him and pulled a pillow up to my chest in a hug, needing to wrap my arms around something. I laid on my side away from him and curled my legs up. I heard a couple of steps, and he pulled the blankets up over me. He pulled my face up, so I was forced to look at him. It made me flinch, but I needed to put my brave face on and try and reassure him, "I am okay, Luca."

He watched me for a minute, "We need to talk about some things. Nothing to be worried about, we must have open communication Ana. That is the only way I am going to be able to keep you safe. Some people want to hurt you right now. It is hard sometimes for me too, to trust someone. I just want to keep you safe. For now, relax. Watch some TV but please stay in this room."

"Okay fine Luca. You win. I will sit here and watch TV. Just don't do anything that my father would do. That is how we ended up in this mess. Be a different man than he was," I said as he walked away from me. He didn't say anything, but I could see the tension in his body as he exited the room and my words sunk in.

Time flew by and I sat in silence listening to the TV talk on some random show. There was a small tap on the door, "Can I come in please?" It was the only female I knew that was on my dad's crew.

"Sure, come in Evelyn," I said slowly, sitting up on the bed a little bit.

I watched a tall thin blond walk into my room and close the door behind her. She was about five feet seven inches tall. She was a healthy skinny woman with a waistline most girls would die for. She was a platinum blond-haired person and had bright green eyes. She was married to Angelo and spent too much time involved in my father's business. That's why my dad just hired her. She sat down next to me on the bed, "Are you okay?"

"Sure," I was playing with my hands as she stretched her legs out and half laid half sat up next to me on the bed.

"It's okay Ana. What you experienced was not okay. It is fine to say that you are not okay and let me help you."

"Did they send you in here to check in on me," I asked, trying to force some amusement into my voice to distract her. I couldn't talk loudly due to the pain in my throat.

"They may have thought a woman would make you feel a little more at ease considering what happened. I didn't even know that you dated Xavier. You know we used to talk a lot more. You know those guys just want to make you feel better. We have all spent most of our lives with you and your family," she went on a ramble.

"You got married to Angelo. We have all been a little busy. I didn't think it was worth mentioning, especially since it has been over for a long time. It was a stupid little fling and I thought he was over it," I said, my heart hurting at the mess my father and I both caused. Maybe I wasn't that different from him after all.

"You have had a rough couple of days. It has been a minute since we talked. I am sorry about that. Getting married has distracted me and made me a bad friend," she said, watching my face.

"What is Luca going to do to Xavier," I asked, turning to look her in the eyes as she turned toward me.

We both lay on our sides facing each other, and I watched her examine my face, "If he saw the bruises that are beginning to appear on your face and neck, nothing good." She saw me grimace and I watched her eyes tighten a little, "It is going to be okay Anastasia. Xavier did this to himself."

"Evelyn, I just want to be alone. It wasn't just him. I am the one who didn't take his heart seriously. I am the reason he lost his mind. I don't need a babysitter especially since Luca has them stationed outside my door. I can't go anywhere, and I am stuck in a room where all I can do is think about my life and mistakes. Now you can tell the two overanxious men out there that I am fine and just want to be left alone."

She sighed, "Alright Ana. Try and relax. I won't be far if you want anything, food, water, or company. I am still your friend, and I am sorry that I went MIA for a bit, but I still want to be your friend. Please don't blame yourself."

I watched her leave the room and a bubble of hysterical laughter exploded from my chest, "Relax? Is everyone high? I have been chased from my home, shot at, listened to my father die, separated from my family, killed a man, and then attacked by someone who was sworn to protect me. All they seem to be able to say to me is to relax."

I sank to the floor, my body shaking with laughter as I realized how incredibly insane I sounded right now. It didn't take long for the laughter to turn into sobs, and I held myself tightly trying to comfort myself. I don't know how long I was on the floor hiding and I heard the door open. I peeked over the bed and saw Luca closing the door behind him. He turned as I sat back down, and must have seen the top of my head, "What are you doing on the floor?"

"I just had a mental breakdown and let my brain exhaust the rest of my body again because no matter what I do at this point, my life will never return to the way it was and I will never return to my normal self."

He was standing at the end of the bed watching me. I saw a flash of sadness before he recovered, "Well that is an awful deep amount of thinking. I am sorry to hear that is how you were spending your day. How about you get dressed?"

"All right. I can do that I suppose," I slowly got to my feet. My limbs were numb from sitting so long on the floor, I went over to my suitcase and grabbed sweatpants and a T-shirt. I went into the bathroom and pushed the door closed but it was unable to latch due to the damage it had seen earlier today. I quickly put on the sweatpants and T-shirt. I caught a glimpse of my reflection and saw the bruising on my neck and face. I didn't like what I saw and moved quickly away from the mirror and back to the bedroom. Luca was sitting on my bed, and I saw he turned the TV off, "Luca?"

He looked at me, "I do not want you to argue. I want you to listen to me and please just do what I ask." When I didn't say anything, he took that as a sign of compliance, "Come with me."

"Okay, Luca. Lead the way," I said, throwing my arms out as if to say after you. I followed him out of the room and down the hallway. We came to a small accessible area that looked like a living/dining room. I saw them gathered around the table and some pizza boxes and two liters of soda were on the table. I let my hair fall into my face to hide the bruises that would only get darker with time.

"I would like you to try and eat something please," he said as I came to a stop.

I sat down at the table without saying anything and he put a plate with some pizza and a glass of brown soda in front of me. I picked up the greasy pizza and began to eat.

The more I ate the worse I began to feel. I finally ate one whole slice and pushed the plate containing another slice away from me. I took a drink of the soda and decided that was plenty to last me a minute. I was lost staring at the table in front of me with the sound of conversation everywhere, when suddenly I heard my name, "Anastasia?" I looked down at the table and saw that it was Apollo who was talking to me.

"I am sorry. I cannot eat anymore. I am full. It hurts to keep forcing food down," I returned my face to the table in front of me and tried to keep my face hidden.

"Hey, it's okay. You at least got some food in your body," Evelyn said, trying too hard to be my friend again.

"You should go lay back down. I don't think you've had enough rest," Ace said somewhere in the room.

I heard the room grow quiet as everyone stopped talking and I grew uncomfortable with the attention I was drawing, "I was hoping I could sit on the balcony. I could use some fresh air."

"I don't think that is a promising idea right now," Jace said, the tension in his voice at the thought.

The rage that coursed through me took over, "Fine!" I shoved the chair away from the table and stomped my way through the top floor of the hotel until I found the room once again. I slammed the door shut and wanted to scream at the top of my lungs. So, I let my emotions out, "I don't like being locked up!! I am not a prisoner! You all work for me!"

Despite yelling as loudly as I could and cursing my rage was not subsiding. The pain in my throat was growing worse. I began to pace the length of the room until the door began to open, "Anastasia?"

"Go away. I am not in the mood for company or a lame-ass lecture right now," I snapped.

"I am coming in," Luca said, opening the door enough for him to come in and closing the door behind him again, "You need to calm down. You are being a bit dramatic."

"I don't care! I hate this! You are all keeping me locked up like I am a mental patient. I believe I told you to leave me, the hell alone. How do you take that as please come in?"

"Well luckily, I take orders from adults, not bratty teenagers. You want to bitch and moan about it. Yell at all the people who are trying to keep you alive," he yelled back at me.

My anger just kept building and I couldn't stop myself anymore, "You mean the same people who failed to protect my family. The same people who were friends with the man that attacked me?!"

"Who the hell is this?! This is not the Anastasia that I know. This is some imposter. Some ungrateful girl acting like she is five."

We were screaming at each other. I had some angry tears spill over as I could not stop them, and I watched his face soften ever so slightly, "I am sorry. This is not easy for me. I lost so much in just a short amount of time. That includes me."

I turned away from him and just tried not to let my body collapse, "Ana…"

"Luca, I am asking you… Scratch that I am begging you, please. Leave me alone. I won't leave this damn room.

I just need some time alone please," I said, trying to keep the strength behind my words so that he would listen to me.

"No," he said, spinning me around and making me look at him. "I am worried about you," He pulled me into an unexpected hug, and I froze. Even though the tension entered my body the anger completely drained out of me, and I hugged him back.

Chapter Three

The Kill

After a few minutes, my body relaxed and I tried to keep a calm head when I asked, "What am I allowed to do?"

He was quiet for a minute, "For tonight? Can you please just relax? Get some sleep. I will let you do something tomorrow, but it's been a long day, and we all need some rest."

I felt the little anger I had left just leave my body. I felt completely defeated. I sighed, "Fine, I will be good tonight. Luca, I won't stay locked up for long."

"Thank you," he said, not bothering to try and cover up the relief that flew into his voice.

He pulled away from me and I couldn't bring myself to look at him. He pulled my face up by my chin and ignored me when I flinched away from him as he moved my hair out of my face. It was like he was afraid he would break me if he moved too fast. I saw a slight twitch in his expression as he saw the bruises on my face and neck, "How bad is it?"

His expression softened a little bit more, "It's not bad Ana. Let's get you into bed please?"

I stared at him trying to see if I could see any more in his expression, "Don't lie to me, Luca. You are bad at it."

He smirked but it didn't quite reach his eyes, "I'm not. You are still as beautiful as ever. Now please let's get your stubborn butt in bed."

Before I could react, he scooped me up into his arms. I felt the blood rush to my face, and I must have been red as a lobster. I didn't want to ruin his good mood, but I had to know, "Luca…? What are you going to do with Xavier?"

His whole body tensed, and I knew the fun teasing was over. He set me down on the bed gently, "That is none of your concern, Anastasia…"

"The hell it's not. He attacked me. He works for my family. It is my business," I said, my temper flaring again.

He stared at me for a moment before he chuckled. It was humorless and I could see on his face that he hated he was having this conversation, "He is going to be punished for his awful behavior. He should live."

"Is this nightmare over yet," I asked as I pulled my knees to my chest and hugged them tightly.

"It will be soon enough. We just have to keep you safe until we can get you to Texas safely, find him, and end this war," he said, looking at my face. I couldn't stop the shiver that his words brought on. He sat down next to me, "You need rest, or it will be harder for your body to recover. We need you at your best too."

I thought about his words and just sat there frozen. I very slowly laid my head on his shoulder giving him plenty of time to move away if he wanted to, "I just… I don't want to do this anymore. I don't want to eat or sleep. I was awful to him, Luca. I hated him. I wasted so much time being angry at him."

"I understand Ana. If I could change it, I would. Neither can you. There is no point dwelling on things that can't change. We can only focus on the things we can. Now please lay down. I will be back in a bit to check on you," he said, getting up from the bed slowly, so I had time to move my head.

I sighed and lay down. I pulled the blankets over me and had them up to my neck. He set the TV remote next to me, "I will lay here like a good girl, but I don't think I will sleep."

He smirked at me again and this time I saw that it did touch his eyes a little, "I can live with that for now. I will be back soon. Just please stay in your room."

I saw him hesitate for just a moment and then he turned. He walked right out of the room without looking at me. I heard voices on the other side of the door. My irritation bubbled because I was stuck in the room. I have been nothing but crammed into small spaces for a week. I gave up with silence, it was beginning to drive me crazy. I decided I could watch some TV. I turned on a chick flick and snuggled into the blankets against the fluffy pillows. My eyes closed at some point without permission, and I slowly sunk into a dreamless sleep.

****

I woke up to voices, "How long has she been asleep?"

"Maybe an hour. She's been muttering and whining. She feels a little warm. I don't know if it's the blankets or if she's getting sick. I don't think we should move her until we can get her to eat some real food," Angelo said, his voice quiet.

"Okay, go get some sleep with Evelyn," Luca said softly. "I'll take the next watch," both men were trying their damnedest to not wake the girl who was already eavesdropping.

There were no responses, after a minute I heard the door close, and someone moved silently across the room. I felt a hand on my forehead and decided to open my eyes. Luca's face looked so sad, "Are you okay Luca?"

His face changed and I could see there was concern and a flash of something else in his eyes, "Yes. I am fine. How are you feeling Ana?"

"I am okay. You should get some rest. I promise to stay in my room. I know you haven't gotten much sleep lately," I said looking at my hands.

I peeked up at his face and saw him staring at me, "Move over." He said giving me a small nudge so that I moved over on the bed, and he got in next to me. He lay down exhausted on top of the blankets. Before I could get any words out, he said, "I am not moving. Do not argue, it is easier if you have a nightmare or something."

I felt the blood rise in my face as he lay in the bed next to me looking disheveled and handsome. I laid down and pulled the blankets up to my chin to try and hide my embarrassment, "Luca?"

"Go to sleep, Anastasia. It has been a long couple of days, we could both use a good night's rest. You also might be getting sick, and we need you to not be sick so we can get on the road," his voice was growing rough.

I was overwhelmed by the amount of sadness that filled me in such a brief time. I sat up and felt dizzy, but I suddenly couldn't stand the thought of lying here any longer. I pushed off the bed just as Luca grabbed my wrist, "Please let me go."

He got off the bed and spun me around, so I had to look at him, "Get back to bed."

Those words would have been exactly what I wanted to hear if he had felt the same way about me that I had felt about him. I grew weary of myself and him. The sudden urge for my razor blade came hard and fast. I needed to distance myself from him again. My vision began to blur and then it went black, and my knees gave out. I felt his arms circle around my waist, and I could hear the change in his breathing, "I-I'm okay Luca…"

"Ana? Apollo?!" Luca scooped me up in his arms and set me gently down on the bed.

"What's going on Luca?"

"Get Angelo now!"

My eyes felt heavy, "Luca I am okay really. I am just suddenly very tired."

"Shh, I need to hear it from someone who knows medicine," he said sitting down next to me on the bed and pushing my hair back from my face.

The door opened and I looked over to see Angelo walking towards us looking exhausted, "What is going on?"

"She collapsed. Her whole body just seemed to stop working. I don't know what happened," Luca said, the tension flowing freely into his voice.

"It's okay Luca. She's just sick, let me see," Angelo said, trying to reassure Luca. "Anastasia, can you look at me please?"

I looked at him, "I don't feel good Angelo."

"I know honey, but Luca is worried about you. He said your body just collapsed and that is something to be concerned about," he said softly.

I felt the concern flow through me. I didn't want him to do a checkup. He'd see the scars and fresh wounds. "I told him I was fine. I just stood too fast and lost my balance. Nothing to freak out over. I just want to get some sleep now. He worries too much," I grumbled letting my eyes slip shut.

I heard him chuckle, "I am just going to check a few things quickly to be safe, okay?" I nodded back and tried not to think about what he would find if he tried. He took my temp and blood pressure, "She will be fine. Just let her get some sleep. It is just a combination of everything and a small fever. She hasn't been able to eat much either since Tony."

"Thank you, Angelo," Luca said, relief flowing freely into his voice. I heard them walk across the room and I heard the door close. After a few minutes I was drifting back to sleep, and I felt the bed move. I wanted to move towards him, but I forced myself to stay in one place, "You scared me, Ana."

"I'm sorry Luca. I didn't mean to. I just needed to move," I mumbled as I got comfortable once again on the bed.

I felt his hand on my forehead and the touch was gentle, "You are safe, Ana. Please get some rest. You need it to feel better."

"Okay, don't forget to get some rest too please."

"I won't honey. Now please go to sleep. Your body needs rest," he said, soothing me with his voice. He pulled the blankets over me. I felt myself begin to drift off into a dreamless sleep and I began to slip into unconsciousness.

****

I woke up unwillingly in a warm and comfy place. I had to talk myself into opening my eyes because it was not appealing at all. I let my eyes flutter open, and I saw that I was lying on Luca's shoulder. I looked up at his face and saw he was still fast asleep with one arm under and around my waist pulling me to him. My face flushed red in embarrassment as I didn't know how long we had laid together like this. I stretched and grabbed the TV remote and turned it on. I moved away from him ever so slightly and Luca started to grumble, "Quit moving Ana."

I forgot for a minute what my life had turned into, and a giggle escaped, "Quit grumbling at me Luca."

I saw the corners of his mouth turn up and then his bright hazel eyes opened and trained themselves on my face, "How are you feeling, Anastasia?

"I feel okay. Still not a hundred percent but I feel much better," I said, sitting up and looking back at him.

My long black hair fell around my face, and I took a second to gather myself and try not to let my feelings overwhelm me. I tucked my hair behind my ears and looked back at him. He was rubbing the sleep from his eyes and sitting up, "Good. How about you take a nice shower, while I talk to our team about the next step," he turned to look at me and I saw his eyes harden ever so slightly.

"Okay Luca," I said slowly getting to my feet and off the bed. I was standing and stretching some more. I went into my suitcases and grabbed some clothes without really looking at what I was grabbing. I turned and almost ran right into Luca.

"Anastasia, I need you to listen to me. You are still possibly sick, and I need you better so we can get back on the road. We shouldn't be staying but you are sick and the only way to get you healthy is food and rest," he said softly.

"Can I please sit on the balcony or go to the pool? Anything?" I asked, trying to hide the hope in my voice.

He stared at me for a moment and then sighed, "Sure Ana. I just need you to eat first and eat a little bit more than last night."

I couldn't stop myself from smiling as I won a small victory, "I can do that. Let me shower first."

He smiled back and my heart almost jumped out of my chest, "Go get in the shower. I will make you some breakfast, and we will go from there."

"Okay Luca," I walked to the bathroom with some clothes in my hand. I quickly got to the door I closed it as much as possible and turned on the water. I got under it, cleaned myself up, and shaved again. I got out of the shower and dried myself off. I quickly got dressed. I decided to look at myself in the mirror and decided to keep my hair down to try and hide all the bruises that were forming. I did some light makeup and had to stop when the bruises were too sensitive for me to continue. I went out of the bathroom and looked around for my team. I saw that Evelyn was sitting on my bed.

"Hey Ana," Evelyn said, moving towards me quickly. "Wait a minute."

"What is going on? Why do I have to wait," I asked looking up at her.

"They are moving Xavier. He is going to let him heal up a little before we move out. We need to keep you two away from each other. Luca told me to take you to the balcony and he said he would meet you out there when he was done," she said, pulling me outside into the warm air.

I felt the light breeze on my face, and I didn't care what was happening inside our hotel suite. I was just thrilled that I could be in the bright sun. I moved quickly to the railing and stared out into the world and looked at all the nice shiny buildings. I closed my eyes and took a deep breath, "Oh how I have missed this."

"I will be right back. I need to go help the guys out. Keep yourself safe and away from the edge, please. Do not leave the balcony," Evelyn said quietly.

"Okay you be careful please," I said softly.

I turned to look at her as she walked into the suite. I turned back to the beautiful view of the city. I jumped when a gunshot rang through the suite, and I turned in time to see Xavier running out onto the balcony and blocking the door. My heart stopped, "Hello Ana."

He had been beaten. His face was all swollen and he stared at me with one eye as the other eye was swollen shut, "Hi. Where is everyone?"

I heard banging on the door, but I couldn't see anyone, "They are busy."

"I want to go inside now," I said, feeling myself losing my nerve. My knees began to shake, and my throat felt tight like it was closing.

He held up a gun and pointed it at me, "I don't think so. You and I have some talking to do."

My blood ran cold, and my hands went up, "What do you want from me Xavier? I can't change. I can't change how I feel, and I can't change what has been done. You and I made a mistake, and I am so sorry that I hurt you."

I could see the anger flash across his face, "No we were not. The mistake was you leaving me and then pretending like it was nothing. It was everything to me!"

I began to panic and try to figure out how I was going to get out of here. My heart was racing, and I thought it might explode out of my chest, "They are going to kill you for this Xavier. You have messed up way too much and pushed it way too far."

He moved to me faster than I thought possible for someone in his condition. He grabbed my face and pain pierced through as he pushed the bruises, "I am taking you with me, Ana. I am not leaving this world without you. If I can't have you, no one can."

I could feel the panic taking over, but I refused to give in or to cry. I tried to calm myself down, "What the hell Xavier? I don't think I need to go anywhere with you. I certainly am not dying with you."

I hit him hard in the groin with my knee and bolted towards the door. He recovered faster than I initially thought, and he hit me hard in the back of the head with the gun. I fell to the ground. The light disappeared and the pain seared through the back of my head. He put the gun to my head and his voice was surprisingly soft, "Get up."

I slowly sat up through the pain and he pulled me up by my bicep. He was dragging me towards the railing on the balcony. The tears spilled over as I looked down at the ground. He picked me up and set me down, so I was sitting on the railing. My heart leaped again, and I let a small scream pass through my lips. I weaved my legs around the bars so that I would not fall, "Xavier stop! Please don't do this. This is crazy."

He moved to me and sat down next to me on the railing, and my breathing stopped for a split second, "It's the only way for you and me to be together and to be happy again. That is all I wanted. I want us to be together and happy, that's all."

"Killing us is going to do that?!"

He didn't respond. I looked at the door and looked through the small window on the balcony door and I saw Luca's face. He had a look of horror on his face, and I let a tear slip down my face. I closed my eyes, and the gun pressed against my head. I whimpered and I knew it was a matter of seconds before I fell. The one thing that gave me a little bit of relief was that it was about to be over. He would pull the trigger and I would be gone. I let a small sob escape as I imagined my mother and brother alone in the world. Just as I was ready to die, I heard gunshots, and I heard glass shatter. I opened my eyes in time to see Luca holding a gun and he had shot Xavier in the shoulder. Xavier lost his balance, and he began to fall backward and grabbed me. I had my legs still weaved in and out of the bars and that was the only reason that I didn't fall. I screamed as I felt his weight pulling hard on my muscles and bones, "Hold on Ana!"

"Luca help me!!" I screamed as the pain seared through my shoulder, abdomen, and legs, "Xavier let go of me!"

I felt someone's hand on my legs, "Jace take the damn shot."

I looked down at Xavier and he pulled the gun up and aimed it at me. I heard one final gunshot and it hit Xavier right between the eyes, and I felt the relief of him letting me go and the fact that I was still alive. I was quickly pulled up. Luca pulled me down and into his arms. I felt completely limp as I hugged him back and cried into his chest. We heard screams as his body hit the sidewalk below, "What do you want us to do Luca?"

I could feel my body shaking as he held me tightly, "Evelyn, call the police. You, Angelo, and Apollo go down and talk to them. Go now, the rest of you clean up this suite," his arms were still tightly around me, "Hey you. I need you to come with me."

"Okay Luca," I barely whispered but I could not bring myself to move.

He wrapped his arms tightly around my waist. He gently pulled me back to my room and helped me down on the bed. He kneeled in front of me, "Ana? Honey, are you okay?"

I broke down, "He tried to kill me!!"

"Shh, you're safe now. Please breathe," he moved my hair out of my face. "Anastasia, I thought we were going to lose you. I-" his hands went through his hair.

I touched his arm desperately wanting to make him feel better, "I am okay Luca."

He put his hand on either side of my face gently and stared at me for a minute, "I was very worried about you."

I slowly put my hands over his, "It's okay Luca. I am okay really. Just a little shook up."

He gave me a rare smile, "Well I am going to get some food in you. Why don't you sit here, and I will be right back."

I laughed despite myself, "I am not hungry Luca, but I can try if you want me to."

His smile got a little bigger, "Thank you, Ana." He moved away and stopped for a second to look at me. After a few seconds, which felt like an hour, he leaned down and kissed my forehead. The blush filled my face, "I will be right back."

"Okay, I will be here," I said quietly.

Then he was gone. I moved up to the pillow and hugged myself. My muscles screamed from the motion, but it was a nice reminder that I was alive. There was a light knock on my door, "Anastasia the police want to talk to you."

"Okay," I said slowly. I watched Angelo and Evelyn come in with two officers.

"We need to ask you some questions about what is going on, Miss Balistreri," One officer said.

"I will answer to the best of my abilities," I said slowly.

Luca rushed in with some toast, "Hello officers." He moved right to me, "Here you go Anastasia. Please try to eat."

I slowly took the toast and began to nibble on it. The two officers began to drill us with all kinds of questions about what had happened. I ate until I began to feel the bile rising in my throat again. At the end of this long interrogation my stomach was churning, "I am sorry, but she is sick. We have answered all your questions, and she has had a grueling day. Is there anything you need from her," Angelo asked.

"No, you can answer my other questions. Thank you for your time and cooperation," the officers both left the room with Angelo.

"Luca?"

He must have seen something on my face, "Hey it will be okay Ana."

"I just feel weird. I almost died more than I care to in the brief time that I have been away from home," I said looking down at my hands.

He moved to me quickly, "Hey stop. You are sick. You have had a rough couple of days."

"Luca-"

"Stop Ana. Please. We had a rude awakening today. So, I want you to rest. Angelo will be in, in a bit to check the flu. Make sure Xavier didn't do any severe damage to your body," Luca said, pulling my face up, so I had to look at him.

"Please don't punish anyone. It wasn't anyone's fault…"

"No one is getting punished. The only one I would punish is dead on a sidewalk. As for you, your only job is to rest," he gave me a small smile, "Now please relax. I will be back soon."

"Okay, Luca. You should relax too," I said, laying down in the bed and pulling the blankets up. I was warm and comfortable in bed. I watched him leave and I turned the TV on and felt my body try to relax. I stretched myself out and cringed under the pain my body felt. I rolled onto my side, and I let my eyes close.

****

I felt like it had only been five minutes since I shut my eyes when someone was pushing my hair back and irritating me, I groaned, "Leave me alone."

I heard Luca chuckle and my irritation melted away as quickly as it had appeared, "I am sorry sweetheart, but I came to check in on you."

I opened my eyes and saw that Luca was sitting down next to me on the bed, "Are you okay Luca?"

"Yes, I am fine Ana. How are you feeling," he asked, moving the hair off my face and he froze for a split second.

"I am feeling okay. Are the police officers gone?"

"Yes, they are gone. No need to worry Ana. Do you want to try and eat some food," he asked, overly hopeful. I could tell he wanted to do something to help me, and this was his way of doing it.

I sighed and summoned all the energy I had left in me, "I guess I can try some more food." I pushed myself into a sitting position, "Just let's start slow."

He smiled and stood up, then stretched his hand out to me. I took a deep breath and took his hand. He pulled me to my feet and my entire body hurt, "Let's get some food for you."

He pulled me through the upstairs floor slowly because it hurt to move. My men were scattered throughout the suite doing endless tasks, "What time is it?"

"It's just a little after four in the afternoon. You needed sleep, and we were going to let you get all the rest you could. Now time for some food," Luca said, pulling me to the small kitchenette.

Evelyn was at the stove cooking and grumbling under her breath as she stirred something in the pot, "So much food to cook. You are all a bunch of pigs."

I giggled and moved to her quickly, "How are you doing Evelyn?"

She looked at me with tension causing the veins in her head to bulge, but she still managed to smile at me, "Hey you. Glad to see that you were able to get some sleep. Want to help me cook for all these hungry men?"

"Of course, us girls must stick together. Let's feed this pack of wolves," I said, moving behind the counter to assist her. We cooked spaghetti, we made a salad and garlic bread. We needed them to eat healthily. We set the table, and it was already for them, "Let's call them to the table. Dinners done! Come and get it!"

The guys came rushing in and sat down. They began to dish themselves some food and the room was filled with conversation and laughter. This was the first time I had felt relaxed since we had to flee my house. I grabbed a plate and gave myself some food. I felt eyes on me and looked up to see Luca was watching me. He was sitting at the head of the table slowly picking at his food. I sat down at the island, so I wasn't crammed between all the men. Evelyn was sitting down next to me, "You are being watched."

The blush rose to my face, and I could not let my hope spread, "It's kind of their job to watch me, Evelyn."

"Eh, I know men. He is not watching you just for his job right now," she said, nudging me and winking.

My face somehow managed to grow even more red, "What else could it be? He just must protect me due to his job."

"You can say what you want my dear, but I know that look. It's why I am married to Angelo," she said, smiling at me.

"He sees me as a child. Besides, Luca is six years older than me. I am more of a job than anything else. It's okay though I can accept that," I said looking at her.

"Well, my dear. I am way better at this, so I am going to bet against you this time," she smiled at me with such confidence.

I looked down at the food on my plate and began to put food into my body again, "Hey Anastasia."

I felt my heart jump at the sound of his voice, "Hey Luca. What's up?"

"How are you feeling," he asked, his exterior very tense.

"I am fine. How are you," I said in a quiet voice so as not to draw attention to us.

"I am good. Did you still want to go to the pool," he asked, watching me closely.

The shock went through my body as I thought I would be on house arrest, "Yeah. Is that still, okay?"

"Yes, go get changed and we will go," he said, his voice still hard.

"Okay," I said and quickly went to my room. I changed into my black bikini. I was confused by Luca and his sporadic behavior. He is sweet and kind one minute and a hard ass the next. I sighed as I realized my life was never going to be simple.

There was a knock on the door, "You ready to go Ana?"

I opened the door and saw Angelo and Evelyn dressed for the pool as well, "Yeah. Let's go."

We went down the hall to the elevator and hit the button to go down to the first floor. We went into the pool room, and I waited a few minutes before I jumped into the heated water. I just needed to work off the nervous energy that I had. I swam for what seemed like minutes but according to the clock by the door, I had been swimming for two hours. People began to leave and before I knew it, I was the only one swimming in the pool. I heard a door slam shut and I saw Angelo with Evelyn sitting in the hot tub. Someone jumped off the diving board and I knew I wasn't alone in the water, but I tried not to look. I began to swim again but I moved towards the edge of the pool, my paranoia and panic took over. As I went to pull myself up, I was yanked under the water. I was pulled back up and was gasping for air. I went to yell at the person and saw Luca, "Hey."

I smacked him out of instinct, "You scared me half to death."

He had a small smile on his face, "I am sorry. I didn't mean to."

I splashed him, "I see you are taking a break from being the boss."

"Yeah, I needed a break. I needed to feel human again," he said, his voice growing softer as he spoke to me.

He grabbed me and pulled me to him, "I don't understand you, Luca." I didn't want to get my hopes up with how he was acting.

"Shh, just relax with me," he said, hugging me. He was hugging me tightly like he was scared that I was going to run away from him.

I giggled at the tension I felt in my stomach. I giggled again because he spun me around into the water, "You know you spin me for a loop. No pun intended."

He chuckled at my lame joke, "I don't know how to act around you, Ana. I know it's not fair and I am trying to figure it out," he said, moving a hand to the side of my face to keep me from looking away from him.

The blush rose on my face, "What does that mean?"

He made me look at him and I looked right into his amber eyes, "It's complicated."

I gave him a small smile even though the confusion was taking over my mind. He was staring at me, and I saw a look of hesitation on his face. He leaned down and pressed his lips against mine in a gentle kiss. He pulled away and we just looked at each other for a moment, "Luca…" My voice was a little shaky.

"Shh, you are safe I promise. I don't quite understand my feelings, but I know they are there," he said softly.

I laid my head on his shoulder, "I-I believe you. I am scared."

His arms tightened around me, "I understand Ana. I will show you I promise. Just trust me."

"Luca? It's getting late. Should we head up," Angelo asked quietly.

I tensed up because I forgot that we had other people here in the pool room with us, "Yeah. We should. We will be leaving the hotel tomorrow."

I heard Evelyn and Angelo leave, "I am sorry Luca…"

"Why are you sorry," he asked, pulling me away from him so I could look at him.

"I don't know…" I said, not wanting him to admit that I was an embarrassment to him.

"Let's get you upstairs, warm, and in bed. One step at a time," he said, pulling me to the stairs. He got up and grabbed a towel off the bench. I followed him out of the pool and wrapped it around my body to dry off. We both headed upstairs, "Go take a warm shower. I will check on you in a bit."

"Okay Luca," I said going into my room. I went into the bathroom with the broken door. I took my swimsuit off and quickly showered. I changed into shorts and a T-shirt. I lay in bed and turned off the TV. My body was exhausted, and I let my eyes slip shut. I looked up and around the room not wanting to fall asleep. I sat up and saw Xavier standing across the room. He had a gun in his hand, and the panic took over, "Get away!!!" I screamed and moved quickly across the bed and got out as fast as I could. I ran into Apollo and screamed again, "I'm sorry!!!"

"Shh you are safe Anastasia," Apollo said, hugging me. "Come on, let's get you back to bed."

"No! He's back! Please don't make me! He will kill me this time," I said, trying to get away from him.

"I got it from here, Apollo. Get some rest," Luca said somewhere behind us.

"Are you sure," Apollo asked looking past me.

"Yes, get some rest. I have it from here," his voice was hard and tense.

Apollo let me go and I wrapped my arms around myself. Luca grabbed my elbow and pulled me back toward my room. The panic took over once again, "No Luca!" He pulled me into the room, "Please listen to me! Xavier-"

He closed the door and put his hands on either side of my face, so I had to look at him, "Xavier is dead. You had a bad dream. No one is here but me and you baby."

I collapsed into him, and I could feel myself shaking, "It felt so real. He was right there. I swear."

"Relax please," his voice was soft and gentle.

My eyes closed as I laid my head on his chest and let his heartbeat relax me, "Luca, I don't want to sleep. I am scared."

"No reason to be scared Ana," he said, picking me up and putting me on top of the blankets on the bed. He got in next to me. He pulled the blankets down and over me, "You don't have to sleep."

"You are making me tired," I groaned as I laid my head on the fluffy pillow and my eyes grew heavy.

"Do you want me to go," he whispered. I shook my head, and he laughed as I let my eyes finally slip shut, "Good night, Ana. I will be here when you wake up," He kissed my forehead, and I began to drift into unconsciousness.

****

I woke up to Luca shaking me, "Time to get up and get dressed."

I rubbed my eyes and sat up, "Okay Luca."

I got up and went into the bathroom. I put on a light blue sundress and sandals. I did a little makeup which included eye shadow, eyeliner, and mascara, "Anastasia's car is ready. Let's move."

"I am coming," I yelled back. I grabbed my purse to find my suitcases were already gone. I went out to find the group of men. I had Jace walk me to the car. I climbed inside and saw Angelo, Evelyn, and Apollo, "Where's Luca?"

"He's in the other car managing some things. Come on Ana," Evelyn said, closing my car door.

My phone went off in my purse. I didn't remember Luca giving it back to me. I shrugged off the feeling of confusion and answered, "Hello?"

"Hello, my sweet. You look wonderful in that dress. I can't wait for us to meet," came a cold dark voice. We were now driving down the road. Someone ran into the back of our car and my heart stopped as I dropped the phone.

Chapter Four

The Accident

I looked at my phone on the floor and looked over at Evelyn, "Where's our other car?"

"In front of us somewhere. Who was that," she asked as someone hit us again.

I screamed, "It's him. He's here for me. What do we do Evelyn? I don't want to go with him. I don't want you to get hurt."

She pulled her phone out of her pocket and dialed. It began to ring, and she put it to her mouth, "Luca he's here."

We were hit again, and the car swerved as the guys tried to avoid hitting another car, "Evelyn?!" My breathing began to pick up into hyperventilation.

She reached over to me and helped me buckle up. I watched her put her seatbelt on as well, "We are going to crash. It's going to be okay Ana. I just need you to remain calm. Luca is going to be ready to turn around and grab us as quickly as he can. Just breathe."

My breathing didn't slow and as I tried my best efforts couldn't help the racing of my heart. We got hit once again and our car fishtailed a little. I closed my eyes, grabbed the door, and squeezed it with all the strength in my hand. Before I could tell myself, it was going to be okay, we were getting hit from multiple sides and then we were rolling. I threw my hands over my mouth and my seat belt snapped. I tried to stop myself from going anywhere I threw my arms out to grab or stop myself. I couldn't grab anything. I just kept flying around, unable to control where my body tumbled. I was surrounded by glass and broken car parts. You know how they tell you; that your life will flash before your eyes? Well, the world went into slow motion, but I wasn't thinking about my life. I was just thinking about last week. All too soon we came to a stop, and I felt pain everywhere. Everyone else groaned, "Ana are you okay?"

I went to sit up and was surrounded by shattered glass from the crash. I felt a sharp pain in my side as I collapsed back to the ground, "What happened?"

Before anyone could respond to me gunshots were bouncing off the car. I screamed as one went into the roof of the car next to me. I tried to make myself as small as humanly possible and just froze with fear. Evelyn, Apollo, and Angelo, all unbuckled themselves. Evelyn moved to me and grabbed me by my arm and began to pull me out. We were sitting along the side of the car hiding from the raining gunshots. We were waiting for a second limo to pull up so we could get the hell out of here.

I looked over at the people who had seen me through the worst and a lump formed in my throat. This was all my fault. Evelyn had tears streaming down her face, "This is it. This is how we are going to die."

I tried to think of something I could say to help, but our second car pulled up to a screeching halt. Luca flung the door open, "Everyone in now!" Angelo grabbed Evelyn and Apollo grabbed me while shielding me with his body. The limo was speeding away before we even had the door fully closed.

Luca was checking everyone and making his rounds around the small space. I was on the floor gasping, every breath was painful, but it felt like freedom because I was alive and not in the presence of some mafia man. Luca knelt in front of me, "Luca?"

"Hey, it's okay. No reason to panic or to make yourself freak out. You are safe. Let's get you off the floor and into a seat," he held his hand out to me, and I reached over to grab it. As he was pulling me up from the floor the pain in my side became too unbearable and I collapsed back onto the floor, "Ana?"

"I-I'm okay," I said, putting my hand to my side out of instinct. I took a deep breath and when I moved my hands to push myself up, I saw there was blood, "Luca...?"

He looked down at me and stopped dead when he saw the blood on my hand, "Angelo get over here!"

Angelo was next to me in a flash of a moment, "Alright Ana. I need to move your dress so I can see what is going on."

"No. Luca please no. There are too many people. I have- I don't want-" I was trying to focus on the car full of men, instead of the scars; fresh and old. I also didn't need the men in the car to see what type of underwear I wore.

His eyes softened as he took in my face, "Jace, can you hand me my jacket please." I watched Jace hand Luca the coat and he draped it over me. He looked up at my face, "Now no one can see. Now please let Angelo do his job and keep you from bleeding everywhere."

I took a couple of deep breaths when no words came to me. I looked at Angelo who was still right by my side and nodded, "Alright. This may hurt Anastasia. Deep breaths."

He moved my dress up carefully so he could see the wound. He put a little pressure on my side, and I gasped, "Stop!"

His hands moved quickly away from my side, "Jace, come here. I need you to keep her legs still. Apollo-"

"I will hold her shoulders," Luca said, his voice hard and tense, leaving no room for arguments, "Let's do this before she loses too much blood."

"No, wait," Jace grabbed my legs, and the panic took over. "NO!" I tried to get away from the group of guys that were trying to help me. Luca grabbed my hands and I stopped to look at him, "Luca stop!"

"You listen to me, Anastasia. You are not dying. Not today or anytime soon. So, I suggest you dig your nails into my arms or whatever you must do, to get through this. Get ready," he said his voice was cold and determined.

"This is going to hurt. I must get this bar out, clean out the glass, and stitch it up. I need you to just try to be as still as you can little boss," Angelo said, his voice gentle.

I felt the pressure again. I dug my nails into Luca's arm to try and keep myself still. It felt like I was being cut open as hard as I tried. I couldn't stop the scream that slipped past my lips. Then there was this popping sound, and the pain dulled a little bit as he took the bar out of my side. I took a deep breath and more tears slid down my face, "Are we done yet?"

I looked at Angelo and his eyes were sad as they met mine, "Not yet honey. We still must get the glass out and stitch it up."

"But it hurts Angelo," I sobbed and looked away before I lost my shit more than I already was, "Please can we stop?"

"No, we cannot stop Ana. Breathe and get ready. We are going to do this, and we need to do it now," Angelo responded.

"I am not ready," I whined and moved my head from side to side as if to say leave me alone.

"Get ready. We don't have time to wait for you to be ready honey. We need to stop the bleeding," Angelo said using his doctor's voice.

I felt him picking out the glass and just felt tense. After half an hour of him picking at me and me whining and crying. He finally began to stitch me up and I screamed the first time he pierced my skin with the needle. I lay on the floor exhausted and drained with him putting a bandage on my side, "Ana?"

"Luca," I mumbled, turning my head towards the sound of his voice.

He moved my hair out of my face, "Honey I am going to move you off the floor."

I groaned and shook my head weakly, "It hurts Luca. I don't want to move."

I could hear the pain in his voice as he spoke softly, "I know baby. I will make it better I promise. The first thing I want to do is get you off the floor please."

He scooped me up and I curled close to him, "I feel sick."

"When we get to the hotel, I will make it better. I just need you to hold on until we get you there," he said quietly.

I slowly opened my eyes and found his hazel eyes were mostly green today, "I am trying Luca. I am. I just really hurt."

"Just relax. We will get you all set up," he gave me a weak smile that didn't quite reach his eyes.

I let my eyes slip shut again, "Okay…" I tried to force my body to relax but it caused searing pain. I was slipping unconscious while I listened to the hum of the car.

****

I moved and the pain hurt enough to wake me up. I groaned, "Are you awake Ana?"

I opened my eyes, "Hey Evelyn. Where are we now?"

"We are in Tennessee, we went until Luca made us stop for you," she said, watching me. "He's been out of his mind. I am going to get him before he does anything else to drive everyone crazy."

I let my eyes close again and tried to push away the pain. I heard the door squeak open and close quietly, "Ana, are you okay?"

I opened my eyes, "Luca I am okay. Are you okay?" I looked him up and down. I saw his posture was defeated. I got back to his face, and I saw dark bags under his eyes. He moved next to me, and I rested my hand on the side of his face, "When is the last time you have slept?"

He closed his eyes at the touch of my hand, and I resisted the urge to smile, "I couldn't sleep. I wasn't sure if you were going to be okay. You had lost so much blood. I was so worried."

His eyes opened and I stared at his hazel eyes that were back to a golden brown, "How about you come lay down with me? We can watch TV and just relax."

I watched the corner of his mouth kick up as he thought I was amusing, "Of course, I will lay with you. Try and stay still. I do not want you to tear your stitches."

He laid down next to me and I could feel the tension slip out of his body. I turned on the TV and put on the first movie I could find. I looked over at him a few minutes later and saw his eyes were closed. His breathing had steadied out and I dared hope that he was asleep. I finally let myself smile and went to sit up when the pain in my side made me collapse into the mattress. I was gasping and trying to get up when my bedroom door opened, "What are you doing?"

I looked up to see Apollo, "I want to sit up."

"You are ridiculous! You must be careful. You have a nice deep wound, and Angelo didn't have the proper equipment. We do not have the means to give you a blood transfusion," he said, moving to me.

"I can't just lay here. Apollo, I hate just laying here. I feel useless and much more vulnerable than I ever have. Please I must do something," I said. I froze when Luca stirred and I lowered my voice, "This isn't me."

"Lay back down and I won't wake him up to tell him. You can get up in a little bit, but I need to make sure you are fine," he stared at me until I groaned and nodded. He gave me a sad smile, "Thank you. I will be back in a little bit." I watched him walk across the room and leave as quietly as possible.

I was lying there listening to the movie and staring at the ceiling. I felt like I was losing my mind just sitting here counting the cracks. After what felt like years instead of a few hours I heard a gentle groggy voice, "Anastasia?"

I turned my head to look at Luca. He had his eyes opened but they were still a little droopy, "Well good morning you. I am glad you finally got some sleep, but it looks like you could use some more."

"Yeah, it was good. I can't sleep anymore," he said sitting up. "How about you? Did you get any more sleep?

"I am losing my mind, Luca. I can't sleep anymore. I can't just lay here. I must do something. Please I need to move," I said, my voice whinier than I wanted it to be.

He gave me a small, crooked smile that melted the walls I had surrounding my heart, "Alright, but baby steps. You need to take it easy."

"I promise. Now, please help me sit up," the excitement leaked into my voice.

He sighed and gently slipped his arm under my back to help me sit up. I gripped the bed and squeezed it hard as the pain seared up my side. I was in a sitting position, but I kept having to hold my breath to get through the pain. I was finally able to let out the air and was breathing heavily. He sat down in front of me and watched me until my breathing returned to normal, "Take an easy, Ana. Nice slow breaths."

"I am okay," I said as my body was fighting me to relax.

He put his hands on either side of my face, "Breathe. I need you to relax your body and take deep breaths."

I felt the warmth of his hands and tried to focus on that. My shoulders and back relax. My breathing slowly became easier, "I am okay."

He stared at me for what felt like forever, just studying my face, "Ana, I don't want you to do anymore. That was too much."

"No, please Luca. I need to get up. I can't lay here anymore," I was close to begging, and I hated myself for it.

"Honey please listen to me. I was worried about you. You could've died. You almost died and that is far more than I am ready for. I need you to stop and just do as I say," he said, his eyes bearing into my soul.

I felt ashamed and that surprised me. I didn't have anything to be ashamed of, "Okay Luca. I will be a little more patient. I just don't want to be stuck here."

I let my hair fall into my face as his body relaxed. I just needed a few seconds to compose the crushing disappointment I knew was on my face. He moved my hair out of my face and tucked it behind my ear, "Thank you, Ana. How are you feeling?"

It took everything I had not scoffed at the question. Didn't I just explain to him that I was not happy about the situation? I wanted to grab the razor but instead, I took a deep breath and thought about my body before responding, "Tender but good. Thank you, Luca. I need to move. I am feeling like I am losing my mind."

His eyes were soft, and I knew he wasn't going to budge, "I understand baby. I also need you to take it easy please."

I felt frustration and blood rush to my head. I loved hearing it, but I knew he was doing it just to make me not argue, "When will I be back on the road?"

"Not for a couple of days. I need you to get your strength back up," I felt embarrassed so I looked down at my hands. They were folded in front of me, and I don't know how long I was looking at them when he pulled my face up and made me look at him, "Ana. I cannot express the fear I felt in my heart. I thought you were going to die in my arms.

I didn't like the fear of knowing there was nothing I could do about it."

My throat began to restrict the emotion I was feeling and the emotion I was seeing on his face. I felt selfish and I could see the truth in his eyes, "I am okay Luca. Please relax."

He went to respond when a small knock interrupted him, "Come in."

I looked over at the door and saw Angelo coming in and closing the door, "I need to check your stitches."

I sighed knowing that I was going to have to lay back down, and it made me want to scream. I felt the sudden urge to cry as well. The men helped me lay down, "I feel fine. You guys worry too much," I said, trying to keep the anxiety and pain from taking over my voice.

"I know but you need a new bandage. I also brought some pain pills to help relax you," Angelo said, lifting my shirt so he could see my side. I froze when I realized that someone had changed my clothes.

The pain brought me out of the embarrassment and concern that they saw the marks, "Please stop."

"We are almost done. Ana, just hold on a little bit longer," Angelo said, his voice soft as if talking to a child.

I squeezed my eyes shut and had my hand in a tight fist so that my knuckles were white. I finally was able to take a deep breath when the pain began to dull down a little bit. My body felt weak from that little bit of tension it had endured. "Open your eyes, Ana," Luca said, his voice gentle.

I let my eyes open a touch, "But I am tired now."

It surprised me when he chuckled, "I need you to take these pills that Angelo has in his hands,"

I looked over at Angelo, "Do I have to?"

"It will help you be able to get some more rest, little boss."

I sighed, "Alright. Give them here."

I took the pills out of his hand and put them in my mouth. Luca helped me sit up enough to drink out of the bottle of water to wash them down, "Get some sleep little boss. You need it."

I let my eyes slip shut the rest of the way and my body turned to jelly. I was slipping into a state of unconsciousness when I heard a strange voice, "You are mine."

I whimpered, "Please leave me alone." I wanted to scream, to yell. I just couldn't take the sound of his voice, "I didn't do anything."

"But you will be mine whether you like it or not. You will give me children. This is the payment you will pay for what your father has done to me and my family," he said his voice dark.

"NO!!!" I screamed and popped into a sitting position. The pain had me gasping and it was something fierce. I had tears streaming down my face. I put my hand to my side and when I pulled it away to move my hair off my sweaty face I saw blood, "Luca... Angelo..." I tried to yell but my voice came out weak and quiet.

I stopped and listened, but I did not hear anyone. My voice was growing weaker and weaker. I felt my body grow dizzy. I took a deep breath and pushed myself out of bed and onto my feet. I had to stop for a minute because the pain was too bad. Once I was ready again, I managed to get close to the wall. The pain in my side began to get worse, but I leaned against the wall and moved slowly through the suite. I was searching desperately for someone, keeping the pressure on my side, but the blood was still seeping through my fingers. I had managed to get out of my room down the hallway. I stumbled on something and fell over. I hit the floor hard and silent tears went down my face. I heard someone close by, "Did you hear that?"

"Please help me," I tried to shout but I just felt my strength draining from my body. I let my eyes close as my hope of living through this disappeared.

"Anastasia?!"

I pried my eyes open, "Ace? Please help me…"

"Hey, I am here. Shh, please save your strength. Angelo! Luca!" He yelled, putting pressure on my side and causing me to gasp in pain.

I heard people running toward us and I turned my head to see Angelo and Luca running toward me, "What the hell is going on?"

"I am sorry. I had a nightmare, and I tore my stitches fighting in my sleep. I don't know when or how long I was bleeding. Please don't be mad," I said as loud as I could, looking between the group of men slowly forming around me.

Luca was moving my hair back from my face, "I am not mad. No one is mad. Let's just get you all fixed up Ana."

I felt so drained, and I felt more pain in my side. My life is nothing but pain and misery currently. I wasn't hopeful for that to change anytime soon. They fixed my side and Luca put one arm under my knees and the other under my back. He picked me up and I wrapped my arms weakly around his neck. I hid my face in his shoulder. He bent down and set me down on the bed, "Luca?"

"Shh, please. Let me get you cleaned up and then we can talk," he said, his voice thick with tension.

I didn't know what to say or do. I felt weak and pitiful. I was feeling hatred towards myself. I was sinking and I felt like my father would be ashamed of me. Luca came back with a washcloth and some new clothes for me, "Luca, I-"

"Ana, please just stop. I want to get you cleaned up. You are covered in blood, and I want to get you back to sleep," he said before I could try and finish a sentence.

"Oh okay," I said, looking anywhere but at him. I hated that he was seeing me this way. He had only seen me since I've been in this mess. Then the hatred for my father began to bubble. This is his fault. I should be enjoying my summer before I go off to college with my friends. I didn't want to be sitting here trying not to bleed to death.

He began to wipe the blood away, "Alright. Now we need to get you into clean clothes. This is going to hurt."

"No," I said, not wanting to take my pants off.

"Yes."

"Luca…"

"Ana, we will fight about whatever you want to after," he said quietly.

He pulled me to my feet, and I was gasping as pain seared my side. I waited for it to become a dull ache. Once I had clean clothes on, he changed the bedding on the bed. Before I knew it, I was in a clean bed sitting down trying to control the war that was happening inside my head. I felt like I was being torn in half and not just because of the pain in my side, "I am sorry Luca."

"Shh, you need to be more careful baby. You scared me once again and I do not like coming to find you in a pool of your blood. You better get used to me because I am not leaving your side until you can walk without holding on to the wall," he said, pulling my face up by my chin, so I was forced to look in his direction. I couldn't bring myself to look into his eyes.

I hated that I felt relief at the thought that I might die. I sighed, "I am tired. I am going to lay down and try to sleep." I couldn't bring myself to look at him. He helped me lay down and I tried to make myself as small as possible. The bed moved and I knew he was lying down on the bed next to me.

"Good night, Ana."

I lay there staring at the wall trying to be the positive person I used to be before my father ruined it. After a couple of hours, I couldn't keep my eyes open anymore. I let them slip shut and I drifted into a dreamless sleep.

****

I woke up with the sun shining through the window and it made me want to groan. I did not want to be awake. I wanted to be asleep. I froze when I heard people saying, "We must keep an eye on her, Angelo. She has had too many close calls."

"We will Luca. She is an adult. She needs to have some freedom. We just flipped her entire world upside down. She has had to experience way too much in such a short amount of time. Our next step needs to be getting some food into her body," Angelo responded to Luca.

That was enough eavesdropping, and I should join society again whether I wanted to or not. I took a mental deep breath and opened my eyes, "Do I have to eat?"

The guys turned to me as I slowly rolled over to face them, "Yes, you need to eat. I need to see how your mother and brother are doing. I need you to put some food in your body please," Luca said like he was coaxing an abused dog out from under a porch.

"I am not hungry. I do not want to eat…" I saw the sadness begin to flood his eyes and it made my chest tighten, "I guess I could try…" I said as he helped me into a sitting position.

I tried to keep my breathing under control as I waited for the pain to dull back down, "Just try and relax. You are getting better with your breathing through the pain."

I pushed the lump that wanted to form deep down. I need to work on being numb and strong like my dad. That was why I hated him. He had to do this to keep himself sort of human in this job, "I am trying. It does hurt but I want to get better."

Luca looked away from me, "I must go call your mother and brother. Angelo, help her get to the kitchen and get her something to eat. She needs to get some substance in her body. No ifs and's or buts."

Angelo moved towards me, "Ready?"

I heard Luca leave and I took a deep breath. I was pulled to my feet, and I had to take a moment to get myself back together. Angelo waited patiently and then pulled me through the suite. I couldn't bring myself to say anything. I just kept my gaze down with no complaints. Someone put toast in front of me and I nibbled at it. I could hear Luca in the next room talking and my stomach churned ever so slightly. I still nibbled knowing that if I didn't eat it would just hurt him more. I looked up from the table to see that I had six sets of eyes on me, "Please stop. I am fine."

They all looked away as if caught peeping on someone who was changing. I sighed and got up from my seat. I moved slowly but luckily no one dared to stop me. I walked over to the balcony door and sat down in the cool fresh air. My side was tender, but I was starting to adjust to the pain. I was finally feeling a little hopeful that I could do this. The door opened behind me, and I heard Evelyn talking, "Ana, you should come inside before Luca sees."

My irritation flared, "Eve I want to be out here. I do not care what he says. I am in charge here and he keeps forgetting it," I said, my voice sounding numb. "Now please leave me alone."

"Fine it's your war," she said, closing the door. I sighed, finally happy to feel sort of in control of what was happening in my life.

I sat down and watched the sunrise. I just enjoyed the little bit of peace before the world got busy again. All too soon it was over, and Luca was storming out onto the balcony, "What the hell are you doing out here? Get inside now!"

"No, Luca. I am not going inside. I want to sit outside, and feel like a person. I am not fragile. I am not a child," I said, my voice growing hard.

He sighed and picked me up ready to start a fight. He carried me to my room quickly. He set me down on the bed and I was ready for the fight, "You will stay here. You are not free to do what you want. Someone is trying to get you! What do you not understand by that?!"

"The hell I am not free! I will do what I want! I am

92

my own person. I am capable of handling myself," I said, my anger growing along with the volume of my voice.

I looked at him and saw he was fuming right back at me, "Make yourself comfy. You won't leave until we leave the hotel if this is how you are going to be. I am trying to do my job, you selfish brat," he slammed my bedroom door closed and I heard the click of the lock.

"Are you kidding me?!" I moved to the door, trying my best not to tear my stitches. I grabbed the doorknob and sure enough, I couldn't get it to turn, "You are such an asshole!"

I screamed and wanted to punch something but given my physical state, I didn't think that was safe. I sat down on the floor instead of punching things. I hugged myself as I hid in the corner. The pain in my side grew as the pain meds wore off. I was still so angry. He locked me up; this asshole locked me up. I can't believe he locked the door so I couldn't leave. The door opened and two people stepped in. I looked up to see Angelo and Evelyn. Evelyn set a food tray down on the floor in front of me, "You shouldn't be on the floor. You are going to tear your stitches."

"I am fine. Go away," I said, not making eye contact with either of them hoping they would get the hint.

"Ana, you need to eat," Angelo said, his voice pleading with me. I know he was trying to get me to understand but I still couldn't see past my blinding rage.

"No," I said, the determination flowing freely into my voice. I was not caving. I was angry and they all were going to know it.

"Luca-"

"Luca can go to hell. Get out of my room now. I do not care what that man has to say about anything. He locked me in here like I am a common criminal. Now please get out. GET OUT!" I yelled as the anger flowed freely from my body into my voice.

I heard one of them sigh, "We will leave the food in case you get hungry." They both got off the floor, "Look I know you are upset. I would be if I were being forced to stay in a room but take it easy on him. He doesn't know how to act. He has been in this for way too long. He doesn't mean to be this way," they both left, and I heard the click of the lock once again.

I hugged myself again and pushed the tray of food as far away from me as possible without getting up. I leaned my head against the wall in the corner. I let my eyes close, and I hadn't realized I was drifting off until the door opening jolted me awake, "What are you doing now?"

I gagged and a trash can was in front of me suddenly. I threw up the little bit of food I had gotten into my system. I couldn't get myself to stop and had my eyes in the trash can until my body was dry heaving, "Just leave me alone. I won't be going anywhere. You made sure of that. Just please go away."

"I am not going anywhere, and I am not trying to trap you. I am trying to keep you safe. You are not making that easy," he grabbed the trash can and moved it away from me, "Let me help you up."

I had the sudden urge to cry and fought it with every fiber of my being. I didn't want to cry anymore. I just wanted to make my dad proud. I just stared at my hands in hopes that he would leave me alone. He pulled me gently to my feet and the pain was sharp in my side, "I don't feel well Luca. Please just leave me alone."

His eyes softened ever so slightly. He pulled out his phone and sent a quick text message, "I am not going anywhere. I am not leaving you alone like this," There was a knock on the door and Luca had me sitting on the edge of the bed, "Come on in Angelo."

Angelo opened the door and stepped in. He took one look at me, "Hey you. You look a little rough around the edges."

I couldn't stop the small smile that appeared on my face, "I am not feeling well."

He gave me a small smirk back, "Well how about I do a little check-up on you then and see what is going on."

He moved to me with his medical bag. He opened and began to check my stitches and changed the bandages again, "Is she okay?"

"Calm down Luca. It just looks like a small infection is forming. Luckily, it was caught early but it must have occurred when she tore her stitches. We caught it plenty in time to nip it in the bud," Angelo turned to me. "Take these pills, little boss. Take it easy."

I took the pills and swallowed them down with some water. I wanted them to leave me alone. I was still upset, "Thank you, Angelo."

"You two must figure out how to not yell at each other. She is fragile despite how she holds herself. You don't know how to have a relationship and she can't let herself be vulnerable. There must be some other way other than yelling at each other," Angelo said trying to keep his voice down as he talked to Luca.

"I got it. Go, let me handle this and talk to her," Luca responded to him.

I heard the door close. After a few minutes, the bed moved under his weight, "I am fine Luca. I do not want to keep repeating myself."

He made me roll over so that I was facing him. He pulled me gently into a hug as to be careful of my side. I kept my eyes down not wanting to look or talk to him. He moved my hair out of my face and tucked it behind my ear, "Ana... Baby the way that my mind works I-I just want to keep you safe. I am sorry. Seeing you out on the balcony reminded me of when you almost fell because of Xavier..."

I gave myself a pep talk in my head and looked up at him, "I was raised a certain way, I-I can't just turn it off. I was taught not to take crap from anyone. I am sorry that I hurt you that way..."

"Stop. We have some stuff that we need to figure out but not right now. Right now, I need you to relax. I know that you are feeling sick," he said, his voice soft.

I let my body relax ever so slightly and I laid back against the pillow, "How are Mom and Dom?"

"They are both good. On their way to Texas. The safe house will be a good place for you all to be a family again. We will meet them there soon."

"Okay, it will be nice to see them again," I said, my voice numb.

He pulled my face back up, "I am deeply sorry for how I acted Ana. I don't mean to be this way."

I felt an overwhelming urge to hug him. I reached out to him and pulled him down, so he was lying next to me, "I am sorry for being a pain in the ass."

He laughed as I laid my head on his shoulder, "This is going to be a trial-and-error thing, Ana." It was quiet for a minute, "Alright little lady. Come on," he gently pulled me into a sitting position. He reached over and grabbed a jacket; he helped me into the jacket. He pulled me slowly through the suite.

He brought me to the balcony door, and he opened the door, "Thank you."

He gave me a heart-stopping smile, "I will have some food brought out to you and I expect you to eat it all. I have some stuff that I need to manage. Please don't leave the suite."

"I won't. Thank you so much, Luca," I turned and hugged him as tightly as I could. "Thank you, this means so much to me."

He smiled and hugged me back, "You're welcome baby. I will see you soon. Now please be good." He left me out of the warm fresh air.

I sat down in one of the two chairs out on the balcony. There was a table next to me and the sun on my skin was warm. I felt the smile on my face, and it felt like forever since I had felt peace like this. The door opened and I saw Ace come out with a tray, "Here is some food, little boss."

He set the food down and left me to be alone. I had time to think and relax. It was a good, wonderful feeling to just be myself instead of prey. I looked at the food and saw grilled cheese and pretzels. I did what I told him I would do and began to eat. Evelyn came out in a little bit of time, "Hey you."

"Hi, Eve."

"Are you doing better?"

"I think so. He's hard to read. I have never been this involved in my father's work before. This is hard to adjust to as well," I said looking out at all the buildings.

"This is a hard life. It takes a lot out of you and the relationships that you form. If you are lucky to form one. It doesn't mean that it's not possible to maintain them," she said.

We sat there in silence for a while, while I thought about her words and the way she phrased them. I just don't see how that could be possible, "Hello ladies." I looked up and saw him with his hair a little wet and wearing a black T-shirt that hugged him tightly. I watched her leave. He turned to me, "He was spotted in the city. We can't wait for you to heal. I am sorry it's time to leave."

I froze and suddenly felt exposed. It was amazing how fast I could go from loving the outside to hating being out here. "Okay," I went back to my room; it was getting a little easier to ignore the pain in my side. I changed into a set of leggings and a T-shirt that was long enough to go over my butt. I packed the remainder of my things into the suitcases and put my hair up into a bun. Ace came in and grabbed my bags and quickly left the room. Apollo came in after him, "Time to go?"

He nodded, "Let's move Ana."

Chapter Five

The First Meeting

Now that we were on the road again it was nice and quiet despite all the people in the car. My side was tender, and I tried to sit at an angle to keep the stitches from being moved. I had my seatbelt on, Luca insisted after the last accident and I just didn't have the energy to argue with him. Everyone was in the limo talking amongst themselves, just trying to keep their voice down but not to be bored. Luca was sitting and looking at his phone intently as he texted. I moved my gaze to the outside world cruising by us, "What is wrong?"

I just shook my head knowing my words wouldn't have the effect that I wanted them to have. After a few seconds, I heard Evelyn, "Being in the car this much sucks Luca. We haven't been able to stop and do anything. We go to the hotel; we sleep and eat then we get back in the car. Sometimes we need to get out and do things."

"I understand that I do. It's just too dangerous. We must keep going and put as much space between us and Luther as we can. He knows that you are not at your strongest and he is going to try and take advantage of that."

I quit listening to the back and forth between him and Evelyn. They were talking about needing to do something and how we couldn't. I just wanted it to be over and at this time I didn't care if that meant I had to die. I felt the strongest urge to reach for the razor in my purse. I felt my hope sinking with the sun as the day droned on and we only stopped for a few minutes to use the bathroom. That was fine by me. I had bigger problems and wasn't hungry, "I want this to be over."

Suddenly the bickering came to a stop, and someone was taking my hand, "It will be over as soon as I can end it. We must make sure you are safe first. I just need you to listen to me. Ana, I know you are your person, but I need you to listen." I was frustrated but I could see the sincerity on Luca's face that I pushed it deep down into my soul. I agreed so that I wouldn't have to continue this conversation and I needed to give myself a pep talk. He pulled my face back up with his hand under my chin, "I will keep you safe, Ana. Just keep yourself alive."

I forced a smile, "Okay Luca."

"How about you lay down?"

I just nodded and laid my head down on his lap after I took the seatbelt off. I closed my eyes so it would appear as though I was sleeping even if I couldn't fall asleep. I just listened as the conversation picked up around me, "How do you think she is doing?"

"She is doing as well as she can be expected considering her life has been completely uprooted. I hate that we must do this to her. I hate that we had to take her away from her life just to keep her safe."

"She will be okay. It will help once she is around her mother and brother again. It is hard to be separated from your family," Apollo said his voice across the car.

It was like a light bulb going off and my heart started to race as the panic set in. I sat up and demanded that the car be stopped. The car came to a screeching halt and Luca threw his arm out to catch me. I pushed it off and got out of the car in a matter of seconds. I heard Luca yell behind me, "Are you out of your mind?! What the hell?"

I was moving as fast as I possibly could, the fear making me run. The adrenaline coursing through my body made me forget about stitches and I ran as fast as I could for as long as I could. I didn't care that I was in the middle of nowhere. I didn't care that I was stuck with these people or that someone was hunting me. I needed to get out and I couldn't wait any longer. I heard shouting behind me as they all tried to get me to stop. I didn't know where I was or where I was going but I knew that I could not go to Texas, "We can't meet Mom!"

"Anastasia, you need to get your ass back here!" I heard Luca yelling at me. The pain in my side became too much and I collapsed to the ground. I was trying to get the pain and breathing under control at the same time. I looked up and saw my team had surrounded me and were staring at me as if I had lost my mind. Luca had my face between his hands making me look at him, "You cannot run off like that! You are being hunted! You almost died! You are still injured."

My hair had begun to slip out of my bun and was looking like I was attacked by a wild animal, "I need you to listen to me. For once please listen to me. I need you to acknowledge the words that I am saying to you, and you need to agree with me." He looked stunned by my words like he didn't know how to respond. My words had brought silence to my team, and I moved my eyes with my face still trapped between his hands. Angelo was the first to speak of his concern for my stitches. I interrupted him, "We cannot go to Texas. He will follow me to Texas. I can't let him find Mom or Dom. We can't go to Texas," I said, tears filling my eyes despite my best efforts.

Luca put his hand to his temples as if he were going to push the headache away. "I need a moment to think!"

I wiped at the tears that went down my face. I looked down at the ground and that's when a couple of drops of water hit my head. I looked up at the sky and dark clouds. I felt a couple more drops as it began to sprinkle. Apollo looked up at me, "It is going to be okay little boss."

I hugged myself as the rest of my team argued and went back and forth with Luca. Discussing if we should go to Texas and if not where we should go. More shouting and talking over each other and I couldn't take the chaos anymore. I covered my ears to try and block out the yelling and yelled over them, "STOP! Stop it. I am not going to Texas. I will not get back in the car if the plan is to take me to Texas."

Luca kneeled in front of me, and I watched his lips move to try and calm me down. He pulled my hands down so I could hear what he was saying, "Okay I won't take you to Texas. I will figure something out. Right now, I need you to come with me back to the car now."

The rain began to come down a bit more, so we were getting wet. I stared at him for a minute for any sign of deception. I was not going to put my family in danger. After I saw that he was being honest with me, I responded that I would go with him. Apollo and Luca pulled me to my feet, and we began to walk back to the car. I was surprised at how far I got. I walked back with the men and Evelyn watching for any signs of the enemy. I stared at my feet as I began to feel soaked through my clothes and to my bones. I tuned everyone out once again and just tried to keep one foot in front of the other. Apollo opened the back door for me, and I climbed quickly. I buckled up and stared out the window, the pain in my side growing. I leaned against the door and felt my body slowly growing colder and colder. My clothes were beginning to dry when we came to a rest stop, "What are we doing?"

"Everyone out. We need to stretch, use the bathroom, and produce a new plan as to where we are going to go," Luca said, his voice hard.

I looked down at my hands as everyone got out of the car and went about their mini-break. I heard the door close and just sat there. I waited and fidgeted with my hands trying not to think. I nearly jumped out of my skin when the door opened next to me, "Come on little boss." I looked up and saw Angelo was holding his hand out to me.

I took his hand, not in the mood to argue with him. I unbuckled and let him pull me out of the car, onto my shaky legs. I followed him up the walkway and into the building. He turned to face me, "Stay here. I will be right back."

I wrapped my arms around my waist and looked out the large windows, I could see the group of people whose job it was to keep me alive, amongst moving around and discussing things themselves. I watched the wind blow the trees in the dark, "Ana?"

I turned to find Luca standing in the middle of the room. His body was tense, and he looked uncomfortable as he looked at me. I gave him a small smile in hopes that would relax his rigid frame. After a few minutes and his body didn't relax, I sighed, "Hi Luca."

"I need you to listen to me. I can't have you running off like that. That was irresponsible and stupid Anastasia. I need you to stop and use your head. You could've hurt yourself," he said his voice was gentle despite his harsh words.

I watched him and realized his behavior was my fault, I have been selfish and irresponsible. I have been making his job and everyone else's much harder than it needs to be. I crossed the small room and hugged him, "You are right. I am sorry. I won't do it again. Please don't be mad."

He hugged me back and I peeked up at him to see his facial expression turned to one of compassion rather than disappointment, "We will be going west. I am not sure exactly where yet, but we will be going as far from Texas as I can get you."

With those words, my entire body had relaxed. All the tension left my body, "Thank you so much. I just don't want any more people to get hurt."

He smiled at me, "Don't thank me yet. It is still a long drive. I need you to try and relax. I also would like you to change into some dry clothes, so you don't get sick." He pulled my face up and I stared into his hazel eyes that were as green as a field. I agreed because I was hopelessly staring into his eyes. He smiled and it reached his eyes, "I am going to grab you some clean clothes from the car."

"No, I can go. You get the team together and do bossly things. I will take Apollo and Jace so that I can run to the car quickly," I stretched up on my toes to give him a quick peck on the cheek.

"Be careful please."

I gave him a small smile and walked out to the car. I don't know when they appeared but suddenly Apollo and Jace were on either side of me and it took everything I had not to roll my eyes at them. I stopped in front of the trunk and opened it. A couple of bullets were shot and Jace knocked me out of the way. I heard people yelling and more shots were fired. I tried to crawl under the car but was dragged out. I was hit hard by an unknown force and hit my head so hard off the back of the car I lost consciousness.

****

I woke up with a sharp pain in my head and winced when I tried to move. I groaned as I felt stiff and wondered how long I had been lying here. The memory of what had happened came flooding back. I opened my eyes and saw that it was still very dark wherever I was. I went to reach out my hand, but they were zip-tied together. My heart began to race as reality began to set in. I moved both of my hands to reach out in front of me and my hand stopped when I felt something hard in front of me. I was in a small space, and it was cramped. The panic took over my mind as I realized I was in a trunk, "Oh god no."

"It's okay little boss. Don't panic. We will be fine," Apollo said next to me.

"What is happening Apollo? Where are we," I needed him to say the words out loud for me to believe them fully. I tried to keep control of my anxiety which was restricting my heart and making my chest hurt.

"We were put inside of a trunk. Ana, I know it is hard, but I need you to remain calm. Luther caught up to us and that is who has us right now."

The panic took over, "No, no. NO!! Apollo, I was careful. I don't want to be here. I can't be here," I said, trying to move my hands apart and having the zip tie dig into my wrist. "Do you still have your phone? Where is Jace?"

"Ana, I saw Jace get hit. I don't know if he made it. I was hit in the head. I am sorry. I did manage to get his phone after he went down," he said, putting a phone between both of my hands.

I took a deep breath and turned the phone on. The bright light caused pain in my eyes, and I had to resist the urge to cry. Once I adjusted to the newfound light, I quickly scrolled for Luca's number. I stared at the phone for a minute before I hit the call button. I put the phone up to my ear without letting the zip tie go deeper into my wrists, "Please answer your phone."

"Jace, where the hell are you??"

The tears quickly filled my eyes when I heard his voice against my best efforts, "Luca! I am in a trunk. I don't know where I am. Apollo is with me, but I am scared."

It was quiet for a moment, "Hey baby. I am so glad to hear your voice. I know you are scared but I am going to find you. I want you to try and hide this phone until I find you. Is everyone okay?"

My heart hurt as I heard him being gentle and I desperately wanted him to hug me, "My head hurts. Apollo has been talking and seems fine. We think Jace might be dead…" My voice broke as I talked about one of my friends being dead.

"Hey, it's okay honey. I am glad you and Apollo are safe. I just need you both to stay alive. I will get you both and bring you home, I promise. I hope Jace is okay too. I am so sorry," his voice was soft as I heard the guilt in his apology.

"Ana, we are slowing down. You need to put the phone away," Apollo said quietly.

"I must go. We are stopping. Bye Luca," I hung up before he could respond, and I lost my nerve. I needed to be strong. I couldn't get caught up in fear. I turned it off and went to hand it back to him, but he pushed it back to me.

"You keep it on you. You were searched when you hit your head and passed out. Remember to breathe and try to stay calm. I am right here," he said, helping me tuck the phone into the waistline of my jeans.

We came to a halt, and I heard the doors close as people got out of the car. My heart began to race as I tried to prepare myself for what was to come. The trunk flew open, and I couldn't stop the scream that flew out of my mouth. I was blinded by the sun and couldn't see who grabbed me, but I heard Apollo yell out trying to get them back. I was pulled out of the trunk and immediately pushed onto my knees. I looked up with my eyes squinting to see a tall maybe five feet eleven inches to my five feet and three inches. He was very muscular with a large build. He was covered at the neck and arms in tattoos, "It's nice to finally meet you, Sunflower."

I took a minute to make sure my voice was steadied, "Please don't hurt my men. They were just doing their job and didn't deserve this. No more death," I was looking at the ground by his feet not wanting to look at this mountain of a man.

It was incredibly quiet while he thought about my words. Jace was on one side of me, and Apollo was on the other, "I understand. I need them to behave, and no one will die."

Apollo was to my right, and I heard him speak first, "I won't fight if she is safe. It is my job to protect her, and I will continue to do so."

"Well good. We have an understanding. Get them up and in the house," Luther's voice was rough as he spoke. He pulled my face up, so I had to look at him, "You know where I want you to put them."

I was pulled to my feet and screamed as the pain seared through my side. Apollo moved to me quickly. He had me pulled into a hug, and I heard Jace fighting with people. I tried to cling to Apollo as he tried to calm me down. They managed to pull us apart and the pain grew as I tried to get away from these men. I saw Jace fighting to get to me. I watched Luther pull out a gun and shoot him twice in the chest before I could do anything. I screamed as he hit the ground and Apollo used the opportunity to grab me again. Luther turned and pointed the gun at Apollo, "NO! Don't hurt him, please! I will go with you." I pushed myself in front of Apollo and someone grabbed me. I was being pulled away from him when I turned back to see him, "I'm so sorry Apollo."

He was still trying to get away from them and back to me, even though we had just watched him shoot Jace. They started to hit him and tried to get him to subside his anger. I heard Apollo shout, "It'll be fine, boss. Just do what they say. It is going to be okay!"

I was pulled out of Apollo's sight. I was being pulled through a large mansion, "Let me go. You got what you wanted; my father is dead."

"Shut up," the man said, pulling me along.

He pushed me into a room and pulled me right to the bed. He pushed me down, so I was sitting on the mattress as he chained my ankle to the leg of the bed. He cut the zip ties from around my wrists, and I saw a red mark from it cutting into my wrists. He walked out and left me alone with my thoughts and panic. I looked at my side and there was no blood, so I assumed my stitches were still intact. I tugged at the chain as hard as I could and to no surprise I was stuck. The bed was bolted to the floor. I wasn't going anywhere anytime soon, "No… Please no."

I pulled the phone out from my waistline, surprised no one felt it in the struggle. I turned it back on and took a deep breath. I once again found Luca's number one more time and dialed, "Ana?"

"We are in a large mansion. I don't know where we are, and I was separated from Apollo. Luca... Jace was alive... They just shot him for trying to protect me. I am scared. I don't want to be scared. I want to be strong. Please find us soon," I barely whispered while looking at the door.

"I know Ana. I need you to try and be brave. You are doing great. Leave the phone on while it's on, I can track you. Don't let them find it. I will be there as soon as possible. I won't stop till I have you back," his voice was cold as he went on.

I heard some shouting, and I knew I had to move quickly. I turned the phone on mute and turned the volume down. I hid it under the nightstand by the bed. I had just sat back on the bed when the door opened. Luther walked in and my heart began to race. A lump formed in my throat while fear tightened in my chest. I moved to the middle of the bed and pulled my knees up to my chest, "Hello Sunflower. Mind if I sit?"

I shook my head, "What do you want?"

He sat down and watched me, "A family. Mine was taken from me by that father of yours. It is only right that you give me back what your family took."

Unwilling tears filled my eyes, "Please let me go. I didn't know what he was up to. I have nothing to do with any of this. I don't want or need any of this. I didn't start this; I shouldn't be the one to finish it."

"I know, I didn't want to lose my family either. I am sorry but sometimes we have to pay for our parents' mistakes. We don't always get what we want," he pulled at the chain until my legs were straight in front of me.

A tear spilled over from the pain in my side. I wrapped my arms tightly around myself, "What are you going to do?"

He reached for my face, and I cringed away, "Tomorrow we will get married, and we will start our life and family. You should try and rest. I know you sustained a head injury. You'll be here for the night."

I watched him stand up and leave. I heard the lock click and I took a shaky breath. I tried to gather my composure before I grabbed the phone again. I unmuted it and turned the volume up a bit, "I need you to help me, Luca. You need to hurry."

"I will be there as soon as possible Ana. I just need you to hold on," the tension was in his voice and made me feel even worse.

"I can't do this Luca. He says we are getting married tomorrow," I said, my voice growing thick no matter how many times I tried to clear it.

I heard him growl in frustration. Just then the door swung open, and I screamed. I dropped the phone, and I could hear Luca yelling at me. I thought Luther was large, this guy made Luther look like a doll. His face was red with anger, "What the hell is this?"

This giant man came further into the room. He was at least six feet five inches, and he could've been a professional wrestler with the way he was built. I tried to hide under the bed, but he grabbed the chain, "Let me go!!"

"Where the hell did you get a phone?! How did they not check you!?" He pulled the chain until I was right by him. He grabbed me by the hair causing me to scream once again.

110

"Let me go!!" I screamed while I tried to claw his hand so that I could free myself. The pain searing through my scalp and side was too distracting.

He grabbed the phone and put it to his ear, "Who is this?"

He let me go and I crawled away feeling some relief that my head was now free. My side still hurt but at least my scalp was free. I had tears streaming down my face against my better judgment. He looked at me one last time before he left the room taking the phone with him. I moved quickly under the bed and hugged myself tightly, trying to gather my courage again. Multiple footsteps came into the room, "Come on out Sunflower."

"I just want to go back home and live my life. Please just let me go," I said my voice thick as I ended up begging instead of standing my ground.

"Get her out Blade," Luther said, his voice harsh.

I was dragged out by the damn chain, and I screamed as I clawed at the floor trying to stop myself from being yanked out. I was flipped onto my back and looked up to see Luther bent down next to me. He was holding the phone and I quickly realized that he had put it on speakerphone. "Luther, please. Leave her alone," Luca's voice was begging, and I had never heard him beg, even as children.

My heart hurt as I heard the pain in his voice, and a sob escaped, "I am so sorry Luca."

"You want to keep an eye on her, Luca. Well, then you can listen to her pain. You can listen to her be tortured before I kill her. Blade, you know what to do," Luther said, setting the phone down on the dresser.

I watched him close the door and sit in a chair that I was now noticing in the corner. I heard Luca shout, "Don't you dare touch her! You will regret this!"

I tried to get away from the monster of a man who approached me, but he grabbed the chain around my ankle. I screamed as he pulled me back towards him quickly. I felt my shirt ride up and the cold hardwood floors against my back. He smacked me hard against my face. I kicked at him without actually seeing if I was close, and he stood up to avoid me. It worked because I did not connect with him. Just when I thought he was done; he surprised me by kicking me hard in the ribs multiple times. I screamed in agony, and I could feel the stitches tear. I gasped and collapsed to the floor losing all the strength I had mustered up. I was coughing and some blood came out of my mouth. He rolled me back onto my back and I spit in his face and held onto my side as the pain spread. He was instantly pissed, "You bitch!" He hit me hard in the face and I hit my head hard against the floor so hard that I heard a ringing, and my vision grew splotchy.

"She has stitches! You are going to kill her! I will kill you for doing this to her!"

After twenty minutes of nothing but abuse, I was lying on the floor bloody and gasping for air. I was trying to get up on my hands and knees when Luther kneeled by me with the phone, "Say goodbye to Luca. Time to go be with your father."

A sob escaped as my whole body hurt. I had felt some relief in knowing that it would be over in a few minutes, "Goodbye Luca. I am so sorry."

"Deep Breath Ana. I'm so-"

He was cut off because Luther threw the phone on the floor by me and shot it three times. I screamed and covered my head as if that would protect me, "Blade run a bath for her please."

I heard footsteps and someone grabbed me. I flinched away, "I thought you were going to kill me."

Pain shot through my body as Luther pulled me into a sitting position. I hope he didn't notice that I was bleeding from my side and the hope that I would die was to the surface. "I don't want to hurt you. Despite what you might think. I am not killing you," he pulled my face up, so I had to look at him. "Don't do that again. He thinks you're dead now. You will be punished if you try again," I couldn't use my words, so I just nodded, "Good girl. Let's get you cleaned up."

I watched him unchain me. He pulled me gently to my feet but the pain that coursed through my body caused me to cry out and I collapsed back to the floor, "I am sorry. I am trying. I just hurt all over."

He didn't say anything. He just stood up and walked right out of the room. I took a shaky breath and after a few minutes, I heard footsteps, "You can help her to the bathroom. I need you to try and calm her down. Nothing else," Luther came back in and this time he had Apollo with him, "Help her up and follow me."

I couldn't make myself look at Apollo. I could only imagine what I looked like to him, "Hey Ana. I am going to pick you up. We must get you cleaned up."

"Okay Apollo," I said quietly.

He picked me up and I tried to keep the pain out of my voice as I groaned. He followed Luther through the house, "You have half an hour. She is mine. So, don't think of doing anything inappropriate."

We went into the bathroom, and I heard the door lock. Apollo set me down gently in a chair, "Look at me." I refused to look at him, "Ana?"

I finally made myself look at him once I prepared myself, "He found the phone. I was punished for lying and calling for help. I am so sorry Apollo. He told Luca he was going to kill me. They probably think we are both dead now. I blew our chance to get home."

His eyes were soft, "Shh it's okay honey. Are you okay? How are your stitches? Let's get you cleaned up."

"I hurt. Blade sure does know how to beat someone up. I can see why he gets paid to do it. My stitches are okay. I suppose I should get cleaned up," I said as he pulled me to my feet again. I was gasping for air as the pain shot harshly through my body.

He held on to me until I had steadied, "Get in the tub. I am going to watch the door," He turned his back to me.

I got undressed very slowly and I saw a little bit of blood coming from my side. I grabbed a washcloth and held it tightly to my side unsure of what I wanted to accomplish. I lowered myself into the hot water and tried not to cry. The water came up to my shoulders so Apollo couldn't see anything even if he wanted to. I cleaned the blood off of me the best I could, and it felt like there was no time when the door was being opened. Blade walked in with Luther and my blood ran cold, "Please no… No more."

Apollo stood up and went into protector mode, "Hey she is in a bit of pain because of what your man did. She is scared. Leave her alone."

"Apollo, I need you to go with Blade. No more harm will happen to her. I promise she will not be harmed. I just want to get her to bed," Luther said, watching him.

I didn't want to see Apollo get hurt and I could see him getting ready to fight, "Apollo, go with him. Please. I will be fine," I said, trying to sound braver than I felt.

I saw his back relax ever so slightly, "Is that an order?"

"Yes."

"Okay boss," he said, leaving with Blade. I could see his hesitation as he walked out of the bathroom and the door closed behind them.

I felt sick to my stomach as Luther moved his way closer to me. I pressed harder on the washcloth on my side unsure if I was helping or making it worse. He grabbed a towel from the cabinet and held it out to me, "Let's get you back to bed."

I used the edge of the tub to pull myself up. I was shocked to see that he was looking away from me. I grabbed the towel and wrapped it tightly around myself. I grabbed a dry washcloth and pressed it to my side to try and keep the bleeding under control. I moved slowly trying to keep the pain contained. I found clothes on the counter and got dressed as quickly as I could. I turned to him, "I-I'm ready."

He opened the door and walked back to the room he was keeping me in. We went inside the room, and I saw that someone had cleaned my blood off the floor. I sat on the bed, and he chained me back up, "Get some sleep Sunflower. We have a big day ahead of us tomorrow."

He didn't leave me alone. He just went and sat in the chair where he watched me get beaten down. He just stared at me, and I finally managed to lay down, "Please go away."

"I will once you are asleep," he said looking down at his phone as if this was boring to him.

I took the opportunity to get out. I began to pull on my stitches until the blood flow was stronger under the blankets so he couldn't see. I tried to fall asleep, but my body wouldn't let me. I hurt all over and every time I moved it reminded me of what had happened. It was also a reminder that I was not close to death yet. It was taking too long to bleed out. I was terrified of what would happen after I went to sleep. Would they find the wound and fix it? Would I go to heaven? Would I be in hell? After another hour of just lying there trying to close my eyes, there was a small knock at the door. I shot up fast and the pain took over completely, so I folded in on myself, "Who-"

"Come in. Breathe Anastasia. I asked our doctor to come and have a look at you," Luther said as another man came in. He looked more like an accountant than a doctor. He was short with dark hair, and glasses, and he was scrawny, "Hello Eric. She can't sleep. She had a run-in with Blade."

"I can see that," Eric said, moving towards me.

"NO! Get away from me," I yelled even though I was too weak to move away from him. I didn't realize how little energy my body had left.

"It's okay Anastasia. Let him look at you. No one will hurt you," Luther said softly.

It took everything I had not to scoff. He moved to me and examined me, "Luther I need some more equipment. She's bleeding out."

Luther jumped up and my eyes slipped shut at the same time, "What the hell? He didn't do anything to stab her..."

"This isn't a new wound. But the beating seemed to have caused it to reopen," Eric said quietly. "Anastasia, I need you to open your eyes for me."

I pried my eyes open, "I just want to die... I can't do any of this anymore..."

"Eric, go get your equipment now," Luther said quietly. "Sunflower, open your eyes and look at me."

I slowly did as he instructed, "I would say I'm sorry, but I am not. I saw an opening to be free. At least now you didn't lie."

"You are not going anywhere. We are going to get you fixed up," he said, surprisingly full of concern.

"I can't keep my eyes open anymore," I said, breathing heavily as my eyes slipped shut.

Eric must have come back into the room. I felt my side being stitched up but didn't hurt. My heart began to slow down, and I heard some yelling. I popped up gasping and there was an oxygen mask on my face, "We got her back. Hook up the blood. We need to get some flooding back through her body."

I was gasping and I watched the people moving around the small room, "She must be in a lot of pain. She has some serious damage to her ribs. Without an x-ray, it's hard to say the actual damage. Then based on the bruising I'd say she did something bad. She should live now that we got some blood in her."

"What can you give her? She needs some rest without dying," Luther said looking at me.

I can give her some morphine. I also have a muscle relaxer. Won't do too much for the pain but either of them will put her to sleep so she won't care until we pull her out of it," Eric said.

"Please… Stop… Just let me die…"

"Shh, save your strength. You are not going anywhere. Let's give her whatever you can."

I felt a pinch in my side, "No!"

Eric pushed me down when I tried to get up, "It's okay. It's going to help."

"Why can't you guys just let me die," I barely whispered, not sure if they could hear me or not.

"Blood transfusion is set up, so she will be fine that way. She will be asleep in a few minutes," Eric said, then I heard the door close. My eyes began to grow heavy as the pain began to dull just a little bit. I stared at the wall as my eyes got harder and harder to keep open. They finally slipped shut and I was in a state of complete and utter exhaustion. I let myself drift off, finally falling into the darkness of my unconsciousness.

****

I woke up with a jump and saw the sun was shining. The pain was back but I couldn't let it win. There was a knock on the door, "Go away."

The door opened anyway, and I watched a girl come in with some food, "I am here to help you get ready."

"Please go away."

"I need you to eat. Then cover the bruises with the dress and make-up. Get that thing out of your arm and change your bandage," she said, setting the tray down in front of me and ignoring what I was saying.

The anger inside of me took over, "I said no!!" I threw the tray and the dishes shattered while the food hit the floor and walls, "Get out!"

"Anastasia, we can do this one of two ways. You can get dressed with me or I can get Luther or Blade," her voice was calm as she threatened me.

I looked down at my hands, "Okay."

"Good," She moved to me. She pinned my hair up and began changing my bandages. She got the needle out of my arm and then started to tackle the job of covering all the bruises that covered my skin, "You will look beautiful." I didn't say anything. After a couple of hours, I was in a long white dress. Then there was a knock and Blade came in, "Hello Blade."

"She looks nice, Scarlet. You did an excellent job. Luther will be happy," he turned towards me. "Time to get married."

I didn't say anything back. Blade grabbed me and unchained me once again. He pulled me along and I didn't bother to look around. I knew I wouldn't ever leave and there was no point in trying. We came to a large ball-like room with three dozen people inside. Luther stood in front of a priest, and I was pulled to him. To any fool, it looked like he was walking me down the aisle. Once I stood next to him the priest began, "Ladies and gentlemen. We have gathered here today…"

I let my mind wander, not caring about what was coming out of his mouth. The feeling of despair and depression flooded my body. My body hurts, "I do." Luther said, looking at me.

The priest did the same spiel and then looked at me. The lump in my throat was thick and I tried very hard to push it down, "I-I do."

"I now pronounce you husband and wife. You may kiss the bride."

I closed my eyes and tried to imagine when Luca had kissed me. I felt his lips against mine and quickly kissed him back. He pulled back and I heard people applauding, "Let the party begin."

Luther pulled me to another room where the tables were set up. He held out a chair for me and I sat down. I kept my gaze on the table as he walked away, "You can do this. Just push through it."

He came back and set a plate of food in front of me, "My friend said that you didn't eat this morning."

He sat down next to me, "I wasn't hungry. I still am not hungry."

"I need you to eat please," he said, pulling my face up. I looked at him and I nodded, "Good girl."

I began to nibble on the pasta had he gotten me, "Luther?"

"Yes, Ana?"

"Are we-Are we married?"

"Yes, we are," I had to keep myself calm as the words inspired panic, "Sunflower?" I looked up at him, not ready to trust my voice to talk, "Have you been taking any form of birth control?"

I looked away, back down at my food, "Yes."

"It's time for the first dance," Someone announced. Luther stood and held out his hand to me. I took it slowly and he pulled me to my feet. He pulled me to the middle of the dance floor and pulled me close to him.

"What type of birth control have you been using," he asked, pulling me closer to him, so now we were slow dancing.

"I got the Nexplanon almost two years ago. It seemed easier. I would forget to take the pill," my stomach was churning. "Why did my father kill your family?"

I felt him tense, and he squeezed his hand, and it was over my stitches. I bit my lip to keep from crying out in pain, "He thought we were going to take him down first."

I knew he was looking at me and his grip loosened ever so slightly. I looked up at him right into his dark brown eyes, they were so dark they were almost black, "Was he right?"

He stared into my eyes for what felt like an hour, "Yes he was."

The song ended and I pulled away from him, "Excuse me. I need to use the bathroom."

I walked away from him quickly. I saw Blade was next to me in an instant. I went into the bathroom and closed the door. I moved to the toilet and threw up all the food I had just consumed. After half an hour the door opened and I saw Eric peeking in, "Luther sent me in here. He is worried about you."

"Tell him I'm fine," I said my voice was tense.

"Let me take a look at you," he moved to me, and I tried to move away.

"Get the hell away from me!" I shouted, moving to the wall.

The door opened and Blade came in, "Need some help, Doc?"

"Yes, I have my orders. Be careful of her side. She has stitches that you already tore once," Eric said, and my blood ran cold.

Blade came in and closed the door behind him. He moved towards me, and I tried to run. He grabbed me and I screamed, "Let me go!" I gave it my all to get away. He held me down while Eric cut my Nexplanon out of my arm. I fought with everything I had but it was no good. After they were done, they let me go. I crawled away and hugged myself. I was surrounded by the fluff of this white dress.

"Are you feeling sick," Eric asked.

I didn't respond at first and then carefully picked the words I wanted to say, "Go to hell."

In two strides Blade slapped me hard across the face, "Watch your mouth."

The door opened once again and Luther, my new husband, stepped into the small bathroom, "What the hell is going on in here?"

I had tears in my eyes, and I didn't want them to fall, "She was being difficult Luther. I had to step in."

Luther looked at me huddled on the floor, "You two get out." They got up and moved to the door. Luther grabbed Blade's arm, "Send everyone home."

The door behind them closed, "Anastasia, I need you to get up off the floor."

I stood up and kept my eyes on the floor. Not blinking in hope that the tears wouldn't fall, "Just kill me already and get it over with. This is not fair. I don't deserve this. I am a good person. I was going to be a photographer."

He moved to me quickly, "No, I never said you deserve this. I lost my entire family and I believe eye for eye. Your family owes me a family. Now come with me." He pulled me along and to a new room, "This is our new room. This is where you will be from here on out." He locked the door and moved to me faster than I wanted him to, "There is always a guy outside my door." He pulled my face up, so I had to look at him, "Get out of the dress."

I let the tears slip down my face, "Luther... Please don't make me do this."

"Now," he almost yelled.

I jumped at the sudden change in the volume. I slowly began to take off the wedding dress while he watched me. I was shaking and trying to keep my eyes on the floor. I was soon down to my bra and panties, hugging myself tightly as he moved to me, "Please don't do this..."

He reached for my face, and I flinched away from him, "We are married now. Luca isn't going to come to find you. He thinks you are dead, remember that. You are mine now. So, get in that bed so we can consummate this marriage."

I let a small sob escape as I moved to the bed. I stood over it for a moment and just stared at the dark bedding. I looked up at Luther with more tears in my eyes, "I know you don't owe me anything but please... Don't make me do this."

"I will not ask you again, Sunflower," he said, his voice harsh as he undressed. I laid down in bed under the blankets. I hid under the covers and waited for him to come to bed. I felt the bed move under his weight and he pulled me to him, "Don't fight me. It will be easier for you." I tried to calm myself down as the night went on and I was forced into having sex.

Chapter Six

Reunited Again

I woke up the next morning and my body hurt. Not only from being beaten but from being forced into sex that I couldn't help but fight which led to more abuse. I curled up in a ball and hugged myself as tightly as I could without any pain. Luther was getting dressed when I looked over at him. He moved slowly to my side of the bed and kneeled next to me, so I had to look him in the eye, "I want you to eat some food today."

I looked at him with what I hoped was not a pitiful look, "I'm not that hungry."

"I know, Sunflower, but I need you to eat. You didn't get much sleep last night. Are you in any pain," he asked, moving my hair that had slipped in my face.

"I am fine…"

"Are you sure? I need you to eat some food," he said, making me look at him. Finally, I just nodded not wanting to say anything else and he kissed my forehead, "Good girl."

I watched him stand up and leave. I lay down and thought about my life. I felt myself sinking into depression. The door opened and Scarlet brought food in, "Time to eat."

"Okay," I said watching her leave the room after she set the tray down. I slowly sat up and grabbed the large white T-shirt that was on the floor and slipped it on. I went over the tray and saw there were eggs and toast. I threw it away and covered the food up with napkins. I went and hid in the giant walk-in closet, "I want to go home."

I heard the door again. I just stayed in the corner of the walk-in closet. I was huddled in on myself trying to be small. I didn't want to move and the voice I heard made it worse, "Ana?" I heard a deep voice, and my body froze. It was Blade and I knew I had to keep quiet and keep myself safe. I had to be strong and fight through fear. I couldn't bring myself to do or say anything. I was going to be strong, not stupid. The closet door opened, and I saw his towering body in the doorway, "There you are. What are you doing?"

I had to try and control my voice as I responded, "Nothing. Just sitting here thinking about my new life."

I looked at my hands, "Well enough hiding. Come on, get out."

"No."

"Yes, it is time to get out and be a wife. We have things for you to do," he said, his voice growing harsher as he grew more irritated.

"I said no. I was a wife last night. I get to be me today. Now leave me alone," I snapped back at him.

He growled as he heard the attitude slide into my voice. He moved in three strides to me and grabbed me by the bicep. He pulled me aggressively to my feet. Out of peer instinct, I slapped him hard across the face. He slapped me just as hard back and I hit the floor under the impact. He knelt on the floor next to me, "This is my house. You will do as I say."

"Go to hell Blade," I said, getting up on my hands and knees. He stood up and kicked me hard in the ribs. I collapsed to the floor gasping for air. Luckily, it wasn't in my stitches, but I could feel them tug a little. I was gasping for air, "Does it feel good to beat me up?"

He grabbed me by my hair, and I screamed as he dragged me out of the closet. I tried to get him to release me by clawing at his hand. He froze when he walked back into the bedroom. I saw a shadow in the doorway and then I heard the cold hard voice of Luther, "What the hell is this?"

"She needs her ass beat. She doesn't know when to listen. She shows no one any respect," Blade said, the anger flowing freely into his voice.

"Let go of my wife now," Luther said. Blade did as he was told and let go of my hair. I dropped to my hands and knees again. I crawled away from him as fast as humanly possible. I sat against the wall and hugged myself trying to reassure myself that I was safe, "I don't want to catch you touching her again. Get out now." I had my hair in my face as I tried to gather my composure. Of course, this meant that I couldn't see where they were. I heard someone getting closer to me, "Anastasia?"

"I am sorry," was all I could think to say to keep myself from being hit anymore. I tried to make myself as small as humanly possible, "I didn't mean to. Please."

"Look at me, Anastasia."

I peeked up at him through my hair, "I'm sorry."

"Can I get you off the floor," he asked, his voice gentler than it has ever been. I shook my head and told him no, "Okay." He just sat there for a minute, and I assumed I was too distracted to notice when he left. I couldn't get myself to move even a little bit. I heard the door open again and couldn't help but cringe a little, "Go sit with her."

"Ana?"

My head shot up and I saw Apollo sitting in front of me, "Hey."

"What are you doing down here," he asked, moving my hair out of my face. He froze, "What-"

"I am okay. I just want to go home," I said, looking at his face.

"I know. I am working on it. Just hang in there, please. Can I look at your stitches? Have you been able to eat since we got here?"

"Not really, I haven't been very hungry," I couldn't bring myself to look at him or acknowledge my stitches.

"Well, how about you sit and have lunch with me," he said trying to give me his best smile considering the situation.

"Okay I will try," I said, watching him very closely.

He picked me up and set me down on the bed with no hesitation. I watched as he walked over and grabbed the food. He set it down in front of me and sat down next to me, "Let's eat."

We ate some food, and I began to grow tired. My body was in a lot of pain from all the trauma that I had gone through in the last few days. This is the most relaxed I have felt since we were kidnapped. Apollo turned on the TV and I tried to focus on that, "Okay you can look at the stitches."

He smiled, "Thank you."

He moved to my side, and he lifted my shirt. I let my eyes slip shut and my shirt was pulled back down, "Please don't leave."

"I wish I could promise that. I wish I could," he pulled a blanket over me. I felt even more relaxed. "Just hold on Ana. I will take you home. I just need you to hold on. I just need you to hang in there a little bit longer," I fell asleep listening to him talk and play with my hair. That was the first good night's rest I have gotten since they gave me the muscle relaxer.

Someone was getting into bed with me. I moved away and felt instantly sick. I quickly got out of bed and found the nearest trash can. It has been a little over a month since Luther took us. I was throwing up and I heard him groan, "Again?"

"I am sorry. I am fine. Just go to bed. I'll be there in a minute," I said between gagging and throwing up. "I think I have the flu."

I heard him walk over to me, "Are you done?"

I sat back on my feet, "I think so."

"Come on let's go brush our teeth," he pulled me up to my feet by my elbow.

I went to the bathroom and brushed my teeth, so I wasn't reminded of the smell of vomit. I took a deep breath and walked back into the room. This was a ritual, every night since we got married. I would beg him not to and he would try and impregnate me. I sighed at him from across the room, "Do we have to tonight?"

"Yes, every day until you get a positive test. Now come on," he said, pulling the blankets back for me.

"Then let me take a test. I don't want to do it every night. I am tired and I don't feel well," I said as my attitude got the best of me, "I can't get a positive test if you never let me take one."

"Get undressed and get in the damn bed," his frustration was leaking out to his voice. When I didn't move, he got mad, "NOW!"

I jumped and did as he told me. I got undressed and got back in bed, "I don't feel good Luther."

"Quit complaining and just let me do the job. The sooner you shut up the sooner it will be over."

"Gee, how romantic."

A Few Hours Later

I woke up to people screaming and gunshots. Luther was already up and dressed. He turned to me, "Hide in the closet and do not move until I come back for you."

I grabbed my clothes off the floor and quickly hid in the closet. I got dressed faster than I thought was possible with my whole body shaking uncontrollably. I hid in the back of the closet and tried to make myself as small as humanly possible in case this was not my friend. The door flew open, and I saw Blade standing in the doorway again, "Boss won't know it was me with everything going on."

"Get away from me you pig," I screamed as he moved towards me quickly. He grabbed me, pulled me out of the closet, and threw me on the floor. I kicked at him and tried to keep him away from me. He hit and kicked me until I was weak, and it was hard to fight him.

I spat in his face, "You bitch!" He kicked me hard over one more time in the ribs and I screamed. I curled up into a ball, "You are going to pay!"

He jabbed me with a needle in my side, and I got dizzy. My body suddenly felt heavy. He was working on getting my pants off. I started to struggle to get away as I tried. I screamed again as I felt myself beginning to lose the battle against this mountain of a man. All I could think of was this cannot happen. I can't get raped by him. I felt him pull my panties down. Just as he was working on his pants my body was glued to the floor. Just as he was getting ready to lean over me someone shot him; I was covered in his blood as he collapsed to the floor. I was gasping for air and moving as far away from whoever pulled the trigger as possible. I looked up and saw Angelo standing in the doorway holding a gun. I collapsed to the floor and passed out.

****

I woke up screaming as the night before came flooding back and I was not ready to die. Angelo came running in, "Hey Anastasia you need to calm down. You are safe."

"No! This isn't real. I died," I screamed at him and moved as far away from him as I could.

"Whoa, easy. Okay," he had his hands up in the air as he slowly walked away from me, "That's okay. Let me go grab someone."

I watched him leave and I just sat there shaking wondering if I had died or maybe I was just in a coma. I needed to wake up and face reality, I was currently in. I hugged myself tightly ignoring the pain I was feeling throughout my body. The door opened again, and my head snapped up to see Luca stepping into my room. I felt a sob escape my lips as I stared at the man who was supposed to find and protect me, "Luca…?"

He moved slowly across the room and stopped when he reached the end of the bed. He had his hands raised slightly so that I could see them, "Hey baby. Do you mind if I have a look at you, please?"

I couldn't say anything yet. I was stunned and couldn't take my eyes off him. I just shook my head and wanted to cry. "You are not here. You are not real. This is a dream or I'm already dead," I said. He shook his head and slowly moved towards me. I backed myself into the corner as he slowly moved towards me. His hands were up as if I had a gun. He closed the distance between us. He gently placed his hands on either side of my face and looked into my eyes, "You can't be here. It's not possible."

He gave me a sad smile, "Yes baby I can be. I am here. I am so sorry it took me so long. I swear you are never going to leave my sight ever again."

It still felt like a lie. I gave him my best smile as a couple of tears spilled over. I wasn't completely convinced that this wasn't a dream to avoid what was happening, "You are here? Promise?"

"I promise. I am right here in front of you. This is not a dream, and your brain is not playing a trick on you. I am not going anywhere either," he moved a little closer to me. "I am so happy you are here and safe. I need to ask you a question."

"What?"
"Do you know what they gave you? You've been in and out of it for a few days," he asked, his voice soft and gentle.

"I don't know. It was in a needle. It made me dizzy, and cloudy and made me feel very heavy. Like my pockets were filled with rocks."

"Hey, it's all right. You are safe now," he said, tucking my hair back behind my ear.

"It feels fake. Like I am going to wake up any second and-" My sentence was cut off by the lump forming in my throat.

He slowly moved so that his forehead was resting on mine, "Ana, I am here. This is real. I don't know what happened to you while you were with them, but we will figure it out together."

There was a light knock on the door before I had a chance to respond to Luca. I looked at him and asked, "Who is it?"

"Come on in Angelo. It's okay Ana. Please breathe," he watched me move as far away from both. I was still sitting on the bed, but I was on the edge with my knees pulled up to my chest.

"I-I can't."

"Let's start small. Can he look at your head," Luca asked his gentle voice, but I could hear the hurt and frustration leaking through.

"No, no one is going to touch me."

Angelo took another step towards me, and I flinched away from him. He put his hands up causing me to flinch again, "No one is going to touch you, Ana. Not without your permission. I know you are scared, and this doesn't feel real. Just take your time."

I was shaking and I could feel the tears sting at my eyes again, "I don't... I am scared."

"I know Ana. I just want to make sure that you are okay. Can you let me check your head first? Then we can go from there," Angelo said, his voice soft and so were his eyes.

I took a deep breath. He won't know if I was abused just based on the head injury or if I hurt myself. I steadied myself and I knew that they wouldn't do anything to hurt me, "O-Okay. I can do that."

He gave me a small smile that barely reached his eyes, "Atta girl." He sat down next to me and slowly moved towards me as he examined my head. I think he could sense my nervousness, "Talk to me."

My heart was racing at the thought of not knowing what was going to happen. I couldn't stop my body from shaking while he checked my head. I knew he just wanted to distract me but the only thing I was curious about, and I needed to know he was okay, "How is Apollo?"

"He is fine. He got a little roughed up in the fight, but he will live. I wouldn't worry too much about him," Angelo said. "We need to talk, you and me."

He sat back down across from me this time so that I had to see his face. I pulled my knees back up to my chest and hugged them tightly ignoring the pain that shot through my body, "What do you want to talk about?"

"Luca, I need you to give me a moment with her."

"Angelo-"

"Luca, please. This is for her. It will help her talk to me so we can get it handled," Angelo said looking at him and I could hear the tone of his voice.

Luca looked at me and took a deep breath, "Okay…" He moved to me slowly and made me look at him, "I won't be far. Please try and relax Ana."

I watched him leave and I looked back at Angelo, "What do you want to know?"

His eyes were filled with sadness, "Honey you are covered in bruises. I also know that you have other scars. What happened to you while you were gone? Have you still been hurting yourself?"

"I got in trouble when I was caught with the phone. That's when Luther made Luca listen... I was roughed up a few more times for not being compliant. I didn't listen and I didn't want them to win. Then-" I stopped and thought about everything I had endured and that had almost killed me. "I haven't hurt myself since I almost died. I don't want to talk about this anymore." The tears had filled my eyes as the memories hit me hard. They spilled over and I moved away from him and covered my ears with my hand, "NO! NO MORE!"

Luca was there in an instant. He took my hands away from my ears so I could hear him talking to me, "Shh, I need you to stop. You are safe. It's okay Anastasia." His voice was bleeding with worry, but I still couldn't stop hyperventilating, "Angelo, I need you to help me calm her down."

I felt a slight pinch in my side and my muscles turned to jelly, "I don't want to sleep, Luca. I don't."

"It's okay honey. Let me help you lay back down. You don't have to sleep," Luca said, helping me lay down. He moved the hair and pushed it off my face to the side, "That's it. Just breathe."

My eyes grew heavy, and they slipped shut, "Luca?"

"What baby," he said, playing with my hair.

I opened my eyes and looked at him. A lump formed in my throat, "Luca...He-" My voice dropped, and I tried to swallow the lump that had formed, "He wanted to get me pregnant. He wanted me to replace the family that my father took from him. So, he would- Every night we would-"

I saw his body tense up, "Hey it's okay Ana. Don't think about that anymore. You are safe and will not be forced into anything ever again. I won't let that happen again."

I let my eyes slip shut, "I am sorry, Luca…"

"Shh don't worry about a thing. You have nothing to be sorry for. Just relax and rest now honey," he said, his voice gentle again.

A few minutes and nothing but silence. I started to feel okay enough to finally go to sleep. Then I heard Angelo say, "Go for a walk Luca. I can see you shaking."

"Because of what that bastard did-" he cut himself off after he started to get louder and louder. He took a deep breath when I moved away from the sound of his voice, "I am sorry. I will be right back."

I heard the door close and after a couple of minutes I forced my eyes open, "I'm sorry." My voice broke as I apologized. "This is all my fault."

"Hey, no. It's not. This is not your fault," Angelo said softly.

"It is though. This is my fault," A sob escaped my lips as I continued to talk. I rolled onto my side and hugged myself as tightly as possible, "He's after me. He hurt Apollo. He raped me every night until you guys found me again."

"Hey shh. Please breathe," Angelo said, moving closer to me.

"Go away," I said, my voice breaking again.

"Ana-"

"Please, Angelo. Just go away."

"I will be right outside Ana," he said, and I heard his footsteps going away from me.

I heard the door close, and I couldn't stop the tears now that they had started again. I just closed my eyes and cried until my body was exhausted. After a couple of hours, I was mentally and physically exhausted. I was getting the feeling back in my body which told me the medication they gave me was wearing off. I felt the bed move and not fully aware I moved away, "No-"

"Shh, you're safe Ana. I promise," Luca said softly, kissing the top of my head. "Angelo and I had an idea. Can I help you up?"

"Luca…"

"Please, Ana."

I sighed and nodded. I saw the relief on his face as he pulled me out of the bed. I was on my feet and a little wobbly with his arm tightly around my waist to keep me steady. He pulled me through the house and pulled me into another room. I hadn't paid attention when he pulled me through, I would explore later. I saw Apollo sitting on the bed, "Hey little boss."

"Apollo!" I moved across the room as fast as Luca would let me. I hugged him tightly once I was on the bed, "I am so glad that you are okay! I was really worried about you."

I had so much excitement seeing him alive, relief took over my body, "Yes. I am fine. Please relax. Nothing is your fault. I know that is where you are at. Just calm down. Let your body heal."

"It is my fault. It is my family that started this. Jace is dead because of me," I said looking down at my hands.

"It's not you though. We all knew what we signed up for when we took this job. It was always a risk to get killed," Apollo said softly.

I sighed, "Okay. I will try."

He smiled at me, "Good. Try and look at the positive thoughts."

I couldn't say anything back to him. Luca held out his hand to me and I took it without hesitation. He wrapped his arm around my waist again after he pulled me to my feet. He pulled me back to my room and helped me back to the bed, "Please relax. You are safe now. Now you also know that Apollo is okay."

"Luca-"

"No, baby stop. I need you to lie down and relax, okay? Please," he said to me softly.

I didn't say anything at first. I just laid down and pulled the blankets over me. I couldn't shake the feeling that I had, "This is my fault. I know you say it's not but it's my family. It's my shitty situation, Luca. It is all my fault."

He was quiet for a minute. I thought maybe he had left but then he started to talk. "Hey now. That's not acceptable. This is not your fault. You didn't do anything to deserve any of this," he sat down on the bed next to me. He began to rub slow circles on my back which made me want to fall asleep.

"I feel like it's my fault," I barely whispered.

He was still rubbing slow circles on my back and that is what I tried to focus on as this bad feeling inside of my body just got worse, "It's not. You have had a long month. I just want you to stay lying down and try to sleep."

"I don't want to sleep. I want to not be broken and not be in this situation," I said, hugging myself tighter, and moving away from him.

"Ana," he pulled me to him and made me look at him. His hazel eyes were sad, and it made my heart hurt just a little bit, "Baby nothing will change how I feel about you. I mean that. I need you to relax a little, please. All this stress your body isn't going to be able to handle."

"Okay," I moved up to the pillows and tried to get myself to calm down. I felt so freaked out that I didn't want to feel this way anymore. After a few minutes of just sitting here, "I think I am going to take a shower."

He watched my face for a couple more minutes, "Okay. Just be careful. The muscle relaxer hasn't fully worn off yet. While you shower, I am going to go make you some food," He stood up and moved towards me. He kissed my forehead again before he left the room.

I slowly got off the bed and headed to the bathroom that was attached to the bedroom. I walked into the bathroom and closed the door. I moved immediately to the shower and turned on the hot water. I tried to avoid the mirror as much as possible because I was not ready to see myself in the mirror. I took off my clothes and got under the hot water. I felt my muscles instantly relax. I scrubbed my skin and washed my hair. I even had the motivation to shave my body. Once I was all done, I wasn't ready to go out and face the world again. I sat down and let the water hit my skin. I had my knees hugged to my chest and once again ignored the pain that came with it. I jumped when there was a knock on the door, "Yeah?"

"Anastasia, you've been in there for a while. How about you come out and eat some food," Luca asked in a gentle voice.

I took a deep breath before I responded, "Okay Luca. I will be out in a minute," I didn't hear anything for a minute and figured he walked away. I slowly got up to my feet and I stumbled for a moment. I quickly steadied myself using the door to the shower. I turned the water off and wrapped myself up in a towel. Once I was out of the shower, I took another deep breath and decided to look at myself in the mirror. I saw the bruises marking my face, neck, and other parts of my body. The towel was covering up quite a bit of the bruise and my heart began to race. This wasn't me, and I didn't like who I was seeing in my reflection. I felt the room begin to spin as I didn't recognize myself anymore. I didn't know what was going on, but I couldn't get a breath deep enough. Before I could stop or catch myself, I collapsed on the floor and passed out.

Chapter Seven

The News

"Anastasia, are you okay? Can you hear me," Evelyn asked as the panic flowed freely into her voice. "She is covered up guys if you want to come in."

I felt someone's hand on my head, and I wasn't sure who it was until I heard his voice and the complete and utter stress it was soaked in, "Ana? Are you okay?"

I laid there for a moment before I forced my eyes open, "I am sorry. I am not sure what happened. I just got dizzy, and I think I passed out."

"Oh, thank God. Ana, you hit your head when you fell. Do you feel any pain?" Angelo asked. I shook my head and told him I didn't notice any pain. He nodded back, "Evelyn is going to help you get dressed."

"Okay."

I watched as Angelo and Luca, who barely spoke, left the room. I wondered why Luca didn't say anything to me. Was he rethinking his situation and seeing that I was not worth all of this? I wouldn't blame him. Yet, this caused pain to flow into my chest as I thought of him leaving me. Evelyn pulled me into a sitting position, "Let's move slowly. I don't want you to get dizzy and pass out again."

"I'm sorry. I don't know what happened."

"I know Ana. Let's get you up in a robe. Angelo wants to look at your head. You didn't have anything to catch you, so you hit your head hard. I am impressed you aren't feeling it yet. I also know that Luca wants to see you and not when you are lying half-naked on the floor," she said, pulling me to my feet.

She helped me into one of my fluffy robes. I tightened the waistline quickly so that I knew it wasn't going anywhere. We both walked slowly out into my room where the guys were. Luca moved to me instantly and wrapped his arm around my waist, "I am okay Luca. I promise."

"Come sit down. I have a little fruit salad that I want you to eat. I don't want you to move until you have eaten the whole thing," he said, helping me sit down on the edge of the bed.

Once I was situated, he put the bowl of fruit on my lap. I looked down at it and took a deep breath. I began to eat the fruit. When I was about halfway through the salad my stomach began to churn. Angelo moved more and started checking out my head to make sure I didn't injure myself more than I currently was, "It doesn't look like she did any physical damage to her head. She got lucky."

"I can't remember the last time I ate. Maybe that was the problem," I said, choking down some more fruit.

Luca moved and sat down by my legs, "Eat as much as you can then please. We brought your clothes in here so you can get dressed. We will be staying here until we get rid of Luther so it's okay to get comfy."

"Where are we?"

"We are on the west coast in Washington. That is all you need to know. You can go out and explore," he said, his voice soft and full of hope.

"Okay," I said, setting the bowl down on the nightstand next to me and the bed. Angelo and Evelyn had left us alone in the room. I felt the bile rising in my throat and I grabbed the trash can closest to me to throw up in. I felt my body get tense as I emptied the little amount of food I was able to consume.

"Whoa," Luca said, pulling my hair back for me quickly.

I sobbed as my body hurt and I just wanted to eat, "It keeps happening. I can't make it stop."

He froze and I felt the tension that flooded his voice, "It's okay baby. You said he tried to get you pregnant?"

I kept my head down, trying to make sure that I was done throwing up. I also was not ready to face him, "Yeah. Every night we would have sex."

"Did you take a pregnancy test," he asked. His voice was quiet, and he was talking to me as if I was a small child.

I felt the tears fill my eyes as my chest restricted, "No. Not yet. He wanted to wait until I missed my first period."

He must have heard my voice growing thick, "Are you done?" I just nodded, not trusting my voice anymore. He took the trash can from me, "How about I go out and get a test so we can rule it out? Then we can relax a little bit." I couldn't look at him. I didn't know how he was staying so calm. I just nodded again not wanting to say anything. "Take it easy. I will be back soon," He kissed my forehead and brushed my hair back before he left. Then he was gone from my sight.

I took a deep breath, and I felt a little relief that I was alone. I was alone and able to think about what was happening. I moved off the floor and towards the window. I just wanted to see the view that we had. I saw someone move outside and I collapsed to the floor terrified that Luther had found me again, "Help!"

143

Angelo came running in and saw me huddled under the window too scared to move, "Why are you hiding? Are you okay?"

"I saw someone outside," I said looking at him.

He looked out the window with his hand on his gun ready to use it. I saw him relax, "Oh Ana." He knelt in front of me, "It's just Ace, Ana. No reason to hide. He is here to protect you."

Angelo pulled me to my feet and over to the bed, "I don't know if I can do this anymore Angelo. I don't seem to be surviving well."

I heard him sigh and stand up, "Stay here till Luca gets back. We can't be thinking this way, Ana." He moved my hair out of my face and pulled my face up, so I had to look at him, "I need you to try and think positively for just a few minutes."

I just nodded and watched him leave the room. I just sat on the bed and hugged myself tightly. It felt like no time had passed when the door to my bedroom opened. Luca came in with a bag of stuff, "Hey honey. How about you take one of these?"

"Okay Luca," I took the pregnancy test he was holding out to me. I went into the bathroom and closed the door. I looked at myself in the mirror and took a deep breath. I quickly peed on the stick and set it on the counter so I couldn't see it. I sat down on the floor and waited for the results to show up.

It felt like forever when Luca knocked on the bathroom door, "Look at the test, Ana. It's been five minutes. It should be ready now."

I stood with shaky legs and approached the counter. I went and reached for the test with shaky hands. I took a deep breath and turned it over. I saw two pink lines that said it was positive, and I dropped the test. I sank to the floor and screamed as loudly as I physically could. Luca was there before I could look up. I panicked and tried to move away from him, "No!! No! I can't do this. I-I can't do it! I-I am-"

He moved my hair that fell in my face and made me look at him as the tears slipped down my face, "Shh. It's okay Ana. I need you to calm down baby."

I tried to pull away from him as fast as I could, "I can't do this Luca. I can't. I don't think I can handle this. I can't be pregnant with a mafia boss's baby who forced me into a marriage I didn't want. My father started a war, and I am the one who is suffering from it all."

I pulled away and lay down on the cold tile floor. He laid down next to me after a few minutes and watched me, "Don't say that. I am right here, Ana. I am not going anywhere."

He put his hands on either side of my face and wiped the tears away with his thumb. I just didn't know what to say to him. He watched me and he moved closer. He kissed my forehead and I wanted to cry. I moved closer to him and just inhaled his scent, "I am sorry Luca."

"Don't be sorry, Ana. Let me help you off the floor," He pulled me into a sitting position. He didn't wait for me to respond and scooped me up in his arms.

I gasped and felt him chuckle, "Luca-"

"Just stop. Get out of your head for just a few minutes please," he set me down gently on the bed. He pulled my face up, so I had to look up at him again, "You are safe. It is just me here." I looked at him and I leaned forward and kissed him. I moved closer but he pulled away when I tried to unbutton his shirt, "Honey stop. I don't think that we should."

"Why? I want to," I said looking at the buttons on his shirt, not able to look him in the face.

"Ana, I don't think that you do. You just found out some unexpected news. You haven't had time to think or to process all of this. I think this is just a reaction to the positive pregnancy test," he was talking like he wasn't listening to me. I froze and he made me feel silly. Like I wasn't capable of making a rational decision.

I couldn't sit here anymore. I pushed away from him and got up from the bed, "I am going to go for a walk."

"Wait," Luca said, grabbing me by the wrist. He pulled my face up and I quickly pulled away and let my hair fall into my face, "Hey." He pulled my face back up, "I am crazy about you. I just want you to be okay before you and I do anything. I don't think having sex right now is the best thing for you. I don't think it would be fine with anyone, not just you."

"Okay, Luca. I just want to feel normal," I said, staring into his eyes.

"I will help you baby. Just not with that right now. Not in that way," he said, tucking my hair behind my ear.

"Okay, Luca. I would still like to go for a walk. I'll be back soon," I said pushing past him. I quickly found the way out of the house and went down by the river. I followed the river until I couldn't see the house anymore. I took the pregnancy test out of my pocket; that I snuck out of the room. I took a deep breath and felt relief as the fresh air filled my lungs. I came to a stop when I thought I was far enough away. I sat down and leaned against a tree that was by the bank of the river. I looked at the water and the lovely chaos it was in.

"I knew I would find you."

I gasped and stood up quickly. I saw one of Luther's men, "Get away from me."

"Oh, I don't think so. I will be rewarded for bringing you back home. I will be a hero to Luther," he said, smiling at me.

I backed up away from him slowly and the test slipped from my pocket. I kept moving, unaware that I had lost the test. He was moving closer to me, "No, please. It's not worth it." I stumbled when I got to the edge of the river, "Please um-"

"My name is Oliver, and I will not betray Luther the way that you have. You must go back," he said, taking another step. He stepped on the test and my heart stopped as I saw him bend over and pick it up, "Especially now that you are pregnant."

"No, I don't think I will go back. I didn't have to, and it was hell. I am done being held prisoner for my father's mistake," I jumped into the river without much more thought. It was cold enough that I was shocked by the water. It carried me down and closer to the house. I broke the surface gasping for air and coughing. I heard Oliver swearing as the current swept me away from him. I turned around in time to hit a log that knocked the wind out of me, and I slipped below the surface. My hand went up and stopped me from going further down. I pulled myself back above the surface and I clung to the log for dear life. I coughed out the water that I had inhaled and started shouting for help.

"Ana?!"

"Evelyn, please help! Luther has a man nearby. I had to jump in," I shouted as my body slowly got colder and colder. I began to shiver and had to keep my grip tight on the log.

I slipped back under the surface of the water for a few seconds. When I pulled myself back up, I heard Evelyn, "Hold on Ana! We are coming!"

I heard some shouting and arguing. My whole body was shaking from the cold, and I couldn't do anything but hold on for dear life. I then heard a splash and some more shouting. I saw someone swimming towards me, and I thought for a split second that it was Oliver. I was preparing to let go of the log when I saw Luca's face, "Luca! There's one of Luther's men out here."

"I've got some of our guys on that. I am here to get you back to shore," he said, grabbing the log which made it rock in its place.

"I am s-sorry L-Luca. I-I went too far," I said, grabbing him so that he wouldn't slip off the log.

"Hey, it's not your fault honey. I've got a rope. Come here so they can pull us back to shore," he said moving around the log.

"I am shaking too much. I-I c-can't move," I stuttered as I felt the shivers run through my body.

"It's alright. I am coming to you. Just hold tight," he began to move closer to me as he moved along the log. I felt his arm go around my waist and it felt just a touch warmer than I was. I let go of the log and wrapped my numb arms around his neck. He yanked on the rope, and we were being pulled back to shore.

We slipped below the surface a few times and they resorted to me coughing up water, "Grab Ana first. Luca is attached to the rope," I heard Angelo shout and then I was pulled out of the cold water.

I was gasping and shivering uncontrollably. Luca was pulled out of the water next and was coughing up the water he inhaled. He moved to me without hesitation and scooped me up into his arms, "Let me know when you find him."

"L-Luca?"

"Shh. Right now, the only thing I want to focus on is getting you warmed up before you are too sick. I have a feeling you are going to be a little sick after this," he said, taking me into the house.

He moved through the house quickly, not wasting any time. He set me down in the bathroom and I just stood there hugging myself trying not to collapse every time I shivered. I watched him turn on the shower. Once he got the temp where he wanted, he turned back to me, "I-I am s-sorry."

"Come here Ana," he said, holding his hand out to me. I slowly took it, and he pulled me into the shower, clothes, and all."

I gasped as the warm water touched my clothes and soaked down into my skin, "L-Luca?"

"Shh, just sit in the warm water with me and get warm again, please. We can talk after. I just need you warm," he pulled me into a hug. I leaned against him, and my body slowly stopped shaking. I was exhausted and my stomach began to churn, and I moved quickly from Luca to the toilet. I threw up and felt my whole body tense with every heave. Luca pulled my hair back, "Shh it's okay Ana."

When I was done and lying on the floor, I worked up the courage to talk to him, "Luca…"

"Let me grab you some dry clothes," he said leaving the bathroom. After fifteen minutes he came back in dry clothes and set some down on the counter for me "Get dressed and come out to the bed please."

He left and I stood up. I slowly changed into dry clothes. I was in pajama shorts and a big T-shirt. I dried my hair with the towel, so I wasn't dripping. I took a deep breath and tried to prepare myself for what was going to happen. I walked out to the bathroom and saw him pacing with his phone in his hand, "Luca I messed up."

He froze and turned toward me slowly, "What did you do?"

I looked down at my hands not ready for the fight that was about to come, "I-I had the pregnancy test with me. I dropped it. I just needed to clear my head and think about everything that was happening. Oliver picked it up though."

"WHAT?!"

He yelled and it made me jump, "If you don't find him, then Luther will know that I am pregnant."

"How could you be so stupid?! I can't believe you did that," he was pacing and yelling. "You better hope that we find him!"

I lost my temper and control of my mouth as my emotions took over, "Get out! You are a selfish prick. This is my life! It has been messed up because of my father's mistake!!"

He froze, "Ana…"

"I said get out. I won't say it again," I had tears building in my eyes and I batted my eyes desperate to keep them from falling, "Please leave me alone."

He watched me for a moment and then he turned around and left. I went and locked the door, and I went to the corner of the room; I slid down the wall until I was sitting on the floor. I screamed as loudly as I could trying to expel the toxic energy out of my body. I had my knees pulled to my chest and cried. I just cried until my tears dried up and no more would come. I was completely exhausted both physically and mentally, "Ana?" Evelyn said gently.

"Go away, Eve. Please just go away."

I sounded defeated even to myself. Minutes turned into hours, and I couldn't bring myself to move, or even attempt to fight the direction my life was going. Multiple members of my team tried to talk to me. I just told them all to go away. Each time my voice grew thicker and thicker. Then the voice that kept breaking my heart was on the other side of the door, "Ana?"

I cringed in response and didn't move, "Go away, Luca."

It was quiet for a minute, "Baby let me in."

"No, please go away. Please," I said, my voice low trying to sound stronger than I was.

"Ana, I am so sorry. Please let me in," his voice was full of pain and regret.

I sat there looking at my hands as the lump formed in my throat, "I didn't mean to. I didn't do it on purpose…"

"I know honey. I was an ass. I am so sorry. Please let me in," he said pleading with me, and it just made my chest restrict.

I sighed and got up off the floor. I moved like a turtle to the door and unlocked it. I moved faster back to my spot on the floor and was back there when the door opened. He walked in, "I don't know what to do."

He didn't move towards me. He just closed the door and watched me from across the room. He looked like he was trying to figure out what to say, "How about we sit on the bed together?" I nodded and we moved to the bed, and I sat down. I pulled my knees up to my chest, "It's going to be okay Ana."

"What do we do now," I asked looking down at my hands.

"We wait for him to call. We couldn't find his man. Which means he will know you are pregnant soon," Luca set my phone down next to me on the pillow. "We can talk more about this tomorrow. I would like you to lay down. I am worried you are going to get sick."

I looked at him, "I am not feeling well."

His eyes softened and he moved to me slowly, "Come on baby. Lay down." I slowly laid down with his coaxing and he pulled the blankets over me, "That's it, sweetheart."

He put his hand on my forehead, and I groaned, "Don't tell me I am sick. I don't want to be sick. I am already pregnant. There is only so much I can take."

He laughed without humor, "You do feel a little warm Ana. I want you to lay down and try to rest please."

I went to move and felt my phone go off. I froze and looked at Luca, "I-I can't do this."

"It's okay Ana. I am right here. Go ahead and answer your phone," he said, taking my hand. I picked up my phone and stared at it for a moment.

I stared at it for a moment and then I answered, "Hello?"

"Hello Sunflower. Miss me?"

"No, not really. I am enjoying my freedom. I bet you miss me though," I said as the acid leaked into my voice.

There was no humor in his laugh either, "Put me on speaker Ana." I did as he asked and clicked the button. I let him know he was on speaker, "Hello Luca."

"Luther."

"Is she and the baby, okay?"

"She is fine. I haven't checked the baby yet. It would be very early in the pregnancy and may not have a heartbeat yet," Luca said, squeezing my hand.

"I want my wife and child back."

"That must suck. It is my job to protect her. You are not getting her back considering the state I found her in the last time she was in your care. Especially since you made me think she was dead," he said, the venom leaking into his voice.

"She is mine. The baby is mine," Luther growled.

"I am not property. This baby is not property. I belong to no one," I hung up and threw my phone angrily across the room. I was hyperventilating and I felt him put his hands on the sides of my face, "I-I am okay."

"It's okay, just breathe. I know it's a lot. I just want you to breathe. Nice slow breaths," he said, watching my face. I began to take slow deep breaths, "Good job baby. How about you lay down?"

I laid down and he pulled the blankets back over me, "Luca?"

"What Ana?"

My eyes were barely open after the day that I had, "Can you lay down with me? I know you are busy… I just…"

He pushed his fingers against my lips, "Shh. I must go talk to our team. I will be back soon for all the cuddles your heart desires."

I tried not to let my disappointment destroy me, "Okay."

I watched him leave and I hid deep under the blankets. My body and mind were completely exhausted after today. I couldn't believe the turn of events that happened. My eyes slipped shut and I began to fall asleep. I felt the bed moving and I cringed away from whoever it was, "Please not tonight. I don't feel good. I just can't tonight."

"I don't want anything from you baby. I just want to lay down and I want to keep an eye on you," he said, his voice gentle and soothing.

"I missed you. Can you lay down with me please," I asked, not opening my eyes, just moving my head a little.

I felt the bed move again and the warmth of his body surrounded me. I felt his arms wrap around me. I turned towards him and felt his lips on my forehead, "Good night, Ana."

I buried my face in his chest and took a deep breath, "Good night, Luca."

****

I woke up still cuddled into Luca. I took a deep breath and sighed. My stomach churned and I groaned as I ran to the bathroom to throw up, "Oh Ana. It's okay."

"Why me? I don't want to be sick or pregnant," I said as I threw up more than was in my stomach.

I felt him pat my back, "Get dressed when you are done. We must get you to your baby appointment today."

"I wasn't aware that I had one."

"Eve made one for you. I forgot to talk to you about it amongst the chaos yesterday," he said uncomfortably.

"Okay, Luca."

I stood up slowly and moved to my suitcases. I haven't finished unpacking yet. I got dressed in a pair of jeans and a T-shirt. I put my long hair into a ponytail and went into the bathroom to brush my teeth. I walked back into my room to see Luca dressed in jeans and a tight white T-shirt, "I am ready to go whenever."

He moved to me and pulled my face up, "We will be teaching you how to fight. I want you to be able to take care of yourself. If you decide to keep the baby, then we will train every day until you can't anymore. I need to know that if something happens to me you will be okay."

I moved my face away, the emotions hitting me in multiple waves, causing me to be distracted, "Okay Luca."

He pulled me back into a hug, "Please relax Ana. I am not planning on going anywhere. I just really need to know that you will be okay if something happens to me."

I hugged him tightly, "I understand Luca. But please don't let anything happen to you."

I could hear the smile in his voice, "I am not going anywhere baby. So don't worry. Now let's get you to the doctor and we can go from there," he kissed the top of my head.

He grabbed my hand, and we walked through the house and to the parked car out front. I climbed into the front seat and Luca got behind the wheel. I quickly put on my seatbelt, "I don't think I am ready for this."

He stopped the car and took my hand, "It's okay. We can wait a minute, Ana."

After a few minutes and some deep breaths, "Okay let's go."

We drove about an hour to Seattle to see a doctor. Before I knew it. I was sitting in the waiting room waiting for someone to call my name. I was playing with my hands as the anxiety began to set in. My name was finally called, I stood up and followed the nurse alone. I lay on an uncomfortable bed as a lady did an internal ultrasound to measure the fetus. Once that was done, I sat on a bed waiting for the doctor to show up. After about fifteen minutes the door finally opened, "Hello Anastasia. I see here that you had a positive home test. According to the ultrasound, you are about five weeks."

"Hi. Um yes."

"Well, your urine and ultrasound confirm the pregnancy. So, do you want to go over all the options?"

"Yes please."

"Well, the baby doesn't have a detectable heartbeat until about six weeks. You can terminate, keep, or put the baby up for adoption. Termination is the only option until twenty-seven weeks, but is frowned upon late in a pregnancy," she said watching me.

"I-I don't know," I said as a lump formed in my throat.

"That's okay honey. You have time. Let's schedule you for your twelve-week visit. We can go from there," she patted my hand. I went to the front desk and got my next appointment scheduled. I felt Luca's gentle hand on my back.

"We will see you in about seven weeks," the nice receptionist said.

I walked out of the office with Luca's hand always on my back, guiding me, "How did it go?"

"The doctor said I am about five weeks along. They told me my options and that I should decide before my next appointment. I just want to go home now. Please."

"Okay, Ana. Let's get you home," he pulled me into an unexpected hug. He pulled my face up, "We are in this together. I will support any decision that you make but you have seven weeks to decide."

He pulled away from me and opened the car door for me. I got in and he got in next to me. We drove away and all I could do was stare out the window and think of the way my life had flipped upside down.

Chapter Eight

Taken Again

I took a deep breath as he pulled up to the house, "Can we train?"

He seemed surprised, "Of course we can."

I gave him a small smile and went to change out of the clothes that restricted me from moving. I needed something mindless to do right now and I needed to get all my energy into something. I went out to the front yard and saw Eve, "Let's train Ana."

I nodded in agreement, not wanting to talk about anything. We trained hard for hours. I learned how to duck, block, and strike consistently while getting hit very little. We did this for at least six hours. I didn't want to stop, and I didn't think I could. I was gasping for air as the sun was setting, my hands on my knees, "That's enough ladies. Get inside and clean up."

Eve went inside and I gave myself a few more minutes before I followed behind her. I went through the house and straight to my room and bathroom. I stripped and got under the hot water, "Ana?"

"Luca, please. I don't want to talk yet. I just-"

I cut myself off not sure how to finish the sentence. "That was a lot of training. How are you feeling," he asked somewhere nearby.

"I am fine. Please, Luca. Just please leave me be," my voice broke as I was pleading with him.

He was quiet for a few minutes and then I heard his footsteps fade. I heard the door close, and I just let myself scream as the day came flooding in. After an hour I got out of the shower and dressed myself quickly. I could feel my body growing sore as time went on from the amount of exercise I had just done. It is not used to that much all at once. I sat on my bed and stared out the window that was in front of me. I felt someone's hand suddenly on my back, "Hey baby."

"Hi, Luca."

"Can I sit with you?"

"Yeah," I said, not bothering to move.

"Can you tell me what's going on inside your head please," he asked gently.

"I'm thinking about what has happened to my life."

He hugged me from behind, "It's okay, Ana. It's going to be hard for a while. It's going to be confusing and upsetting while we figure this all out."

"We?"

He pulled my face up, "Yes, we. Ana… You are not alone. We are a team. The time that you were away, and I didn't know if you were okay, was the worst for me. We will do this all together. You will never be alone again."

I leaned over and kissed him, "Thank you, Luca. That helped but I'm still not sure what I should do."

"Well honey what do you want? That's all that matters here. I will support you whatever you want to do," he said, his voice gentle as he tucked my hair behind my ear.

My heart began to hurt as the answer popped into my head. I didn't want to be doing any of this but given the situation, I knew what I wanted, and it was impossible. I looked away from him, and he pulled my face back up, "I-" I couldn't seem to bring myself to form the sentence. I couldn't fathom how to bring my thoughts to actual words or if he would even like what I had to say.

"Tell me, Ana. Please," his eyes were soft as I looked at them.

"I wish it wasn't Luther's..." I pulled my face away from him and played with my hands on my lap. I was too scared to see what his face would tell me.

He grabbed my face with both hands, so I had no choice but to look at him. I couldn't move away, "It's not Ana." I froze and he moved his hand gently to my stomach, "If you want the baby and decide to have it and keep it, it's mine."

Before I could stop myself, I threw myself into his arms, "I love you, Luca. I have since we were kids and I tried not to so I didn't get hurt again but I can't help it."

He wrapped his arms tightly around me, "I love you too, Ana. Sorry, it took me so long to realize it, but I am never letting you go."

We sat like that for a while. Then there was a knock at the door, "Dinner is done you two."

"We will be right out," Luca said quietly, "Now it's time to get you two fed, and hopefully it will stay down."

"Okay," he pulled me to my feet, and we walked out to the kitchen together.

"Hey, boss. I hope you are hungry," Apollo said, smiling at me.

"I will eat," I said, giving him the best smile I could manage.

I sat down at the table and Luca put a plate of shrimp pasta in front of me. I slowly ate it as the world around me erupted in conversation. I heard laughter and teasing. The sounds made my shoulders relax. I focused on the task at hand which was eating and keeping it down. I managed to get a little more food down before I had to stop because I thought I was going to throw up, "Are you doing okay Ana?"

"Yeah, I just can't eat anymore. Can I go outside? I could use the fresh air?"

Luca was watching me closely, "Yes. Just stay close to the house, please. We don't need a repeat of earlier. I mean it, you need to stay in sight."

I didn't need to be told twice. I got up and walked out of the house with no hesitation. I went down by the riverbank and felt relaxed just the few minutes I had been there. I sat down by a tree and leaned against it while I watched the running water. The sunset stole my attention when the reds and oranges began to take over the sky. I just sat there and tried to think about the decision I was supposed to be making. What was I going to do? To keep the child or do I get rid of it one way or another? I could always have it and put it up for adoption or I could just terminate the pregnancy.

One Month Later

I am now nine weeks pregnant, and I train every day to make myself feel a little less useless. I also need it to help get my anxious energy out. I still haven't figured out what I need to do for myself. So far there has been no sign of Luther, which made my anxiety worse. I was in the shower after a long hard day of learning how to kick someone's ass, "Ana, hurry up. I want you to come out so we can talk please."

I sighed, "I'll be right out Luca." We still haven't decided if we are going to keep the baby. I kept going back and forth about it. I wasn't sure if I was ready to be a mom. I was only eighteen years old. It was a harder decision than anyone I knew had led me to believe. It was something that needed some thought. I quickly finished the shower and got dressed. I haven't started putting on weight yet because of the morning sickness so it was still me in the reflection. I walked into my room and saw Angelo, Apollo, and Luca watching me, "What's going on?"

"Well, Dom has been taking over the family business. Well, he pissed off another family," Luca said, watching me closely to measure my emotions.

I froze instantly and felt the fear hit me, "What happened now?"

Angelo looked worried as I stumbled forward, "The safe house in Texas was ambushed. We lost all communication with everyone."

I felt the blood drain out of my face. I stood there and swayed a little as the bile rose in my throat and my heart rate sped up, "Ana? Are you okay?"

There was a loud roaring sound in my ears. I felt my knees give away and I couldn't stop the anxiety that had overtaken my body. Apollo caught me as the realization that the rest of my family could have been killed hit me like a brick wall. I may never see my family again. My dad is gone, and my mother is missing along with my brother. Everyone was trying to talk to me, but I couldn't hear what they were saying. I was set down on the bed and Luca grabbed my face and had me look at him, "Breath Ana. Please focus and breathe."

I just watched him focus on his words and took deep breaths with him, "That's it, Ana," Angelo said softly.

"I-What do we do Luca?"

"Just keep breathing. We will figure this out. We don't know where they are. They could be completely fine. I just need you to remain calm," he said, trying to reassure me.

I felt sick to my stomach and tears filled my eyes, "Are they gone? Did my father destroy our family?"

"Shh, we don't know anything. Let's not go to the worst-case scenario unless we have proof. You are safe. I am sure we will find them. I just really need you to remain calm," he said, wiping the tears that had spilled over.

Before I could respond to him there was shouting. Then we heard gunshots being fired. I froze and knew deep in my gut that it was Luther. He had finally come for me. Angelo and Apollo went running out of the room. I looked at Luca with panic in my eyes, "He's back for me."

"It's okay, Ana."

I stood up as the panic got the best of me once again and I wanted to scream with everything I had. I wanted to run, "Luca I can't. I haven't even decided if I want to keep this baby. He is-"

My throat started to grow thick as the shouting and shooting started to grow louder. He moved to me quickly, "Hey you are okay." He hugged me tightly to him, "Here's what we are going to do. We are nothing. If he knew, we both would be dead. The baby is okay, and we can figure the rest out. I love you; Ana and I need you to stay calm and alive."

I looked up at him with tears filling my eyes, "I love you, Luca. You must stay alive too please."

He leaned down and kissed me, "I will baby. Now we are going to get you out that window and you are going to make a run for it."

"No, please don't make me go without you," I said as the tears spilled over.

"Shh. It's okay baby. You must go. I love you and I need you to be safe. For me, that means you are going to try and run. Stay out of the river. It is too cold, but I need you to try and get out of here," he said, his voice and eyes pleading with me.

He pulled me over to the window and opened it for me. I was crying as he picked me up and slid me out, "I love you, Luca. Please stay alive. I will be back for you if I get away."

He kissed me, "Do NOT come back. Run and get away. I will call you if we get away," he handed me my phone and closed the window. I ducked as the door inside slammed open and I covered my mouth and listened to the conversation, "Where is she, Luca?"

"I don't know. My guess is as far away as possible. I told her to run and run fast," he said, his voice oddly calm. I heard some struggling and I took off running before I could change my mind. I was running in the dark and heading only God knows where. I ran as hard as I could, and sobs escaped as I ran.

I saw flashlights and tried my best to avoid them. I ran into someone and hit the ground hard under the impact. I looked up to see Oliver smiling down at me. My stomach churned, "Hey you. Ready to be returned to your husband?"

"Go to hell," I said, standing up and getting ready to fight. I wasn't great at it yet, but I bet if it was just the one, I may have a chance.

He threw his head back as he laughed, "Well this should be interesting. Let's see what you got, little girl." He tried to strike, and I ducked and hit him in the nose. He swore at me and took another blind rage swing. I moved again and punched him in the gut, "You bitch!"

"You ready to get your ass kicked by a little girl," I said smiling.

We fought a little more between the two of us. I got kicked in the legs and screamed out as I hit the ground. He jumped on the opportunity, "I've got her!! Someone come over!!"

"Get off me!!" I screamed, doing everything I could to get away from him, I kicked and clawed at him. He had me pinned on my back with both hands above my head.

I kicked him as hard as I could in the nuts, and he groaned as he rolled onto his back. I stood up and kicked him as hard as I could again. I took off running, and I went straight for the river. I didn't see any other options for me to get away quickly. Just as I was about to jump, I froze, "I wouldn't do that Sunflower."

I turned to look at Luther who had a gun pointed at Evelyn's head. I felt sick instantly, "Put the gun down Luther."

"Then I suggest you come with me. I would hate to use this on her. She looks so nice," he said, giving me a sick smile.

I saw that she was crying but her words struck me hard, "Ana, don't do it. I'll be okay. Get out of here now."

I heard the waiver in her voice, "Eve I am not going to do that. Put the gun down. I will come with you. Just don't hurt her please."

"Get away from the river, Anastasia. I will put the gun away once you are in front of me where I can reach you," he said, watching me closely.

I slowly walked towards him. My body was shaking, and I tried to keep what pride I had as I moved towards him.

I fought every instinct I had. I watched Eve as I moved closer. I stopped when I was directly in front of him, and he put the gun down. Oliver who had joined us grabbed Eve and Luther grabbed me right above my elbow, "Put her with the rest of Ana's men. Then Ana can be put in my new room."

A guy I hadn't met before took me from Luther and pulled me back through the forest to the house. He pulled me into the house, passed the staircase, and into a room, "Boss will be here soon."

I watched the man leave and I began to pace the length of the room. I was in the same crappy situation once again. I felt the panic, fear, and sadness all begin to flood into my brain and take over, "What the hell am I going to do now!?"

The door opened and I froze as Luther stepped into the room, "Hello Sunflower."

"Hello, Luther. How are my men."

"They are fine. No one was hurt. All shots fired were fired to scare not harm. A few men were lost but there was no helping that and it was on my side," he closed the door and watched me like I was a caged cat set free, "How far along are you?"

I began to play with my hands as my anxiety set in, "I'm a little over nine weeks now. The baby is healthy."

He sighed, "When is your next appointment? Can you sit down please," he said, moving slightly closer to me.

I took a step back away from him, "I want to see all my men. I need to see that they are okay with my own eyes."

"Tomorrow, for now, I want you to rest. Eric is on his way to check you out. I need to know that you are okay," he said, watching me closely.

"I have a doctor. His name is Angelo. I want him and only him to look at me," I was trying desperately to stand my ground.

He moved to me and pulled my face up, so I had to look at him, "Fine. I will get you, your doctor. Now quit being so difficult."

I sighed and he pulled me over to the bed. I sat down trying to make myself numb to the situation I was in. I wanted this to be over. There was a knock at the door and my heart jumped as Luther told them to come in. Angelo and Eric stepped in. I ran to Angelo and threw my arms around him, "Everyone's okay boss."

I saw Luther watching us, "I want you to check the baby. She still looks so thin."

"Come here, Anastasia. Let's check the baby," Eric said, pulling me to the bed again.

I laid down on the bed, "Angelo is the only doctor touching me." Eric handed the equipment over to Angelo. He put the doppler on my stomach and then we heard the heartbeat. I saw the three men in the room instantly relax.

"Why is she so small?"

"Morning sickness. The baby has had her sick most mornings and nights," Angelo said, squeezing my hand.

Luther pushed him away, "Let go of my wife."

I jumped up instantly and pushed him away from Angelo with all my strength, "Back away from my men Luther."

Before I had time to react, he smacked me hard. I lost my balance from the impact and Angelo caught me before I heard Angelo growl, "Back off Luther."

"Don't tell me what to do or how to treat my wife," he turned to me. "Fine, you want to be with your men. You think I am so bad. I will show you just how bad I can be. You can go in a cell with your men. We'll see how long you are in there before you realize how good you have it with me."

I was dragged away, and I heard Angelo yelling behind me. I was dragged through the house to the kitchen. Oliver opened the door and dragged me down the stairs. I didn't know we had a basement that was lined with cells from one wall to the next on each side. I was put into a cell by myself at the end of the room. It was cold down here and we were in fall, "Boss said to let him know when you are ready to be a family."

The door closed and I heard the lock click as he locked me in the cell. I looked around at my surroundings. I saw a small bed and more cells down the little hallway hidden in the very back of the basement. I sat on the floor, my back against the wall by the bars. I hugged my knees to my chest and had a tight grip on them. I rested my head on my knees trying to keep myself calm and to stay warm. I heard Angelo return and my team started talking to each other. I couldn't get myself to focus on them or to hear anything they were saying. I felt someone touch my head, "Ana?"

I looked up and saw Luca next to me, "Hi Luca."

"Are you okay?"

"Yes and no. The baby is good. Its heartbeat is strong," I was trying to distract myself from the situation I was once again in. I laid my head back down on my knees, but I had it turned so I was looking at him.

"That's great baby," he pulled my face back up not wanting me to rest it, "But I am worried about you."

I pulled away and laid my head back down, "I don't know what to do Luca. I can't go back. I ran as fast as I could. I even fought with someone. It just wasn't enough."

"It's okay. You did your best. I just need you to breathe and try to remain calm. I promise we will be okay. Why don't you lay in the bed," he said, nudging me. I just shook my head no longer trusting my voice, "Please get in bed baby."

I looked back at him and felt completely defeated, "Okay Luca."

I got up and went to lay in the small hard bed. I curled up under the thin blanket to keep whatever heat I could, "How is she doing?"

"She's in bed now, but she is not herself," I heard Luca say in his soft voice.

I closed my eyes and forced myself to sleep. Not wanting to listen to the conversation that was flowing around me. I woke up with a scream as I watched the bullets fly, "Please no more." A sob escaped, "I can't handle this anymore."

I noticed someone was in my cell, "Hello Sunflower. Are you doing, okay?"

"Just go away, Luther. I'm being punished, remember? I didn't ask for you," I looked away and wiped the tears away, "Please."

"No, it's time to get you out of here. Luca told me-"

"What? Luca?" I moved to the bars that separated us from each other, "Why?"

"Because it's freezing. You need to be warm. You need food and a comfy bed. I don't need you to catch a cold. My job is to protect you, not watch you suffer," he said, moving towards me ever so slightly.

"No," I turned back to Luther, tired of everyone making decisions for me. "Did you know that I love him? He loves me. He is more than a bodyguard. Do you think he gets paid enough for this? I am not leaving this basement without my men."

I heard Luther growl. He was pulling me away from the bars aggressively and he forced me to face him. He stared at my face for a moment, and I saw the rage building. He smacked me again and when I hit the ground, he had me on a short chain to the bed, I am sure it was just for his pure enjoyment, "Let me know when you are done lying and trying to piss me off. I get you want to hurt me but try to be smart. You don't bite the hand that feeds you."

Then he was gone, "You are lucky he thought you were lying. What the hell were you thinking Ana?"

"I can't go back up there! You don't understand! I have been through this before! I-He-" I couldn't think of how to phrase the crushing disappointment and fear that coursed through my body. I screamed out of frustration and desperation to make him understand.

"Whoa, easy."

I hid under the bed and caved into the depression. I didn't move unless necessary, which was either to puke or use the bathroom. Everyone tried to talk to me. To coax me out of the dark place I had found myself. Soon a couple of days had passed by, "Alright what do you want?"

"For you to get Luther now," Luca said, his voice full of concern and urgency. I heard the footsteps fade, "Ana? Baby please."

"I just can't right now Luca. It hurts too much."

"Come here please."

I took a deep breath and focused all my energy on moving towards him. I got as close as I could with my ankle chained to the bed. I laid on my stomach facing him and felt my heartbreak at the look on his face, "I do love you."

"I love you too. Which is why I need you to fight. You are going to get sick if you aren't by some miracle already. Please, baby for me. Don't give up."

I watched him for a minute, "Okay, for you."

He gave me a sad smile in response and then we heard footsteps, "Good. Now close your eyes and rest. I will handle this."

I did as he asked, and then I froze when I heard Luther's voice, "What do you want, Luca?"

"She needs out of here, Luther. She's not doing well. She won't move and she's getting sick from the baby. So, she said some stuff that you didn't like. She is pregnant and overly emotional. Not to mention the shitty situation you put her in," Luca said.

"Oliver, unlock her door."

I took a deep breath and tried to prepare myself, "Is she even alive?"

"Yes, Oliver. Now, shut up," I felt someone next to me. He put his hand on my forehead, and it took everything I had not to cringe away from him, "Anastasia?"

I opened my eyes, "What now?"

"I think it's time for you to come upstairs. What do you say, Sunflower?"

I sighed, "Okay Luther."

He smiled and unchained me, "Come on. Let's get you cleaned up."

He pulled me to my feet and out of the dark cell. I was moving off of instinct and passed all the cells and up the stairs. I knew where the room was and headed towards it, "I am tired."

"You can sleep after you shower," he led me to the bathroom. "Come on out when you are done."

This is where Luca and I spent our time together. I hated that it was now tainted with Luther. I closed the bathroom door that was adjoined to the bedroom. I got in the shower not realizing just how cold I had been until the warm water had touched my skin. I showered, quickly scrubbed my skin and changed into the clean clothes that were left for me on the counter. I walked into the bedroom to see Eric, "What's going on?"

Luther stood up and approached me like I was a bear cub ready to attack, "Eric is here to check on the baby. Come sit down."

My stomach churned and I moved to the trash to throw up, "I'm sorry."

Luther came and helped me back into a standing position again. He helped me walk over to the bed and I got up into the hospital-looking bed. It was just much bigger, "It's okay Ana. Eric if you please."

Eric came over and tried to find the heartbeat, "I am having a hard time boss. Let me go get the ultrasound machine."

I started to breathe heavily as I realized I had hurt the child. It hadn't done anything. It was innocent in all of this. The tears filled my eyes as the panic set in. I may have killed my child, the thing I was supposed to protect. I was too stubborn. My chest hurt as the panic took over. I looked up at Luther, "Did I-"

His eyes softened ever so slightly, "Breathe Ana. It's okay."

"Did I just kill the baby," I asked, my voice growing thick.

"Shh hey easy," he moved to me. "Let's not panic yet."

A tear spilled over, "I'm so sorry."

He hugged me as I cried as if I had done something unspeakable. Eric came back and I closed my eyes as he did the ultrasound, "Open your eyes, Sunflower." I opened them slowly and Luther pointed to the screen, "That's the baby's heartbeat. It's a little weaker than we like but a little food, water, and some rest will help." He turned the volume up so I could hear it.

"Is the baby really, okay?"

"Yes, honey. Now lay down. I'm going to go make you some food," Luther left as Eric followed him out the door.

I lay down and tried to remain calm. I took a deep breath and pushed the panic away the best I could. I had my hand on my stomach and the tears slid down my face. I groaned and wiped them away, "Well I guess I am going to have you. Just not sure if I am going to keep you for myself or not."

The door opened and Luther came back in with Eric. Luther had toast on a plate and Eric moved to the side of the bed I was lying on. Eric started to set up an IV and I went to protest but Luther stopped me, "It's to get fluids into you more quickly. It will help the baby," I let them put the IV in with no complaints, "Good. Thank you."

They finished and my arm was cold from the fluids flowing freely into my arms, "Leave it alone while we get you rehydrated."

Luther walked over to me, "Eat this please."

He gave me a plate of toast and I began to eat. He sat down on the bed next to me and watched me eat. I finished and handed him back the plate, "We are going to put something in your IV so you can sleep."

"I don't want to sleep," I said softly.

"I know, but you need to sleep," I tried to move away.

"No, Luther, please. I don't want to sleep," I tried once again to move away but was trapped by him and an IV.

"Relax Ana. We just need to sleep so we can heal. We are going to keep an eye on the baby. You need to lay still," he said, grabbing me.

They got me settled back on one side of the bed. I had my arms wrapped around myself and the despair was crushing me, "I'm so tired."

"Go to sleep Ana," Luther said sitting on the bed next to me.

My eyes grew heavy, "I don't want to. I want to go home."

"You are home. Now go to sleep," he said as my eyes slipped shut. It was quiet and he was speaking softly trying not to wake me, "She needs to be watched closely until the baby stabilizes."

"Yes sir," Eric said. "I will stay with her tonight. Go take care of your business."

"Alright, I will be back soon."

****

I woke up screaming and was being pushed down. I couldn't remember the dream or why I was so scared. I just knew I had to get away, "Get away from me!"

"Shh calm down," Eric said, trying to calm me down.

"Stop! Let me go! I want to go!"

Luther came running in, "What the hell is going on?"

"She is having a panic attack. Grab her so I can get her something that will calm her down," Eric said.

Luther came and held me down while Eric moved away, "Please let me go! I just can't handle this right now!"

"Anastasia, stop! You are going to hurt yourself! Hurry up, Eric!"

I couldn't stop trying to get away from them. This isn't the life I wanted. I did everything I could to avoid my father's business. Then suddenly all the fighting left me. The panic was still there, and I was gasping for air trying to calm down, "Please leave me alone."

"Breath. You are going to hurt yourself," Luther said he was trying to soothe me.

"No-I-Just-"

"Eric, sit with her," Luther said before he quickly left the room. I tried to move my arms, but I couldn't. After a few minutes, Luther came in with someone, "Go calm her down."

Eric moved out of the way, and I saw Evelyn, "Eve!"

178

"Hey Ana. Are you okay," she asked as she moved to me and squeezed my hand.

"No, I want out of here. Please help me," I said, trying to get my breathing under control.

"It's okay. Just close your eyes and take some deep breaths."

I closed my eyes, but my heart rate wouldn't slow. I was still struggling to take a deep breath. Luther came and grabbed her, "No! Don't hurt her!" I screamed and fought again with everything I had as she was pulled from the room crying. Eric tried to calm me down again.

The door opened and only one person came in this time, "Stop Anastasia."

I froze, "D-Dom?

Chapter Nine

The Family Reunion

"You need to calm down. If something happens to you or the baby he won't like it," Dom said moving to me.

"What are you doing here? Where is Mom?" I started spewing questions.

"Calm down. When the safe house was hit, we were taken. How are you," he asked quietly.

My stomach churned, "Dom... Why are you okay?"

"Ana-"

"Dominic, unless you are going to tell me what is going on, I want you to get out," I said as my stomach churned again.

I watched him leave and I collapsed to the bed. I cried and I heard the door open, "Ana?"

"Luther I can't. Please just go away," I said through the tears.

I heard him sigh, "Eric, help her sleep. I will be back shortly."

I felt tired and let my eyes close. I slipped back into a state of unconsciousness.

****

I woke up and looked around the room. Luther was next to me in a chair. I took a deep breath, "Luther?"

He lifted his head and looked at me, "Are you okay, Ana?"

"I am fine. How is the baby," I asked. My voice was quite soft sounding.

"The baby is good and improving quickly. We can take you off the monitor soon," he said, stretching.

"Is Eve okay," My voice was growing thick.

"Your friend?" All I could do was nod because I was scared my voice would betray me, "Yes she is okay."

I sighed as a single tear slipped down my face, "Where is my mother?"

"Ana… We- The house was being attacked as we got there. Your mother died on our way here. She is buried out in the backyard."

My whole body began to shake as I listened to him while staring at my hands, "Why is my brother alive?"

"We are using him right now."

I let out a shaky breath and looked up at his face, "I don't feel well." I gagged and he put a trash can under my head quickly. I began to throw up and empty my stomach, "Why…? How are you using Dom?"

"I think you should get some rest Ana," he said, pulling my hair back.

"Answer me, Luther. I need to know," I said, keeping my head down.

I heard him sigh, "Your brother started his little gang. I was his gang that was attacking the house. It's made up of some old-fashioned Texans with a whole lot of guns. We are using him to keep them back."

A sob escaped and I threw up more as my body couldn't handle the stress or news, "What the hell is happening?"

"Please take an easy Ana. I don't know how much more your body can take," Luther said, his voice gentle.

"Can I go see my men?"

"If you try and eat," he said, the tone of his voice stating this was not up for discussion.

"Okay," I slowly sat up and waited to make sure the vomiting had ended, "Bring me some food."

He watched me for a minute, "Alright. I'll be right back," I watched him leave and felt my body go limp in defeat. I heard the door open and saw Luther come in. He handed me a bowl of fruit, "Eat while I talk." I nodded and began to eat the fruit, "Ana I am not stupid. I know you don't love me, and I honestly don't expect you to. I am here for you though. I know you don't trust me and again I don't blame you, but we need to work together. I need your team."

My stomach began to churn, "Why? Why should we? You took my father, me, my mother-"

"I know. It's not fair but if we don't your brother will destroy us both. If we do this, I will let you go. I just want to see our child, but we will be free of each other," he said, watching me intently. "I just want to be a better man and father than I had."

"Let me go talk to my men," I said, my voice sounding weird.

"Okay let me help," he stood up and unhooked me from the monitors. He helped me take out the IV. I was pulled to my feet, "Go talk. We will go over everything after. Oliver will take you down."

I went to the door and saw Oliver standing on the other side, "I want to be alone when I talk to my men."

"As you wish. Help her to her men then come back and find me," Luther said to Oliver.

"Are you sure that is wise," Oliver asked astounded.

"I gave you an order."

Oliver nodded and I followed him through the house. We went down the stairs and I saw the cells with my team in them, "We will be right upstairs."

I didn't say anything, just watched him leave. I heard the door at the top of the stairs close, "Where are the keys?"

Eve stood up, "Over there by the wall."

I walked over to where she had pointed and grabbed them. I began to unlock each of their doors. I finally got to Luca's door and unlocked it. I couldn't look at him as I looked over and I saw Dom sitting in a cell towards the back of the basement waiting for me to come unlock the door. I turned my back on him. I was shaking and I wasn't sure how much longer my legs would hold me. I felt someone's arm go around me, "Ana?"

Luca pulled me to the bench and had me sit down. He stood up with the team in front of me. I was surrounded by them. Tears sprung to my eyes as I looked at the closest thing I had to a family now, "I'm okay guys. We need to talk." I talked to them and brought them up to speed about everything. Then I told them the deal I was just given, "So I need to know."

Luca came and kneeled in front of me, "Ana, we can't trust him."

"What other choice do we have? Dom had my mother killed. Plus, I want to be free." Tears filled my eyes as I digested his response. "I want to be free Luca. To be with who I want," I took a deep breath, "I won't do anything unless we all agree."

A couple of tears spilled over and slid down my face. Luca reached out and wiped them away, "I don't trust him but if this gets me out of this cell and closer to you then let's do it."

I heard murmurs of agreement around the circle. I sighed and hugged Luca, "Thank you. Thank you all. You are my family now."

"Well let's go talk to Luther," Luca said, tucking my hair behind my ear.

"Ana wait!!!"

I froze when I heard Dom say my name. I turned around to look at him and mustered all the strength I had in me, "No. You had our mother killed. I was tracked down and beaten. You rot in that cell."

"They will kill you all to get to me. It doesn't matter if you are pregnant or not. They do not care. They just want me back," he smiled at me.

Luca moved so fast that I didn't have time to react. He reached through the bars and slammed Dom's head into the bars as hard as he could and spit on the body lying on the floor. He moved back to me quickly, "Come on Ana, let's go."

I was pulled up the stairs trying to compose myself. My team pulled me to the nearest chair and made sure that I didn't collapse. I heard Luther and Luca talking. My hand had fallen to my stomach, and I had three guys in front of me looking at me like I was a bomb about to go off. I looked to see Luther, Luca, and Angelo, "I'm okay."

"No one is going to let anything happen to you or the baby," Luther said. "Luca and Angelo are going to take you to your room that you will be sleeping in now."

"Okay, what is going to happen to Dom?"

"Don't worry about that right now. Come with us," Angelo said.

I was pulled to my feet by these men. I was pulled through the house one on each of my arms. I was pulled into a room with two beds and Eve was sitting on one of them, "Are we okay for now?"

Angelo went over and hugged her, "Yes honey. Now go in there and take a nice hot shower. I want you to be able to get some real sleep."

"Okay," I watched her disappear through a door at the back of the room.

Luca pulled me to the other bed, "You don't have to sleep but can you lie down?"

"Why?"

"Because you look completely exhausted, baby. We are not doing anything today. We will be showering and resting," Luca said, his voice gentle.

"I don't want to sleep. I don't want to lay down. I want this to be over," I said watching his sad eyes watch me like a hawk.

He kneeled in front of me again, "Baby we have a war to prepare for. I need you at your best. The baby does too."

"I am scared, Luca. My brother-He... I thought I could trust him. How do I know who to trust? It's all so messed up."

"You trust me, Ana. I will keep you safe but there's only so much I can do. Please lay down baby," he pulled my face up, so I had to look at him.

It took me a minute before I could respond, "Okay Luca. I will lay down, but I do not want to sleep."

He smiled at me, "Thank you."

He pulled the blankets back and I laid down by the wall. He pulled the blankets over me, "I don't want to sleep yet."

"That's fine baby. You don't have to sleep. I just want you to get some real rest," he moved my hair out of my face.

"Will you lay down with me," I asked looking down at my hands.

He pulled my face back up, "After I shower. Until then you just lay here and be comfy."

My eyes grew heavy, and I just watched Luca. Eve and Angelo both showered and were lying down on the bed. They were quiet like they were sleeping. They were lying down across the room from us. Luca stood up and looked at me, "I will be right back. Angelo and Evelyn are here."

He walked away to the bathroom. My stomach churned, so I tried to focus on just my breathing and buried my head further into the pillows. I let my eyes close. I don't know how long I laid there like that, but I jumped when someone got in bed next to me, "Luca?"

"Yeah silly. It's just me. I'm sorry I woke you up. I was hoping you'd sleep more if I got into bed."

I moved to him and felt his arms close around me, "It's okay. I'd much rather be awake."

He chuckled, "Go back to sleep, Ana. I am right here if you need me."

I let my eyes slip shut as I buried my face into his chest, "Good night, Luca. Please don't go anywhere."

"I am not going anywhere baby," I felt him kiss the top of my head. "Good night, Ana. Please don't worry about anything, just get some rest."

****

I woke with a scream as the flash of dead bodies was still fresh in my mind. My breathing was heavy as the night before came flooding back. Luca moved into a sitting position, and I saw Angelo and Evelyn jump, "I'm okay…"

I watched Angelo and Evelyn lay back down. They murmured to themselves. I looked over and Luca flopped back down on his back and was rubbing his eyes, "Just breathe. Nightmares are completely normal considering. I just need you to stay calm."

He was rubbing small circles on my back. I took a deep breath, "I'm going to get some water. I will be right back."

He grabbed my wrist, "I am coming with you."

He looked completely exhausted, and I needed him to get some more sleep, "Luca I am going to be fine. No one is going to hurt me. Get some more sleep. I will be right back."

He sighed, "Okay honey. Just please be careful and hurry back."

"I will, Luca," I said, kissing his head. I quickly got off the bed and hurried out of the room before he could change his mind. I went to the kitchen and grabbed a glass from the cupboard. I filled it with water and was looking out the window as I sipped from it.

"Are you okay?"

I gasped and dropped the glass as the sudden sound made me panic. It shattered as it hit the floor and I turned to see Luther, "I'm sorry."

I bent down to clean up the glass that had scattered across the kitchen floor, "Let me do that. Here," he picked me up and set me down, so I was sitting on the counter, so I didn't cut myself I assumed. He cleaned up the glass and once he was done and sure it was all cleaned up, he turned back to me, "Are you okay?"

"I just needed some fresh air and something to drink. I am sorry I broke the glass," I said quietly.

"Don't worry about it. It's a cup, it can easily be replaced. You should go back to bed. You are starting to look a little bit better. I am sure some more sleep will help with that," he said watching me.

"Okay," I said as he walked over to me and helped me off the counter. I walked back to the room we were occupying. I sluggishly crawled back into the bed with Luca, and he instantly pulled me to him, "Sorry," I mumbled realizing it took me longer than expected.

"As long as you are safe, baby. Now go back to sleep," he said, kissing my forehead.

I lay next to him unable to turn off my thoughts as he fell back asleep. My stomach began to churn, and I felt the bile slowly trying to rise in my throat. I got up and moved to the bathroom to throw up. I sat down and emptied the contents of my stomach. I didn't know anyone was awake until someone grabbed my hair and pulled it back, "I'm sorry."

"Don't be sorry. You should have woken me," Luca said, patting my back gently.

"You look so tired-" I was cut off to throw up some more stomach acid. I didn't know it was possible to keep throwing up like this and not die, "I want it to stop."

"I know Ana. Just a little longer," he said, soothing me.

"I can't. How can I keep this child alive if I can't keep anything down? This doesn't seem possible," I said, getting completely frustrated.

He chuckled, "It is part of the process. You got this, Ana. It's going to be a little while longer and then it should be easier."

"Well, it sucks," I grumbled resting my head on the toilet seat, my body completely exhausted.

"I know it does. Come back to bed," he said, scooping me up in his arms. I wrapped my arms around his neck as he carried me back to the bed. I curled up and felt him lay down next to me, "Good night, Ana. We will figure it out. Just one step at a time. The next step is to get to tomorrow."

"Okay, Luca. Good night," I said, closing my eyes. I willed my body to go to sleep, but I couldn't help but think of my broken family. My mother and father both died alone and in fear for not only their own lives but their children's. Before I fully understood myself, I had tears streaming down my face. My brother, whom I had trusted, was now my enemy and my enemy was now helping me. My life had completely flipped, and a small sob escaped. I didn't want to wake anyone up, so I very carefully got out of bed. I practically ran out of the room; I was desperate to get outside.

I was on my way out of the house, but someone grabbed me by the elbow just as I was about to reach the front door, "Where are you going?"

"Please, I just need some air, Oliver. I have nowhere to go. I certainly wouldn't be safe out there by myself. Please let me go outside," I said as the panic attack caused me to hyperventilate.

He stared at me for a long moment, "Fine, but stay where I can see you."

"Thank you," I stumbled out of the house. I sat down by the nearest tree. I didn't move, and I certainly didn't care if the air was cold as I took a few deep breaths. I sat there for hours but only felt like a few minutes. Soon the sun was rising, and I was all out of tears. I was lying on the ground in a tight little ball for warmth and comfort.

Shouting erupted from inside the house, and I am sure it had to do with my sudden disappearance. I couldn't make myself move to calm them down. I heard the front door open, "She's still out here!" I heard Luther shout. I heard his footsteps as he approached me, "Ana?"

I looked up and saw his face full of concern, "I-I needed s-some air."

Luca came running out behind him, "Is she okay?"

"I-I'm s-s-sorry. I-I l-lost track of t-time," I shivered as they both kneeled in front of me, and my teeth chattered.

"Hey, can we move you? We need to get you warm and check the baby," Luther said, his voice soft.

As cold as I was, I was enjoying the fresh air and space, "D-do I h-have to?"

Luca gave me the best smile he could muster up, "Your lips are blue boss. Can I pick you up?"

"O-okay," I said watching his face. He leaned down and once again scooped me up in his arms. I curled in towards the heat and closed my eyes.

I was set down on a soft surface. He pulled away taking the heat with him and I had to resist the urge to groan, "We need a heated blanket, a regular blanket, and some food," Angelo said.

"C-can L-Luca s-sit with m-me," I asked, opening my eyes slowly to look at the group around me.

"Of course, I can," he moved my head, so it was on his lap.

Soon I was covered in blankets and my body was thawing out. My eyes closed again as I began to warm up inside and out. Luca moved my hair out of my face, "She trusts you completely. That is quite odd for her. Why does she trust you?"

"I've known her since we were kids. We used to be best friends but then I kind of disappeared for a while," Luca said his voice was quiet as he tried not to wake me up.

My stomach churned as these two people talked, "Luca, I don't feel good."

"I'm sure you don't. Do you still feel cold," I opened my eyes and shook my head. "Okay, we are going to check the baby quickly."

"I'm really bad at being a mom," My voice dropped as they freed my stomach to check on the baby.

I didn't think anyone was listening to me when I heard, "No, you are just learning how to be a mom. It's hard to learn. I am sure the baby is just fine, Sunflower," Luther said back to me.

I heard the baby's heartbeat and promised myself I would be better for my child, "You hear that. The baby is fine Ana."

I smiled at my stomach, not sure if the smile looked real. Evelyn came into the room, "Most of the guys are training. Here, Ana, I made you a grilled cheese."

I sat up and took the sandwich slowly. I began to eat it slowly trying not to throw up. The warmth felt good, "Ana?"

I looked at Luca, "Yeah?"

"Luther and I must plan and train. I know you have been training but maybe you should rest today with Eve," Luca said, pulling my face up when I looked away.

"But I want to help," I could feel myself being defeated, and the depression began to take over my mind.

"You can help honey. I just think you could start helping tomorrow."

I sighed, "Okay… I'll rest today but that is it. I will be helping tomorrow."

Both men smiled at me. Luther got up and walked away, "Thank you, baby. I love you. Try and keep some food down. I will see you for lunch."

"I love you too, just be careful please," I said as he got up and walked away.

Evelyn sat down next to me and turned the TV on, "Don't worry. They will be fine."

"Eve, this whole thing has me worried. What are we going to do? Dom was supposed to be my rock. I was supposed to be able to trust him out of all people. Now I'm working with someone who killed my father, kidnapped me, rape me, and got me pregnant," I went on a rant. I didn't know how to stop the words from coming out of my mouth.

"Hey, it's going to be okay. We got each other. Just because we are working together doesn't mean we trust each other," she said, trying to reassure me.

"I just hate the unknown. I also hate treating my brother like a criminal, but I am doing it. He was my hero growing up. I wish my mom was here to help me through this," my heart ached as I thought about my mother and brother. I couldn't believe my life had turned into me.

"He said she's buried here. Let's go look for her. Maybe being close to her will make you feel better," Eve said, standing up and getting off the couch.

"Yeah, but I don't even know where to begin," I said standing up and following her.

I followed her through the house barely paying attention to where we were going. Before I knew it, I was going out the back door with her, "It's okay let's look together."

We wandered around the big space. After an hour of searching, I came by a white cross at the edge of the tree line. I went over there, and Eve followed but decided to leave a few steps between us as I registered what this meant. I came to a stop and collapsed on the ground in front of it, "I think we just found her."

"Are you okay, Ana?" Evelyn asked if her voice was gentle as my world shattered even more than I thought possible.

"My mother is buried here. I don't know how that makes me feel. My mother is on the ground, I will never hug her again. My brother is in a cell in our basement, we use him to keep gun-crazy gangs away from us. My father is dead. It has only been a few months. How did this all happen in a few short months," I said, unable to take my eyes off the little white cross?

"It's okay to feel conflicted. If it was my mom I would be conflicted and devastated at the same time," she said, her footsteps approaching me.

I went to respond when I heard a low growl, and I heard her steps falter. I froze and when I looked up, I saw a large wolf staring at me from within the tree line, "Eve go get help now."

"Ana-"

"No, I can't look away. We have already made eye contact. I must stay here. You can. I need you to go get help before we both get eaten by the large dog. Go get help now!"

"I'll call on my phone. I am not leaving you. Hell no, to having that conversation with Luca. I would rather stab my eyes out," she said, her voice shaky.

"Are you guys okay," A man asked somewhere behind me.

"No, we need help! There's a large wolf and she can't move," Evelyn said. "I'm Eve and this is Ana."

"My name is Elijah. Let me help. Eve, slowly move towards the house," he said his voice was quiet like he didn't want to startle the wolf.

"Hi, Elijah. Eve, you need to do what he says. I need you out of the way and safe," I said keeping my eyes on the wolf praying the pack wasn't close by.

"Okay, Ana. I will do what you ask. Listen here you, you better keep her safe. She can't get hurt. We all need her. I'll find Luca and Luther and have them come back this way," she said quickly.

"Alright Ana," After the footsteps began to fade, "I need you to slowly get to your feet," Elijah said, his voice soft.

I slowly began to move without moving my eyes from the wolf. The wolf began to growl again, and I flinched, "I'm scared. I don't think I can move… What if there is a pack nearby?"

"Trust me, Ana. I am just as scared right now. If there was a pack nearby, we would've seen it by now. It's either a lone wolf or out on a hunting mission. I've got my gun, and I am ready to use it if I have to. I would just rather you be out of the way when I do. I would like you to try and move closer," he said, sounding abnormally calm.

I took a deep breath, "Okay I guess I can try." I slowly began to rise to my feet once again. The wolf let out a small bark and made a small lunging gesture. I let out a little scream as I moved back as fast as I could. I watched the fur on the back of its neck stand up. It slowly went into a pouncing position as it watched me.

"Good job. You are doing great. Here comes the hard part. I need you to move very slowly backward. I am behind you so you can stop moving when you run into me. I just need you to move until you hit me," he said, his voice growing more and more tense.

I felt my stomach churn, "I can't do this. I don't think I can do this."

"It's okay. You can do this. Please just start moving back towards me," he said his voice was soft.

I felt the tears start to threaten me as I thought if I were to die here, after everything. I took a deep breath and willed them away, "Okay. I will just start to back up." I took one slow step back and I watched the fur rise even higher on its neck and the low growl in its throat getting louder. The wolf stalked forward slowly, following me, "Elijah..."

"It's okay Ana. Just keep going. You are doing great. I am not going anywhere," he said, trying to control his voice so I wouldn't panic.

I took another deep breath as one tear managed to escape and just took another step backward. With each step I took the wolf would take one forward. It was fully out of the woods and in plain view, "What do we do now?"

"Just keep moving back slowly. You are going to be okay. I promise," he said, trying to reassure me as much as he was trying to convince himself.

I stopped when I ran into him, "I found you."

His laugh was humorless as he began to slowly move himself around me so that he was going to be blocking me with his body, "Yes you did. Now I need you to take a couple more steps so that I am in front of you."

"Okay," I said as I took another step behind him, and he moved in front of me.

"I'm going to try and scare it back. When I tell you to, run and run like hell," he said as he stretched his arm out in front of me, "Are you ready?"

"What kind of question is that? Not even a little bit but let's do it anyway," I said, taking a deep breath to try and prepare myself. I took one more deep breath to steady my nerves. He shot the gun in his hand twice and I flinched away from him. He shouted at me to run, and I was sure as hell not sticking around for the wolf to figure it out. I took off and I ran as fast as my body would let me.

Chapter Ten

The Truth Comes Out

We were running as fast as we could. I felt something hit me and I fell to the ground and tried to get back up. I couldn't move too fast. I rolled onto my back and screamed when I saw the wolf lunging at me. I heard Elijah shout, "Stay down!" I screamed and covered my face. I tried to make myself as small as humanly possible. I heard two gunshots and the wolf fell on me covering me in a warm sticky liquid I could only assume was its blood. I felt the wolf being pulled off me, "Ana?!"

I was gasping for air and staring at the large wolf that almost ended my life. I heard more shouting and running. I collapsed to the ground and tried to get my breathing under control. Elijah sat next to me, and I could see he was close to my age with brown eyes. He was on the smaller side with a small to medium build, "I'm okay."

He sighed and sank to the ground next to me, "Nice to meet you, Ana."

I laughed despite myself with no humor in my exhausted body, "Nice to meet you too Elijah."

"Please call me Eli. I think we are to that point," he said lying down next to me.

We were both trying to get our muscles to relax. Before we had time to process anything, we were surrounded by people, "Ana what the hell happened?"

"Please Luca give me a minute. My heart is still racing from the near-death experience," I groaned as Luther, Luca, and Angelo sat down on the ground next to me.

"Sunflower, we are happy you are okay, but we need an explanation," Luther said quietly.

I slowly sat up and looked between Luca and Luther, "I am sorry. I began to panic, and it made me want my mom." I watched both tense up at the mention of my mother, "Luther told me she was buried out here and I just needed to find her." I looked down at my hands, "I was so focused on finding her that I didn't think about the wildlife that could be out here. I just needed my mom." My voice broke as a few tears fell. I quickly wiped them away because I was tired of crying.

"Ana, honey you can't just go off like that. You must be careful," Angelo said.

I looked at him with more tears in my eyes, "I was with Eve. I did everything right. I have been doing things right. I just needed my mom. I didn't know there was going to be a giant wolf looking for their next meal out there."

"Shh okay. I'm sorry," he said softly.

"Good job Eli. Go inside everyone," Luther said looking around at the group of people that had formed around me and Eli.

They dispersed, and Luther and Luca pulled me to my feet, "Let's get you cleaned up."

I followed the guys without saying another word. The two men pulled me to and through the house by my arms. I was pulled into our room. I sat down on the bed and my legs suddenly couldn't hold me anymore, "I'm sorry guys. I just needed to see where she was. I just needed her."

Luca kneeled in front of me, and Luther sat down next to me, "It's okay, Ana, I promise you that it is okay. We were just very worried about you."

Luther was rubbing my back, "Things are okay now. We were just worried. You can't just go off like that."

"I know. I'm sorry. I didn't mean to make you worry. I feel fine besides a little shaken up. I just feel a little tired now," I said, rubbing my face.

I pulled my hands away from my face and saw they were covered in blood, "Oh, I am sure you are."

"Yeah, but I suppose I should take a shower," I sighed as I just wanted to lie down.

"Yes, you should. You need a shower, and we need to get some food for you," Luca said, smiling at me trying to calm me down.

"Okay," I stood up and grabbed some comfy clothes from the dresser that held all my clothes. I went into the bathroom slowly and turned on the shower. I didn't bother locking the door, I didn't think it would matter at this point. I got under the hot water and scrubbed my skin until it felt raw. After half an hour and I was clean, shaved, and feeling a little bit better, I turned off the shower and got out. I dried my body quickly and put comfy clothes on. I couldn't help but feel sad given the circumstances I was in and a little angry. I walked back into our room and Luca stood up instantly.

Luca grabbed me and pulled me into a hug, "I'm sorry honey."

I hugged him back tightly, "I'm sorry for just going off. I know that was not smart. I don't know how to explain it, but I just needed to see where she was."

"Do you need or want to talk to me about what is going on in your head," he asked in a soft voice.

"I just... I don't know. I hate how I feel right now. I'm sad, angry, betrayed, and way too emotional. I miss my mom and brother. I even miss my father. I miss the way my life used to be a little bit," I said looking down at my hands.

I watched him pull me into another hug, "I'm sorry baby. Get into bed. Luther is going to be bringing some food in here."

"I'm not hungry," I pulled away from him and climbed into bed.

"I know Ana, but it's not just for you. You must feed the baby too. It needs all the strength it can get," he said, pulling the blankets over me.

"Okay, Luca. I will eat, but I want to spend some time alone please," I said not wanting to look at him again.

"Okay, I will go and give you some time, but I need you to eat please," he said.

I just nodded and I heard the door close. I let out a shaky breath that I had been holding since the wolf almost mauled me to death. I laid there and stared at the ceiling counting the tiles. The door opened and Luther came in slowly. I caught the smell of cooked tomato and had to quickly throw up all my food, "Oh boy. I'll be right back."

I emptied my stomach, and I heard the door open again, "I'm sorry. I guess the baby didn't like that smell very much. That hurt."

"I'm sorry. I brought you a salad instead," Luther said from the room.

"Thank you. Please go. I'll eat the salad, but I want to be alone right now please," I said, getting up and brushing my teeth.

I heard the door open and close once again. I rinsed off the toothbrush and tried to stop my hands from shaking. I went back out to the room and sat down on the bed. I grabbed the plate with a salad on it and began to eat. Once I finished, I set the plate down. I laid down and hid under the blankets. I stayed there for what felt like hours. The doors opened, "Ana what are you doing?"

"I am lying here trying to imagine my mom here. I just want her here to tell me. It will all be okay," I said my voice was tight, "Eve how do I do this without my mom?"

"You do it with me. We got this Ana. You just can't hide out. This isn't how either of them raised you. You must be an adult and handle this with us. Don't hide from us," she said sitting down next to me.

I pulled the blankets down so I could see her, "I just am so tired of fighting and being an adult Eve. I feel exhausted."

"I'm sure you are. Part of that is the baby," she said, giving me a small smile.

"This is an incredibly uncomfortable situation. I don't want to be pregnant or doing any of this," I took a deep breath."

"I know but you are. Time to handle the situation. No more hiding, no more feeling sorry for yourself," she said, her voice gentle, but her message was harsh.

I took a deep breath and got out of bed. I wiped the tears from my eyes, "You're right. Let's go train. I just can't lay here, or I'll be stuck in a constant state of depression."

"Alright, let's go," she said, smiling back at me.

We headed out of the house, and I began to put all my energy into learning how to be a better fighter. We did it for hours. After I got knocked on my ass, I saw Luca and Luther standing by a tree with their arms crossed against their chest, "I think I might be in trouble."

Eve laughed as she saw the two men staring at us, "I think I am going to go find Angelo. I don't want to listen to a lecture just yet."

"Run and run fast," I chuckled. I took a deep breath and moved towards the two guys who were staring and scowling at me. I stopped in front of both, "Hi guys."

"What are you doing?" Luther asked, his voice full of rage.

"I-"

"Anastasia, I thought we agreed that you are resting today. Then we find you out here overworking your body," Luca said frustration leaking into his voice.

"Okay. I get it. You are both mad and frustrated. I understand. Can you finish yelling at me after we eat? I'm starving," I said looking between the two of them.

They both froze and I saw their eyes widen at my words, "You are hungry?"

"Yes, and I know you are angry, but can you please yell at me while we eat," I said, smiling at the look on their face. "I promise to take you seriously while you yell at me."

They both smiled, unable to hide their happiness, "Yes, please. Let's go eat." Luther said walking towards the house ahead of us, like he was scared I was going to change my mind.

Luca stared at me with a big smile on his face. Once Luther was out of sight, he picked me up and spun me around. I laughed, "Let's get some food in you. I am so happy you are hungry."

"Okay Luca," I couldn't stop myself from smiling as he set me back down on the ground. I felt a little more at home. The most relaxed I have felt since we fled the house of gunshots.

We walked back to the house together. We walked up the back porch and into the house to see Luther making sandwiches, "Sit down. I will bring the food to you."

I went and sat down at the table with Luca and folded my hands on my lap. I knew it was only a matter of time before they both remembered they were angry with me, "I am so happy you are eating but what were you doing? We told you to take it easy."

I couldn't look at either of them and I knew they were looking at me, "I was trying to not be depressed. I needed to do something that made me not think," I said looking at my hands on my lap.

"You can't overdo it, Ana. You must take things slowly. How are you feeling?" Luca asked his voice gently as he lectured me as he was worried about my mental state.

Luther set a sandwich down in front of me and Luca. That took me by surprise, "Eat. It's been a busy day."

"It's barely started," I said, eating the food, still refusing to look at either of them in the eye.

"It's already over," Luca said as I heard him eating.

I finished the food that was on my plate and sat there waiting for them to finish so the yelling could begin. It was quiet for a long time and then finally I heard, "Ana, I think you should rest now."

"No," I didn't even hesitate as the word left my lips. "I just can't rest while everyone prepares for a war. We must all prepare together. You guys have been preparing all day," I said, finally looking up at Luther.

"The baby-"

"The baby is fine. I am only ten weeks pregnant," I said looking between the two men trying to stand my ground as they both stared at me. "I can't go back to doing nothing. My depression will win. I-" I had a tear spill down my face

I hadn't realized was in my eye and I hated myself for looking weak.

Luca reached over and wiped the tear away gently, "Ana-"

"No. Neither of you understand. Please. I have been shot at, in car accidents, I've been attacked, raped, killed a man, and beaten, and now my brother has turned against me, and my enemy is now on my side. I-I really can't," I moved away from both of them, moving my eyes to the floor.

I heard the chair scrape as someone stood up, "Hey Ana. You need to calm down."

I hadn't realized how panicked I had gotten until I was gasping for air, "I-I can't go back to doing nothing."

I heard another chair and Luther moved towards me. I moved back and trapped myself against the wall while they stood in front of me, "Sunflower you have to breathe."

Luca moved to me and hugged me, "Stop." I tried to pull away from him desperately not wanting to break down, "Ana stop!" I felt my knees give out and I sunk into his chest as he held all my weight. I felt him squeeze me tighter, "I have you. Please breathe."

Tears went down my face as I couldn't hold them in any longer, "Please don't make me do nothing. I don't want depression to win."

"Shh, I'm not asking you to do anything. I just want you to take some deep breaths. I want you to keep the food down that you just ate," he said gently. My breathing slowed down and finally went back to normal, "That's it."

I moved away and he let me. I wiped my tears up on the sleeve of my shirt, "I'm sorry. I didn't mean to have a panic attack."

"It's okay Ana. I just worry about you and the baby. I am sorry," Luther said, watching me very closely.

"I think I just need some air," I said, turning around and going out to the back porch. I had a seat on the stairs and took some deep breaths. I heard the back door open and close again. I sighed, "I'm okay really. I don't need a babysitter."

"I am not here to babysit. I want to talk to you for a minute," Luther said sitting down next to me.

My anxiety suddenly spiked, and I sat up a little straighter, "Sure Luther. What's on your mind," I asked, folding my hands on my lap again.

"I want you to be honest with me. No lying. What is going on with you and Luca," he asked quickly.

My whole body tensed up and I tried to keep my breathing under control as my husband asked me about the man I was seeing. Not that this was a real marriage but flashbacks of being hit came back hard, "What do you mean?"

"He's the only one you don't flinch away from. The only person you will let touch you for more than a few seconds. Something is going on," he said his voice was soft which just put me more on edge.

"Luther-I-" I couldn't seem to find any logical reason besides telling him the truth. My whole body and soul screamed at me to keep my mouth shut but it all spilled out,

"I love him. Despite all I've been through he has always been there. He-"

I looked at him and saw he was staring at his hands, and I couldn't tell what he was thinking. I did know that I needed some distance, "I see."

"I'm so sorry. I-I must go," I stood up suddenly unable to sit there anymore. I moved away from him, and I began to run. I didn't stop, didn't take a break, I just ran. I ran for about an hour when I collapsed to the ground in pain and exhaustion. I screamed all my anger and frustrations out.

"Ana?"

I looked and saw Luther running towards me and the panic set in, "Luther is everything okay?"

He came and sat down next to me, "Yes everything is fine. Please don't run again."

"Luther, please. I really can't do this right now. I know it's not fair given what our families have done to each other, but I can't help who I love," I said, staring at the ground.

"I know Ana. I'm not mad. I was very upset about everything at first, but I want to be better for our child. I want to be better than both of our fathers," he said his voice was gentle. "I want you to be happy despite everything I have done to you and what your father did to me."

"I want to not fear you, Luther. I don't know much about how I feel about this baby, but I do not want to fear you. It's just going to take time," I said looking over at him.

He stood up and held out his hand to me, "It's okay. I have plenty of time. We have plenty of time to figure everything out."

I slowly took his hand, and we went back to the house. We found Luca sitting on the steps of the back porch. Luther didn't hesitate; he walked right into the house. Luca moved and stopped right in front of me, "What happened? Are you okay?"

"He knows about us. I'm okay. We just talked about things with the baby and how to move forward when I am terrified of him," He pulled me into a hug. I hugged him back, "I promise Luca I am okay."

"We are done for the day. Come with me," he said, pulling me into the house. He pulled me through the house quickly and soon I was standing in our room. I moved and sat down on our bed, "Baby how are you feeling?"

"I am fine. I don't feel sick or anything. I am sorry," I said looking at him.

Luca sat down next to me, "You looked good training today."

"Thanks," I said, trying not to blush.

I stood up and took a few steps towards the window. I wanted to see the sun and where it was in the sky. I took another step and the window shattered. I screamed as Luca pulled me down to the floor. He covered my body with his and I heard multiple gunshots. He slowly inched me towards the bed so that I could hide under it. He yelled out a couple of times, "Get under the bed now!!"

"Luca! No! What about you?"

"Get under the bed now!! This is not up for discussion," he yelled as he shoved me towards the bed. I screamed as a gunshot went right by my head.

He moved quickly and I ducked as he pulled my head down, "Luca!"

"Get under the bed NOW!!"

I moved under the bed, losing my argument with him, and made myself as small as possible. The gunshots were all that I could hear as they hit the house. He moved under the bed with me and continued to cover me with his body, "Luca? Please say something?"

"We don't move until the gunshots stop. You stay right here and stay small," he said his face was pale.

"Luca, I'm scared. Please be okay. I need you to be okay," I said as the tears streamed down my face.

He pulled my face up, so I had to look at him, "I'm not going anywhere, Ana. Just stay here with me. We will be fine."

It felt like hours, but maybe twenty minutes went by when the gunfire finally ended. He moved out from under the bed and was breathing heavily. I followed him when he threw his arm out, "Be careful."

I moved slowly and got to him, "Luca! Are you okay?" I saw blood coming out of three different places and the overwhelming urge to cry was strong. I tried to put pressure on the wounds so that I could stop the bleeding, "Angelo!!!" I screamed as loud as I could. "Luca, please stay with me."

I had tears filling my eyes, "I am okay baby. I will be okay," he said, gasping for air.

"Angelo!!!" I screamed as loud as I could. "I love you, Luca. You must be okay!"

The door opened and Angelo, Apollo, Eve, Eli, and Luther all came in, "Are you okay??"

"Please you have to save him, Angelo," I said, my voice growing thick as everyone started to help with each wound.

"Ana," Luca said. I was now covered in his blood, and I looked at him, "I love you too Anastasia, so much…"

I watched his eyes roll in the back of his head, "LUCA!!!"

"Luther, get her out of here now!" Angelo yelled at him while starting CPR on Luca.

I felt Luther grab me and I shoved him away. He wrapped his arms around my waist and pulled me to my feet. He was yanking me out of the room no matter how hard I tried to get away from him. I was screaming and fighting with everything I had, "Let me go!!"

I was pulled upstairs to another room. He set me down on my feet and I just hit him. I screamed at him that I needed to go downstairs and see Luca. I needed to save him. He just let me hit him until I collapsed gasping for air, "Shh calm down Ana."

I just sat down on the floor and cried hysterically, "He died… He's gone. He kept me safe, and we worked so hard over the last six months. Just for him to die."

"I will be right back Ana. Do not move," Luther said walking to the door without looking back at me.

I sat on the floor and hugged my knees tightly to my chest. I stared at my shoes where I could see the blood stain forming. I didn't move, didn't talk. Minutes turned into hours, and I hadn't heard from anyone. I couldn't bring myself to do anything. I couldn't stop the tears. I just kept repeating to myself, "Please live."

There was a light knock on the door, and I couldn't bring myself to move. I didn't know what time it was. The door opened when I didn't respond and Apollo came in, "Ana?" He saw me huddled against the wall. He came to kneel in front of me, "Ana, honey. Can you look at me?"

I looked up at him and saw he had recently showered, "Is… Is he-" I couldn't bring myself to finish the question.

"He's alive, Ana. Now I can take you to him, but we need to get you cleaned up first," his voice was gentle as he spoke to me.

"Okay," I said as my body went numb. He pulled me to my feet and out of the room. We walked down the hallway together to the bathroom. I felt like a zombie, not sure how to feel and just focusing on putting one foot in front of the other. He had me sitting on the toilet while he put clothes and a towel on the counter. I had my head in my hands, unable to watch him anymore as he moved around the bathroom.

"Clothes are on the counter. I'll be outside when you are done," he said, stepping out of the room.

I got into the shower and washed the blood from my body. I scrubbed my skin hard and waited till the water was no longer red. I got out and dried my body off. I quickly found the clothes and got them on, so that I could see him breathing for myself. I opened the door and saw Apollo was waiting and grabbed me by my elbow. He took me downstairs and to a room down a long hallway, "He's... He's in here?"

"Yes, now he was shot three times. He's in rough shape, Ana. I'm not going to sugarcoat it. He isn't out of the woods yet, but if he can make it through the night, he's looking good at recovering. None of us know when he is going to wake up," he said softly.

"Okay," I reached for the doorknob and slowly twisted it so the door would open. I pushed it open and walked in. I froze at the first sight of him, he was in a hospital bed. I had no idea how we got our hands on them. He was hooked up to a bunch of machines. I reminded myself to ask them how we got our hands on hospital equipment. I moved to the chair they had ready for me next to the bed. I sat down and took his hand, "I am right here Luca. I am not going anywhere."

After a few hours, I laid my head on the bed by his hand that was in both of mine. I laid down so my face was facing him, and I could still see him. After a few more hours my eyes closed unwillingly. I must have drifted off because I woke up to someone trying to move me and I mumbled, "Shh Ana. It's okay."

"No, stop. I'm not moving," I pushed them away from me.

"Ana you should lay down. He's okay," Luther said quietly.

"No, not yet. Please not yet," I said, pulling away from him. I grabbed Luca's hand again.

"Okay, Ana. I am going to go get you something to eat and drink. I will be back," Luther responded as he walked towards the door.

I couldn't take my eyes off Luca, "I just want you to wake up. Please wake up so I can see your hazel eyes again."

I was crying when the door opened, "Hey." Luther came and sat by me once again. I looked over at him, "I know Sunflower. Can you drink some water?"

"Okay, I can drink some water," I took the cup he held out to me and began to sip it. I realized I was very thirsty and drank more.

"Good, how about some food? I made some toast. It's light," he stated, trying to get me to relax.

"Okay, I can eat some food," I said, picking up the toast and nibbling at it.

"Great job honey. How much sleep did you get," he asked.

"I don't know. I just want him to wake up. I can't handle this Luther," I said looking back at him with tears in my eyes.

"It's going to be okay Ana. He will wake up," he said, rubbing my back.

I laid my head back down, "I want him to live."

He just sat down next to me rubbing my back. More hours went by, and my eyes slipped shut. I felt someone playing with my hair. I opened my eyes and saw Luca's Hazel eyes looking at me, "Hey baby."

I sat up, "Luca!"

I felt Luther jolt at my sudden burst next to me, "Well hey. I am going to go get Angelo and Eric. I will be right back," Luther said, standing up and exiting the room quickly.

I had tears fill my eyes, "Luca, I am so happy that you are awake."

He touched my face slowly, "Are you okay?"

A tear spilled over as the relief of him talking to me hit, "Thanks to you I am."

He wiped away the stray tear, "It's okay Ana. That is my job to protect you. Come closer."

I moved and sat on the bed next to his legs. I was trying to be as gentle as possible, "You scared the hell out of me Luca. You died."

He cupped the side of my face with his hand and gently rubbed circles on my cheek with his thumb, "I'm so sorry Ana. I didn't mean to scare you."

The door opened and Angelo came rushing in with Eric. Luther was closely behind them. Angelo moved to me, "Ana, I need you to move so we can check him out."

Luther helped me off the bed, "Let's go sit on the couch. Maybe you could lay down," I had seen him place a pillow and blanket on the couch and started to slow down.

I looked over my shoulder at the two doctors and Luca, "I-I don't know." I moved my eyes to Luther, "I don't know if I can."

"You don't have to sleep Ana. Just lay down. Rest your body a little bit. He can't go anywhere, and the worst is behind him," Luther said in a gentle voice.

"Okay, I can lay down," I said as he rearranged the pillow and blanket. I laid down on the couch and he pulled the blanket up. I was instantly tired from barely sleeping, "Can I have some more water please?"

"Of course, you can," Luther handed me a glass of water.

I drank from the glass and handed it back to him. I laid my head back down on the pillow and my eyes grew heavy. I let my eyes close, and I could feel how exhausted I was, "No... Help..."

"Hey shh," I felt someone brush my hair back from my face. I heard Angelo talking to me, "Why are you asking for help?"

"I'm going to fall asleep. I don't want to fall asleep yet. What if I have a nightmare," I barely whispered.

Angelo stuttered over his words as he couldn't form a full sentence. "Go to sleep, baby. I will be here. Just please get some sleep," Luca said, taking over and soothing me from across the room.

"Okay, Luca. I love you," I said as my mind began to drift off.

****

I felt like it had just been a few minutes when I popped up screaming after Luca had been filled with bullet holes. I was gasping for air, "Breath Ana. Angelo will be here soon."

I sat up and hugged myself tightly, "I can't. I just can't sleep anymore. I keep seeing you die. It's awful and I can't watch it anymore."

The door opened before he had a chance to respond to me and Angelo stepped in, "What's going on?"

"It's Ana. She only slept for like an hour. She's going to collapse from exhaustion. What do we do?" Luca asked from his bed.

"I need you to relax before you tear your stitches. That will not help the situation," Angelo moved to me. He kneeled in front of me, "Ana??"

I looked at Angelo and I knew that I must look exhausted, "I keep seeing him die. He died, Angelo. I-I can't keep watching it in my head… It's too much."

Angelo hugged me and rubbed my back as I cried, "Shh it's okay. I understand that was not a happy experience. He is alive and right there. You must sleep, honey. You need it to live. I don't think your body can handle much more if you don't sleep."

"I'm sorry. I'm so sorry," I said close to sounding like I was more animal than human as my throat grew thicker and thicker.

"Shh, it's okay. I'm going to go talk to Luther so we can get a plan. Go see Luca. That will help you relax and maybe we can try sleeping again when I get back. I just need you to stay calm," Angelo said, pulling me to my feet in one quick movement.

He walked me over to Luca to make sure that I didn't collapse, "I don't want to sleep. I just keep seeing him die."

"Ana please just breathe and relax. I will be back soon," he said quietly. He walked towards the door, "I will be back you two."

Luca pulled my face up and made me look at him, "Come here." I shook my head not trusting my voice, "Ana come here."

I shook my head again and tried to swallow the lump down, "I don't want to hurt you."

"To hell with that," he pulled me to him by my arms and I gasped surprised by the strength he still had. My head was on his chest, and I froze, scared to hurt him, "Please relax. Listen to my heartbeat. It's here and steady. I am alive and I am with you."

My eyes closed instantly, "Luca you must be careful. Please. I don't want you to tear your stitches or to get hurt. I shouldn't be lying on you."

"Shh I am fine I promise," he said, adjusting the bed, so we laid straight down. I just focused on his breathing to try and keep the anxiety away, "That's it, baby. Go to sleep, please. I am right here."

"No, what if I hurt you? Or something happens while I'm sleeping? I can't risk it. I-I can't-" I cut myself off and wiped away the tears that fell on my face.

"Ana, you won't hurt me. You will be the first to know if something happens to me. I need you to sleep. Your body can't handle it anymore and this will help you. I promise nothing will happen. I am just going to sleep too."

I felt my body relaxing against my will, "I am scared Luca."

"I know, baby. I have you though. Please just get some rest," he was speaking quietly. "I love you."

I gave in, unable to keep myself from falling asleep anymore, "Okay Luca. I love you too," I focused on his heartbeat and let that be the thing that lulled me to sleep. I finally gave in and let my body sink into a dreamless sleep.

Chapter Eleven

The Damage

I woke up to someone trying to move me away from Luca, "Angelo let her stay here. She's finally sleeping. I don't want her to be in any more distress."

"Luca, if she moves wrong and hurts you, she wouldn't be able to forgive herself. You know that is true. I'm not sure her current mental state could handle it."

"Please, Angelo. Leave her here with me," I could hear the strain and the panic in his voice. "Just let her stay here for a bit. I can do something to help."

"She can come back later. We've already left her there for three hours. We need to check your stitches and change your bandages. She needs food and water."

"Let her sleep. Is it that hard to just let her stay here? She needs sleep," Luca said, his voice gentle as he squeezed me gently to him.

"She can cuddle with you in a little bit. Let us get you guys all taken care of," Angelo said quietly. "Go ahead and take her, Apollo."

"STOP!!"

I jumped at the sudden outburst that came from Luca and the panic that followed in his voice, "Calm down. She is not being hurt. She is safe. It's me and Apollo."

"Just a little longer, please. She's sleeping and not screaming or fighting. I need this just as much as she does. I thought we were going to die... I was so worried about her," he said, rubbing my back.

"Luca-"

"Angelo, I need this. I need this for a little bit longer. Please. At least another hour. That's all I'm asking for."

I heard Angelo sigh, "Fine, but then we will be moving her. No more arguing or having a freak out."

"Thank you. I promise," Luca said, and I felt his body relax.

"We will be back in an hour," Angelo said. I heard the footsteps begin to fade and then I heard the door close quietly.

I opened my eyes and looked up at him, "You okay Luca?"

"Hey, honey. Yes, I am okay. I'm so sorry I woke you up. Why don't you go back to sleep," his voice was gentle.

I was still exhausted, so it didn't take much convincing. I let my eyes close again, but my body was suddenly very awake. Like I had been electrocuted, "Okay Luca. I can do that."

He kissed the top of my head and I just laid there enjoying the time I had with him. I couldn't help but feel sad that I would have to move. Then the door opened, "Alright Luca. It's been an hour. We need to get you all checked out and new bandages. She needs to eat some food."

I could feel the defeat in his body as he knew that he had to wake me up, "Okay let me wake her up," Luca said. Then he was gently shaking me, "Ana? Honey, I need you to get up."

My heart started to hurt at the thought of moving away. I didn't want to move away from him. I could feel his heartbeat and every breath he took. It came out sounding more pathetic than I wanted it to, but I whined, "But I want to stay here with you."

I heard the sadness leak out of his voice as he spoke to me, "I know baby. I would love for you to stay here, but we both need some stuff taken care of. I need new bandages and you need some food," he moved my hair out of my face and tucked it behind my ear.

"Okay," I gently sat up and Apollo reached up to help me stand on my feet.

He pulled me over to another bed, "Get in bed little boss."

I sighed and got into the bed, "Okay. What are you going to do?" I asked while watching Angelo check Luca's stitches, "How does he look?"

"He is healing slowly, but he hasn't torn them," Angelo said.

I went to respond when Eric lifted my shirt and put jelly on my stomach, "Let's do a quick check on the baby. Gotta make sure it's okay."

The room went silent as everyone watched me. He put the fetal Doppler down for a terrifying moment, and nothing but silence. He moved it and the heartbeat appeared.

Me and everyone else let out the breath we were holding, "How's the baby Eric?"

"The baby is good. Strong heartbeat. You on the other hand are completely exhausted and a little dehydrated. I'm going to put an IV in again," Eric responded, getting my arm ready.

He got the IV in and moved to Angelo. I looked up at Luca, "What are they talking about?"

"Probably how to get you to sleep without risking me and my stitches," he said, giving me a sad smile.

"Oh," I looked at my hands, "I don't want to go to sleep."

"Ana…"

"No, just stop. I am trying to work through all this crap that is happening. I haven't been able to process any of this because we are always moving. I just need some time. I thought you were going to die…" I folded my hands on my lap looking at how much they have changed in such a short time.

Angelo moved to me, "Hey you. It's time for you to get some real sleep without putting Luca at risk."

"I don't want to sleep."

"Eric has already put something in your IV while we have been talking," Angelo said, trying to keep me calm.

The panic and anger coursed through my body making me feel too much at once, "Why? Why the hell would you do this? I'm just going to have nightmares. I'm not ready to sleep and I don't like that I am being forced to sleep, don't you see how wrong that is?! I am not ready to sleep!"

"You need to sleep. It is time for you to get some real sleep. I am sorry it had to come to this, but you are exhausted. Your body can't keep going," Angelo said quietly.

My eyes began to grow heavy, and the panic began to grow, "Leave me alone. Just leave me the hell alone!"

I watched them walk away from me. I saw Angelo look back at me before he left and then turned back to walk out the door. I heard the door close, "Ana-"

"Luca, please. I am being forced to sleep. No one is taking me or my feelings into consideration. I need to do things on my own in my own way. I do not want to have these nightmares or keep feeling this way. I do not like watching you die over and over again," I said as my eyes slipped unwillingly shut.

"I will be right here Ana. I promise. Just try and relax. I know you are upset but you do need some sleep," he said as I began to drift off.

I was walking in the woods. I could feel the breeze as it moved my hair and cooled down my face. It felt really warm. I was looking around and enjoying the feel of the tall grass and the smell of the fresh pine. I looked straight ahead of me and froze when I saw Anthony. My heart rate spiked, and I felt a little sick, "I am so sorry Tony. I was so wrong. You didn't deserve what I did to you, and I would take it back if I could." He went to respond when his eyes glazed over, and he started to bleed from a bullet hole that was between his eyes. He started to yell that I was a murderer. I screamed and backed away from him. I backed up until I ran into something. I froze when I felt it move and realized it was a person. I turned slowly trying to get my breathing under control, "NO!" I screamed when I saw Xavier standing before me with a sick smile on his face.

"Hello, Ana. I've missed you," he said smiling down at me.

"Get away from me!" I stumbled away from him as fast as my feet would let me. I was tripping over some above-ground roots, "Leave me alone! Just leave me alone!"

"But I love you. I just want to be with you," he said as blood began to pour out of his head as well.

I finally tripped over a root and fell. I was backing up as quickly as I could on my butt, "I want to wake up! Please someone wake me up! Help me!"

"Ana?"

My head shot up and I saw Luca standing off to the side staring at me like I was an exploding bomb, "Luca? What are you doing here?"

"Ana you are safe honey," he said moving towards me. I felt relief as he moved carefully and gracefully towards me, "I am here to protect you."

He was right in front of me squatting down as he went to reach for my hands. While he was trying to pull me to my feet, he was shot three times. I was covered in his blood, and I moved to him quickly as he collapsed to the ground, "I'm sorry. Please don't die. I am so sorry. This is all my fault."

Dom was suddenly standing on the other side of Luca holding a gun. I was still trying to stop the bleeding, "Don't take it personally Ana. It's just business."

He held the gun up to my head and the panic took over, "Dom please don't do this."

"It's already done," he said as he pulled the trigger.

I woke up screaming and fighting with what little strength I still had. I didn't know who was with me or around me nor did I care. Luca was shouting but I couldn't focus on anything he was saying. Luther was trying to hold me down so I couldn't hit him. I couldn't breathe and I just kept pushing him to get him away from me, "Help! Stop! Let me go now!"

"Ana stop!" Luther yelled at me trying to get me to listen long enough to stop fighting him, "You are safe!"

"There's no such thing as safety! I will never be safe! Let me go please," I yelled back, not caring about anything. I just wanted to be free.

"Get me out of this damn bed now," Luca yelled trying to sit up and get to me.

Apollo moved to him quickly and pushed him back down, "Stay down before you hurt yourself."

"I need to help her. She is going to hurt herself. Luther, stop holding her down. Pull her into a hug," Luca yelled over me and my screaming.

Luther listened and pulled me into a tight hug, "Please breathe. You are safe, I promise. We are all here to protect you."

I sobbed with my hands in fists on his chest, "No more sleep. Please just no more. I can't handle it anymore."

"Okay, we won't make you sleep anymore. Just calm down please," he said, his voice soft and full of concern.

I laid back down and my body was completely exhausted. I worked on getting my breathing under control, "I'm sorry."

"It's okay. I can't say that I blame you. Just keep breathing," Luther said sitting on the edge of the bed next to me.

He sighed as he watched me and my breathing return to normal, "Relax Luca. I'm okay. I didn't mean to freak you out."

He was staring at me; all the tension was in his body as he watched me. He was still pushing against Apollo, "I just want you to be okay."

"I'm okay. Just a little shaken up. It was not a good dream to be trapped in. I will be okay Luca. Please don't hurt yourself. I need you to not tear your stitches," I said as my body collapsed in on itself.

"Don't worry about me, Ana. We must find a way for you to be able to sleep. Your body needs sleep," his voice was gentle as he spoke.

I looked down at my hands not wanting to talk about sleep anymore, "Can I get something to eat please?"

"Of course," Luther said, smiling at me, it didn't quite reach his eyes.

He left and I closed my eyes. I thought I could try and force my body to relax if I focused enough. It was quiet for a few minutes, "Angelo she sleeps better when she's by me. Can we push the beds together or something? Just put her by me so I can help."

It was quiet for another few minutes, "We will get some food in her, and we will go from there."

"Okay, Angelo but remember who is in charge here. I need her to be okay and I am in charge of this team," Luca pretty much growled at him.

The door opened, "Here you go- Ana?"

I opened my eyes and took a bowl of soup. It was brown with little potatoes and various veggies in it. I slowly ate the soup and tried to ignore the room of anxious men who were staring at me like I was a bomb that was ready to explode, "Please don't stare at me."

"Sorry Ana, we are worried about you," Apollo said somewhere amongst the men.

My stomach churned and I gagged. The bowl was pulled away and was replaced by a trash can. I threw up all the food I had just eaten, "I-I'm okay."

"Oh, Ana. You need sleep. You need to let us help you get a good night's rest. Your body isn't going to be able to handle anymore," Angelo said, the worried plain in his voice.

"Please no. No more sleeping. I can't do it. I can't take the nightmares. They are awful. All I see is death," tears sprung to my eyes.

I heard someone sigh, "Alright we are going to push the beds together, but no laying on each other. You need to be careful and not risk hurting anyone. You can stay next to each other. You won't be forced to sleep, Ana. I just think you should try."

"Thank you," I said, swallowing the lump that formed in my throat.

The guys quickly went to work on getting us moved together and moving all the machines closer together. Before I knew it, I was lying on a bed next to Luca. I was lying on my left side looking at him and he was lying on his back. His head was turned towards me watching me, "Hey honey. I think it's time you got some sleep."

"No, no sleep Luca. I mean it. I just see all the death and destruction of the last few months," I said looking away from his eyes.

"Shh okay. Just lay here," he said, giving me the arm that wasn't anchored down by wires and tubes, "Come somewhat cuddle."

"Luca, that will make me tired," I said, finally looking up at him.

"I am right here if you fall asleep Ana. I will stay right here. Come on," he said, smiling over at me.

I laid my head on his arm. My eyes instantly shut, and I took a deep breath, just taking his scent in, "Good night, Luca."

I heard the relief flow into his voice, "Good night, Ana."

****

I woke up to the sun shining, "What time is it?"

"Hey good morning you. How are you feeling," Luca asked, looking at me. His hazel eyes were like liquid, and he looked so handsome in the light.

"I feel okay. How long was I asleep for," I asked, watching him trying to get a straight answer.

"A couple of days of in and out of sleep. I take it you don't remember much though. We were starting to get a little worried about you," he said, giving me a small smile.

"I am sorry if I worried you at all. I feel pretty good though. I guess I did need to sleep," I said, stretching my body out on the hard hospital mattress.

There was a knock at the door, "Can we come in?"

"Yeah, come on in," Luca said, taking my hand when he noticed my whole body tense up.

"Hey everyone," I said as Luther, Angelo, Apollo, and Eli came into the room.

"How are you feeling?" Luther asked as they made their way to our beds.

"A little nauseous, but I feel better," I said sitting up.

"That's normal considering the whole situation you have been in," Angelo said, moving to Luca. "Let me check your stitches."

"How is Luca looking?" I asked sitting up.

231

"Healing well. Should stay in bed for a few more days," Angelo said, changing the bandage on his side.

"Can I get up and walk around? My body feels so sore from just laying here," I said looking at each of the men.

"No."

"Yes."

Luca and Angelo said at the same time. I sighed and grew frustrated, "Luca, please. I'll take guards. I'll be good. I just want to go out and do something."

"Luca let her go on a walk. She's had a long couple of weeks. A little walk won't hurt her," Apollo said looking at him.

"Can we agree to just be outside for half an hour? For my sake and sanity please," he looked at me with the worry and stress plain on his face.

"Okay, I can agree to that. Help me out of this mess please," I said looking around at one of the guys to help me.

Angelo and Eric took out my IV and unhooked me from the multiple machines. I got off the bed and moved to Luca. He put his hand on the side of my face, "Be careful, please. Stay with Eli and Ace."

"I will. You just rest and I will be back soon," I kissed his cheek and Eli followed me out of the room.

Ace found us and we went through the house. There were bullet holes everywhere from the ambush. I rushed outside upset by all the destruction of what happened to the house. I took a deep breath once I was outside and even though the air was cold it felt good. I wanted to go see my mom but given what happened last time, I decided against it.

I decided to just move forward. We moved our way through the trees, "Where are we going, Ana?"

"I just need to walk. I don't care where we go. I just can't stop yet. The house is a mess. People are dying left and right. I just need some fresh air," I said walking further away from the house. I decided we were far enough away. The cold air felt good and bad. I walked up to the riverbank and just looked at the chaos of the moving water.

The guys hung back by the tree line and let me have as much privacy as I was allowed to at this time. I watched someone come out from across the river. I froze and watched him carefully. He watched me for a moment and then started to talk, "We want Dominic back."

"Not going to happen. He betrayed my family. He gets to be punished for his crimes," I said my voice is hard.

"Then you give us no choice. We will do what it takes to get him back. Even if we must kill every single one of you," he said, and half a dozen men came out holding guns and stepped out from the tree line.

I turned and took off towards my team. At the same time, Ace was running towards me. He pulled me back and pushed me behind a tree with his body shielding the front of me. I screamed as the gunshots flew and that is all you could hear, "What do we do?"

"You do not move. You don't do anything," Ace yelled at me over the sound of gunfire. He turned and looked at Eli, "We need to shoot as soon as they reload. Shoot and run."

"Alright let's do this," Eli said as he grabbed his gun out of nowhere. I looked back at Ace and saw that he was holding his as well.

The gunfire ceased for a minute, "Run!" Eli yelled. Both guys pushed me forward and I heard them firing as we ran as fast as we could from these crazy people. More of the automatic gunfire went off and Ace tackled me to the ground and covered my head. I heard him yell out in pain, "Shit!"

"Grab her Eli," Ace yelled.

I was pulled away from Ace and was shot in my thigh. I screamed out in pain, "We have to get out of here or we are dead."

"Breathe. Let me look at your leg," Eli said, standing behind the tree.

The gunfire stopped, and Eli was still working on my leg. After a minute I pushed him away and crawled over to Ace, "Ace are you okay? Can you hear me? Eli, call for help!"

I slowly helped Ace sit up and lean against a tree. I heard people running and Eli was talking on the phone frantically, "Ana come here please."

"No. Ace, are you okay? Please say something."

He coughed but it was a sign of life. That was until I saw the blood coming out of his mouth and he was bleeding from a hole in the middle of his chest, "Ana, get your leg looked at."

I wanted to laugh and cry. Just then mine and Luther's teams came running up and making sure no one was close enough to hurt us anymore. Eli was filling everyone in. I was holding Ace's hand and just rambling on, "You are going to be okay."

His eyes were drooping as he was breathing heavily. I had taken off my sweatshirt and was holding it to his wound to try and stop the bleeding, "Ana, you need to get your leg looked at please."

"Not yet. I want them to look at you first," I said with tears springing into my eyes. Angelo and Eric both came running up while the others made sure we were all safe and looked for the men with guns, "Help him."

"We need to look at your leg. Make sure no major arteries were hit," Angelo said softly.

"No! You save him first! He is in worse shape than I am," I yelled pushing him away from me.

Eli moved to me, "I will help her with the bleeding while you guys help him. Help him so we can get her to relax."

Eric and Angelo both started to work on Ace. I still had a hold of his hand and was squeezing it. Eli put pressure on my thigh, and I yelled out and squeezed Ace's hand a little harder, "I'm so sorry Ace. This is all my fault."

"It is not your fault. You both are going to be okay," Eli said, making sure to keep the pressure on my leg.

"You are going to be fine Ana. Don't blame yourself. It's not your fault. We signed up for this no matter what," Ace said in between coughing.

I went to respond to Ace when his hand went limp in mine, NO!" I tried to move but Eli grabbed hold of me. He let go of the pressure on my leg to keep it in place. Meanwhile, Eric and Angelo both started CPR, "No! You must save him!"

I was covered in his and my blood as Eli hugged me, my back was pressed against his front. I tried to get to Ace, but somehow, I thought I could bring him back, "Hey shh. I don't think you should be seeing this."

He turned to me, so I looked at him instead and I saw he was also covered in blood. He carefully went and put pressure on my leg again, "He needs to be okay. They need to save him, Eli," I said as one tear slipped down my face.

"It's okay," Eli said softly. "I need to get you back to the house. We must get this bleeding to stop, or you could lose the baby."

"No, I-I can't. That will waste time. You need to get it to stop now. I-I can't lose the baby," I said, pushing him away as he tried to pick me up."

I turned to see them covering Ace with a coat and I screamed out in anguish, "I'm so sorry Ana. He's gone."

"No! Please no," I screamed as I collapsed to the ground. My body was shaking, and I felt like I was being stabbed, "Please save my baby."

Eric and Angelo moved to me and began to work on my leg, "Alright we must get this done and get it done now. I'm sorry we must get the bullet out and stitch you up to get the bleeding to stop.

I just lay there and tried not to cry and to keep myself from screaming. Eli came and held me down as they began to dig the bullet out of my leg and I couldn't stop the scream that came out, "We are almost done. You are doing great," Eric said softly.

Soon I was stitched up and they were wrapping a bandage around my leg. I was breathing heavily but the pain had stopped for the most part. At least it didn't feel as bad as when they were digging. Eli moved my hair out of the way, "I think it would be faster if I carried you back to the house. Do you mind if I pick you up?" I just nodded, not trusting my voice to talk. He picked me up and almost ran back to the house. He got me inside quickly and up the stairs. He opened the door and I saw Luca shoot into a sitting position when he saw me covered in blood, "She's okay Luca. Breath."

He set me down on the bed next to Luca and I curled up in a ball as small as I could manage, "What the hell happened?"

"They were waiting and ambushed us. Ace didn't make it," Eli said quietly. "She was shot in the leg. They got the bullet out and stopped the bleeding. She's just in shock now."

"Want to give us the room for a minute," Luca said to Eli.

"Yeah, I'll be right outside if you need anything," Eli said as left the room. He looked back at me before he closed the door.

"Hey, baby. Can I please see you? I need to see that you are in one piece," Luca said, playing with my hair.

I turned to look at him, "Hey Luca. I'm okay."

"Come here Ana," he said, pulling me towards him.

I moved towards him not caring that I was covered in blood. I cuddled into his side and my thigh began to have a burning sensation from the wound, "You were right. I should've just stayed here. I should've listened. Ace would still be alive if I had just listened."

He was rubbing my back as I talked, "It's okay, Ana. Don't feel bad. This is not your fault. How are you feeling?"

"I'm feeling okay. My leg hurts a little. I think the baby is okay. No cramping. I don't think there is any blood hard to say with me being covered in it," I said my voice was numb as I tried to turn off the pain of getting someone killed.

"I'm sure the baby is fine. We will see what we can give you for the pain that is baby-safe," he said softly.

My hand was on my stomach, and I knew then that I didn't think I could give up the baby. Even if I was unprepared to be a mom, "Do you think the baby will make it through all of this?"

He pulled my face up so I had to look at him, "We will keep you and the baby safe. No matter what. Have you decided if you want to keep the baby or if we are giving it up?"

I looked down at my hand on my stomach, "I'll be twelve weeks tomorrow. I will have kept the baby alive for twelve weeks. I just want the baby to be safe and it's not safe right now."

He pulled my face back up, so I had to look at his eyes, "Ana, just answer the question, please. Do you want to keep the baby?"

I looked into his eyes and thought about the question. I knew I wouldn't be able to give it up but keeping it would be so hard. The answer was clear, "I know it's crazy. I know I shouldn't, but I want to keep it. I am terrified."

He gave me a small smile, "It's normal to be scared. We will do this all together. One step at a time."

I smiled back at him, "Thank you, Luca. I trust you."

"Good. Now no more wandering off until we get rid of this gang your brother so graciously brought into our lives," he said, kissing the top of my head.

"Luca I'm going to ask you for something, and I need you to listen to me," I said sitting up carefully.

He tensed up immediately, "What?"

"I need to talk to Dom."

"No," he said as the venom flowed into his voice.

"Please let me talk to him. Maybe I could end this. Then we would be safe and could enjoy the baby growing. Enjoy our lives together," I said, making him look at me. His jaw was tense, but he looked at me with cold eyes, "Please for the baby if not for me?"

He searched my eyes for a minute, and I watched his expression soften ever so slightly, "Ana... I don't trust him."

"I don't trust him either, but even if we could get away just so I could have this baby... then maybe we could end this. Get the baby to safety. See my point please."

I heard him sigh and the door opened across the room. I looked over to see Luther moving over to me, his eyes trained on all the blood, "Are you okay?"

"Deep breath. I am fine Luther. Just a little wound on my leg. Most of this is Ace's. I want to go talk to my brother," I said slowly hoping I could convince him to let me.

"I told her no. It's just too dangerous. Look what happened when you just went for a walk," Luca said, his voice tense and ready to argue.

"I want to go talk to him. I think I can talk some sense in him, and this could be over. At least a temporary truce. Why can't you let me do something that might make a difference?!" I was growing frustrated, and the volume of my voice was changing with me.

"Alright, you two enough. Stand down. Fighting isn't going to get either of you anywhere. This is what he wants. Us to turn against each other," Luther said as he was sending a message.

I flopped back on the bed as far from Luca as I could get, "I am trying to help any way I can. I just want to keep the baby safe. I want to keep the rest of you safe."

"Just take some deep breaths, please. Both of you. Luca, you need to rein in that temper," he said sitting down.

"She is being completely unreasonable. Why would I let her go see him? He has threatened her life and got her into this mess. It's not something I am about," Luca said his voice growing louder with his growing anger.

My temper flared as he talked of me as I was helpless, "Luca I am not a child! Do not think for one minute you can treat me like one," I yelled at him.

"Stop!! Both of you!" Luther yelled, making me jump and cringe away. He sighed and steadied himself, "Just sit in silence while we wait for everyone to show up."

We both sat in silence letting our anger stew and grow. Finally, our room was filled with the main members of our teams, "I want to talk to Dom."

"I told her no," Luca responded instantly.

"I think I can talk to him. Maybe call a temporary truce. Something to buy us some time. Get a regroup, a new headquarters, save our lives," I said looking around the group.

Luther moved to me, "We have to keep you and the baby safe."

"I am in charge. Luca you seem to keep forgetting that," I pushed off the bed and past Luther. I ignored the pain in my leg as my anger only continued to grow.

Luther stood up and blocked me from getting too far, "Not of me or my men Ana. Sit your ass back down."

I stood my ground not letting him scare me anymore. My temper only continued to get worse, "No. I am not useless. I am not someone who always needs protection. I am not going to hide and grow a person while you guys keep dying for me. I have been training too. I am not useless."

"I said sit down. That is my child you are carrying. You do not get to make these decisions by yourself."

I pushed at him as hard as I could, "Look around you Luther! My men are dying! My family is dying! You just decided to play nicely but remember who started this. You don't get to pretend and be the hero now."

I could see Luca getting out of bed while everyone was distracted, "Stop. It's not just your men that are dying Ana. You keep forgetting that."

"You started this!! Don't try to stop me! You put me in that danger and now you have to deal with the consequences."

"Because we got paid to do the hit!!" He yelled in my face, his anger letting loose.

My blood ran cold, and I lost my footing as I lost my focus. Luca caught me just in time, "What...?"

"I have you Ana. Just breathe," Luca said as Luther helped him get me to a chair that was nearby.

"We had gotten a note promising half a million dollars to make the hit. We came up with a plan and a time to meet. They put a hit on the whole family... You included. I went to meet him the night my family died but he didn't show. Just some scrawny man held the duffel with my money. I thought it was suspicious and thought it may be a trap by your father. It turned out that it was one of his henchmen," Luther said, pushing his hair back. "I thought it was a setup to get me killed, so I left."

A flashback of Tony begging for his life and telling us that he just wanted to save his family. That I wasn't supposed to get hurt. The bile rose in my throat, "I'm going to be sick…"

Angelo handed me a trash can barely in time, "Ana…?"

I just threw up what little food my body had and then some stomach acid. I didn't know how I missed it for so long, "It was Dom the whole time… This was all his plan from the beginning. He put the hit on our family… He told my dad about the hit. He destroyed us all within a few days."

The whole room was dead silent. You could hear if someone dropped a needle, "Are you sure, Ana?"

I looked at Luther as my stomach began to churn again, "It's him. It's always been him. I just mistook him for leaving as a lack of interest. He just wanted it all for himself." I felt sick and stupid to not see this sooner, "I am talking to my brother. Someone help me downstairs."

"Ana-"

"This man killed my whole family! Had me hunted! My child is not safe because of him! I trusted him! I loved him and adored him! Let me talk to him now," I said as my anger boiled over. "Eve, please help me."

Angelo held her back from me, "No Ana."

I pushed anyone close to me away. I just tried to push myself out of the room, "Fine. I don't need your help. I can do this by myself. Now get out of my way."

Eli moved right between me and the door, "I don't think that is a good idea right now."

"Get the hell out of my way Eli," I growled through my teeth.

Someone grabbed and I tried to move away from them as fast as possible, "Ana-"

"Get off me! Just let me handle this! Stop letting this go on! I am tired of watching everyone around me die while I sit and do nothing," I said pushing people back.

"Alright. Everyone out," Luther said, standing up and moving towards me. I watched the room clear out except for Angelo, Luther, Apollo, Eli, and Luca.

"Let me go. Now," I said, trying to stand my ground.

"No. Not right now," Luther said, his voice and eyes matching mine. The hostility between us was visible to anyone near, I was sure.

I screamed as loud as I could, "Let me see that bastard now!! I am no longer your prisoner!"

Luca grabbed me, "Give me the room guys." I tried to move away but he just hugged me closer to him. I heard the door close, "Ana... I know you are angry, but I need you to calm down please."

"He took everything from me. He took my life," I said my hands in fists against his chest, not sure what I was going to do.

He pulled my face up, so I was looking at him, "Not everything Anastasia. You still have me. You still have our baby. You have all of us. I need you to see the bright side and not just the dark."

I buried my face in his chest, feeling ashamed of myself, "I love you, Luca. I am so sorry."

He hugged me tightly, "I love you too, Ana. It's hard to see it all the time but we are all here for you."

He pulled my face up and kissed me. I kissed him back and I couldn't help but cling to him. My hormones took over and the desperate need to show him how much I needed him to believe in me. He pulled away and we were gasping, and he kissed my forehead, "We should get you in bed before you tear your stitches."

"Only if you come with me," he said, giving me a butterfly kiss.

"I am filthy. I should take a shower first," I said, trying to keep my focus.

"You can shower shortly. Come to bed with me for a while," he said, leaning his forehead against mine.

I couldn't think clearly with him being flirty and close, "Okay. I'll go with you."

He chuckled as he saw he won, "Good."

He wrapped his arm around my waist, as a way to make sure I came with him. We moved to the bed slowly with my limp and his torn side. We were lying down next to each other. He moved my hair out of my face, "You are so beautiful."

I felt the blush on my face, "Thanks. I know the bandages are a big turn-on. At least you can't get me pregnant."

He chuckled again, "Rest today. I will take you to see Dom tomorrow."

I sighed, "Fine Luca. I am going to see him tomorrow no matter what."

"Agreed. Don't forget you have a doctor's appointment tomorrow," he whispered.

I kissed him and it turned into a wonderful make-out session. I went to pull him close and grabbed him right where he had been shot. He groaned and I pulled away instantly, "I'm so sorry…"

He laughed, "It's okay. That's not your fault."

He laid back down next to me, "I just hurt you. I am sorry."

"How's your leg feeling honey," he asked softly.

"Hurts a little bit. I feel tired somehow and cold," I said as my eyes grew heavy. He pulled the blankets over us and moved as close as he possibly could to me.

"Go ahead and take a nap. I'll wake you up soon to take a shower," he kissed my head.

"Okay honey," I said, letting my eyes close. I was getting warm and comfy, "Don't leave."

"I have nowhere I'd rather be than right here. good night, Ana," he said, his voice soft.

Chapter Twelve

The Surprise

I was being shaken by Luca, "Come on baby. Time to take a shower. You need to get yourself cleaned up."

I shook my head and groaned at him, "I'm comfy. No one tried to kill me in my sleep."

I felt him kiss my forehead and my heart warmed at the action, "Come on baby. You were begging for a shower not too long ago. You will feel so much better after a shower."

I opened my eyes and looked at him, "Okay Luca. Although I wouldn't consider that begging by the way." I went to move and froze as he chuckled. I saw Luther and Eli standing there, "What's going on?"

"Please breathe. Everything is okay. We were just checking on both of you," Luther said quickly.

"Can I help you off the bed," Eli asked, moving to me slowly.

I looked at Luca and he smiled at me. He gave me a small nudge to push me forward and I looked back to Eli, "Okay. Sounds good."

Eli helped me down from the bed. The moment my feet hit the ground, pain shot up and through my leg, "Go get some time alone. Shower. Relax. Feel like a person again."

"Okay. I will be out shortly. Just take it easy too," I went into the bathroom slowly trying not to cause any more pain than necessary in my leg. I walked over to the shower and turned on the hot water. I quickly stripped off the blood-soaked clothes. I got under the hot water and took a deep breath as the hot water started to loosen the muscles in my body. I scrubbed the blood off me.

I heard the door open and froze, "Don't panic. Just dropping off some clothes for you, baby."

"Okay, I will be out in a few minutes," I said as I heard him leave the bathroom again. I slowly got out of the shower and wrapped a towel tightly around my body. I began to dry off the water and get dressed slowly. I limped my way across the bathroom and opened the door. I froze when I saw the group of people that had come into the room, "What is everyone doing?"

Luca moved towards me slowly, "Everything is okay. Just relax."

I took a step away from him as fear coursed through my body. I didn't want him to lie to me and he had so many times. I moved out of instinct, and I saw the pain on his face, "Luca what is going on?"

Angelo stood up and moved to stand next to Luca, his eyes gentle, "It's okay Ana. We are okay. There is nothing to be concerned about."

"Then why is everyone in here," I asked, watching the group of people that had formed in the room while I was in the shower.

Luca took another step towards me, and I once again took another step away from him. My stomach churned but I couldn't just give in and let it happen. He needed to learn to take me seriously and not hide things from me, "Hey whoa. You guys are freaking her out." Apollo moved to me without hesitation, "Hey honey. Everything is okay. We were just planning on what was to come next. Take a deep breath."

I took a deep breath and just focused on his words, "Promise?"

He smiled and gave me a small hug, "I promise." He pulled back from me to look at my face, "Let's sit down."

Luca looked sad as Apollo helped me back on the bed. I lay on my side and listened to everyone talk around me. I closed my eyes and felt someone pull the blankets over me, "I think she's asleep."

"Luca relax. She is going to be scared. She is going to be skeptical. We have lied and hid things from her, she will be scared. She's had a lot happen in the last few months," Apollo said softly to him.

"I don't like it when she doesn't trust me. I just want to keep her safe. I have done everything for that reason. I hated that she moved away from me," Luca said, sitting down next to me.

I opened my eyes and looked at Luca. The guilt was eating me alive, but I couldn't stop the feeling of why he would lie to me to keep me safe. I need to know about things. I sighed, "I know you want to keep me safe Luca. You can't keep hiding things from me. You scared me by having everyone here and telling me everything was fine. When has it ever been fine when there is a meeting going on?"

"Oh, hey honey. I'm sorry we scared you. I understand how you feel. I am just trying to do my best here. I don't have all the answers," Luca said, looking down at me.

"What were you guys talking about," I asked, looking back at him.

"Just the plan. We have to figure out what we are going to do with your brother. We have to figure out what we are going to do with the gang. We must be careful with them out there waiting to strike us again," Luca said softly.

I looked away knowing that I was about to start a fight, "Can I please talk to Dom?"

I heard Luca sigh out of frustration. I pushed off the bed and moved away from him. The anger already started to bubble. He grabbed me, "Stop Ana."

I yanked my arm away from him as hard as I could, "No. Let me help. I am pregnant and not injured. We are going to lose this fight if you don't let me help."

"Not now Ana!" Luca yelled, causing me to jump and move away from him. "Just listen to me! Why is that so hard? I will let you know when you can!"

I watched him storm out of the room as he finished his fit. I hugged myself and looked down at the floor, "I want to be alone. Please?"

I heard the footsteps as they all began to file out of the room. They left me alone and I sighed in relief. My leg was burning, and I made it to the wall. I put my back against the wall and slid down to the floor. I felt a tear slip down my face, "Ana? Sunflower?"

I looked up and saw Luther. I quickly wiped the tear away and cleared my throat, "Hi Luther."

"Can I help you off the floor," He asked as he squatted down in front of me.

I shook my head, "I want to stay here."

He sighed and sat down next to me, "Ana, I agree with Luca. You need to stop this. You can see him tomorrow. Not today. We all need the day to prepare for the danger we are putting ourselves in. The danger you are insistent to put yourself in."

"Why don't you get this? He destroyed my family and yours. How are you so calm? He hasn't hurt me yet. He has given me useless threats," I said as my throat began to grow thick again.

"I do get it. I am upset with him too, Ana. I also want to keep you and our child safe. This isn't about you. You are carrying our child. You were already shot so I wouldn't consider his threats useless," Luther said as he moved next to me.

I slowly laid my head on his shoulder, "I just want this all to be over. I feel like I can help that if I could just talk to him. I know you don't like this, and you are correct, this is your child too. I didn't ask to get pregnant."

"I know you do. It will be over soon. You will talk to him but not right now. Just for our sake right now please give us a day. Relax," he said quietly.

I just nodded, not wanting to speak to him anymore. The door opened and my body instantly went tense as Luca stepped in, "Can I have a moment with her please?"

"Are you done yelling?"

"Yes, Luther. Now please give us a minute alone," Luca said with tension in his voice.

Luther stood up and left the room. Luca moved in front of me and didn't say anything, "Luca…"

"I know Ana. Please let me help you off the floor," he said, pulling my face up.

I sighed trying to pick my battles, "Okay Luca."

He pulled me to my feet. My leg was burning as the pain began to spread along my leg. He pulled me to him and into a hug. His arms were tight around me, "I love you. Just please I don't want to worry about you for one day."

"I understand Luca. I won't ask again. I love you too," I pulled away from him so I could see his face.

He put his hand on the side of my face, "How is your leg feeling?" I looked down and just shrugged his question off. "Ana? Tell me about your leg."

"It hurts a bit."

"Well let's go lay down in the new bed in our new room downstairs. I want out of this room," he said, wrapping his arm around my waist.

He helped me move downstairs. I moved slowly as I hobbled down the stairs with great effort. We finally got to the bottom, and he pulled me through the rest of the house that everyone was desperately trying to fix up. He pulled me into a room that had been cleaned up, "Well this is nice."

"We need our own space that isn't tainted by violence," he said, closing the door. "Go sit on our bed. I am going to ask Angelo to come in here."

I moved over to our bed and sat down. I sat there and played with my hands when there was a knock on the door, "Come in."

Angelo, Luca, Luther, Eli, and Apollo came in. I sighed, "Lay back down so I can take a look at your leg."

"I-I need to take off my pants. Do I need an audience?" I asked, looking at Luca with I am sure there was horror on my face."

"Everyone just wanted to check on you. Everyone can come back once we are done," Luca said, looking at the group of men.

I watched the disperse until it was just Luca and Angelo, "Now can we see your leg?"

I sighed again, "Fine." I slowly stood enough to be able to take off my pants to show the wound. I sat back down on the bed and quickly moved myself into a lying position. Luca moved to sit by my head while Angelo went to look at my leg. I tried to ignore the pain that was caused by them looking at it.

"Her leg looks fine, Luca. Just a little tender. It's from today. I can give her a little bit of Tylenol. Not too much that is considered safe for the baby," Angelo said, more to Luca than to me.

I sat up and began to work on putting my pants back on. I felt a bit of pain as I pulled it over the gunshot wound. I gasped but finally got them up and buttoned, "I am fine. I don't want anything. I just want this mess to be over."

Luca sighed, "You need to take something. You are in pain. Please let me help you."

I shook my head ready for the fight, "You won't let me help you, you don't get to help me.

I watched the tension go into his body, "I'm going for a walk. Get some rest please."

I watched Luca walk out of the room and when Angelo went to say something to me, I just held my hand up, "Please just leave." I watched him stare at me for a moment and then walk out of the room. I moved to look at the window even though it made me want to panic. I needed the fresh air though. I slowly opened the window knowing it would piss Luca off. That made me smile a bit. I felt the breeze on my face and took a deep breath and closed my eyes.

"I would close that before Luca sees that," Eli said from behind me.

I gasped and spun around, "You scared the shit out of me. Make some noise when you enter a room!"

"I'm sorry. I didn't mean to scare you," He moved past me and closed the window. "Come sit down. I think it's been a long day."

I sighed as he pulled me away from the window, "Eli I need to do something. I have been losing my mind here. He is being ridiculous. I just want it all to be okay and to stop any more people from dying. He is not letting me do that."

"You are being stubborn and a pain in the ass," Eli said sitting down next to me. "Why can't you see what you are doing to both of them is a little bit selfish."

"Get out. You are being a jerk. You all seem to keep forgetting what he did to me. What he made me do and go through," I said looking at him as the emotion tried to bubble through. "I mean it. Get the hell out."

He stood and left the room without another word. I wanted to scream, to throw things. I wanted to make them all understand one way or another. I couldn't explain the rage that coursed through my body right this moment. I began to pace, ignoring the pain in my leg the best I could. After an hour there was a knock on the door, "Can I come in?"

I sighed, "Fine Eve."

She came in and saw me. She quickly closed the door, "What are you doing?"

"What does it look like I am doing? I am trying to calm down before my overprotective boyfriend and baby daddy come back," I said, running my fingers through my hair.

"Ana... Are you bleeding?" She moved to me quickly.

I sat down when she pushed me to the bed, "What are you talking about?" I looked down and saw the blood on my shirt. "Eve stop..."

"I am looking for the source..."

"Eve it's not mine," I said as loudly as I could trying to get her attention.

"What do you mean it's not yours?"

I was trying to keep the fear out of my voice, "That is not my blood..." I saw her freeze and look up at my face.

"Ana..."

I looked up and saw there was blood leaking from the ceiling above where I was pacing. I swallowed and slowly stood up, "Eve grab that chair."

"Ana... I don't think we should do anything. We should find Luca," she said her voice mirroring her fear.

"Get me the chair now," I said looking at her for a minute.

She stood up and went over to the chair in the corner and grabbed it. She moved over to where I was standing and set it under the blood-stained tile. I slowly stood up on the chair and took a deep breath. I pushed the ceiling tile up and popped it out. I slowly moved it out and Scarlet came flying out of the ceiling. She hit me on the way down and Eve screamed at the top of her lungs. I gave out a small scream and hit the floor hard, "I'm okay Eve."

She sobbed, "Ana?! Luca! Angelo!!"

I pushed Scarlet off of me. I sat up and looked at her. She had been shot twice, once in the stomach and once in the head. I moved away until my back was against the wall. I had her blood on me to the point I could feel it on my skin. I couldn't bring myself to look away. I could hear Eve sobbing trying to talk to me to get my attention away from Scarlet. I saw Angelo come in and grab Eve. Luther and Luca came running in and froze when they saw the scene that was before them, "What do we do?"

"I'll get Scarlet out of here. You handle her. Then we all need to sit down and talk. They somehow got to her and put her in this room. We can't stay here," Luther said quietly. He grabbed a blanket off the bed and put it over Scarlet so I couldn't see her expression anymore.

The trance seemed to have broken at that one moment. I took a deep breath and Luca was sitting in front of me, "Ana?"

"How did she get up there, Luca?"

"Baby, can I please help you off the floor? I think you might be going into shock," he said, his voice gentle.

"How did they get her to the ceiling? Someone has been in the house. How are we going to get out of here," I said, unable to look away from where Scarlet had been lying before Luther took her out of the room.

He pulled my face up, so I had to look at him, "Ana baby... I need to get you off the floor please."

I stared into his hazel eyes and just nodded. He gently took my hands and pulled me to my feet. Once I was standing, he began to look me over, "I'm fine. I wasn't hurt. She was already dead when I found her."

He finally stopped, "How about a shower and some clean clothes?"

"What happened to her? Someone has been in the house and killed her... Luca, I don't know if it is safe anywhere. What should I do? I'm so sorry," I said as my voice began to grow thick.

"Hey shh. It's okay honey. Let's get you cleaned up, please. I need to talk to our team," Luca said, putting his hands on either side of my face. "I know this is scary. I will have someone stand outside the bathroom door the whole time you are in the shower."

I stared at him trying to think through what he was saying, "It's not safe. I will never be safe as long as he's alive... Will I?"

He froze, "Hey baby... I need you to take a deep breath for me please." I watched him for a minute and finally listened to him. "That's it. Now the next step is to take a nice hot shower. Eli is going to stand outside the door. You are safe. We are all here for you. I need you to understand and trust that."

"Okay... I can try and do that..."

He gave me a small smile, "I'll take what I can get." He pulled me into a big hug, "It's okay to be okay, Ana. Let's go."

I was almost to Eli when I felt someone grab me. I turned and saw Luca. He pulled me back gently for a kiss, "I love you, Ana. I mean it. You will be safe, I promise. I'll see you soon."

"I love you too honey. I will do my best. I am going to take a shower. I will see you soon. Just please be careful," I said, turning and walking to Eli.

"Hey, you, let's go get you into the shower," Eli said, holding his arm out for me. He had done his best to relax his face. "Are you okay?"

"No, she was in the house. He- I don't know how this happened. None of us are safe. I know he is trying to make me feel safe, but I don't know how I am supposed to feel safe when they are picking us off one by one," I began to ramble as the panic took over.

"Hey, take it easy. We are here for you. No one is going to let you get hurt," he said, his voice soft.

"What about all of you?! I don't want any more people to die. I care about all of you and it's not fair. I have had to watch all of you being hunted," I felt the tears fill my eyes.

"Get in the shower. We can talk once you are clean and a little more relaxed," he said, his voice was quiet as he tried to reassure me.

We came to a stop in front of the bathroom door. I sighed, "Okay." I went into the bathroom and tried to keep calm. I turned on the shower and waited for the water to get hot again. I looked at myself in the mirror and I looked like a mess. I was covered once again and covered in blood and looked crappy. I moved to the shower and took off my clothes and quickly got under the hot water. I just sat down at the bottom of the shower.

After thirty minutes I heard the door open, "Hey baby. Are you okay?"

I tried to cover my face so he couldn't see me and stifled my sobs. I swallowed the lump in my throat, "I'm okay Luca."

"Oh, honey. I can hear your voice. Are you ready to get out?"

"No, not yet," I said, shaking my head.

I heard him sit down outside the shower door, "Sweetheart, I am here for you. I know this is a lot to take in. I will keep you safe."

I felt the tears slip down my face, "But who will keep you safe!"

The words left my mouth in a shout that ended up with sobs before I could even think to stop it. It was quiet for a minute, "Ana... baby please come out."

I hugged myself tightly and thought about what he was asking me, "I will get out in a minute. I just need a second to compose myself."

"I understand honey. I will be right outside the bathroom. I will see you in a minute and we will be talking about a lot of things. Just take a deep breath."

I heard him stand and walk out of the bathroom. I took a deep breath and stood up. I washed my hair, shaved my body, and washed my body. Once I thought I was even remotely clean I stepped out and wrapped a towel around my body. I took a deep breath and avoided the mirror. I found clothes on the counter and put them on. I walked up to the mirror and slowly looked at my reflection. My green eyes were sunken and black as if I hadn't slept in years. My hair now brushed was as long as it's ever been and now made its way gracefully down my back. I walked away and out the bathroom door to find Eli and Luca, "I'm okay."

Luca had no hesitation, he grabbed me and pulled me into a tight hug, "Come with me. We are going to talk to the group now. Figure out what we are going to do next."

"We can't stay here. They somehow found a way in. It's no longer safe," I said, my voice lacking emotion as if I had turned into a robot.

I felt him kiss my head, "Come on Ana."

He pulled me through the house, and I just kept giving myself a pep talk as if I could keep it together. I just wanted to disappear into a better life. We came to a stop in the living room where the two gangs had crammed themselves. Luther stood up slowly and moved over to me. He looked down at me, "Are you okay?"

I swallowed the lump, "I am fine. Just a little shook up."

He nodded and stood next to Luca, "Alright all. Someone got into this house. I am not sure who or when, but it is no longer safe. We have to leave. It's time to go somewhere else. The question is where? Also, do we leave Dom here as a distraction?"

That made me falter. I didn't want to use my brother as bait. Despite everything that has happened, he was still my brother. The room erupted in conversation while everyone suggested where we could go and that we should either leave or kill him. I looked between Luca and Luther. They both looked so serious and when I returned my gaze to the floor, I felt someone's hand on my back, "Do you have anything you want to add?"

I looked up at Luca surprised, "I think we should go back to New York and use the private jet to leave the country. I don't see how staying in the United States is going to be helpful. It hasn't been so far." I turned to the group, and I felt myself sinking back into a hopeless depression, "I don't know what to do about Dom. I am so sorry you are all here. This is all my fault. I can't decide this."

Someone guided me to a chair and Luca was kneeling in front of me, "Hey. You are the boss. We will listen within reason. Think hard and decide what you want to do with him. We can leave him, kill him, or take him with us as leverage."

I stared into his hazel eyes unsure what to think but I also felt such gratitude for him in that moment. He was trying to help me, even if it was hard to see. He was leaving the decision up to me. I thought about him and my dad, I didn't want to be like either of them. That's when I knew what I wanted to do, "I think I have a plan. It's a little crazy but I think it's enough to get us out of here and on our way back to New York."

He gave me a small smile, "I like a little bit of crazy. The room is yours."

I looked at the room and began to explain my plan of diversion. The room was silent as I explained that we would set the house on fire and leave him as bait to escape. I explained that it should get us some distance we needed before they would be ready to come after us. I took a deep breath and looked at Luca, "We need to do it tonight. Use the night to give us some coverage."

He nodded, "You heard her. Start getting ready. This will give us four hours to get ready. Let's move it."

"Luca?"

He turned to me, "Yeah? What can I do for you?"

"I need to talk to him. Please? I need to talk to him before we leave," I said, avoiding his gaze.

I heard him sigh and was trying to prepare myself for the argument that was surely to come, "Okay Ana. You get ten minutes. That is it. We have to get ready, and you need to be ready yourself."

I was completely surprised, "Thank you, Luca." I moved to him quickly and threw my arms around his waist in a hug. I was so eternally grateful he was listening and taking me seriously.

"You're welcome, Ana. Come on. Let's get this over with so we can focus on the rest of the day," he said, pulling me along slowly.

We went to the basement door, and I took a deep breath, "Any chance I could have a few minutes alone with him?"

I felt the tension go into his body and once again prepared for the argument to come, "You get five minutes alone. The last five minutes. Then you come up. You stay away from the bars. Away from the windows."

I smiled at him, "Thank you. I promise."

He smiled back at me, but it didn't quite reach his eyes. I could see how hard he was trying for me, and I knew I needed to try better for him. I reached for the door and opened it. I took a deep breath and descended the stairs to go confront my brother.

Chapter Thirteen

The confrontation

I was walking down the stairs in the dark, holding the railing to keep myself from stumbling and falling down the stairs. I was feeling my stomach twist up in knots the closer I got to my brother. I think Luca could sense the tension flooding my body because he took my hand, "It's going to be okay. I am right here if you need me."

I gave him the best smile I could muster up, "Thank you, Luca. I just didn't expect this to happen. I thought Dom was the one consistent. I could always count on him."

"I don't think any of us saw this coming. Just take your time. Say what you have to say. Do what you have to do. Just don't let him sway you. I know he's your brother, but we can't trust him," he squeezed my hand gently.

We came to a stop at the bottom of the stairs. I stopped and took a deep breath. Once I had gathered myself mentally, I took a step towards the little cell my brother was in. Luca let go of my hand and slowed down, so he was behind me. I know he was doing it to show my brother that I was in charge. It just made my heart race a little bit. I walked till I was standing in front of his cell, "Wake up Dom…"

I saw him lying on the small bed. He groaned and sat up, "What can I do for you, Ana?"

I tried to keep myself from shaking as I watched him move. I was standing about a foot away from the bars. I knew Luca was behind me and I tried to take courage in that, "Why are you doing this? I thought we meant something to you. I thought I meant something to you. You made it to everything for me when Mom and Dad couldn't... I don't understand... I looked up to you. I loved you."

Dom stood up and moved to the bars, staring me down the whole time. Luca pulled me back away from the bars ever so slightly and I saw Dom's mouth twitch as he fought the smile, "Calm down Luca. I am not going to hurt her."

"Pardon me if I don't take your word for it. I don't think I have seen any action from you proving otherwise," The acid in Luca's voice made me want to flinch away from him. I managed to resist the urge and stood my ground.

Dom turned his attention back to me, "The family did not mean anything to me. We were separated and cold. We didn't have parents, Ana. They cared more about the money and being successful than about you or me. I do, however, care about you. You are the only reason I ever came back to the house. I love you. You were never meant to get hurt in any of this. I didn't know Luther was going to react the way he did, you were always meant to be safe."

It took everything I had not to laugh and cry at his confession. I so desperately wanted to believe him but how could I after all the lies? I subconsciously moved towards the bars. I hadn't realized that I was until Luca grabbed me by the belt loop of my jeans and stopped me from getting any closer, "How am I supposed to believe that?! Look what you did to me. To our family. It wasn't great, but they were our parents."

"Look around, Ana. Do you think he would have done a better job of keeping you safe? I mean really. You were kidnapped and now you are pregnant. Even his men couldn't keep you safe or him."

"Dom, you destroyed me. You did this to me. Not Dad. Although I did expect it from him… I never expected it from you. You were nice and good. You were the one who kept me safe. This is on you not Dad," I said, watching his face closely.

I saw his face falter as my words sunk in, "Ana… I do care and love you. That is the truth. I just wanted you to have it better than I did. You are so young. I could see how they were hurting you by simply ignoring you. I knew you tried to close yourself off. I can't tell you how great it was every time I came home and how happy you were to see me. I mean it. I didn't want to do this to you. I just wanted you to be happy. You were never supposed to get hurt."

I could feel the tears building at the sincerity on his face and voice, "Luca…"

"What Ana?"

"I need time alone with him now," I said each word slowly, hoping to keep the lump out of my throat.

I could feel the tension radiating off him, "Ana… I don't know if that is a good idea right now. I don't think that will keep you safe."

I turned to look at him with the best boss face I could muster, "Please Luca. I need this. I promise to be careful. I need you to trust me. Not him but me. I need that five minutes alone with him."

He stared into my eyes until a tear slid down. He gently wiped it away and his face melted at the sadness I am sure was there, "No more than five minutes. I mean it. I will be here in five minutes exactly. I want you to stay away from the bars."

I gave him a small smile, "Thank you, Luca. I will."

He leaned down so I was at eye level with him, and he lowered his voice so that only I could hear him, "I love you. Please listen and be careful."

"I love you too," I whispered back.

Then Luca turned to leave, and I waited to talk again until I heard the door close, "Well that was an interesting encounter. I've never seen a boss argue with an employee. Let alone an employee that is protective or hands-on."

I turned to Dom, the annoyance creeping back into my body, "Who was in the house?"

I watched his face once again falter before he got his poker face back into place, "What do you mean?"

"Oh, quit the crap. You hurt me, Dom. Please tell me who was in the house. Why are you still here if someone made it into the house," I said trying to compose myself and the confusion I felt.

"Sit down. You look like you are going to collapse. Why are you so shaky? Are they taking care of you," he said, watching me as I swayed on my feet.

I took steps backward until I felt the bench on the back of my legs. I sat down, "Dom… How could you do this to me? You don't get to ask what's wrong with me. I am so exhausted. I have lost men. My family."

My voice had grown quiet, and I was looking at my hands as the tears spilled over, "Ana… I mean it. You were never supposed to get hurt. I had Tony to keep an eye on you. You were supposed to be safe. Then Luther went rogue. He didn't do anything I thought he would do, and I suddenly couldn't keep you safe. I wanted Dad out of the way, that was it."

265

I wiped the tears that had fallen, "Who was in the house?"

"I didn't know anyone had been in the house, Ana. If they got that close, they were supposed to let me out," he said, his voice straining, "Ana?"

I looked at him, "You hurt me, Dom… I don't know how many times I have to say it. You took not only Dad but Mom. I lost my life and who I was. I have a child you have threatened on countless occasions and one of your men shot me. I have lost my friend and now I can't do this. I can't be your sister. I have to be the person who gets everyone out of here."

"Someone shot you?!"

I heard the door open upstairs, "Sounds like our five minutes are up."

I stood up and walked towards the stairs before Luca could come down and see me in a mess of emotions, "I love you, Ana. I didn't mean for this all to happen. You have to believe me."

I moved quickly, feeling myself about to snap after the heart-to-heart I had with him. I wasn't paying attention and ran right into Luca. I was so close to hyperventilating and without hesitation, I wrapped my arms around his neck and hugged him tightly, "Whoa. Are you okay? He didn't hurt you, did he?"

"Get me out of here."

He leaned down and scooped me up a second after the words left my mouth. I hid my face in his neck as the tears started to fall and I tried to get my breathing under control. It was a task that proved to me to be impossible. He quickly carried me upstairs acting as if I weighed nothing. I couldn't see where he was taking me, but he didn't slow. He sat down with me on his lap, "Let me see your face, Ana."

I shook my head and had more silent tears going down my face, "No."

I felt him start to rub small circles on my back, "Baby girl. Let me see you please. I just want to make sure you are okay," he said, his voice soft as he tried to coax me out.

I gave myself a little pep talk, took a deep breath, and slowly pulled away from the safety I was feeling, "I'm okay Luca."

He pulled my face up, "You don't look okay. I can't tell you how badly I wanted to hit him when I saw you in tears."

"I'm okay Luca. I just want to believe what he is saying so badly, but I can't. I can't trust him. He was the one person I could count on. He was at every game, concert, award ceremony... Now I don't know what to do," I said, fighting with my body as my voice tried to grow thick.

I got up and moved away from him as I tried to gather myself, "Baby don't do that. I am here. You can count on me. I love you and the baby more than anything. You are going to be a little more emotional than you are used to."

He moved to me and gently pulled me into a hug, leaving plenty of time for me to pull away, "I love you too Luca."

I felt him smile into my hair and kissed the top of my head, "How are you feeling?"

"I'm okay. Just a little tired and I am not feeling great. I had a dead person collapse on me..." I went with the list of reasons why I felt like crap. My head started pounding, "I'm sorry. I am acting like you weren't almost killed..."

He pulled my face up and kissed my forehead, "Lay down honey. I am okay. You have a lot going on. I think you are doing great considering all the things."

I rubbed my fingers at my temples, and I saw him freeze when I did, "I'm okay Luca. Really. Let's go get together with the group."

He watched me and followed me out of the room. I walked into the living room where I saw everyone standing around and talking nervously, "Hey are you okay? You look a little rough."

I gave Eve the best smile I could manage and recited like I was in a play, "I am fine." I turned to the group of people with Luther on one side and Luca on the other. "We need to start packing. They have found a way into the house, and I will not have any more people dying. Load up our stuff in the cars. We leave tonight. I will come up with a diversion."

I saw that everyone wanted to ask me more about it, "You heard her. Get on it," Luther shouted, and I saw his men disperse. My men stayed for a moment before they followed suit, "Ana, you look like your head is going to explode. What's going on?"

I have a small headache. I promise I'm fine," I said, resisting the urge to push my fingers into my temples again. As if that would help.

Luca wrapped his arm around my waist and pulled me to the couch, "I told her to take it easy. The woman never listens to me."

I lay down on the couch without hesitation and let my eyes slip shut. I felt the slightest bit of relief from closing my eyes, "I'm sorry. I am trying. I just want all of us to be safe."

I felt a blanket get draped over me, "I know Ana. Please get some rest. You have a small human growing, and you need to take it easy."

"Okay, Luther. Go help him. The sooner we get everything done, the sooner I can tell you what we are going to do to get out of here," I mumbled trying to put some energy behind my words.

I heard a chuckle, "Always with the orders. I will go. Luca, get her settled before you join us," Luther said before his footsteps faded away.

I slowly managed to pry my eyes open, "Luca go help everyone. I just needed to lay down for a little bit."

His face was gentle, "Are you going to be, okay?"

I smiled, "Of course. I am surrounded by two of the craziest teams possible. I will be fine. Go do what you have to do."

He smiled back at me, "Okay honey. Just shout for me and I will come to you. I am going to help the team get things packed up. Just relax. I don't want you to do anything for a bit, okay? Just rest."

I just nodded and closed my eyes again. I could hear the chaos around me as everyone tried to get what they could of our lives packed up from here. I was heartbroken to be leaving. I was comfortable for the first time in a year, and this was the closest I came to feeling happy. I sighed and tried to reassure myself that I would have this peace again. This was not the end of the quiet, it was just the beginning. I needed to get us far away. Maybe we could go visit our summer house in Venice. I jumped when I was starting to fall asleep by relaxing my body, "Are you okay Ana?"

I opened my eyes to see Eve, "Hey Eve. I am okay. I guess I was just trying to fall asleep, and my body said no."

She smiled and sat down on the floor in front of me, "How's your head doing? The guys said you had a headache?"

"Yeah, my head is killing me. I just don't know how to make it go away," I said, my voice a little whiny.

She giggled, "I think that is just how things go sometimes. How do you plan on getting us out of here with the rednecks that have a lot of guns."

I smiled, "I am thinking we make them feel like Dom is trapped in the basement. We are going to set the house on fire. It is going to be the easiest way. They have to work fast to get him out of the basement before the house collapses. While they are busy trying to get to him and put the fire out. We will be speeding off to get back to New York. I am thinking of going to the house in Venice."

"Venice is gorgeous. That will be a great place for us to set up camp while we get this all settled. Ana, are you sure about setting a fire? What if they don't get to Dom in time," she asked quietly.

I froze suddenly wide awake, "I think I am going to help get some stuff packed up. I'll be in my room if anyone is looking for me."

I walked away before she could say anything else. I closed the bedroom door behind me and took a deep breath. My head was pounding and only got worse as the day went on. I heard a small knock on the door, "Anastasia?"

I sighed, "What Luther?"

"Hey, we are getting a little worried about you," he said, coming and sitting on the bed.

I was getting a little dizzy and was trying to hide it. My headache was only getting worse, "I am fine. Just trying to get today done and over with."

The pounding grew and was crippling, "Ana?" I was breathing heavily, and I had my eyes closed. My fingers were pressing into my temples as if I had convinced myself that it would help, "Luca? Angelo?"

I felt myself collapsing and then I felt his arms around me, "I-I'm okay."

"Ana, hold on. Luca! Angelo! Eric!" Luther shouted. I felt the bed under me and a hand on my forehead.

I heard running as someone came into the room, "Ana?"

"I'm sorry I was trying to help… My head just hurts so much," I said to Luca.

I couldn't open my eyes at the risk of searing pain. I lay there and tried to follow the sound of his voice, "It's okay. Don't be sorry. You are not doing anymore for the rest of the day."

"I can help… I know I can," I said as the pain just spread from the little bit of movement I tried.

"No, you have done enough today. You are done," Luther said, his voice leaving no room for arguments.

"My head has nothing to do with the baby. I can help," I said, opening my eyes a little. Luca was sitting on the bed next to me and Luther was standing at the end watching me, "I am okay. It just feels like someone is driving a spike into my head."

Luca's touch was gentle, "I am going to go get the doctor. They are going to help you. Just lay here until I can get back."

"Okay, Luca."

I watched him leave and I let my eyes slip shut again. I groaned at the slightest bit of relief I felt by closing them, "Are you okay? Can I help in any way?"

"It just hurts, and I felt a little bit better with my eyes closed. I'll be okay. I'm probably just too stressed and all the crying didn't help," I said, trying to soothe the pain.

The door opened again, and both the doctors and Luca walked in. Angelo moved right to me, "Hey you. How are you doing?"

"My head hurts," I said, as my voice gradually got quieter.

"Well let me see what we have that we can give you for that," he said, his voice straining as he continued to talk.

"Don't worry Angelo. I will be fine either way. It's probably just stress," I said, cutting him off. I tried to lighten my voice so he could worry a little less. "If we don't have anything that will help and is safe then I will be okay."

"We have something. Just give me a minute, okay?"

It was quiet for a while and I think I was starting to drift off when someone touched me, "I'm so tired. My head feels like it will kill me."

"I know Ana. I have something for you. We are going to help you sit up," Angelo said.

I groaned and shook my head, "When I sit up, I get dizzy. It makes the pain slightly worse. I don't want it to get worse or to get dizzy."

"That's why I am going to help you silly," Luca said, his voice full of concern and stress. I felt him tuck his arm under me and gently pull me into a sitting position. The change in position gave me a sharp pain in my temples. I opened my eyes with great strength and took the pills Angelo had in his hand.

"What are they? Are the medications baby safe? I don't want to hurt the baby," I said as the pain began to take over my focus.

"It's just Tylenol. It is baby-safe. Please take it. It's the best I can do," Angelo said, helping me with a glass of water.

I popped the pills into my mouth and took a drink of the water. I was relieved when Luca helped me lay back down without collapsing, "Is she going to be, okay?"

"Yes, she's just tired. She had a lot today and even more in just a couple of months. It's just harder on her since the baby is getting bigger."

"I just want her to be okay. She has been through way too much. I just want to keep her locked away, where no one can get to her," Luca said with his hand on my forehead.

"I'm going to get back to it. Get her settled back in and come join us. She will be okay. You are keeping her safe," Luther said, his voice soft.

I heard the door open and close again. I opened my eyes, "I'm okay Luca. Please don't worry about it. I know this is hard for you. I'm sorry I tried to be okay."

"Hey, you. Just get some rest. It's really okay. I just want you to feel okay and keep the baby safe. I love you. Please relax," he said, pushing my hair off my face.

"I love you too honey. I am trying my best here. I am going to get some rest. Let me know if you need me?"

He kissed my forehead, "Of course sweetheart. Just get some sleep for now and I'll come get you soon."

I let my eyes close and felt instantly relaxed. Luca pulled a blanket over me and relaxed my nerves. I curled up and he pulled the curtain over the window to help block out the light. I felt like I was floating. I must have drifted off because I woke up to Luca shaking me, "Is everything okay?"

"Everything is fine. It's time to get ready to go. We need to set up the fire and get the hell out of here," he said, helping me sit up once again.

I sighed, ready to be left alone, "Okay. Let's do this thing."

I slowly stood up, I was a little dizzy and I still had a bit of a migraine. I stretched my body out and looked up at Luca, "We are going to tie Dom up in the basement but open his cell door. Is that okay?"

I thought about it for a moment, "It gives them a chance to get him out and still enough time for us all to drive as far away as possible. I think it will work."

He smiled at me with relief that I liked his plan, "We have the cars loaded up and any unnecessary people are in the cars. I think you should go get in the car now."

"Are you getting in the car?"

He looked away and I knew that it was him. Him and Luther were going to be the ones setting the fire and he didn't have the balls to tell me, "No. I am helping Luther. You need to be out of danger. We can't focus if you are in danger."

"Luca, I will be worried about you. I can't put you both in danger while I sit in the car. You are trying to fix a problem my family made," I said, my head starting to pound again.

"Anastasia, we need you to be safe. Let's get you to the car please," Luca said, holding his hand out to me.

I sighed, "Fine. You have five minutes to get out of the house. If you are not out of the house in five minutes, I will be going in the house to get you."

"Deal. Come with me please," he said as I took his hand. He pulled me out of the house, and I saw the five cars that we had now. I was stunned. I saw a group of people dispersing themselves into the cars.

Luther walked over to us, "Everything is ready. I have her in the car with me, you, and Apollo. We need to get this done quickly. We haven't seen anyone yet but that doesn't mean they aren't close by. It just makes me a little worried no one has tried anything yet."

"I'm sure it's going to be okay. They might be keeping their distance. You two have five minutes. I will run into a burning building if you don't come out in five minutes," I said looking between the two men, trying so hard to be in charge.

"We will be fine. Please get in the car," Luther said, giving me a small unsteady smile.

Eli walked over to us, "Go ahead guys. I will watch her. Let's get this over with.

I watched Luther and Luca walk away from me and it made my heart hurt. I stared at where they disappeared into the house, "Five minutes Eli."

"I understand Ana. I think you need to stay out of there though. You need to be safe. It's not just you. You can't just go into a burning building," he said, his voice was tense.

"They have five minutes," I said looking at him.

He watched my face for a minute, "Let's just wait and see what happens."

I saw smoke start to billow out of the house. I looked down at my phone to start the timer I had prepared. Once the countdown started my heart raced and I returned my gaze to the house. After what felt like an hour I looked down and saw that only four minutes had gone by, and I still hadn't seen Luca or Luther. My heart somehow managed to move faster, and I started to take one step closer to the house. Eli grabbed me when I could feel the heat coming off and I turned to yell at him when I heard two gunshots. I froze and slowly rotated back towards the house, "You can let me go, or I will hurt you."

I could feel his eyes on me and then followed by a sigh, "I am coming with you."

"No, you need to stay out here. Where is Oliver, I'll take him," I said my voice shaking as my uncertainty began to rise to the surface.

I heard someone approaching, "Let's go." It was Oliver as if the sound of my voice had called him. I felt slightly guilty because I knew if he died in that house with me, I would still be okay.

I followed Oliver up the front steps and to the front door. It was hot and as we crossed the door frame Oliver moved so he was in front of me, "Be careful Oliver. The house could come down."

He laughed as if I had just made a joke, "We are in a burning building. I am pretty sure that being careful is just a silly dream. Just stay behind me and keep your hand gripped to my shirt."

I grabbed his shirt tightly, and we started moving again through the house. I coughed as the smoke began to take over all my senses. I couldn't hear anything but the crackling of the building as it continued to burn. I felt his body pull mine along, "I don't hear anything! Do you think they are okay?"

"Just keep moving. We can't stop. We need to see what's going on and get the hell out of here. If this gets any worse you will be leaving," he said, his voice tense and rough as the smoke flooded our way.

We somehow found the door to the basement and by this time we were both coughing so much it was hard to stand, "Luca! Luther!" I didn't hear any responses to my shouts.

"Alright, let's go see if they are downstairs," Oliver said, as he started to go down the stairs.

It wasn't quite as smokey downstairs, but it was starting to come down the stairs as the fire devoured the house, "Luca!? Luther?!" I went walking around the basement. I froze when I saw someone lying on the ground in the back. I moved quickly and saw that Luther was here, "Oliver over here!"

Oliver came running over to me and we approached him slowly. Oliver began to shake him aggressively, "Boss wake up!"

Luther groaned and I felt my heart grow with worry and panic as I didn't see Luca anywhere. Luther rolled onto his side, and I saw some blood on his head, "What the hell happened? Where is Luca?"

"Why is she in this building, Oliver? Dom was ready for us. I don't know where Luca is. Let's find him," Luther said. He moved slowly as I am sure he had a great deal of pain in his head.

"She was going to come in one way or another. I decided it was better to have her with me instead of looking for three people in a burning building," Oliver helped pull me back to my feet.

"So, Dom is free?"

My leg was starting to hurt from all the movement, but I couldn't stop until we found Luca. Luther's voice brought me back to the present, "Ana. Let's just focus. I need you to get out of the house," Luther said, his voice gentle as he tried to be nice.

"I'm not going anywhere without Luca. Let's go look for him," I said, staring him down as he watched me.

He sighed, "Alright Oliver. I will be in the front; you stay behind her. Do not lose sight of her. If we separate, get her out of the building immediately," he turned to me. "Hold on to my shirt and do not let go. No wandering off."

I nodded and we began to move again. The smoke was getting worse as we went upstairs. We all started coughing and Luther stopped long enough to tear his shirt so that he could give me something to cover my mouth with.

He had me loop my finger through the belt loop of his jeans after that. I heard another gunshot upstairs. We moved quickly because I started to push Luther. We started searching room by room and when we went into the third room, I saw Dom holding a gun to Luca's head. He was coughing and on his knees in front of Dom. I moved out of instinct in front of Luca. I was so close to Dom I could touch him if I reached out, "Don't do this Dom. We need a running start. If you really did love me or do love me, then you will let us go."

Dom watched me and I was taken over by a coughing fit. He moved towards me as if to help but froze when he saw Luther take a step towards him, "Ana. I never wanted you to get hurt. I need you to get out of here now."

"I'm not leaving without Luca. We need ten minutes Dom... Please," I said watching him as I inhaled more smoke.

His eyes grew sad as I spoke. He thought about what I had said then responded, "Go. You have ten minutes. Get out of this house before you get hurt."

I watched him as I spoke, "Luther, Oliver help Luca up. We need to get out of here."

Another coughing fit came over me as I inhaled more smoke. I had an arm circle around my waist, "Oliver, you help him. I am going to help her," Luther said as loudly as he could without coughing. He started to cough despite his best efforts, and I hadn't caught my breath yet. He scooped me up in his arms and he moved through the house. Once my face touched fresh air, I took a deep breath causing me to start coughing, "Get him in the car. I will get her in the car, and we need to get out of here quickly."

"Is he okay," I asked, my headache slowly creeping back.

"He is fine. I'm going to put you in the front so I can look at Luca. I want you to sit down and rest," Luther said, setting me down in the front seat.

Apollo helped me buckle up and we were speeding off, "Luther? How's Luca?"

I heard lots of coughing behind me. I was also coughing trying to get the smoke out of my body, "Take an easy Ana. Apollo, roll down her window."

"I'm fine. Just wasn't ready for that. I am sorry to worry you all. Is she okay?"

"I am okay," I said, my voice fading because of the coughing.

My phone rang and I looked to see my brother's name on it, "Hello Dom."

"Thank God. I needed to know you made it out." Then his voice changed as he switched his position, "You guys get the night. We will start looking for you tomorrow. I want to make sure you understand. You are not going to get hurt. Or your child. Stay out of my way and let me take care of this," That was all he said then the phone went dead.

I sighed, "Dom is giving us the night. We need to move fast and as far as possible. I don't think we should stop for at least twenty-four hours.

"Well, we are going to need gas. We can stop in about ten-fifteen minutes to gas up, get snacks, use the bathroom, and get on our way. Drive straight through the night and tomorrow and see how far we can get," Apollo said his voice was relieved.

I looked out the window and saw the world flying by as Apollo sped away. The guys were talking, and I let my eyes close to try and relieve the pain in my head. After thirty minutes we came to a stop, "Stay close. Get what you need because we won't be stopping again for a while." I stood up and got out of the car as my muscles were stiff. I stretched and was slightly amazed by the quiet that surrounded us, "Ana?"

I turned to look at Luca, "Are you okay?"

I couldn't bring myself to say anything. I just stared at him for a minute just taking in the fact that he was standing in front of me and alive. I saw that he was fine, and I couldn't see an injury besides his head. Finally, after five minutes I decided to respond, "I'm okay. You scared me. You have to stop almost dying…"

"Oh honey…" He moved to me quickly and pulled me into a tight hug. I was tense and I didn't think it would be possible for me to relax, "I'm sorry. I'm so very sorry. Please forgive me."

I sighed and hugged him back, happy to feel him alive and well in front of me. Just as I went to respond to him, there was an explosion nearby that made the world shake. I lost my balance and so did Luca. We hit the ground, and he held me close to his body trying his best to protect me from what was coming.

Chapter Fourteen

Back on the Road Again

Luca had one arm wrapped around my waist and the other was cradling my head. I was gasping for air as the panic attack set in. I heard people shouting and talking to each other. Then I heard his voice in my ear, "Are you okay?" I was gasping and trying to get my breathing under control, so I just nodded. He must have felt my head move because he pulled back and looked at me, "It's okay. Just look at me. Focus on me." He moved his hand from my waist to my face. I was able to get some deep breaths in and my heart rate started to slow, "That's it."

"Is everyone okay?!" I heard Angelo shout from somewhere nearby.

"We are okay over here," Luca yelled as I slowly got up from the ground, "Are you okay?"

"I'm fine. What do you think that was?"

"Probably the house. The fire must've gotten to the gas line. Let's get you back in the car," Luca said, guiding me to the door of the backseat. "Get in. I will get some food and drinks for you. Stay in the car please."

"Okay, Luca. I can do that," I said quietly. I got into the back seat, and he closed the door gently for me. I sat in the car and watched the two teams move in sync to get things done. Soon enough everyone was in the cars and ready to go. I could see a small glow as it looked like the woods had gotten set on fire. I heard the doors open and people were joining me in the car. Luca was in the back next to me while Luther was driving, and Apollo was in the passenger seat.

We were driving away and off to the next place. I was tired of spending my life on the run but knew that I was better off than the first time. I sighed and tried to make myself comfortable, "It's going to be okay Ana."

"What happened in the house Luca?"

"I will talk to you about it, Ana. I just don't think now is a good time. Just sit here and rest a little bit and I promise we will talk about it tomorrow," he said, his voice gentle.

I sighed too tired to argue with him, "Okay." I could feel the headache coming back and I could see the glow of the forest getting smaller as we moved away, "I think I need to lay down."

I think that took him by surprise because it took him a minute to respond to me, "Lay down baby. You can lay on me."

I laid down across the seat and laid my head on his lap. I felt myself sigh as I closed my eyes and felt the headache lift ever so slightly, "Thank you."

I felt him shuffle and drape something over me. It smelled like him, and I hugged it closer to me, "Good night, Ana. Get some sleep, honey."

I just nodded, unable to say anything else. I wanted to sleep. I needed to sleep, and I was ready for the first time in a year to go to sleep. It didn't take long for me to drift off…

I was back in my house. I was in my room, and I slowly got off the bed. This felt like a trap. I looked around my room and saw everything was still in its place, which surprised me. Shouldn't it be a mess? Shouldn't my suitcases be missing? "Hello?" There was no response and that made my anxiety a little worse. I walked out of my room and down the stairs that were down the hall to the left. Once my feet touched the foyer, I still hadn't seen anyone, "Mom? Dad? Dom?" I heard someone talking from the dining room, but no one said anything back, "Luca?"

I moved to the dining room door and pushed it open. I saw my family sitting at the table but there was no sign of Luca, "Good morning, Ana. Did you sleep well?"

I stared at my mom feeling like this was all a trick, "I slept fine. How about you?"

"I slept fine honey. Come sit down and have breakfast," she said, watching me closely as if I was about to have a mental breakdown.

I went and sat down. I looked around the table and at the food that was in front of me. I couldn't make myself eat. I looked up and saw the sad unfortunate truth. My dad had three gunshot wounds that blood was coming out of. Two in the chest and one in the head. My mother had one that was coming from her stomach, and my brother had completely vanished from the table. I couldn't scream, cry, or even move. I looked down and saw a little bit of a baby bump that was forming. I jumped awake and Luca jumped too, "Are you okay?"

"I'm fine. It was just a bad dream."

He sighed, "Are you feeling better?"

I sat up and rubbed the sleep from my eyes. I felt something hit my lap and saw it was Luca's jacket. I smiled, "I am. I'm ready to leave this behind."

He was looking at me like a confused puppy, "We will go to New York as fast as possible. We will be stopping late tonight. We are talking about switching cars while we are stopped."

"That's probably a good idea. Dom will know what these will look like and there might be a tracker if he knew what was going down," I said looking back at him.

"Ana?"

"Yeah?"

"You seem oddly calm."

I couldn't help the laugh that had escaped my mouth, "I guess I am. I hate what happened. There's no changing it. I will work through the issues I have from this later. I need to focus on what's ahead. Don't worry Luca. I am fine."

He watched me for a minute, his hazel eyes searching for deception in my green eyes. He finally sighed, "Okay. How are you feeling?"

I thought about that for a minute, "My headache is gone. I'm not hungry yet but I'm sure it is coming. I would also appreciate a bathroom break sometime soon."

He laughed, "I am glad the headache is gone. I would like you to eat some food. I'm sure we can make a stop so you can use the bathroom."

"You got it, Ana," Luther said from the driver's seat.

"Which state are we driving through?"

"We are currently in Montana. This state is huge. We are trying to stay North for as long as we can. When we stop to get food and things, we should switch cars. My family owns a dealership near here. We can just pick up cars," Luther said, sounding exhausted.

"Maybe I could drive for a little bit? You sound completely exhausted Luther."

"After we stop, Sunflower. I'll take a break. No point stopping early," he said, trying to reassure me from the front.

I sighed and knew there was no arguing with him. I looked down at my stomach and could see a little bit of a bump forming. I thought to myself just one step at a time. Then I got lost thinking about Dom. What is happening? Why did it seem like he was telling the truth? I could always count on him. He was the one who showed up for everything. He always called. He didn't just leave me behind when he went to college. My father and I never got along though. Then when Dom's girlfriend died it seemed that was the end of their relationship entirely.

"Ana?"

I was pulled out of my thoughts by Luca, "I'm sorry. I guess I'm a little spacey."

He gave me a small smile, "Ready for some food?"

"Yeah, I can eat something."

I slowly opened the door to the cold morning air. I shivered and pulled Luca's jacket around me. I saw him smile as I did that. Luther moved to me, "I'm going to get us some new cars. You and Luca go get some food. There's an IHOP across the street. I'll call when I'm done."

I stared at him for a minute, "Don't forget to get something to eat too. Then you need sleep. You look tired."

He smiled, "Okay. I will. Now go with the team. I'll call in a bit."

I felt Luca's arm around my waist, "Let's go get some food."

I was pulled away and followed Luca, Angelo, Eli, and Oliver across the street. We went in and they managed to seat us all very quickly. There were small bursts of conversation amongst our team as we waited to order. I looked at the menu and nothing sounded good, but I knew I needed to get some food in me. The waitress came by and took our drink order. I felt someone squeeze my knee and looked over to see Luca, "I am okay. I think just last night is catching up with me."

He smiled but it didn't quite reach his eyes, "I understand. I just am going to be checking on you, silly girl."

I laid my head on his shoulder, "I know. I understand."

Suddenly I had the urge to use the bathroom, "I'll be right back."

I stood up and walked into the bathroom. I quickly sat down to pee and froze when I saw a little bit of blood. I took a deep breath and tried to remain calm. I pulled out my phone and texted Eve to ask her to come here for a minute. After a couple of minutes, I heard the door to the bathroom, "Ana? Are you okay?"

"I'm bleeding a little."

I felt her tension through the stall door, "Okay. Well, finish up and come out here okay? I will tell Angelo. I'm sure we have something to look at the baby's heartbeat."

"Okay…"

I heard the door again and I finished. I was washing my hands when there was a knock on the door, "Ana?"

"I'll be out in a second, Luca." I dried my hands and walked out of the bathroom, "I'm okay. I just got worried."

He took my hand and walked with me to the table, "We have a Doppler to listen to the heartbeat. That should put your mind at ease until we can afford to stop at the doctor's office."

I sat down and Angelo was now sitting on the other side of me, "Hey there boss. Mind if I use this quickly so we can all eat?"

I nodded, afraid to say anything else. After a few minutes, I heard the baby's heartbeat and felt all the tension leave my body, "It's okay…"

Angelo smiled, "Yes, the heartbeat is strong. Your body is producing more blood than normal to help accommodate the new habitant. Sometimes that leads to spotting. You should be fine. Just let me know if you start cramping."

"Okay, thank you, Angelo."

The waitress came back, and I watched Angelo put the doppler in his medical bag. We all ordered our food. I sat and looked at my hands trying to figure out if I was really hungry. I spouted my order of strawberry French toast. I didn't know if I wanted it though. I could feel Luca staring at me. I just kept my eyes on the table and thought more about what was going on. I had someone touch my leg and I looked over at Luca, "Hey you."

"Hey, Luca."

"Are you doing, okay?"

"I am okay. I just think I am overwhelmed. I got a little worried with the blood," I said looking at his hazel eyes as they searched my face.

"I get it. How is your head?"

"My head is okay. No headache as of right now. I just want the chase to be over," I said looking away from him.

The waitress came back with our food and the table grew quiet as we all ate. I saw Luther come into the restaurant and find us, "Hello guys. I've got some new cars for us. We can get going once you all finish eating."

"Are you going to eat?"

Luther found me and his eyes were sad, "I think it's best if we just get back on the road sunflower. I'll get some food later."

I felt myself start to panic, "You need food. We need everyone to be at full strength. You are exhausted and hungry."

"I am fine. I paid the bill already. Meet me outside when you are done."

He walked away and my appetite quickly disappeared with him. We were already down men, and I couldn't have any weaker people. I thought about what I could do. Then I heard, "Can we get a box for her food please?"

"Of course, I will be right back with that," the waitress said, keeping her eyes on Luca longer than I wanted her to.

My food got boxed up and I stood up to follow Luca out. He quickly wrapped his arm around my waist. He was carrying my leftovers, and he wouldn't let me go. We went and found Luther in front of our new cars. Luca stopped me and made me look at him, "I love you. I will help but I need you to be quiet and let me do the talking please."

I didn't know what he was talking about, but he looked serious, "I love you too. Okay, Luca."

He gave me a small smile and took my hand. We went to Luther, "I'm going to drive for a bit. I think you could use a break. Here's some food. Eat it." He handed my leftovers to Luther and helped me into the front seat of the car before Luther could respond.

He closed the door, but I could still hear them talking, "I'm fine Luca."

"This isn't just for you. Don't mistake our alliance for friendship. I have no worries or care for you, but for some reason I cannot fathom; she does. I love her. I will do what I can for her. Right now, that is telling you to do this. She is pregnant and dealing with the betrayal of her family. Don't add to her stress. Take care of yourself," Luca said, his voice tense.

"I didn't want to add to her stress. I am fine though," Luther said in a low voice.

"Eat the damn food and take a nap. That will help. Take care of it now. I am driving for a bit," Luca said, moving away.

"I don't know why you are being like this."

"Because she cares about you. I don't have to like it. I just have to respect it. Now get in the car," Luca moved to the driver's side door and opened it. He got in and buckled up, "Seatbelt please Ana."

I quickly got buckled up and Luther got into the backseat with Eli this time. I looked at Luca with more love in my heart than I thought possible. He has done everything for me. It was also a little cute that he was jealous. I took the hand he had free while he drove. I squeezed it, "You are incredible. I haven't thanked you for everything."

He peaked at me and smiled, "I think you are incredible too. I am happy to do it honey." he moved his hand to my stomach, "For the both of you."

I smiled and leaned the seat back ever so slightly. He left his hand, and I rested mine over his, "You are going to be a great Dad. I appreciate you."

"You are going to be a fantastic mother. You just need to rest and let the rest of your pregnancy go by easily. I think Greece is a good place for us to settle and let you have a baby," he said, watching the road.

My eyes grew heavy as the lack of sleep was catching up with me. "I just want us to be safe for a little bit. I want to have a normal life again. I'd love to go to school," I said quietly.

I saw he was peeking at me, "Get some rest gorgeous. I know you haven't been sleeping well. You have been chatty in your sleep. I'll wake you when we stop for the night."

"No, I'm not sleeping. I need to figure things out. In my head," I said, shaking my head.

I heard him sigh and turned to stare out the window. I heard the soft snore of the people in the back as they were sleeping. I hadn't realized that my eyes had slipped shut until I heard a gunshot. I popped up gasping and Luca pulled over quickly, "Look at me, Ana." I found his eyes, but I couldn't get myself to calm down. "You are safe. I am right here. I'm not going anywhere."

I felt a couple of tears fill my eyes, "I am scared…"

His face softened, "Oh sweetheart… It's okay. I'm sorry."

"I can drive for a bit," Eli said, his voice softly coming from the backseat. "Why don't we switch spots."

"Yeah, I got some sleep. Let's get her comfy in the back here," Luther said as the back door opened. I heard my door open, and someone unbuckled my seatbelt, "Get in the back seat Sunflower."

I didn't say anything. I just got up and moved into the backseat. Luca got into the seat next to me and immediately had me lying down on him, "Luca…"

"Shh." He was rubbing my back, and the car was moving again. I could hear his heartbeat, "Get some sleep, honey. I know you are tired. I know you are scared."

I laughed, "Soon I won't be able to lay like this. I am already starting to get a baby bump."

I felt him laugh too, "Well hopefully by the time this happens, you will be safe in Greece where I won't have to share the backseat of a car with you."

My eyes slipped shut without my permission, "I know you are doing this on purpose. I just don't know if I want to sleep yet."

"I know Ana. I think you need to sleep but you don't have to. I just want you to lay with me," he buried his face in my hair. I felt him kiss the top of my head, "Just relax. Enjoy this little bit with me."

"Okay Luca," I said, enjoying the warmth of his arms around me and the sound of his heartbeat. I could feel myself starting to drift off when I felt this flutter in my stomach. I felt Luca freeze, and I felt my heart rate spike, "Luca…"

"This is a good thing, Anastasia."

"Then why do you feel so tense," I said in a gentle voice.

I felt him chuckle, "It's a weird feeling to have on your body. That's the baby moving," he said, his voice soft as his body relaxed. "Relax. Go back to sleep."

I laid my head against his chest and closed my eyes. I suddenly realized that it was the baby moving in my stomach. I felt such a great amount of love in such a short time. I buried my face in his chest and took a deep breath. I felt him tighten his arms around me, "Luca?"

"What Anastasia?"

"You know that I love you right?" I said not taking my face off his chest.

I felt him chuckle, "I know. I love you too."

"Good. You mean a lot to me," I said looking up at him and watching him.

He gave me a small smile, "Well, aren't you feeling a little sentimental today? I think you are past the point of exhaustion. Please rest."

I laid my head back down and I felt him kiss the top of my head, "I don't know if I can sleep right now. There's just so much going on."

"Nothing is going on right now. We are in the car driving. So, rest until we get to the hotel later tonight. Just let me take care of you," he said, giving me a small squeeze.

I sighed and let my body relax, "Fine. I'll try, I make no promises."

I felt him laugh again, "I'll take what I can get." I loved the sound of his laugh. I was exhausted and once I let my brain relax, I slipped into unconsciousness.

****

I woke up to someone picking me up. I groaned, "Leave me alone."

The wind was blowing around me causing me to cling to whatever warmth I could get. I could hear the rain as it was crashing down hard to the earth. I could hear the thunder and flashes of light bounced over my eyelids. We were in the middle of a storm and that must be why we were stopping. "I'm sorry Sunflower. I had to free Luca. Let's get you upstairs," I didn't open my eyes. I just felt Luther pull me closer to him.

It was cold outside, and I moved towards the warmth. I heard people talking around me as we moved. I could hear Luca right next to Luther, "It's getting colder."

"It is fall. It will only get colder as the year moves on. Let's just hope we can get to Greece faster than we got to Texas," Luther said back to him.

Soon I was surrounded by heat as they got me into the building. I let my body relax under the warmth. I heard someone talking and asking if I was alright. I went to say yes but my body felt so heavy. I heard some more talking, and my mind wanted to sink back into unconsciousness. I fought it with everything I had and tried to move, "Put me down."

"I don't think that is a good idea," Luther said quietly.

"I said put me down."

I heard him sigh as he slowly sat me down on my feet. I forced my eyes open, and I swayed a little bit, "Luca get over here."

Luca moved to me quickly, "What are you doing?"

"I am fine. I heard so much talking. I just didn't want to cause any problems. I can't come into places looking drugged or dead," I said trying to move.

He wrapped his arm around me to help steady me, "Ana... You need to slow down. You are exhausted."

"We can't draw attention to ourselves. I am trying to help with that. You guys are carrying me into a building looking like I'm messed up. We are going to get the police to call on us," I said, trying to push away from him.

"Miss, are you okay?"

I looked and saw the man who was behind the front desk, "Yes, I am okay. Sorry, my boyfriend is stubborn. I am pregnant so he is trying to baby me. I promise I am okay."

He looked at me for a long moment. Finally, he seemed to relax, "Okay. Please let me know if you need anything."

"Thank you so much. I will," I said, turning back to the men.

"It is time to get you upstairs," Luca said, his voice tense as he wrapped his arm around me again.

"Fine," I said, resisting the urge to push him away. We went to the elevator, and I stayed on my feet. I resisted the urge to lean into him as I was really tired. I hadn't even realized my eyes had closed again until Luca went to pick me up, "No. Do not pick me up."

I pried my eyes open again and I turned to look at Luca. His eyes were sad and filled with worry, "Baby we are not in the lobby anymore. You are exhausted. Please let me help."

"Luca... I am not a child. I am not fragile. I am pregnant and having a baby. I need to do things on my own," I said, trying to explain how I was feeling.

He pulled me into a tight hug, and it took me by surprise, "Sweetheart, I know you aren't a child. I have never seen you like one. You are fragile though. You have been through so much and are going to be going through so much more. You are going to be doing things on your own and I couldn't be prouder of you, but I am going to be that pain in the ass. I am going to tell you that you need to relax. I am going to be overbearing and tell you that I love you. I am going to drive you completely crazy."

As he was talking, I felt the tears fill my eyes, "I love you..."

He pulled away enough to look at my face. He saw a tear spill over and he wiped the tear off my face, "I know. Now please let me help you."

"You can help support me, but I want to walk. I need to walk. Please just let me do this," I said, looking up at his bright eyes.

They softened ever so slightly, "Okay Anastasia. I am going to be helping you though. I won't pick you up unless necessary."

He wrapped his arm tightly around my waist and I smiled at him, "Thank you."

I went to say something back to him but when I went to the elevator shook. My heart rate spiked, and I wanted to scream. I went to take a step but suddenly the elevator came to a screeching halt. I couldn't stop the scream that escaped as I slammed to the floor and hit my head on the back wall.

Chapter Fifteen

Trapped

"Ana? Please wake up," Luther was shaking me aggressively.

I groaned, "What the hell just happened?"

"I think the storm knocked out the power. The lights are low. We are stuck on an elevator right now," Luther said, helping me sit up.

"Well, what are we supposed to do now…"

"Either wait for someone to come get us. If they even know we are here, or wait for the power to come back on," Luther responded, standing up.

The panic began to hit my chest hard, "What are we going to do? I don't want to stay here. How far up are we? I want out of here."

"Hey, deep breath," Luca said, pulling my face up and making me look at him. "You need to breathe. We can't panic, okay?"

"No, I can't breathe. I am stuck in an elevator," I looked at the wall and saw it was dark. "God knows how many stories up. My life and the life of our child are in the balance of a wire that could break at any minute while we are stuck in a storm," I said, letting my panic take over my body.

"Hey no. None of that. It's going to be okay. We will make sure that you get out of here. I need you to calm down," Luther said, kneeling beside me and Luca.

I had let a sob escape, and I covered my face with my hands. I sat there and tried to focus on getting my breathing under control. I felt someone rubbing my back. Finally, I was able to breathe normally, "That's it, baby. Good job. Keep that up."

I felt a sob cause a small quake through my chest, "I'm scared. I am tired of being scared…"

"I know Ana. I'm so sorry. Just lay down on my lap for a bit. Luther, can you try getting through to someone on your phone please," Luca said, helping me lay down. He shrugged out of his jacket once again for me and draped it over me.

I heard his cell phone ringing as he called someone. Then I heard someone answer and Luther was talking quickly, "We are stuck in an elevator. Oliver, you need to get us out of here. We can't wait. Ana needs out of here."

I hugged Luca's jacket tightly, "I'm sorry I was so mean Luca…"

"Hey shh. Just rest. We are going to be fine. We are just doing a little bit of a campout right now," Luca said, his voice soft. He was playing with my hair, "Just rest honey."

"I can't rest. I am sitting in a giant metal box in the middle of a storm that is hovering off the ground," I said, my voice growing thick.

Luther hung up the phone, "Oliver and Eli are going to figure out what is going on. They will come to get us as soon as they find us. We won't be here too long."

"I don't want to be here at all. I need to get out of here," I sat up and hugged my knees to my chest. Luca's jacket slipped off me as I sat up.

Luca watched me closely but didn't say anything. Luther sat down by the elevator doors, "Well we might be here for a little bit. Let's just take it easy and wait."

I had a couple of tears spill as I thought about my life. The doors to the elevator started to pry open. All three of us jumped up to our feet, "Help!"

The elevator shook with drastic movement and Luca steadied me, "Calm down in there. We are going to get you out of here as fast as possible."

"I need to get out of here… Please get us out of here," I said as my throat continued to grow thick. "Please get us out of here now."

"It's okay. It's going to be okay honey. Just stay calm," Luca said, taking my hand and squeezing it gently.

The only way the doors opened about a foot before it locked up was, "I can't get out… What are we going to do…"

"Miss, we are going to get you out of there, but we have to do it safely. Now there was a malfunction with the elevator. The safety cable is not secure, and we have to move slowly. I need you all to not move around too much," the firefighter said, his voice tense.

"Are you okay Luther," I heard Oliver ask from behind the two firefighters.

"We are fine Oliver. Help anyway you can," Luther said, his voice changing as his boss mode came out.

I started to hyperventilate as I heard the fact that we were not safe. I knew there were systems in place, but it was still terrifying. Now the systems were failing, "I need out of here… Someone get me out," I almost screamed as I grabbed two fistfuls of my hair and tried not to yank them out.

Someone tried to touch me, and I pulled away instantly. I couldn't get myself to calm down and I knew I was only going to make it worse. I felt tears go down my face and I just couldn't get myself to stop. I was pushed against the wall and screamed from the panic, "Look at me!"

I looked at Luca as my heart raced from the panic and the PTSD, "I-I just can't-"

"Ana, I will not let anything happen to you. I need you to take a deep breath and try to calm down. You can't be panicking and moving around right now. It's not safe and we have to try to stay still," he said watching me.

I collapsed and he caught me, "I am scared... I can't breathe. I need to get out of this giant death box."

"I know, baby. I am right here. I just need you to focus and to breathe," he said softly.

"Is she okay?"

"I've calmed her down for now. Can you please hurry up and get us out of here," Luca said looking at the firefighter.

"We will get you out of there as quickly as possible," he said in response to that.

Luca helped me back to the bottom of the elevator and I hugged myself, "I think I am going to be sick..."

Luca squatted in front of me, "I know honey. You are doing great. I am sorry for being rough with you. I am just trying to get you to stay calm. Are you okay? I didn't hurt you right?"

I felt the little flutter again and my hand went immediately to my stomach, "You didn't hurt me, I just want to get the baby to safety."

He looked at my hand and gave me a small smile, "We will. I need you to try and remain calm. Even when it comes to the baby, please."

"Okay, Luca. I will try," I said looking down at my hand.

He stood up and I blocked him out as he started to talk to Luther. I just stared into space, and I laid my head down on my knees. I must have started to drift off because I jumped when the top of the elevator opened and screamed, "It's okay, Ana! It's just me." I saw Oliver above us and tried not to cry from relief.

"How did you convince them to let you come down," Luther asked looking up at him.

"They saw how she panicked and thought it would be better with a familiar face. Also, I'm a volunteer fireman," Oliver said, giving me a small smile.

"Well, that works," Luca said quietly.

"Alright, we need to get the large weights out of here first. Relieve some of the pressure. Luther time to go up," Oliver said, and I saw he was in a harness.

"No, I want Ana taken out of here first," Luther said, his voice hard. There was a snap, and the elevator went down a foot. I screamed and hit the floor again. Once we stopped going down Luther was angry, "She is getting out of here now."

"We need to get rid of some of the weight. You have to come with me now before this thing moves anymore," Oliver said, reaching down and trying to grab him. "Quit arguing and just listen to me."

He sighed and turned to us, "Keep her safe Luca. I will see you in a few minutes, Sunflower."

I nodded and watched as Oliver picked him up and they disappeared. I let out a sob, "I don't want to die…"

"Hey no, no one is dying today. It's going to be okay," he said, his voice gentle. He moved my hair out of my face.

Oliver appeared again, "It's your turn, Luca. This thing won't hold for too much longer. I need you to come with me now."

"You can't take Ana?"

"She's the lightest one, we need to save her for last," Oliver said.

"It's okay, Luca. Go ahead. I will see you soon," I said, giving him a nudge. He reached up for Oliver and was able to get out easily. Once they pushed off the elevator it shifted again. I hugged myself and screamed as it moved another six inches. I moved to the corner and sat there holding myself together.

Then Oliver appeared again, "Alright Ana. Time to go."

"It keeps moving. I don't want to move... What if it goes down because of the movement… Please."

His face softened, "I have to go into the elevator. I need more rope." He climbed down carefully. "We need to get out of here now."

"I'm scared."

"If I don't bring you up there, imagine what would happen. I think I may be more afraid than you. Just come here so I can get you out of here and survive too," he held his hand out to me, and I slowly took it. He pulled me to him, and the elevator started to shake, "Bring us up now!"

I felt the rope pull us up. We managed to get out of the elevator and on top of it when we heard it shift again. I screamed and hid my face in Oliver's shoulder. His arms were tight around my waist, and I had my arms wrapped around his neck. We were being pulled up and I froze when I felt someone grab me, "It's okay miss. Let him go."

I shook my head as tears slipped down my face. My body was shaking with my silent sobs, "Hey it's okay Ana. Let me go so they can get you to safety."

I listened to Oliver and slowly let him go. I was pulled away from him and then I was in Luca's arms again. I sobbed once my feet were on the floor. I turned to thank Oliver when I heard the cable snap, and it came through the open elevator doors. I screamed as I was tackled to the ground. I hit my head on the tile floor. Luca moved off me and I moved quickly to Oliver who lay on the floor. He had gotten hit on the back and was bleeding. I immediately pushed pressure on the wound; it took a minute for the firefighters to surround us. Luca pulled me away gently, "It's okay honey. Let them do their job."

I was frozen in place staring at Oliver, "Get her to the room Luca. She doesn't need to be seeing any of this."

"Alright. Keep me posted on him. We will see you soon," Luca said, helping me to my feet. He pulled me down the hallway. He pulled me so that I could focus on what was in front of me, "Just one step in front of another."

We went up a flight of stairs to get to our room. I was pulled into the room, and I went straight into the bathroom. I turned on the shower and took off the clothes I had been wearing. I got into the shower and let the hot water relax my muscles. I stood in the hot water and watched the blood roll off my skin. I saw a little bit of a baby bump and I hugged myself and sat down. This was the first time in a while I had thought about my razor blade. It would make me feel better, but I couldn't risk it with doctors looking at me all the time. Probably not. I sighed, "Well now that I am almost calm."

"Anastasia?"

"Luca, I'm okay. I just got worked up. I don't like being trapped. I don't like that people keep getting hurt or dying," I said without moving an inch.

I saw him move and he was standing outside the shower door, "Ana... You don't have to like it. You are allowed to be afraid and upset. I need you to be safe though."

"I'm trying to be safe. I swear. I don't want to cause any issues or do anything to make things harder or worse. I just can't help it when I get panicked. I lost my mind. I don't know what happened," I said as my voice grew thick.

"Ana, please come out," he said, his voice full of worry and pain.

"I'm warm and so tired of fighting."

"Alright, I'm coming to help you."

The door opened and I just covered myself with what I could. He turned the water off and kneeled holding a towel, "I don't want to move."

"I know. I promise to help as much as I can. Just let me help you please," he said, trying to coax me out of the shower.

I sighed, "Okay." I took the towel and wrapped it tightly around myself. He pulled me to my feet and wrapped an arm around my waist. He moved slowly, giving me time to get my body to cooperate, "I'm sorry Luca."

"Don't be sorry. Let me just take care of you," he helped me sit down on the bed. He moved me, so I could sit on the bed. He moved around the room and came back to me, "Here I grabbed some underwear and one of my T-shirts for you."

"Okay Luca," I slowly stood up and took the clothes from him. I walked away and back into the bathroom to put my underwear on. I couldn't figure out how to get the shirt on without letting go of the towel. I can't explain why it was important to keep the towel around me but it was.

I felt my body shaking and then I felt him against my back, "Let me help."

I sighed, "Okay Luca."

He lifted the shirt over my head. I felt him pull it down over my chest and most of my body. Once I was mostly covered, I let go of the towel and put my arms through the sleeves. I turned around to look at him; he put his hand on the side of my face, "You ready to lay down?"

My eyes were slipping shut and I nodded as I leaned into him, "I haven't been this tired since you were shot."

He scooped me up quickly before I could protest, "Then we are getting in bed right now." He took me back out to our room and sat me down on the bed. I lazily pulled the blankets over myself, and my body wanting to sink quickly into unconsciousness, "Get some sleep."

I opened my eyes enough to see him. I grabbed his hand, "Please stay. Please lay with me."

"Of course, I'll lay with you. Close your eyes again," he said, coming to the other side of the bed and lying down next to me. I felt him get under the blankets and pull me to him, "Sleep Ana."

My body didn't need any more convincing. I took in the warmth and comfort I was getting from his body. "I love you." I didn't hear him, but I could feel him pull me closer as I drifted off.

****

I woke up and stretched my stiff body. The bed next to me was empty. I slowly sat up and looked around the room. I heard the shower going and figured that was where he was. I sighed and slowly stood up. The blue shirt he had me in came down to mid-thigh. I got up and felt my body relax after a full night's rest. I heard a knock at the door, "Can I come in?"

"Yeah, come in Angelo," I said my voice was quiet to not alert Luca I was awake.

The door opened and Angelo stepped in. He closed the door quickly behind him, "Hey you."

"How's it going? Is Oliver, Okay?"

"He's alive. He's at the hospital right now. We are all going to get ready to see him. I figured we could also have them check on the baby while we are there. You haven't been to a doctor in forever. We should make sure that the baby is okay," he said sitting on the bed.

"Okay, that sounds good. I suppose I should get checked out," I said looking around for a suitcase or a duffel bag with my clothes in it.

He saw me looking around the room, "I'll have someone bring your clothes in here. Ana?"

I looked back at him, "What Angelo?"

He stood and moved towards me, "We care about you so much. Don't forget you have us all. You scared us last night."

I moved over and hugged him, "I'm sorry Angelo. I am fine. I care about all of you too. I love you. Just relax a little."

The bathroom door opened, and I saw Luca standing in the doorway, "I'll have someone bring your clothes. Do you need anything, Luca?"

"No, I am fine. Thank you." He said to Angelo as he left. He turned to me, "Hey. How are you doing?"

"I'm doing alright. How are you doing?"

"I'm good. I was going to wake you up after my shower. I figured you could use all the rest you could get," Luca said, watching me.

Luca's hair was wet, his hazel eyes were a little red and I couldn't figure out why. He was in a black T-shirt that hung off him well, and he had black jeans on. He was watching me closely, "Are you doing, okay?"

There was another knock and Apollo came in with my clothes. He set them down on the bed and just walked right back out, "Okay what is going on?"

"Nothing, it's just been a little tense with everything going on. We've been worried about you. We don't like being in one place," Luca said walking over to me. "Get some clothes, Ana."

I moved to the suitcase and grabbed a pair of jeans, a bra, and a blouse. I went into the bathroom to change as quickly as possible. I couldn't get the jeans to button, and I felt stupid tears in my eyes. I stood and tried to get them to button but it just was painful when I tried. I sat on the toilet seat and wiped my eyes, "God. I know this is stupid."

There was a knock on the door, "Ana? Everything okay?"

"Yeah, I'm okay. I just need a minute," My voice was thick, and I prayed he wouldn't hear it.

Then the door opened, and he was kneeling in front of me, "Hey silly girl. What's wrong?"

"It's stupid," I said, wiping the tears away.

He chuckled, "It's okay. I'm sure it's not."

I looked at him and tears filled my eyes as I responded to him, "I can't button my pants. They don't fit."

He tried to keep himself from laughing, "Honey that is going to happen. How about I go get something a little more baby-friendly."

I wiped at the tears again, "I don't want to get new clothes. I just want to stay in my clothes."

His face was soft, "Oh baby. It's completely normal to feel this way. I will get you something that fits a little bit better. I will be right back." He left and when he came back, he handed me a skirt, "Put this on and I'll see you in a second."

He smiled at me and leaned down to kiss me. Once he walked out of the bathroom, I took the jeans off and put the skirt on. I could hear the voices in my head about me getting fat. I tried to push it back. I brushed my hair, and it was almost down to my butt now. I sighed and knew you couldn't see the bump anymore. I went out to find Luca on his phone. He was angry and hung up when he saw me, "Everything okay?"

"Yes, come on let's go check on Oliver," he held his hand out to me.

I went over to him and took his hand. He was angry, so I didn't say anything. We saw everyone standing in the hallway. I got into my head and could only think he was upset about the weight gain. I mean it was bad enough I was carrying a child that wasn't even his, and now I was losing my body to it. I mean he's never made a move on me. Was he rethinking this entire relationship? I was brought back to Apollo talking, "You ready to go Luca?"

"Yeah, let's get going. I want to get back here and figure out what our plan is going to be," Luca said looking at Angelo.

"You got it, boss. We will keep her safe and close," he said looking at me.

It all made sense. He was tense because I was losing my body and having a baby that wasn't his. It just became more apparent now that I have a bump. He has been trying so hard to still show love, but I think I finally put him over the edge. The rest of the team was just tense because we were stuck in one spot. I felt the itch again slice into my skin. To feel something familiar. This was all my fault. My family did this and now all these people were suffering. I was pulled forward and froze when I saw the elevator doors, "I'll take the stairs. There is only one elevator now anyway."

Luca looked at me with something in his eyes, "We aren't all going to get on all at once. You are still tired. I won't let anything happen to you. We will be safe."

"Do I have to take an elevator? I'm not saying I won't face this fear, but do I have to do it today? I would much rather take the stairs," I said looking back at him.

"The elevator is going to be the fastest way down. I know you are scared, but I need you to be fast. We are already in danger here. Close your eyes and take my hand so we can go down together," Luca said, holding out his hand to me again.

They have been continuously putting themselves on the line for me. I sighed, "Okay. Let's take the elevator."

He gave me a small smile that didn't reach his eyes, "Good. Just focus on breathing."

I nodded and we went into the elevator once it opened. I took a deep breath and tried not to panic. My voice started to restrict, and the panic began to bubble up. I was gasping a little bit, but I tried to remember to breathe. Finally, the door opened, and I was able to get out quickly, "It's okay Ana. Just take some deep breaths." Angelo was talking to me softly.

"I'm okay. Let's just get to the hospital so that we can get things done," I said, pulling myself free from everyone who tried to grab me. I put my hands up to warn them to leave me alone. "I just want to check on Oliver."

I was soon in a car, and we were driving away. I wouldn't let anyone touch me. I was trying not to let the depression and anxiety win but they were making sense of what they were saying inside my head. It was hard to fight against common sense. I took advantage of the quiet and stared out the window as the city went by. We came to a stop, and I saw the giant plus sign and the hospital. I got out of the car and followed Luca and Luther into the hospital with the rest of our teams behind us. We walked in and Luther went right up to the front desk, "Hi my name is Luther. My brother was admitted to the hospital late last night. His name is Oliver."

"Yes, your brother is stable. He needed stitches and he's been given blood. But he is alive and is doing alright. You can go up and see him," she said.

Then Luca walked up, "I was wondering if you could do a check-up on my girlfriend. She was in the elevator and is pregnant. We never got confirmation of how far along she is."

"Of course, we will get her in right away. We just need her information. If you want to give her these forms to fill out, we will take her back once she's done filling them out," she said, smiling at Luca.

He came over to me and pulled me to a row of chairs. I sat down in one and he sat down next to me, "I will take you to see Oliver, but you need to be looked at first."

I went to protest but Luther came over to me, "He's right Ana. Make sure the baby is okay. Please."

I sighed, "Fine." I took the clipboard from Luca and sat down. I started filling out all the paperwork. Once I was done, I handed it back to Luca. He took it back up to the front desk and sat down next to me. He reached for my hand, but I pulled it away. He went to say something, "Please Luca. I just need a little space."

"Okay, Ana. I understand," he said, his voice full of defeat.

I couldn't bring myself to look at him. I just wanted this all to go away. I didn't know if he was just fooling himself into trying to be with me. I was then distracted by another flutter and my hand went to my stomach. Then I heard my name being called and Luca walked one step behind me as we went back. They had me change into a gown and I was lying on a table waiting for an ultrasound. Luca gave me the space I asked for, but he stood across the room. It hurt my heart knowing this was the end of us. We just sat in silence while we waited for a doctor to come in. Finally, the door opened and a woman in her late twenties came in, "Hello you two. Congratulations. Let's check on this baby."

She walked over to me and instructed me to lie still. I had a sheet covering my lower half so that my stomach was exposed. She put the machine on my stomach with this cold jelly. It made me freeze but then she was looking at the baby. I didn't hear anything which made me panic, "Is the baby okay?"

"Yes, the baby is fine. I just have it muted," she clicked a button and the heartbeat popped up on the screen.

Luca moved closer to see, "How far along is she, Doctor?"

"After measuring, she is about seventeen weeks pregnant. Almost halfway there. The baby looks good, but I'd like to run some blood work. One might even tell you if the baby is a boy or a girl. Just to be safe," she said, putting the ultrasound stuff away.

After another half an hour and lots of vials of blood, we sat in a room by ourselves. I was sitting with my legs crossed on the bed staring at my hands. I decided to try to talk to him again, "Seventeen weeks. Crazy that it's almost halfway…"

"Yes, it is," Luca said, back his voice sounding dead and lifeless as if he finally realized I was a lost cause for him.

I sighed, "Okay."

We sat in silence again and eventually, the doctor came back in, "Hello you two. The baby looks great. Just a little bruising on you. Some malnutrition. You need to eat more food. Don't worry about anything and eat. You should be fine though. Do you want to know what your baby is?"

I looked at Luca, and he must have seen something on my face where his facade changed a little, "Yeah go ahead and tell us."

She smiled, "Okay. Well, you two. It appears as though you are having a little boy. Congratulations again."

I didn't know what to think of it. My heart was breaking, and I knew I was only going to sink further away. I just wanted to protect everyone, and I couldn't protect anyone. I just nodded and she told me I could get dressed. She left the room, and I got up and got dressed quickly. I knew Luca was upset with me, but I didn't like the fact that he was. I knew I was going to lose him, but I didn't like it. I didn't know how to make any of it better or what I was supposed to do next. Then I felt someone touch my back, "I'm sorry. I'm so sorry."

"I know, baby. Let's go check on, Oliver, and give Luther the happy news," Luca said, holding his hand out for me.

I took it and it felt good to feel him squeeze my hand. We went through the hospital and found our teams just all around this one room. I went in and saw him hooked to machines, but he was awake. I heard laughter and I sighed, "He's okay."

"Go on Ana," Luca gave me a small nudge towards the hospital bed. I moved easily after that and stood next to it.

Oliver turned to see me, "Well, hey there. I'm glad you are okay."

I smiled, "I was going to say the same thing to you."

"How's the baby?"

"Baby is good. She needs some more food. But after the ultrasound, they said she was for sure seventeen weeks along. So, she is about halfway through," Luca said from behind me. "Do you want to share the good news?"

I was feeling a little sick and I wasn't sure if I was happy, sad, okay, or anything, "She was able to tell us the sex of the baby."

The room went dead silent. Luther was standing on the other side of the bed staring at me, "You know what we are having?"

I nodded and looked down at my hands, "It's a boy."

The room erupted in cheers as the men were excited this happened. I gave my best shot at a smile and then there was nothing but talking. I was stunned by all the excitement considering the situation we were in or even if I was going to give birth before I died. Although everyone kept reassuring me that I wasn't going to die. I didn't know what to think or how to react to all of this. But I could feel my depression taking over my body when I didn't want it to. Or did I? It was a complicated feeling, "Ana?"

I hadn't realized Luca was standing next to me until he spoke, "Hi Luca."

"Hey, do you want to come with me," and he was the only one that I could hear. He was being gentle and quiet. People were still talking around us excitedly about the baby's gender. I nodded and I saw we had Luther's attention, "I'm going to take her to get some food. We will be downstairs. I want to get her some rest so we need to figure out when Oliver can come home and get back on the road." Luther was watching me closely and I looked away as Luca pulled me out of the room. He didn't take me to the cafeteria, he just pulled right out of the hospital. I sighed when I felt the cold air on my face. He found a bench and had me sit down on the bench, "How can I help?"

I looked at him surprised, "What?"

"Ana… Sweetheart I recognize the signs here. How can I help?"

I felt the tears fill my eyes, "I don't want the depression to win… I don't know how to make it stop. I don't know if I should be happy or sad. I don't know how to make the thoughts stop."

He gave me a sad smile and swiped the stray tear away, "It's okay. I think I do. Come on. Let me get you back to the hotel." He took my hand and pulled me back to my feet. I could feel his excitement as he knew how to help me.

Chapter Sixteen

Fighting the Monster

Luca had gone up and talked to the group of men and Eve. He came back down with Luther and Eli, "Let's get you back to the hotel."

I got into the backseat with Eli sitting next to me. I heard Luca and Luther talking quietly in the front of the car, "When can Oliver come back?"

"They just want to keep him overnight and make sure he is good to go. He had a few stitches in his back. So, he can come back tomorrow," Eli said, staring out the window as if he was bored with this conversation.

We were back at the hotel quickly. I sat in the car as the guys got out. I couldn't make myself move. The door opened and Luca was next to me again, "Hey you. I need you to try for a bit longer. I want to get you up to our room."

"Luca…"

"Hey, look at me," he said, his voice was full of life again. I slowly looked up at him, "What is your head telling you?"

I felt the tears fill my eyes again, "I don't know how to explain."

Luther was behind Luca, watching my face, "Well try Sunflower. We are all worried about you."

I looked down at my hands, "I am getting fat. I'm carrying a baby that isn't yours. I am not with the father of the baby. This is all my fault. Xavier, Tony, every death, and

317

injury is my fault. My family has managed to tear everyone's lives apart."

It was dead silent and then I was pulled out of the car swiftly and quickly. Luca had me in his arms and I felt the sob explode from my chest, Ana... I am so sorry. I don't want you to feel like this anytime. None of this is your fault."

He let me go and Luther hugged me tightly too, "You deserve to be happy. Even though we aren't together, our baby will grow up with both of his parents and we will both be happy."

"I'm so sorry."

"No need to be sorry. Let's get the brain of yours figured back out," Luther said letting me go.

Luca immediately took my hand and pulled me into the hotel. We were once again standing in front of the elevator and my heart started to race. I tried not to think about it, but I could feel the panic setting in. Luca squeezed my hand, "It's okay Ana. I just want to get you upstairs."

"I don't want to go up... Can't we just change rooms," I said, trying to clear my throat so he could understand me.

"Alright, let's take the stairs," Luca said, pulling me to the stair corridor. I sighed and felt myself relaxed a little bit. My stomach churned and we started going up the stairs. I didn't pay attention to anything but putting one foot in front of the other.

We finally were up on the fifth floor and pushing the door open. I tried not to let the bile rise, but I couldn't help it. I moved to the nearest trash can in the hallway and threw up. Someone pulled my hair back for me, "Oh honey. Just take it easy."

"I'm sorry. I don't know why this hit me so hard right now," I said, emptying my stomach.

"It's the baby. He just wants you to be all about him," Luther said, his voice soft.

"I think it's time we get you in bed with some food," Luca said, trying not to set me off.

"Luca... The depression... I don't want to just lie down and do nothing. I don't want the monster to win," I said looking at him after I finished emptying my stomach.

"It won't. We are here for you. Right now, you need a little rest. How about just the couch? Can we compromise and have you sit on the couch," Luca asked, helping me stand back up.

"Okay, I'll sit on the couch. Do I have to eat," I asked, as we began walking to the room again.

"The doctor said you needed more food. Not less," Luca said, putting his hand on the small of my back.

I sighed and followed him into our room. Luther was quiet but followed behind us, "The doctor said something about her eating habits?"

"Yeah, she said she was a little malnourished. Nothing to be worried about, but she wanted to try and improve her food intake," Luca was talking to Luther like I wasn't with the two of them.

I sat down on the couch and listened to them talk about my eating habits. Meanwhile, I just heard that I was getting fat and that I wasn't good enough from the monster in my head. That I wasn't taking care of my son the way I was supposed to be. I just stared at the floor and my vision was blocked by two men, "Hey you."

319

"Hi, Luca."

"What's going on with your head?"

I shook my head, unable to talk. Luther took that moment to say his peace, "Hey you. We can see you are about to cry."

I managed to clear my throat again, "I just... I can't eat more..."

"Why not?" Luca asked his hand on my knee.

"Please don't make me say it..."

"Sunflower, I think you have too. We need to know what's going on to help you," Luther said, his voice quiet as he was talking to me.

"Okay... Well, I just have a hard time eating because I don't want to get fat..."

I felt Luca let go of me. I instantly felt ashamed for saying the words out loud. I got up and pushed myself past the two men. I moved straight into the bathroom and locked the door behind me. I sat down on the floor and ignored them as they tried to talk to me. I sank to the floor until I was lying down. I lay on my side, using my arms as a pillow. I lay there and forced myself not to focus on any words that they said to me. I don't know how long I lay there like that when finally, I was able to focus on the two voices with no pain, "Ana?"

"Go away."

"No please come out," Luther said this time.

"No, neither of you understand. I don't think you will," I said, my voice growing thick. I felt the baby move and I knew he was trying to tell me something.

"Baby, I am trying so hard to understand. Can I come in please," Luca asked, his voice quiet as he tried to convince me to open the door.

"No. I want to be alone," I said and let my eyes close. I laid there like that for a while and just let my body melt to the floor. I don't know how long I stayed like that but suddenly my hair was being moved out of my face, "Leave me alone. I'm tired."

"Ana, baby... Let's get you to bed."

"No Luca... I don't want to move," he tried to pick me up and I pushed him away, "Please..."

"Luther, can you talk to her," Luca said while playing with my hair.

"Sunflower, let Luca get you to bed, please. This doesn't look too comfortable," Luther said somewhere nearby.

I slowly opened my eyes and saw Luca by my head and Luther was sitting in front of the baby, "But I am comfortable. I am tired. I am sad. I just want to not feel anything."

"Let's start with one thing. The first is getting you off the floor. Can you let us do that?" Luca asked, his voice was full of tension.

I sighed, "Okay. I can do that."

They both smiled at me, "Okay. Go ahead, Luca."

Luca moved and bent down to pick me up. Luther helped him stand with me in his arms. I wrapped my arms around his neck and hid my face in his shoulder. I felt him sit down with me on his lap, "Come out." I shook my head and kept my face where it was. "Luther, do you mind giving us a moment?"

"Yeah, I'll be by in a little bit," Luther said quietly.

I heard his footsteps and then he was gone. "Please come out." I sighed and slowly removed myself from my safe spot. I couldn't look at him yet, but I could feel him rubbing my back, "Ana... I love you. You are pregnant. You are going to change a little bit and that's okay. You are gorgeous, and this doesn't change anything."

He put his hand on my stomach. I stared at his hand on the baby bump, "I just know that it's been a mess. You left me once, for ten years. I didn't want to lose you again."

He pulled my face up, "I need you to listen to me closely. I am not going anywhere. I will never leave you again. Either of you."

I hugged him tightly and he hugged me back. I felt him chuckle and kiss my forehead, "Thank you, Luca. I love you."

"I love you too," He set me down gently, "Can I get you some food now?"

"Yes, I will eat some food," I said lying down. I pulled the blanket over me and took a deep breath. He stood up and went out of my sight. There was a knock on the door, "Come in."

Luther walked in, "Hey you. Are you doing okay now?"

"I'm getting there. I am sorry. Are you excited to be having a son," I asked, sitting up and looking at him.

He smiled and sat down next to me, "Of course. I mean I would've been happy with a daughter, but I am excited it's a boy. What about you? Any idea for a name?"

I smiled back at him, "I am okay. I don't know how I feel. I hadn't thought about it. Knowing the gender just made it all that more real..." I looked down and felt the little butterflies as he moved, and I gasped.

He stood up and looked at me, not sure how he could help me, "Are you okay?"

I smiled, "Yes. He's just moving, and I haven't gotten used to him moving around yet. It feels weird." He smiled and his eyes had a look of adoration in them. "Do you want to feel?"

He stared at me for a moment, unsure if I had asked him. Then he knelt in front of me with his hand extended towards me, "Can I?"

I took his hand and put it on the bump. The baby moved again as if he knew it was his father. I watched his face as he felt the baby move and a smile broke across it, "It feels a little weird."

"It's incredible. We made something completely amazing," he was in awe of the baby that we had created.

"Do you have a name?"

He looked at me, "I've always liked the name Hayden."

I smiled, "I like that too."

Then Luca came back in and saw Luther, "Hey you two. Is he moving around?"

"Yeah, he's been active," I said, watching him closely.

He sat down next to me, "What are you two talking about?"

"The baby and what to name him," I said, taking Luca's hand as the insecurity was starting to show through.

"That sounds nice," he handed me a plate with a sandwich on it.

"Well, I think I'm going to check on the team. I'll come back in a bit," Luther said, he must be sensing the tension. He stood up and walked out of the room.

"Are you okay Luca?"

"I am fine. Did you guys figure out a name?"

"Well, I think we just agreed on the name Hayden," I said, watching him closely. I could see the tension in his body, and I didn't know how to make it better. I started to eat, and I thought about what could go with Hayden and then the answer was super easy and perfect. "Don't be upset please."

He looked at me, "I'm not upset baby. I just get a little inside my head too. I wish it was just me and you. I'm a little jealous."

"Do you want to know what I want to give him as a middle name?"

"Of course, I do," he said, giving me the best smile he could muster up.

"I want his middle name to be Lucas... So that he knows he has a dad who chose him and not just one by blood," I said looking at my hands.

He pulled my face up and kissed me hard at first, "You surprise me more and more each day. Thank you, Anastasia."

"I love you very much, Luca. You are so important to me. Please don't feel left out," I said looking at his hazel eyes. You know you were the first person to feel him move?"

He smiled, "Please eat. You two need food."

I looked at the sandwich and began to eat. I knew it would make him feel so much better. I ate the whole sandwich and laid back down. He came over and kissed me on the head, "Where are you going?"

"I am just going to shower. It has been a long day and I need to wash off this negativity. Will you be alright?"

"Yeah, go shower. I'm just going to lay here and let the food settle, "I said smiling up at him.

He disappeared into the bathroom, and I closed my eyes. I heard my phone going off and I sat up. I looked through my purse until I found it. I answered it without looking at the name, "Ana?"

I froze, "Dom…"

"How's the baby?"

"He's okay…" I froze. I realized that I had made a stupid mistake. I had just revealed that I was having a boy.

"He huh? Well, that means you were at a doctor's office or hospital. Is everything okay?" Dom asked in his voice tense.

"Dom please stop… I just can't- I need him to be safe. I got hurt," I said, my voice stuttering.

"Anastasia. I told you; you are safe. I love you. I won't hurt you or your son. I just want you to be happy, but I need Luther and possibly Luca gone," Dom said in his quiet voice.

325

"Dom, I love Luca. You take him and I won't be happy. I care about Luther and these men. They have become my family. I don't want to lose any of them," I said, my voice growing thick.

"Ana, no one can threaten my place. They both do. I am sorry," he said as the phone went dead without another word.

I was going to get all the people I loved dearly, killed. I had a few tears slip down my face and I was frozen. The bathroom door opened, and Luca was talking to me. I couldn't hear the words that he said. He stared at me for a minute, "Ana?"

I was gasping for air as I saw everyone who had and would die. I saw everyone who loved me and tried to be there for me. He pulled my face up so I was looking at him, but I couldn't hear anything else he was saying. Dom was going to kill him. I couldn't lose him. I had to get away from him. He was talking, but my brain was still so focused on what to do next that I couldn't hear what he was saying, "I'm sorry… I'm so sorry."

The door opened and I saw Angelo and Eve come in. Angelo moved to talk to Luca and Eve moved to me, "Ana?"

"Eve… He's going to kill them all… It's all my fault…"

"Ana, you need to calm down. You can't get too upset," she said, tucking my hair behind my ear.

"Hayden is going to grow up with just me… I don't want that… He needs to know how loved he is," I said as a tear slipped down my face.

"Angelo, she's not listening. She's not able to focus," Eve said sitting in front of me.

"I will be there in just a second. Luca, what the hell happened?"

"I don't know. She was just frozen when I came out. She started hyperventilating. We had talked about the baby. She told me his name and I needed a shower," he said, his heart breaking in his voice.

"It's going to be okay. Eve let me sit there for a moment," Angelo said moving to me. Eve stood up and stood next to Luca, "Hey Ana."

I looked at him, the tears spilled over because I could not blink it was just overfilled. "He's going to kill you all… I don't know how to make it stop… I don't know what to do to keep you all safe," I said, still not able to blink.

"Who is going to do this?"

"Dom… He says he loves me. He's not going to hurt me, but he has to kill everyone who threatens him. I don't know what he is going to do… I think the only way to keep you all safe is for me to leave," I said as I dug my nails into the skin of my wrist. The feeling was painful and sweet as I felt the pain.

"I don't think you should be going anywhere. You would cause quite a bit of panic if you disappeared," Angelo said, his voice gentle.

"I have to keep you all safe… I can't have any more people die because of me. I can go to Greece alone, and you guys can go to one of the other houses or vice versa," I said rambling.

"Honey, I think you need to calm down. You aren't going anywhere. I am going to go get something and I will be right back," he said, standing up and moving to Luca.

"She's in shock. I'm going to get something to help her rest. I will be right back and maybe we could check her phone."

I just sunk my nails deeper into my skin to try and keep myself grounded. The pain brought back pleasure as I could control something. The bed moved, pulling me back to what was going on around me, "Ana?"

"He's going to take you from me… He thinks you will take over the business… I don't know what to do…"

He pulled my hands away from each other, "You are hurting yourself. I need you to stop."

"I need it. It feels good… Makes me feel like I'm in control. I just want to feel in control of one thing. Please let me go," I said, trying to pull my hands away from him.

He held me tightly, "Honey I'm not going to sit here and let you hurt yourself."

The panic began to take over and I fought with everything I had, "Let me go!!"

He held me tightly and I yanked my arms as hard as I possibly could. I tried to get away from him and eventually, he had me pinned on the bed while I screamed. I yelled and fought. Before I could do anything else I felt a pinch in my side and my eyes grew instantly heavy, "That's it, sweetheart. Just let it relax you."

He moved my hair out of my face, "It's not safe… You have to leave me… I need you to live."

"Baby please relax a little," he kissed my forehead. "Angelo, can you look at her arm please."

"Luca…"

Someone was looking at my wrist, "It's okay, Ana. It's just me," Angelo was quiet as he examined my wrist. "I can wrap it. She doesn't need anything serious. Pretty minor wound because it was just her nails. Just watch her. Self-harm is very common in those with depression, and she has already struggled with it in the past. She is also going to be a flight risk. So, we can't leave her alone at all."

"I'm not a kid... I'm an adult... I didn't mean to do it... It just felt nice to be in control of my pain," I said my eyes slipping shut.

"I know you aren't a kid honey. I know you have a history of this. Just rest please," he said, his voice gentle.

"I can't stay..."

"Rest baby... I won't be leaving. Just get some sleep," Luca said, taking my hand in his. I fell asleep against my will and soon let the drugs win.

****

I was still groggy when my eyes finally opened, "What's going on?"

"Hey, baby. We need to keep you calm so we have an IV with some medicine going into it. You are going to be very tired, but we have to make sure you and Hayden are safe. I don't think you can do that right now," Luca said as he was sitting next to me.

"I don't like it. I feel gross. Can we please stop," I said, my eyes not able to focus on anything I tried to look at. "I am okay. I just want to keep you safe too."

"I understand, but you have to get some rest. I think you will be better once you wake up again."

"No, we have to get back on the road. For that, I need to be functional. Take this IV out. Luca..." I let my eyes slip shut against my will once again.

"Ana, we can do whatever we need to do. You hurt yourself. I am not going to let that happen. You wanted to keep hurting yourself. I think you need the medicine to stay calm. I have to know you are safe and not trying to leave," he said his voice full of worry and doubt.

"It's not safe Luca... I think you... I need you to stop the meds..." My body sank into unconsciousness without my permission. I ended up sitting gasping for air. "I can't do this..." I looked down and saw that my hands were zip-tied together. The panic set in my body, "What the hell? Luca?"

I didn't hear anything, and I could feel my body shaking. I slowly stood up and moved to the bathroom. I turned the knob slowly, and when the door opened, I saw Luca lying on the floor in a pool of his blood. I screamed and launched myself forward. Luca was asleep so he was slow to move. I got off the bed and into the bathroom, before he registered what was going on. I had my phone in my hand and locked the bathroom door behind me. I dialed Dom's number and waited for him to answer. I heard him say, "Ana?"

"Please don't hurt them," A sob crashed through my chest so hard it hurt. "You can't hurt him. I love him and Luther is the father of my child. I need you to leave them alone."

"Whoa. Stop. Breathe this can't be good for you or the baby," Dom said, his voice flowing with worry.

"No. I need you to stop. I can't see them die," I sobbed. There was a banging on the door, and I screamed.

I dropped the phone and Dom must have hung up once he heard my panic or when I stopped responding to him, "Ana, baby let me in."

"No. Just leave me be for a while. I just need some time alone," I said, sinking to the floor and just lying there staring at the tile floor.

"I know you are upset. Can we please talk about it? I haven't given you anything. We also need to get ready to get on the road," Luca said, trying to distract me.

"I can't keep you safe!"

"It's not your job, Anastasia. Open this door right now," he said, his frustration leaking through.

"No!" I screamed back at him as I hugged myself. I saw my arm had been wrapped from where the IV had been. I had a very strong urge to pick at it so it would bleed again. Another sob crashed through my chest and there was nothing left to do but to try and keep it together.

"Angelo, I need you in this room right now," Luca said, the anger and fear flowing in his voice.

"I am working on it. Just keep talking to her. Try and keep her calm," Angelo said, somewhere nearby.

"Anastasia. I need you to open this door. I need to see you. Please," Luca's voice broke my heart, and it just made the sobs come harder. I was going to get him killed and there was nothing I could do to stop it from happening.

"I can't...I just can't," I stared at a spot on the tile. I was as small as I could be, and I could feel Hayden getting stronger with his movements.

"Angelo, get me in that damn bathroom right now," Luca practically yelled.

The door flew open, and Luca was in front of me in a matter of seconds, "Luca, slow down. You need to take your time. Something is going on with her. Breathe so you can help her."

"Ana… Baby, please talk to me," Luca said trying to contain himself. He decided to lay himself in front of me on the floor. I could look at him while he talked. I tried to focus on him.

My body was fighting me, but I was managing to get it to calm down. I was sniffling as I let the tears stream, "I can't lose you. It took me ten years to get you. I don't think I could handle losing you. You are so important to me, and I love you."

He put his hand on the side of my face, "Listen to me. I am not going anywhere. I will be with you for the rest of our lives if I can help it. You are so important to me too, and I will do everything I have to, to keep you safe. I love you. I need you to talk to me before you get to this point. Luther and I can handle ourselves."

"Can you? He almost had you back at the house. I can't handle it if something happens to you," I said as I enjoyed his hand on my face.

"Oh, Ana. It's okay. I think you are just overthinking and overwhelmed."

"He had you at gunpoint," I said thinking back to the house.

"Ana, I would give anything on this planet for you. I don't want this business. I don't want to be in this situation ever again if that means you are here. I just want you, and you to be safe. Please just relax."

Chapter Seventeen

Back on the Road

I lay on the floor for an hour just talking to him. I couldn't help but let him relax me and calm me down, "Are you ready to leave?"

"Do I have a choice? We have to get out of here," I said blinking through the pain in my swollen eyes.

"I need you to be okay. I can't leave if you aren't okay," he said in a gentle voice.

"I'm okay. My body just hurts a little bit. I feel better," I said, staring into his hazel eyes.

"Okay good. Can I help you up," he asked, sitting up.

I stared at him for a moment, and I wasn't sure what I wanted to say or to do. I just knew that I was in pain. Mentally my head and heart were killing me. I couldn't think of responding. I was miserable. I slowly got out of my head and looked into his eyes, "I guess I can get up."

He slowly leaned down and pulled me into a sitting position. He waited to make sure I was steady before he looked at me, "Ana?"

I was thinking about my life and how it got flipped upside down. I didn't understand how so much could happen in almost a year. I felt my heart hurt and I looked at Luca, all I felt looking at him was love. "I don't know what to do anymore Luca. I don't know how I should feel or the way I should act."

"It's going to be okay. Can I please help you up," he asked in a gentle voice.

I nodded and he slowly pulled me to my feet. I stared at him wondering how he could be so calm as our lives just continued to get worse and worse. I wanted to cry. He pulled me into a gentle hug, "I'm sorry Luca. I am trying."

"I know you are honey. I see it. It's hard sometimes. I get it. I just need you to trust me. Trust Luther as much as we can. Just believe we can do what we need to," he pulled away but kept his arm around me to keep me stable. "I'm sorry you are so dizzy. I tried to keep you calm with the medicine Angelo recommended."

"I can still feel it in my system. I'm honestly surprised I could move that quickly and get in the bathroom as fast as I did," I said leaning on him heavily.

"I think it was your adrenaline. I have you. Just let me help," he said, helping me back to the bed.

"I feel very drained now. I just want to sleep. Do we have to leave today," I asked as my eyes grew heavy.

"I'm afraid so. We got Oliver back today. We need to be on the road. I want to get you as far away from your brother as possible," Luca said, moving my hair out of my face. "You can sleep in the car sweetheart I promise."

I groaned and laid down on the bed, "When do we have to leave?"

"We have to leave soon. I will come to get you when we are ready to go. Try and get a little more rest," he said, pulling the blanket over me.

I had my eyes once again focused on him, "Please don't leave. I don't want to be alone. I was scared that you died."

"Ana... I am right here. I won't leave. I just want you to relax. I am alive and right here," he said softly.

My eyes slipped shut, "Can you lay next to me?"

"I may have to move. I am just going to sit here next to you for now."

I whined more than I meant to, "I-Okay."

"I know, baby. I am sorry. Just rest. I am right here, and I won't leave the room," I heard him say in his gentle voice.

I was losing consciousness once again, and I knew it wouldn't be long before I was asleep again. "Okay, Luca."

"Get some sleep, honey. I will be right here," he said as he played with my hair. It didn't take long for me to give in. I whined a little and felt the warmth of my body heat being trapped in the blanket. I fell asleep faster than I expected to.

****

I woke up to Luca shaking me, "What's going on?" I still felt dizzy from the medication, but the fog had cleared a bit. I looked at him and finally got my eyes to focus. He looked worried, "Are you okay?"

"I am fine, Ana. It's just time to go. Can I help you up? Can you walk?"

I sat up slowly testing the waters to see how I was doing. I felt pretty stable, so I put my legs over the side of the bed. He watched me with worry in his eyes, "I think I will be fine. I'm just going to move slowly. How long did I have that IV in my arm?"

"We left it in for a day. I know it wasn't fair, but we needed to keep you calm. You were hurting yourself. I needed you to stop hurting yourself. I will be close to you and make sure that you will be okay," Luca said, his voice gentle.

I stood up slowly and took a testing step. I was fine and decided I could move, "How long have I been asleep?"

"We put off moving for another day. You have been asleep for a whole day," Luca said, watching me closely. "Do you want to get changed?"

"Yes, do I have clothes somewhere nearby," I asked looking back at him.

"I'll be right back." He left and I waited to look around the small hotel room. I was getting a little angry at the situation I was in. I was upset and I didn't know how I should be feeling. I get that he was being helpful, and I also get that he was trying to protect me. I didn't like that I was on medication. I didn't like how I felt. It reminded me too much of how I felt when I was with Luther for the first time. The door opened and he moved with caution, "Here you go Ana."

I opened the bag and grabbed a long skirt and a T-shirt. I went into the bathroom and put the skirt on. I went to put the T-shirt on, and it was tight and wrapped tightly around the baby bump. I stared at myself in the mirror and immediately grew ashamed. I had hurt myself. The place my baby was housed in, and I can't believe I let myself get so close to hurting myself. I mean at the moment it felt good. I took a shaky breath and tried not to let the guilt and tears take over me. There was a knock on the door, "I'll be out in a second."

"Are you okay," Luca asked as he must have heard something in my voice.

I tried to make sure my voice was clear when I responded to him, "I'm okay sorry I just needed a moment."

The door opened, "Hey there gorgeous. You look great."

I turned to look at him, "I'm sorry for hurting myself."

He froze and just watched me for a moment, "Hey… It's okay Ana. I know it's just a response. You are going to be okay. It's just you need to talk to me before these depressive episodes get worse."

"I know it seems hard to believe but I am trying. I don't want to be this way and I don't want to hurt the baby," I said looking down at the baby bump where I could feel him moving.

Luca moved to me and brought my face up. He kissed me, "I know. Let's get back on the road so I can get you two somewhere safe please."

I smiled at him, "Okay."

We walked out of our room and into the hallway to see the men filling the hallway. I took a deep breath and tried to put my brave face on as I followed Luca to the end of the hall where the elevator was. The out-of-order sign was gone somehow and it made my heart race. I looked at Luca and he just held his hand out to me, "It's going to be okay. I know you are scared but we are right here with you."

I took his hand and a deep breath, "I am okay. I can do this."

He smiled again and pulled me gently to his side. "Let's get back on the road," he said, hitting the button and waiting for the elevator door to open. The door opened and I felt my body freeze a little, but Luca gave me a small nudge in the right direction. I was soon in the little metal box with Luca and Luther trying to keep my breathing under control. Finally, the doors opened, and I rushed out of the elevator thinking of the way that I had almost died. I was guided to the car with Luca's hand on my back, "How are you feeling?"

"I feel fine. Just a little tired if that is even possible," Luther went ahead of me and opened the door of the car. I got into the backseat and the door closed behind me. I wrapped my hands around the bump that was my stomach. I felt Hayden move and I couldn't help the smile that spread across my face. Luca got in next to me, Luther got in the passenger seat, and Apollo got behind the driver's seat.

"Let's get out of here," Luca said his voice was loud and bossy.

"Way ahead of you Luca," Apollo said as we began to move. I looked out the window and felt like something was going to go wrong. I was watching and searching for any sign of Dom.

"Relax Ana. We are leaving. We will be safe," Luca said looking down at his cellphone.

I closed my eyes and took a deep breath. I needed to relax. I sighed and stretched out on the seat and removed the seatbelt I had on briefly. Luca looked at me, "I am fine Luca. If danger comes, I will put it on, but I am fine."

He glared at me for a moment, "Anastasia, that is our baby you have in there. You will wear a seatbelt."

"It's uncomfortable. Apollo, are you planning on crashing the car?"

I heard Luther chuckle as I was getting frustrated, "No I am not planning on crashing the car."

"Good. Then I am fine," I said, crossing my arms.

Luca growled in frustration, "Why do you have to be so stubborn? It isn't that complicated."

I didn't look at him, I just stared at my stomach where I could see the baby making little movements. I was so happy to just sit there and watch him move. Luca took my hand and squeezed it, "Don't be mad."

He moved to me and was playing with my hand, "I am not mad at you. I know you are going to be a little crazy. I am a little crazy too. This child is going to have way too many crazy parents."

I smiled and peeked up at his face, "Yeah, he is. He is going to be loved though."

He smiled and I laid my head on his shoulder, "We are safe. I think it will be okay. Just relax a little. I know it's hard, but you need to just rest."

"I will do my best," I said, laying my head on his shoulder.

"Ana, I don't think this will be comfortable. How about you lay down on the seat? I will sit on the floor next to you. I think laying on your stomach will be harder than it used to be," he said his voice was gentle as he coaxed me.

"That isn't safe for you. I don't want you to get hurt," I said, trying to relax my body.

"If you can sit in the backseat without a seatbelt then I can sit on the floor so you can be comfortable," His voice was gentle as he tried to plead with me.

"Luca, I don't think I would be okay if something happened," I said looking at his eyes and we stared at each other for a moment.

"Well then put on your seatbelt miss," he said after a few minutes.

I sighed and grabbed the seat belt and buckled it up. I looked out the window and tried not to let my annoyance show. I watched the world fly by, and I didn't recognize anything nearby. I heard them all talking amongst themselves. They were pretty happy to just talk to each other and I enjoyed the stupid chatter. I wasn't sure when it happened, but my eyes slipped shut. I heard the seatbelt get released and I panicked. I jumped and my eyes opened, "I'm awake."

"It's okay Ana, I think you need to get some more sleep. You are leaning against the door," he said sitting down on the floor next to me. He had me lie down and saw him relax when I laid down with no complaint. "I have a surprise for you."

"What is it?"

"How is it supposed to be a surprise if I tell you," he gave me a small smile and brushed my hair off of my face.

"I just want to know what you are going to take me to do," I said as my eyes slipped shut. I felt him drape a coat over my body. I enjoyed the scent of him that flooded me. "I know you are trying to be sweet, but I just want to know what is going on."

"Just let me give you a nice surprise," he said, his voice gentle. He kissed me on the forehead. "Please? Our relationship has been nothing but crazy. Let me do this one nice thing for you."

I sighed and pried my eyes open to look at him, "I think you are silly. I love you for you. I have since we were kids. You don't have to try and bring romance into it."

"Just rest Ana. We will be there soon. I know you are tired," he said, trying to reassure me.

I let my eyes close again. I started to worry that we were not going to last. I mean we have been running for dear life since we came into each other's lives again. I didn't want him to just want me because he was trying to protect me at all times. What if he was just with me because I needed protection? I didn't want that. I wanted him to love me because he loves me, "We will be there in like an hour."

"Okay, good. I appreciate you guys letting this happen. I want to show her things, besides fear. I want her to be happy and have some good memories with me," Luca said his voice was soft as he tried to not disturb me.

I moved towards the sound of his voice, and I don't know if he saw me do it. I know that he had when he started playing with my hair some more. "Of course. We need to give her some good memories. She's about to be a mom and life will only get harder from here," Luther said, his voice also soft.

"It will be hard to let her unwind. We just need to let her be an almost nineteen-year-old girl. I can't believe it has almost been a year since this all started," Apollo said as he pushed the gas pedal down.

"Luca, I don't think I can sleep anymore. I just have too much on my mind," I said, getting my eyes open slowly.

"Hey, you. What's going on in your mind? Remember you need to talk to me. I know you are tired, I can see it on your face," he said as he looked down at me.

I looked down at my hands, "I don't know."

He pulled my face up and stared at me, "Ana… Please talk to me. I don't like seeing you like this."

"I'm scared…"

"Of what?"

"That you only like me because I need protection. That you are just with me because I am a mess," I barely got the words out.

I tried not to look at him, but suddenly he had my face between both of his hands. "Look at me," his voice was intense and so I forced myself to look at him. "Ana, that is not the reason why I love you. I understand that's why you think that. Just let me show you please."

I nodded, not wanting to talk. I looked back down, and he released my face. I sat in silence as no one had said anything. Before I knew it the car was slowing down. I tried not to make myself smaller. "We are here Luca. I will get her ready," Apollo said, his voice quiet.

Luca moved in front of me, "Can you promise to try and keep an open mind?"

I stared at him for a very long time, "I know you are trying. I will try, I just don't know how I feel yet."

"Well let me show you something incredible. I want to show you how much I care about you," he said, his eyes were this great pool.

I sighed and slowly sat up. He put his hands over my eyes, and I tried very hard to not flinch away from him. "Is this necessary?"

"Let me have my fun please," Luca said, his voice filled with excitement. "Luther, can you grab the door for her and help her out of the car slowly."

"Of course," Luther said, and I heard two doors close.

I heard the door next to me open, "Go ahead and hold your hands out, Ana. Luther is going to help you out of the car so I can keep your eyes covered."

I sighed, fighting the urge to keep the frustration out of my body. I did as he instructed and was slowly pulled out of the car. I moved slowly as Luca still had my eyes covered and I didn't know where we were going. The terrain was bumpy, and I didn't know what to make of it, "Luca, how much further do we need to go?"

"We are almost there, honey," he said, the excitement growing in his voice. I tried to focus on the excitement so I could try and channel my inner happiness. We came to a sudden stop, "Ready?"

I nodded slowly; my nerves were going haywire as I didn't know what was going to happen next. He moved his hands away from my eyes and I saw a sweet little cabin in a small clearing, "This is for you and Luca tonight. We rented other cabins around here. This one is just in the middle," Luther said.

I was indeed surprised, "It's just going to be me and you tonight?"

Luca smiled and I could see his nerves showing through as he didn't know how I was feeling about this, "Only if you want to."

Seeing the nerves taking over him, my frustrations and anxieties seemed to have melted away even if only temporarily. I couldn't stop the smile that spread across my face, "That sounds nice."

I saw his body relax as he was relieved that I wanted to do this. I was a little sad that he thought I might reject his idea. I couldn't believe I was so ungrateful he thought I was going to reject this lovely idea. Luca was talking to the group of men, "We will see you all tomorrow." He turned back to me and took me gently by the hand. He led me down the trail to the cabin door. He took me inside and turned to me, "What do you want to do first?"

I stood frozen as I hadn't heard a question like that in almost a year, "I don't know. It's just so weird and quiet out here."

He chuckled, "Well we can always start with something small. How about a bath or a shower?"

I hugged myself as all the self-doubt started to swim its way back up, "Luca… I just feel weird. I don't know what to do with peace."

He moved back to me with his facial expression soft and full of love. This was a Luca I didn't see often but it made my heart race. He pulled me into a hug, "Please just have fun with me. Let me do this for you. I just want to give you one night of not running, one night we can forget what has happened. Let me do this nice thing please."

I couldn't resist and hugged him back to me, "Okay Luca."

I felt him kiss the top of my head, "Thank you. How about you go take a shower and I will get dinner cooked, that way you can eat when you get out."

"Okay honey," I said, pulling away from him even though that was the last thing I wanted to do. I went back to where he pointed to and where the bathroom must have been. I opened the door and stepped in. I took a deep breath and turned on the hot water. I stripped off my clothes and got under the hot water. My muscles immediately relaxed, and I got myself cleaned up. After thirty minutes I turned off the water and wrapped a towel around myself. I opened the door and shouted down to Luca, "Do I have any clothes you could bring me?"

"Yeah, I'll be right there," he shouted back at me.

I closed the door and just enjoyed the heat that was surrounding me from the steam. I took a deep breath and looked around at my life. It wasn't great but I was finally getting somewhere with it. I took a deep breath determined to make the most of tonight with Luca. There was a knock at the door, "Ana?"

"Come in Luca," I said, turning to the door.

He came in and stared right into my eyes. He moved to me and set the clothes on the counter next to me without taking his eyes off my face. He cupped my face and my heart stuttered as I felt myself wanting him to try something, "You look beautiful. Dinner is done when you are dressed and come out to the table."

I got on my tip toes and kissed him gently, "I'll be out in a few minutes."

He was smiling when I moved around him to grab the clothes, "Alright. Let's get some food in you."

He turned and left the bathroom, and I got dressed as quickly as I could. I put on the large T-shirt that was gray, and the blue underwear he grabbed. I decided not to grab the shorts in hopes that he would take the hint. I walked out to the table and sat down on one of the four chairs. He was plating some food and he walked over. He set the plate down in front of me and I saw that it was chicken, mashed potatoes, and green beans. "This looks delicious," I said, smiling at him.

He sat down next to me smiling. We ate in almost utter silence as I was getting anxious about trying to seduce him. I had never had to try to do that and so it made me nervous. We finished our food and sat and talked. It was nice to just be sitting and talking with him. We felt like people for a little bit of time. He stood up and took the dishes to the sink, "Follow me?"

I took a deep breath, "Where are we going?"

"To the living room."

I stood and he seemed to have noticed that I was not wearing pants because he stuttered a little bit. I had to stifle the giggle that wanted to explode from my chest. I went and sat on the couch, and he sat down next to me, "This was so nice. Thank you so much for doing this for me."

"You deserve a night off. You were thrown into this, and it's been nothing but chaotic feelings for a year. I am happy we get to do this just me and you," he said trying not to look me up and down.

I smiled, "It was a good idea. I just don't know why we waited so long to do this," I said, stretching a little bit.

His face went red, and he looked away, "What do you want to do now?"

"Did you have anything planned?"

"No, not really. I just wanted to spend some time with you," he said, giving me a small smile.

I turned to the TV, and I turned on the first movie I could find. It ended up being A Journey to the Center of the Earth. We were quiet again and he pulled a blanket over my lap. I sighed when I figured he wasn't going to try anything with me. That upset me more than I thought it would. I just leaned against him and got comfortable. Soon I was falling asleep as the night went on. Luca scooped me up, "Luca...?"

"Just relax," he said softly, "I want to get you into bed. That could ruin your back."

I sighed and leaned into his chest, "I was comfortable just lying on the couch with you."

He chuckled, "Imagine how comfortable you would be in bed."

He set me down and I watched him strip his shirt off and change into a pair of baggy sweatpants, "Luca?"

"What's on your mind, Ana?"

"Why... Never mind."

I hid under the blankets as my embarrassment overtook me. I heard him chuckle as he got under the blankets and laid his hand on my stomach, "Why are you hiding from me?"

"Because I am hormonal and crazy," I said, trying to keep my face hidden.

He slowly pulled the blankets out of my hands and came up to stare at my face, "You are not crazy. Hormonal I can't deny but you are anything but crazy."

I stared into his eyes, and he stared back, "I love you, Luca."

"I love you too Ana," He leaned down and kissed me. I felt like my body exploded with the feeling of love.

Chapter Eighteen

Almost there

I woke up to the sun shining in through the window. We had forgotten to close the blinds. My body was a little sore, but I felt pretty good. I was lying on his chest and when I moved, he groaned, "We were supposed to get more sleep. You had to keep me up."

I giggled, "I am sorry. I didn't mean to keep you up."

He looked at me and brought me in for a kiss, "We should get up and get ready to get back on the road. Are you okay?"

I smiled at his concern, "Yes. I am okay. Although I am not sure where my underwear went."

He chuckled again, "It's okay. Let me get up and get ready. You just relax a little bit if you want. I will get you up soon."

I pulled the blankets over my head as he got out of bed, "You don't need to tell me twice. Come get me when you are done."

He chuckled and pulled the blanket back down, "You are grumpy in the morning." He kissed my head and then walked away from me.

"I am tired. I don't know what else to tell you," I said slowly, stretching.

I sighed and got out of bed slowly. I found a bag with clothes. I found some clothes and quickly got dressed. I was in a sundress that went down to my ankles as I grabbed socks and my tennis shoes. Luca walked back in, "Good morning."

I smiled at him, "Good morning. When do we need to be on the road?"

"I came to get you out of bed and put our luggage in the car. So, we should probably go get in the car so we can get to New York. We've got at least another two days before we are there," he said, grabbing the bag of clothes.

He held his other hand out to me, and I slowly took it. He pulled me out of the cabin and into the car. I was giggling as he kept making me blush after last night. I saw Luther and Eli getting into the car that we were in. Luca threw our bag in the trunk and opened the car door for me. I got into the car and avoided Luther's eyes in the mirror, "How did you two sleep?"

Luca chuckled when my face went beat red, "We slept fine. How did you all sleep?"

"Everyone is well rested," Luther said as Eli put the car in drive. We were driving off into the distance. I looked out the window not wanting to see anyone's eyes after last night either. I don't know why I was so embarrassed; I mean I was already pregnant with another man's baby.

I looked at the world driving by when Luca leaned over and pulled the seatbelt over me. He left his hand on my stomach after, "I know I am ridiculous. I just want to try and keep you and him safe."

I smiled at him, "I understand. I suppose I will let you be a little crazy."

I rested my head on his shoulder, and I realized I felt no tension in his body for the first time in a year. I smiled knowing that I had helped him relax. I closed my eyes tired from the night we had. I heard the guy saying, "I think she's asleep. Have we heard anything from Dom?"

After a few minutes of silence, Luther responded, "They say he has two groups. One is heading south to see if we are down there and the other is heading north. We are ahead and it also means he has no idea where we are after we ditch the cars."

I tried to not let the tension go into my body as the bubble of peace was popped by the conversation I was overhearing. Luca put his hand on my thigh, and I felt him rubbing small circles with his thumb, "Well that is good news. We might be able to get out of the country without having to go around him."

"That is the overall goal. I just want to make sure that we keep things in order so we can get to our destination in one piece," Luther said, his voice soft.

"We will get there in one piece. At least our teams have gotten bigger since we decided to work together. Do we know how many men Dominic has?"

Both Luca and Luther listened to Eli with a strange silence. "I think it is hard to say considering that he decided to round up people from Texas with guns and there are quite a few of them in Texas," Luther said.

Luca was still trying to continue keeping me calm. I opened my eyes and looked at Luca, "Are we going to be, okay?"

After a few minutes, Luca looked at me, "We will be okay. We just have to be on the side of caution. We don't know what your brother wants."

"He said he wants the business. He wants what my father had because he thinks he can do it better. He has to take out everyone that threatens that. I want to call him again. I want you to tell him you don't want it. That we want to live our lives away from it," I said, letting it all exit my mouth quickly so that he didn't interrupt me.

"Ana, how would you know all of that?"

"I called him…"

"What?!"

I jumped at the sound of yelling. "Do you think he is smart enough to check her cell phone?"

"I don't know Luther. Where is her cellphone?"

"I think I left it in the last hotel bathroom. That's where I called him from. If you didn't grab it then it is still there," I said, staring at my hands.

I heard multiple people take a deep breath and knew that the peace I had was now gone. "Well, he could know which way we are going now if he thought to track your phone."

"I-I just didn't want any more people to die. I didn't want to continue to let people die because of my father and my brother. I wanted our child to grow up with all the people that love him," I said my voice wanting to waver, but I took a deep breath and pushed the strength into my voice.

I forced myself to look at Luca who had been staring at me as I had talked, "Ana… We have to keep you safe. You talking to your brother isn't great. He could've tracked your phone. You should have told me. We need to get you a new phone. Something he can't call."

"I don't want to do any of this. I just want to be in another country wanting to go away. I want this to not be a problem. I want my brother to not be crazy and my father to have a legal business," I said as Eli slowed the car down. "What are you doing?"

"It's going to be okay. I think we need to stop for a minute," Eli said, looking over at Luther for a moment.

"Let's keep going for a bit. We are fine and now that we know he had access to her phone we need to put as much distance between us as possible," Luther said the strain in his voice was evident as he was trying to cover his anger.

"Look, I know I messed up. I didn't think about him being able to find my phone. I just wanted to make you guys safe. I had a dream about you all dying. I just can't be the one who causes your death," I said, trying to keep myself calm.

"It was stupid. You need to think straight before you do something stupid. I don't know if we should be getting her a new phone. We don't need any more communication between you and your brother," Luther snapped back at me.

"I'm not stupid. You are the one that let him bait you into a war. Don't start to question me and my mental state when he makes you worse than me. He hasn't hurt me. His men did. As far as I can tell I am safe when it comes to my

353

brother. It's everyone else that I worry about," I said, letting the anger leak into my voice.

"Alright, you two enough. Fighting isn't going to fix anything. It isn't going to help anything. You two are just going to sit here and piss each other off and we won't be stopping until very late. So, let's not fight each other in the car shall we," Luca said, putting an end to the conversation.

I sat there and stared out the window again, my temper flaring. It's not like I thought about doing this on purpose. I hated that I was being called stupid and being treated like a child again. I am not a child. I wasn't a child when they decided to start this god-forsaken war between them and now I have to sit here and listen to men talk to me like I was a child. The car was pulling off until we were in front of a rest stop, "Use the bathroom if you need it. We will be back on the road soon."

I watched everyone get out of the car and I just unfastened the seatbelt. I stretched a little bit but refused to look at anyone. I didn't want to get out of the car and Hayden started moving a little bit. I smiled as he moved, "I know buddy. I am sorry."

The door opened and I saw Luca, "Come here please."

I sighed and got out of the car after pushing his hand away from me. I followed him to the large group of people standing by the building, "What?"

"Luther, get over here."

I heard a groan and we moved to the other side of the building, just the three of us. "Alright, you two need to calm down. We are not going to go backward with fighting. I am too tired to handle another little war."

"I wasn't starting anything. I was defending myself. It's not my fault he doesn't know what to do. I am not useless. I am not a child. I am growing a child. That doesn't give you a right to treat me like a worthless girl," I said glaring at Luther and Luca.

I moved away from both of them so no one could touch me. I was mad and they would know about it. "Ana, I don't care about anything but keeping you and Hayden safe. I am going to get angry. I am going to be crazy. How come he gets to be crazy, but I can't?"

"Luca isn't sitting there telling me what an idiot I am!"

They both froze when I yelled at them. I could see they didn't know what to do or say. They both stared at me as I was fuming and for the first time in forever there were no tears in my eyes, "Ana?"

"No Luca. I am done with this bullshit. I am a human. I am an adult. I may be pregnant, and my family might have made some mistakes, but I am the one who is suffering from all of this. Not just you Luther."

He moved to me fast and pushed me against the building. Fear shot through me, and Luca was shouting, "My entire family was killed by your father. You are not the only one who has suffered loss through this!"

Luca had managed to pull him away from me and I just sank to the ground as the men came running over. I saw a few of them drag Luther away and I could feel my body shaking. My hand went to my stomach and Hayden gave a soft kick as if to tell me he was okay. Luca moved back to me and was looking at me like I was a deer in the headlights, "Ana?"

"I am okay Luca. I just need a minute please," I said, my voice quiet and weak.

He nodded, "I will be right back. Please don't wander off."

I watched him walk away and I took a deep shaky breath. I laid my head down on my knees and tried to get the shaking to stop. Someone touched me and I jumped. I looked up to see Luca, "I am okay Luca."

"Did he hurt you?"

I shook my head and moved to him. I wrapped my arms around him, and he wrapped them back around me. He lifted me to my feet, "I am glad you are okay. Let's get in the car, okay? We need to get back on the road so we can get to New York."

I nodded and he let me go so I could walk. We began to walk towards the car and Luther moved towards us. I stopped immediately and Luca put his hand up to Luther, "Sunflower... I am so sorry. Please..."

"That's enough for right now Luther. We need to get into the car. Let's get into the car now," Luca said, still holding onto my hand.

Luther nodded and got behind the wheel, Eli sat next to him, and Luca and I got in the back. I was shaking as Luca helped me buckle up. I looked at Luca, "Thank you."

"I will keep you safe. I mean it. I just need you to calm down, okay? I know you are upset, and I understand why. Just please," he said, his voice starting to sound defeated.

I cupped his face in my hand, "Okay Luca. I am sorry. I didn't mean for my temper to get that out of control."

He smiled and put his hand on top of mine, "Just rest for now. We will be in New York soon. Then on a plane safely away."

I let my head lean back and closed my eyes. My adrenaline was emptying my system, and I was suddenly very tired. "Is she okay," Luther asked in a tense voice.

"What the hell was that, Luther? That was unacceptable and I sure as hell will not see that again," Luca said, trying to control his voice.

"I am sorry. I just couldn't stop myself. I lost control. Please tell me she is okay," Luther said, his voice breaking.

Luca sighed, "She is fine. I think she may be sleeping. So, let's keep it that way please."

"I just want to get as far away from him as fast as possible. I want to get out of the country. Can we just drive through the night," Luther asked, trying to get control of his emotions.

"Fine. I will have her sleep on the seat. Let's just get you a little calmer, please. Then I want you to do the best apology you can to her."

"Of course, I will apologize. I didn't want to hurt her. I swear. I just lost control," I heard Luther say quietly.

I sighed and opened my eyes, "Hey Luca."

"Hey, you. We are going to drive through the night. I am going to move to the floor again while you sleep on the seats," he said in a gentle voice.

"Are you sure?"

"Yes, baby. Let's get you all set up," he said softly. I watched him grab his coat and make it into a pillow for me. Then he helped me lay down. He grabbed a blanket and draped it over me.

"You were oddly prepared for this," I said, letting the sleepy feeling leak into my voice.

He chuckled, "I wanted to be ready if you needed a nap or anything. I was going to be prepared one way or another. Please get some sleep."

"Okay, Luca. Try and get some rest too," I said as my eyes slipped shut. I started to relax as the hum of the engine lulled me into a nice sleep.

"Is she back asleep," Luther asked quietly.

"Yes. You will have to apologize tomorrow," Luca said, his voice tense.

I decided that was enough eavesdropping and I needed to get some sleep. I let myself finally fall asleep.

****

I woke up to Luca playing with my hair. I sighed, "Did you get any sleep?"

"Good morning sweetheart. I did get some sleep. We will be in New York soon. You ready to get up," Luca asked in a gentle voice.

"Man, we made good time. Yeah, I am ready to get up," I said as he helped me sit up and joined me on the seat. He stretched and I saw him wince, "Are you okay?"

"Yeah, my back is a little tender, but I am okay. We will be on a plane in the next couple of hours going to Venice," he said, giving me a little smile.

"That was fast," I said looking down at my hands.

"Hey, Sunflower?"

I froze when he spoke to me, "Hi Luther."

"I'm so sorry. I had no right. I had no right to do that. I am sorry I lost control. I hope you can forgive me," Luther said in his quiet voice.

I thought for a moment before I responded to him, "I understand that you are sorry. I am not saying that I don't forgive you, but I am a little nervous about you right now."

"I don't blame you. I would be worried if you weren't upset with me. I promise to do better," he said the determination began to flow into his voice.

"I can agree that you will do better. Let's just get out of the States and then we can work on rebuilding our relationship," I said as I felt the tension in my body.

"You got it."

Luca took my hand, "You are doing great, Ana. We are almost done with all of this."

I smiled back at him and looked back out the window. I saw the world passing us by and I wasn't sure if I was glad this was happening or if I was worried. I was ready to be somewhere familiar where I had pleasant memories.

That seemed so far stretched and that I couldn't seem to smile anymore. I felt my anxiety getting worse, "Are we sure that the plane is going to be safe?"

"Your brother hasn't returned to the city so the plane should be completely safe. We wouldn't put you in harm's way. We will also do a full inspection. The pilot should be working at that as we speak," Eli said, taking over the conversation.

I sighed, "Okay good. Well, I guess we needed to get to New York quickly."

"I was determined to not waste any more time than we needed. I don't need you getting hurt again or anyone else getting hurt again," Luther said his voice tense.

I felt the fight that was coming, and I couldn't help but want to make him feel better, "I appreciate it, Luther. Thank you."

I saw him smile in the rearview mirror and the tension in my body lessened ever so slightly. I saw Luca smile out of the corner of my eye. He leaned in and whispered in my ear, "You are such a good person. I don't know how I got so lucky."

I smiled back, "I don't know either. I guess someone likes you in the universe."

I giggled as he poked my side, "I'll take whatever they want to give. Thank God someone thinks I deserve you."

The car was soon slowing, and I saw our little airport where we would be flying from. My anxiety spiked and Luca got off the phone with the pilot, "He says it's all clear. We will get the luggage loaded and then we can all get boarded. They are gassing up as we speak."

I gave them both my best smile as they began to talk about the trip ahead. The car came to a stop in front of a large air hanger. I watched as men began loading up the plane and as they started boarding. I slowly got out of the car and walked my way to the private jet. I put my hand on my stomach and went up the stairs so I could get strapped in. Luca stopped me and handed me a cell phone, "Thank you, Luca."

He smiled, "No more secrets and we need to be careful. We will be gone before he can get to us. You can call him before Luther finds out and gets mad. Make sure he's okay. I know you can't stop being family. Just no details."

I hugged him tightly, "I don't deserve you either. Thank you so much, Luca."

I got up onto the plane and I sat down in a chair. I buckled my seatbelt and went to Dom's number that Luca had put in for me. I hit the call button and waited. He picked up on the second ring, "Hello?"

"Hey, Dom."

"Ana! Are you okay??? You had me worried? I haven't talked to you since you were hysterical," he said, saying so much at once.

"Calm down Dom. I am okay. I just had a bad dream. I don't want to lose either of them. I think you should know Luca doesn't want the family business. He just wants to be with me. Please Dom leave him alone," I said in my quiet voice.

"Ana… I want to. I do but I don't know if I can trust that. He's been in Dad's gang since he was ten," Dom said, the hesitation just starting to show through.

I latched onto that and used it, "Dom why would he jeopardize me in any way? He loves me. He loves the baby even though it's not his. Luther just wants his child protected."

"It's not that simple," he said gently.

Everyone boarded the plane, and I began to be vague as Luther got on. Luca sat in the seat next to me and smiled as he saw me get tense. The door to the plane closed and I heard the engines start, "It is that simple."

"Ana, where are you?"

I was surprised by the question. The plane began to move, "You know I can't tell you that. It would be stupid to tell you that."

"Anastasia, you need to tell me now where you are. Did I just hear a plane," he asked as panic was starting to flow into his voice.

"No. Now calm down," I said as we went straight up into the air. I sighed as we were safely on our way to Venice. "Why are you freaking out?"

"You need to tell me if you are on a plane. Right now," his panic was starting to freak me out.

"We are over the ocean and safe now. We will be in Venice in 27 hours. Everyone get comfortable," Luther said, stretching out.

"Tell me you are not on our private jet Ana," Dom said, his voice sounding weak.

I felt the tension flood into my body, "Why?"

Luca saw me and I saw him look at me with a look of confusion. He sat up and reached for my hand, "Ana. You need to get to land now. Right now."

"What did you do?"

"No arguing. Tell them to get you back on the ground-"

The plane shook and I dropped the phone and screamed, "What is happening?"

"I don't know. Buckle back up," Luther said as he headed towards the cockpit.

I looked at Luca, "Dom says get to the ground now. Something is wrong."

I saw his face become pale and then there was an explosion. I screamed again and looked out the window next to my head and saw the engine was engulfed in flames. The panic hit, "Shit."

"Luca…?"

"We are going down! Everyone gets strapped in and ready for an emergency crash. Now!"

Luca took my face, "It's okay. Just breathe. I am right here. I will keep you safe. Just breathe. Close your eyes and prepare to hit the sea."

I felt the bile rise as we began to spin. I heard the men shouting. I closed my eyes and felt Luca take my hand again.

I squeezed his hand with everything I had as we crashed into the sea, and everything went black.

**** The End... ****

Made in the USA
Middletown, DE
04 December 2024